What readers are saying about

One Day in December

★★★★★

'Devastatingly good'
Johnny, Netgalley

★★★★★

'I LOVE, LOVE, LOVED this book'
Vicki, Netgalley

★★★★★

'Wow! What a book!'
Jen, Netgalley

★★★★★

'This kept me turning pages long into the night. I'd highly
recommend it'
Christine, Netgalley

★★★★★

'I can't wait to reread it over and over'
Nikita, Netgalley

★★★★★

'Beautifully written'
Helen, Netgalley

★★★★★

'I just didn't want this book to end . . . I shall be singing its
praises from the rooftops'
Cassie, Netgalley

★★★★★

'The perfect book to read this winter'
Rebecca, Netgalley

One Day in December

JOSIE SILVER

PENGUIN BOOKS

PENGUIN BOOKS

UK | USA | Canada | Ireland | Australia
India | New Zealand | South Africa

Penguin Books is part of the Penguin Random House group of companies
whose addresses can be found at global.penguinrandomhouse.com.

First published 2018

021

Copyright © Josie Silver, 2018

The moral right of the author has been asserted

Set in 12.5/14.75 pt Garamond MT Std
Typeset by Jouve (UK), Milton Keynes
Printed and bound in Great Britain by Clays Ltd, Elcograf S.p.A.

A CIP catalogue record for this book is available from the British Library

ISBN: 978–0–241–98227–3

www.greenpenguin.co.uk

MIX
Paper from
responsible sources
FSC® C018179

Penguin Random House is committed to a
sustainable future for our business, our readers
and our planet. This book is made from Forest
Stewardship Council® certified paper.

For James, Ed and
Alex with love.

2008

21 December

Laurie

It's a wonder everyone who uses public transport in winter doesn't keel over and die of germ overload. In the last ten minutes I've been coughed on and sneezed at, and if the woman in front of me shakes her dandruff my way again, I might just douse her with the dregs of the lukewarm coffee that I'm no longer able to drink because it's full of her scalp.

I'm so tired I could sleep right here on the top deck of this swaying, rammed-full bus. Thank God I've finally finished work for Christmas, because I don't think my brain or my body could withstand even one more shift behind that awful hotel reception desk. It might be festooned with garlands and pretty lights on the customer side, but step behind the curtain and it's a soulless hellhole. I'm practically asleep, even when I'm awake. I'm loosely planning to hibernate until next year once I get home to the nostalgic familiarity of my parents' house tomorrow. There's something soothingly time warp-ish about leaving London for an interlude of sedate Midlands village life in my childhood bedroom, even if not all of my childhood memories are happy ones. Even the closest of families have their tragedies, and it's fair to say that ours came early and cut deep. I won't dwell though,

3

because Christmas should be a time of hope and love and, most appealing of all at this very moment, sleep. Sleep, punctuated by bouts of competitive eating with my brother, Daryl, and his girlfriend, Anna, and the whole gamut of cheesy Christmas movies. Because how could you ever be too tired to watch some hapless guy stand out in the cold and hold up signs silently declaring to his best friend's wife that his wasted heart will always love her? Though – is that romance? I'm not so sure. I mean, it *kind* of is, in a schmaltzy way, but it's also being the shittiest friend on the planet.

I've given up worrying about the germs in here because I've undoubtedly ingested enough to kill me if they're going to, so I lean my forehead against the steamy window and watch Camden High Street slide by in a glitter of Christmas lights and bright, fuggy shop windows selling everything from leather jackets to tacky London souvenirs. It's barely four in the afternoon, yet already it's dusk over London; I don't think it got properly light at all today.

My reflection tells me that I should probably pull the naff halo of tinsel from my hair that my cow of a manager made me wear, because I look like I'm trying out for Angel Gabriel in a primary school nativity, but I find that I really can't be bothered. No one else on this bus could care less; not the damp, anoraked man next to me taking up more than his half of the seat as he dozes over yesterday's paper, nor the bunch of schoolkids shouting across each other on the back seats and certainly not dandruff woman in front of me with her flashing snowflake earrings. The irony of her jewellery choice is not lost on me; if I were more of a bitch I might tap her on the shoulder to advise her that she's drawing attention to the skin blizzard she's depositing with every shake of her head. I'm not a bitch though; or maybe I'm just a quiet one inside my own head. Isn't everyone?

Jesus, how many more stops is this bus going to make? I'm still a couple of miles from my flat and already it's fuller than a cattle truck on market day.

Come on, I think. *Move. Take me home.* Though home is going to be a pretty depressing place now that my flatmate, Sarah, has gone back to her parents'. Only one more day then I'll be out of here too, I remind myself.

The bus shudders to a halt at the end of the street and I watch as down below a stream of people jostle to get off at the same time as others try to push their way on. It's as if they think it's one of those competitions to see how many people can fit into one small space.

There's a guy perched on one of the fold-down seats in the bus shelter. This can't be his bus, because he's engrossed in the hardback book in his hands. I notice him because he seems oblivious to the pushing and shoving happening right in front of him, like one of those fancy special effects at the movies where someone is completely still and the world kaleidoscopes around them, slightly out of focus.

I can't see his face, just the top of his sandy hair, cut slightly long and given to a wave when it grows, I should imagine. He's bundled into a navy woollen reefer jacket and a scarf that looks like someone might have knitted it for him. It's kitsch and unexpected against the coolness of the rest of his attire – dark skinny jeans and boots – and his concentration is completely held by his book. I squint, trying to duck my head to see what he's reading, wiping the steamed-up window with my coat sleeve to get a better look.

I don't know if it's the movement of my arm across the glass or the flickering lights of dandruff-woman's earrings that snag in his peripheral vision, but he lifts his head and blinks a few times as he focuses his attention on my window. *On me.*

We stare straight at each other and I can't look away. I feel my lips move as if I'm going to say something, God knows what, and all of a sudden and out of nowhere I need to get off this bus. I'm gripped by the overwhelming urge to go outside, to get to him. But I don't. I don't move a muscle, because I know there isn't a chance in hell that I can get past anorak man beside me and push through the packed bus before it pulls away. So I make the split-second decision to stay rooted to the spot and try to convey to him to get on board using just the hot, desperate longing in my eyes.

He's not film-star good-looking or classically perfect, but there is an air of preppy dishevelledness and an earnest, 'who me?' charm about him that captivates me. I can't quite make out the colour of his eyes from here. Green, I'd say, or blue maybe?

And here's the thing. Call it wishful thinking, but I'm sure I see the same thunderbolt hit him too; as if an invisible fork of lightning has inexplicably joined us together. Recognition; naked, electric shock in his rounded eyes. He does something close to an incredulous double take, the kind of thing you might do when you coincidentally spot your oldest and best friend who you haven't seen for ages and you can't actually believe they're there.

It's a look of *Hello you*, and *Oh my God, it's you*, and *I can't believe how good it is to see you*, all in one.

His eyes dart towards the dwindling queue still waiting to board and then back up to me, and it's as if I can hear the thoughts racing through his head. He's wondering if it'd be crazy to get on the bus, what he'd say if we weren't separated by the glass and the hordes, if he'd feel foolish taking the stairs two at a time to get to me.

No, I try to relay back. *No, you wouldn't feel foolish. I wouldn't let you. Just get on the bloody bus, will you!* He's staring right at me, and then a slow smile creeps across his generous mouth, as if he can't hold it in. And then I'm smiling back, giddy almost. I can't help it either.

Please get on the bus. He snaps, making a sudden decision, slamming his book closed and shoving it down in the rucksack between his ankles. He's walking forward now, and I hold my breath and press my palm flat against the glass, urging him to hurry even as I hear the sickly hiss of the doors closing and the lurch of the handbrake being released.

No! No! Oh God, don't you dare drive away from this stop! It's Christmas! I want to yell, even as the bus pulls out into the traffic and gathers pace, and outside he is breathless standing in the road, watching us leave. I see defeat turn out the light in his eyes, and because it's Christmas and because I've just fallen hopelessly in love with a stranger at a bus stop, I blow him a forlorn kiss and lay my forehead against the glass, watching him until he's out of sight.

Then I realize. Shit. Why didn't I take a leaf out of shitty friend's book and write something down to hold up against the window? I could have done that. I could even have written my mobile number in the condensation. I could have opened the tiny quarter-pane and yelled my name and address or something. I can think of any number of things I could and should have done, yet at the time none of them occurred to me because I simply couldn't take my eyes off him.

For onlookers, it must have been an Oscar-worthy sixty-second silent movie. From now on, if anyone asks me if I've ever fallen in love at first sight, I shall say yes, for one glorious minute on 21 December 2008.

2009

New Year's Resolutions

Just two resolutions this year, but two big, shiny, brilliant ones.

1) Find him, my boy from the bus stop.
2) Find my first proper job in magazines.

Damn. I wish I'd written them down in pencil, because I'd rub them out and switch them over. What I'd ideally like is to find the achingly cool magazine position first, and then run into bus boy in a coffee shop while holding something healthy in my hand for lunch, and he'd accidently knock it out of my clutches and then look up and say, 'Oh. It's you. Finally.'

And then we'd skip lunch and go for a walk around the park instead, because we'd have lost our appetites but found the love of our lives.

Anyway, that's it. Wish me luck.

Laurie

'Is that him? I definitely got a bus-ish vibe from him just now.'

I follow the direction of Sarah's nod and sweep my eyes along the length of the busy Friday-night bar. It's a habit we've fallen into every time we go anywhere; scanning faces and crowds for 'bus boy' as Sarah christened him when we compared Yuletide notes back in January. Her family festivities up in York sounded a much more raucous affair than my cosy, food-laden one in Birmingham, but we'd both returned to the reality of winter in London with the New Year blues. I threw my 'love at first sight' sob story into the pity pot and then immediately wished I hadn't. It's not that I don't trust Sarah with my story; it's more that from that second forth she has become even more obsessed with finding him again than I am. And I'm quietly going crazy over him.

'Which one?' I frown at the sea of people, mostly the backs of unfamiliar heads. She screws her nose up as she pauses to work out how to distinguish her guy for my scrutiny.

'There, in the middle, next to the woman in the blue dress.'

I spot her more easily; her poker-straight curtain of

white-blonde hair catches the light as she throws her head back and laughs up at the guy beside her.

He's about the right height. His hair looks similar and there is a jolting familiarity to the line of his shoulders in his dark shirt. He could be anyone, but he could be bus boy. The more I look at him, the more sure I am that the search is over.

'I don't know,' I say, holding my breath because he's as close as we've come. I've described him so many times, Sarah probably knows what he looks like more than I do. I want to inch closer. In fact I think I have already started inching, but then Sarah's hand on my arm stills me because he's just bent his head to kiss the face off the blonde, who instantly becomes my least favourite person on the planet.

Oh God, I think it's him! No! This isn't how it's supposed to happen. I've played out variants of this scene every night as I close my eyes and it never, repeat *never*, ends like this. Sometimes he's with a crowd of guys in a bar, other times he's alone in a cafe reading, but the one thing that never happens is he has a girlfriend who he snogs to within an inch of her shimmery blonde life.

'Shit,' Sarah mutters, pressing my wine into my hand. We watch as their kiss goes on. And on. Jeez, do these people have no boundaries? He's copping a thorough feel of her backside now, wildly overstepping the mark for a busy bar. 'Decency, people,' Sarah grumbles. 'He's not your type after all, Lu.'

I'm crestfallen. So much so that I pour the entire glass of chilled wine down my throat, and then shudder.

'I think I want to go,' I say, ridiculously close to tears.

And then they stop kissing and she straightens her dress, he murmurs something in her ear, and then turns away and walks straight towards us.

I know instantly. He brushes right past us, and I almost laugh with giddy relief.

'Not him,' I whisper. 'Not even very much like him.'

Sarah rolls her eyes and blows out the breath she must have been holding in. 'Jesus, thank fuck for that. What a sleaze-dog. Do you know how close I came to tripping him up just now?'

She's right. The guy who just sauntered past us was high on his own self-importance, wiping the girl's red lipstick from his mouth on the back of his hand with a smug, satisfied grin as he made for the loo.

God, I need another drink. The search for bus boy is three months old. I better find him soon or I'm going to wind up in rehab.

Later, back at Delancey Street, we kick off our shoes and flop.

'I've been thinking,' Sarah says, crashed out on the other end of the sofa to me. 'There's this new guy at work, I think you might like him.'

'I only want bus boy,' I sigh, costume-drama melodramatic.

'But what if you find him and he's a twat?' she says. Our experience in the bar earlier obviously hit home for her too.

'You think I should stop looking?' I ask, lifting my heavy head off the arm of the sofa to stare at her. She flings her arms wide and leaves them there.

'Just saying you need a contingency plan.'

'In case he's a twat?'

She raises her thumbs, probably because it's too much effort to raise her head.

'He could be an A-class, top-drawer super-knob,' she says. 'Or he could have a girlfriend. Or Christ, Lu, he could even be married.'

I gasp. Actually gasp. 'No way!' I splutter. 'He's single, and he's gorgeous, and he's somewhere out there waiting for me to find him.' I feel it with all the conviction of a drunk woman. 'Or maybe he's even looking for me.'

Sarah props herself up on her elbows and stares at me, her long red waves the worse for wear and her mascara end-of-the-night smudged.

'I'm just saying that we, *you*, might have unrealistic expectations, and you, *we*, need to proceed with more caution, that's all.'

I know she's right. My heart almost stopped beating in the bar earlier.

We look at each other, and then she pats my leg. 'We'll find him,' she says. It's such a simple gesture of solidarity, but in my boozy state it brings a lump to my throat.

'Promise?'

She nods and draws a cross over her heart, and a great snotty sob leaves my throat, because I'm tired and pissed and because sometimes I can't quite bring bus boy's face to mind and I'm scared I'll forget what he looks like.

Sarah sits up and dries my tears with the sleeve of her shirt.

'Don't cry, Lu,' she whispers. 'We'll keep looking until we find him.'

I nod, dropping back to gaze at the Artex ceiling that our landlord has been promising to repaint ever since we moved in here several years ago. 'We will. And he'll be perfect.'

She falls silent, and then waves her pointed finger vaguely over her own head. 'He better be. Or else I'll carve "twat", right here in his forehead.'

I nod. Her loyalty is appreciated and reciprocated. 'With a rusty scalpel,' I say, embroidering the grisly image.

'And it'll go septic and his head will drop off,' she mumbles.

I close my eyes, laughing under my breath. Until I find bus boy, the lion's share of my affection belongs to Sarah.

Laurie

'I think we've nailed it,' Sarah says, standing back to admire our handiwork. We've spent the entire weekend redecorating the tiny living room of our flat; we're both covered in paint splatters and dust. We're pretty close to done now and I'm feeling a warm glow of satisfaction – I only wish my crappy job at the hotel would make me feel even half as accomplished.

'I hope the landlord likes it,' I say. We aren't really allowed to make any material changes, but I don't see how he can object to our improvements.

'He should be paying us for this,' Sarah says, her hands on her hips. She's wearing cut-off dungarees over a Day-Glo pink vest that clashes violently with her hair. 'We've just increased the value of his flat. Who wouldn't love these boards more than that threadbare old carpet?'

I laugh, remembering our comedy sketch struggle to lug the rolled-up carpet down the stairs from our top-floor flat. By the time we reached the bottom we were sweating like miners and swearing like sailors, both plastered in chunks of loose foam underlay. We high-fived each other after we slung it into a neighbour's skip; it's been there half full of junk for ever, I don't think they'll even notice.

The old oak floorboards have come up beautifully – in years gone by someone had obviously gone to the trouble of restoring them before the current landlord hid them beneath that patterned monstrosity. Our arm-aching efforts to buff them up all feel worth it now that we're standing in our mellow, light-filled room thanks to the fresh white walls and big old sash windows. It's a tired building with glamorous bones, Artex ceiling notwithstanding. We've added a cheap rug and covered the mismatched furniture with throws from our bedrooms, and all in all I think we've performed a shoe-string miracle.

'Boho chic,' Sarah declares.

'You've got paint in your hair,' I say, touching the top of my head to show her where and promptly adding a whole new splodge to mine.

'You too,' she says, laughing, then looks at her watch. 'Fish and chips?'

Sarah has the metabolism of a horse. It's one of the things I like most about her, because it allows me to eat cake guilt-free. I nod, starving. 'I'll go.'

Half an hour later, we toast our newly fabulous living room over fish and chips eaten off our knees on the sofa.

'We should jack in our jobs and become TV home-makeover queens,' Sarah says.

'We'd kill it,' I say. '*Laurie and Sarah's Designer Do-overs.*'

She pauses, her fork halfway to her mouth. '*Sarah and Lu's Designer Do-overs.*'

'*Laurie and Sarah's* sounds better,' I grin. 'You know I'm right. Besides, I'm older than you, it's only fair I should come first.'

It's a standing joke; I'm a few months older than Sarah and I never miss a chance to pull rank. She splutters on her beer as I lean down to pick my bottle up off the floor.

'Mind the boards!'

'I've used a coaster,' I say, grandly.

She leans down and peers at my makeshift coaster, this month's supermarket offers flyer.

'Oh my God, Lu,' she says slowly. 'We've become coaster people.'

I swallow, sombre. 'Does this mean we're going to grow old and have cats together?'

She nods. 'I think it does.'

'Might as well,' I grumble. 'My love life is officially dead.'

Sarah screws up her finished-with fish-and-chip paper. 'You've only got yourself to blame,' she says.

She's referring to bus boy, of course. He's reached near-mythical status now, and I'm on the very edge of giving up on him. Ten months is a long time to look for a complete stranger on the off-chance that they'll be single, into me and not an axe murderer. Sarah is of the vocal opinion that I need to move on, by which she means I need to find someone else before I turn into a nun. I know she's right, but my heart isn't ready to let him go yet. That feeling when we locked eyes – I've never had that before, ever.

'You could have trekked around the entire globe in the time since you saw him,' she says. 'Think how many perfect men you could have shagged doing that. You'd have had tales of Roberto in Italy and Vlad in Russia to tell your grandkids when you're old.'

'I'm not going to have kids or grandkids. I'm going to

search vainly for bus boy for ever and have cats with you instead,' I say. 'We'll start a rescue centre, and the queen will give us a medal for services to cats.'

Sarah laughs, but her eyes tell me that the time has come to pack my bus boy dreams away and let him go.

'I've just remembered I'm allergic to cats,' she says. 'But you still love me, right?'

I sigh and reach for my beer. 'It's a deal-breaker, I'm afraid. Find someone else, Sarah, we can never be together.'

She grins. 'I've got a date next week.'

I clutch my heart. 'You got over us so fast.'

'I met him in a lift. I held him to ransom with the stop button until he agreed to ask me out.'

I really need to take life lessons from Sarah – she sees what she wants and grabs it with both hands. I wish for the millionth time that I'd had the balls to get off that bus. But the fact is, I didn't. Maybe it's time to wise up, to stop searching for him and drunk crying every time I fail. There are other men. I need to make 'What would Sarah do?' my life motto – I'm pretty sure she wouldn't spend a year of her life moping.

'Shall we buy a picture for that wall?' she says, looking at the empty space over the fireplace.

I nod. 'Yeah. Why not? Can it be of cats?'

She laughs and bounces her screwed-up chip paper off my head.

18 December

Laurie

'Try not to make any snap decisions when you meet David tonight? You probably won't think he's your type on first sight, but trust me, he's hilarious. And he's *kind*, Laurie. I mean, he gave up his chair for me the other day in a meeting. How many guys do you know who'd do that?' Sarah delivers this speech while on her knees pulling as many dusty wine glasses as she can find from the back of the kitchen cupboard in our tiny shared flat.

I cast around for an answer and, to be honest, it's slim pickings. 'The guy from the bottom flat moved his bike out of the way to let me through the front door this morning. Does he count?'

'You mean the same one who opens our mail and leaves trails of cold kebab on the hall floor every weekend?'

I laugh under my breath as I immerse the wine glasses in hot foamy water. We're throwing our annual Christmas party tonight, which we've held every year since we first moved into Delancey Street. Though we're kidding ourselves that this one will be much more sophisticated now we've left university, it's mostly going to involve students and a few colleagues we're still getting to know descending on our flat to drink cheap wine, debating things we don't really understand and – for me it would seem – getting off with someone called David who Sarah has decided is my perfect man. We've been here before. My best friend fancies herself as a matchmaker and set me up a couple of times when we were at uni. The first time, Mark, or it might have been Mike, turned up in running shorts in the depths of winter and spent the entire dinner trying to steer my food choices away from anything that would take more than an hour to work off in the gym. I'm a pudding girl; the main thing off the menu as far as I was concerned was Mike. Or Mark. Whichever. In Sarah's defence, he bore a passing resemblance to Brad Pitt, if you squinted and looked at him out of the corner of your eye in a dark room. Which I have to admit I did; I'm not normally one to sleep with guys on a first date, but I felt I had to give it a go for Sarah's sake.

Her second choice, Fraser, was only slightly better; I can at least remember his name. He was far and away the most Scottish Scotsman I've ever met, so much so that I only understood about fifty per cent of what he said. I don't think he mentioned bagpipes specifically, but I wouldn't have been surprised if he was packing a set underneath his jacket. His tartan bow tie was disconcerting, but none of that would have mattered. His real downfall came at the end of the date; he escorted me home to Delancey Street and then kissed me in the style of someone trying to administer CPR. CPR with an entirely inappropriate amount of saliva. I made a dash for the bathroom as soon as I got inside, and my reflection confirmed that I looked as if I'd been snogged by a Great Dane. In the rain.

Not that I've got an impressive track record at choosing boyfriends for myself, either. With the exception of Lewis, my long-time boyfriend back at home, I seem to somehow keep missing the mark. Three dates, four dates, sometimes even five before the inevitable fizzle. I'm starting to wonder if being best friends with someone as dazzling as Sarah is a double-edged sword; she gives men unrealistic expectations about women. If I didn't love her to pieces, I'd probably want to poke her eyes out.

Anyway, call me stupid, but I knew none of those men were right. I'm a girl given to romance; Nora Ephron is my go-to answer for fantasy dinner party guest and I yearn to know if nice boys really do fucking kiss like that. You get the idea. I'm hoping that amongst all these frogs will one day come a prince. Or something like that.

Who knows what David is going to be like, perhaps it will be third time lucky. I'm not going to hold my breath. Maybe he'll be the love of my life or maybe he'll be hideous, but either way I'm undeniably intrigued and more than up for letting my hair down. It's not something I've done very often over the course of the last year; we've both had the upheaval of moving out of the cushioned world of uni into the reality of work, more successfully in Sarah's case than mine. She practically walked into a junior position with a regional TV network, whereas I'm still working on the reception desk at the hotel. Yes, despite my New Year's Resolution I am decidedly not working in my dream job yet. But it was that or go home to Birmingham, and I fear that if I leave London I'll never get back again. It was always going to come more easily for Sarah; she's the gregarious one and I'm slightly socially awkward, which means interviews don't tend to go so well.

None of that tonight though. I'm determined to get so drunk that social awkwardness is a complete impossibility. After all, we'll have the buffer of New Year to forget our ill-advised, alcohol-fuelled behaviour. I mean, come on, that happened *last year* for God's sake. Move on already!

It's also the night that I finally get to meet Sarah's new boyfriend. She's known him for several weeks already but for one reason or another I've yet to lay eyes on him in the apparently incredibly hot flesh. I've heard enough about him to write a book, though. Unfortunately for him, I already know he's a sex god in bed and that Sarah fully expects to have his children and be his wife once he's the high-flying media celeb he's clearly on track to becoming. I almost feel sorry for him having his future mapped out for the next ten years at the age of twenty-four. But hey, this is Sarah. However cool he is, he's still the lucky one.

She can't stop talking about him. She's doing it again now, telling me far more about their rampant sex life than I'd ideally like to know.

I scatter bubbles in the air like a child waving a wand as I hold my soapy fingers up to halt her flow. 'Okay, okay, please stop. I'll try not to orgasm on sight when I finally clap eyes on your future husband.'

'Don't say that to him though, will you?' she grins. 'The future husband thing? Because he doesn't know that bit yet and, you know, it might, like, shock him.'

'You reckon?' I deadpan.

'Far better if he thinks it's all his own brilliant idea in a few years' time.' She dusts off the knees of her jeans as she stands up.

I nod. If I know Sarah, which I do, she'll have him wrapped round her little finger and more than ready to spontaneously propose whenever she decides the time is right. You know those people that everyone gravitates towards? Those rare effervescent birds who radiate this aura that draws people into their orbit? Sarah's that person. But if you think that makes her sound insufferable, you'd be wrong.

I first met her right here, the first year of uni. I'd decided to go for one of the university rentals rather than halls and I'd picked this place. It's a tall old townhouse split into three: two bigger flats downstairs and our attic perched on the top like a jaunty afterthought. I was utterly charmed when I first viewed it, my rose-tinted glasses jammed all the way on. You know that shabby-chic little flat Bridget Jones lives in? It reminded me of that, only more shabby and less chic, and I was going to have to share it with a total stranger to meet the rent. None of those drawbacks stopped me from signing on the dotted line; one stranger was easier to contemplate than a crowded, noisy hall full of them. I still remember carting all of my stuff up three flights of stairs on moving-in day, all the time hoping that my new flatmate wasn't going to crush my Bridget Jones fantasy dead.

She'd tacked a welcome note to the door, big, loopy red handwriting scrawled across the back of a used envelope:

Dear new housemate,

*Have gone to buy cheap fizzy piss to celebrate our new home.
Take the bigger room if you like, I prefer being in stumbling
distance of the bog anyway!*

S x

And that was it. She had me in the palm of her hand
before I'd even laid eyes on her. She's different to me in
lots of ways, but we share exactly enough middle ground
to get on like a house on fire. She's in-your-face gorgeous
with waves of fire-engine red hair that almost reach her
bum, and her figure is amazing, though she doesn't give a
toss about how she looks.

Normally someone as gorgeous as her would make me
feel like the ugly sister, but Sarah has this way of making
you feel good about yourself. The first thing she said to
me when she got back from the corner shop that day was,
'Fucking hell! You're a dead ringer for Elizabeth Taylor.
We're going to have to get a deadlock on the door or else
we're gonna cause a riot.'

She was exaggerating, of course. I don't look very much
like Elizabeth Taylor. I have my French maternal grandmother to thank for my dark hair and blue eyes; she was
quite a celebrated ballerina in her twenties; we have the
prized programmes and grainy press cuttings to prove it.
But I've always thought of myself as more of a failed
Parisian; I have inherited my grandmother's form but not
her grace, and her neat brunette chignon has become a
permanently electrocuted mass of curls in my hands.
Besides, there's no way I'd ever have the discipline for

dancing, I'm far too fond of an extra chocolate biscuit. I'm going to be a goner when my metabolism catches up with me.

Sarah jokingly refers to us as the prozzie and the princess. In truth, she's not got an ounce of slut in her and I'm nowhere near ladylike enough for a princess. Like I said, we meet in the middle and we make each other laugh. She's Thelma to my Louise, hence the reason I'm disconcerted that she's suddenly fallen hook, line and sinker for a guy I haven't even met or vetted for suitability.

'Do we have enough booze, do you think?' she asks now, casting a critical eye over the bottles lined up across the kitchen work surface. No one could call it a sophisticated collection; it's pile 'em high and sell 'em cheap supermarket special offer wine and vodka we've been hoarding for the last three months to make sure our party is one to remember.

Or not remember, perhaps.

'More than. People will bring a bottle too,' I say. 'It's going to be great.' My stomach rumbles, reminding me that neither of us has eaten since breakfast.

'Did you hear that?' I say, rubbing my middle. 'My guts just asked you to make a DS special.'

Sarah's sandwiches are the stuff of Delancey Street myth and legend. She's taught me her holy breakfast trinity of bacon, beetroot and mushrooms, and it took us the best part of two years to settle on our signature dish, the DS special, named after our flat.

She rolls her eyes, laughing. 'You can make it yourself, you know.'

'Not the way you do it.'

She preens a little, opening the fridge. 'That's true.'

I watch her layer chicken and blue cheese with lettuce, mayo and cranberry, an exact science that I've yet to master. I know it sounds hideous, but trust me, it's not. It may not be your average student food, but ever since we hit on the winning combo back in our uni days we make sure to always have the ingredients in the fridge. It's pretty much our staple diet. That, ice cream and cheap wine.

'It's the cranberry that does it,' I say after my first bite.

'It's a quantity thing,' she says. 'Too much cranberry and it's basically a jam sandwich. Too much cheese and you're licking a teenager's dirty sock.'

I raise my sandwich for another bite, but she lunges and pushes my arm down. 'Wait. We need a drink with it to get us in the party mood.'

I groan, because I realize what she's going to do when she reaches for two shot glasses. She's laughing under her breath already as she reaches into the back of the cupboard behind the cereal boxes for the dusty bottle.

'Monks' piss,' she says, pouring us each a ceremonial shot. Or Benedictine, to give the old herbal liqueur that came with the flat its proper name. The bottle informs us that it's a special blend of secret herbs and spices, and on first taste not long after we moved in we decided that one of those secret ingredients was almost certainly Benedictine monks' piss. Every now and then, usually at Christmas, we have one shot each, a ritual we've come to enjoy and loathe in equal measures.

'Down the hatch,' she grins, sliding a glass across the table to me as she sits back down. 'Happy Christmas, Lu.'

We clink and then knock our shots back, banging the empty glasses down on the table and wincing.

'Doesn't get any better with age,' I whisper, feeling as if it's taken the skin off the roof of my mouth.

'Rocket fuel,' she rasps, laughing. 'Eat your sandwich, you've earned it.'

We lapse into sandwich silence, and when we've finished she taps the rim of her empty plate.

'I think, because it's Christmas, that we could add a sausage.'

I shake my head. 'You can't mess with the DS special.'

'There isn't much in life that can't be improved by a saveloy, Laurie.' She raises her eyebrows at me. 'You never know, you might get lucky tonight and see David's.'

Given the last two blind dates Sarah set me up on, I don't let the prospect overexcite me.

'Come on,' I say, dumping the plates in the sink. 'We'd better get ready, they'll be here soon.'

I'm three glasses of white in and definitely very relaxed when Sarah finds me and literally drags me from the kitchen by the hand.

'He's here,' she whispers, crushing the bones of my fingers. 'Come and say hi. You have to meet him right now.'

I smile apologetically at David as she pulls me away. I'm starting to see what Sarah meant about him being a grower. He's made me laugh several times already and he's kept my glass topped up; I'd just been considering a tiny exploratory snog. He's nice enough in a vaguely Ross from *Friends* kind of way, but I find I'm more intrigued to meet Sarah's soulmate, which must mean that Ross from *Friends* would be a regret come tomorrow. It's as good a barometer as any.

She tugs me through our laughing, drunk friends and a

whole load of people I'm not sure either of us even know, until finally we reach her boyfriend standing uncertainly by the front door.

'Laurie,' Sarah is jittery and bright-eyed. 'Meet Jack. Jack, this is Laurie. *My* Laurie,' she adds, for emphasis.

I open my mouth to say hello and then I see his face. My heart jumps into my throat and I feel as if someone just laid electric shock pads on my chest and turned them up to full fry. I can't get any words to leave my lips.

I know him.

It feels like just last week I saw him first – and last. That heart-stopping glimpse from the top deck of a crowded bus twelve months ago.

'Laurie.' He says my name, and I could cry with the sheer relief of him being here. It's going to sound crazy but I've spent the last year wishing, hoping I'd run into him. And now he's here. I've scoured countless crowds for his face and I've searched for him in bars and cafes. I'd all but given up on ever finding bus boy, even though Sarah swears I've banged on about him so much that she'd even recognize him herself.

She didn't, as it turned out. Instead she's presented him to me as the love of her life.

Green. His eyes are green. Tree moss vivid around the iris edges, warm amber gold seeping in around his pupils. But it's not the *colour* of his eyes that strikes me so much as the look in them right now as he gazes down at me. A startled flash of recognition. A dizzying, headlong collision. And then it's gone in a heartbeat, leaving me unsure if the sheer force of my own longing made me imagine it had been there at all.

'Jack,' I manage, thrusting my hand out. *His name is Jack*. 'It's so good to meet you.'

He nods, a skittish half-smile flickering over his lips. 'Laurie.'

I glance towards Sarah, crazy guilty, certain that she must be able to sense something amiss, but she's just grinning at us both like a loon. Thank God for cheap wine.

When he takes my hand in his, warm and strong, he shakes it firmly, politely almost, as if we're meeting in a formal boardroom rather than at a Christmas party.

I don't know what to do with myself, because all of the things I want to do wouldn't be okay. True to my word, I don't orgasm on the spot, but there is definitely something going on with my heart. How on earth has this colossal fuck-up happened? He can't be Sarah's. He's mine. He's been mine for an entire year.

'Isn't she fabulous?'

Sarah has her hand on the small of my back now, presenting me, actually propelling me towards him to hug because she's desperate for us to be new best friends. I'm wretched.

Jack rolls his eyes and laughs nervously, as if Sarah's obviousness makes him uncomfortable.

'Just as splendid as you said she was,' he agrees, nodding as if he's admiring a friend's new car, and something horribly like an apology creeps into his expression as he looks at me. Is he apologizing because he remembers or because Sarah is behaving like an overeager aunt at a wedding?

'Laurie?' Sarah turns her attention to me. 'Isn't he every bit as gorgeous as I said he was?' She's laughing, proud of him, as well she should be.

I nod. Swallow painfully, even as I force a laugh. 'He certainly is.'

Because Sarah is so desperately keen for us to like each other, Jack obligingly leans in and touches his lips briefly against my cheek. 'It's good to meet you,' he says. His voice matches him perfectly; coolly confident, rich, shot through with gentle, knowing wit. 'She never shuts up about you.'

My fingers close around the familiarity of my purple pendant, looking for comfort as I force a laugh, shaky. 'I feel as if I know you too.' And I do; I feel as if I have known him for ever. I want to turn my face and catch his lips with my own. I want to drag him breathlessly to my room and close the door, tell him that I love him, strip off my clothes and climb into bed with him, drown in the woody, clean, warm scent of his skin.

I'm in hell. I hate myself. I take a couple of steps away from him for my own sanity and grapple with my wretched heart to stop it banging louder than the music.

'Drink?' Sarah suggests, light-hearted and loud.

He nods, grateful to be thrown a lifeline.

'Laurie?' Sarah looks at me to go with them.

I lean back and peer down the hallway towards the bathroom, jiggling as if I'm in dire need of the loo. 'I'll catch you up.' I need to get away from him, from them, from this.

In the safety of the bathroom, I slam the door and slide on to my backside with my head in my hands, gulping air down so as not to cry.

Oh God, oh God. Oh God! I love Sarah, she's my sister in all but biology. But this ... I don't know how to navigate safely through it without sinking the ship with all of us aboard. Hope flares bright in my chest as I fantasize running out there and just blurting out the truth, because maybe then Sarah will realize that the reason she's so drawn to him is that, subconsciously, she recognized him as bus boy. God knows I've all but drawn him for her. What a misunderstanding! How we'll laugh at the sheer absurdity! But . . . then what? She graciously steps aside and he is *my* new boyfriend, easy as pie? I don't even think he recognized me, for Christ's sake!

Lead-heavy defeat crushes the delicate, ridiculous hope as reality creeps in. I can't do it. Of course I can't. She has no clue, and Jesus, she's so happy. It shines from her brighter than the star of fucking Bethlehem. It might be Christmas, but this is actual life, not some crappy Hollywood movie. Sarah is my best friend in the entire world, and however much and for however long it kills me, I'll never silently, secretly hold up signs to tell Jack O'Mara, without hope or agenda, that to me he is perfect, and that my wasted heart will always love him.

19 December

Jack

Fuck, she's so beautiful when she's asleep.

My throat feels like someone shovelled sand down it and I think Sarah might have broken my nose when she smacked her head back in bed last night, but right now I can forgive her anything because her scarlet hair is strewn out around her shoulders on the pillows, almost as if she's suspended in water. She looks like the Little Mermaid. Though I realize that thought makes me sound like a pervert.

I slide from the bed and fling on the nearest thing to hand: Sarah's dressing gown. It's covered in pineapples, but I've no clue where my own clothes went and I need headache pills. Given the state of the stragglers last night I wouldn't be surprised to find one or two of them still strewn across the living-room floor, and I figure pine-apples will offend them less than my naked arse. Shit, it's pretty bloody short though. I'll just do a quick dash.

'Water,' Sarah croaks, flinging her hand out towards me as I skirt round the edge of the bed.

'I know,' I murmur. Her eyes are still closed as I lift her arm and carefully tuck it back under the quilt, and she makes a noise that might mean *Thanks* and might be *For God's sake help me.* I drop a kiss on her forehead.

'Back in a sec,' I whisper, but she's already slid under the fog of sleep again. I don't blame her. I plan to climb back in there and do the same thing myself within the next five minutes. Glancing at her again for a long second, I back quietly out of the room and click the door shut.

'If you need paracetamol, they're in the cupboard on the left.'

I pause for a beat, swallowing hard as I open the cupboard door and root around until I spot the small blue box.

'You read my mind,' I say, turning to Laurie. I force a casual smile, because in truth this is really fucking awkward. I've seen her before – before last night, I mean. It was just once, fleetingly, in the flesh, but there have been other times in my head since: random, disturbing early-morning lucid dreams where I jolt awake, hard and frustrated. I don't know if she remembers me. Christ, I hope not. Especially now I'm standing in front of her in a ridiculous pineapple-strewn ball-grazing dressing gown.

Her dark hair is piled high on her head in a messy bun this morning and she looks as if she's as much in need of medication as I am, so I offer her the box.

Sarah has banged on about her best friend so much that I'd built a virtual Laurie in my head already, but I'd got her all wrong. Because Sarah is so striking, I'd lazily imagined that her choice of friend would be equally colourful, like a pair of exotic parrots perched up here in their cage. Laurie isn't a parrot. She's more of a . . . I don't know, a robin, maybe. There's a contained peace about her, and a quiet, understated sense of being okay with herself that makes her easy to be around.

'Thanks.' She takes the tablets, popping a couple out into her hand.

I run her a glass of water and she raises it to me, a grim 'bottoms up' as she knocks the pills back.

'Here,' she says, counting how many are left in the packet before she hands it over. 'Sarah likes –'

'Three,' I jump in, and she nods.

'Three.'

I feel a little as if we're competing to prove who knows Sarah best. She does, of course. Sarah and I have only been together for a month or so, but Christ, it's been a whirlwind. I'm running to keep up with her most of the time. I met her first in the lift at work; it jammed with just the two of us inside, and by the time it moved again fifteen minutes later I knew three things. Firstly, she might be a fill-in reporter for the local TV station now, but one day she's likely to take over the world. Two, I was taking her for lunch as soon as the lift got fixed, because she told me so. I was going to ask her anyway, for the record. And lastly, I'm pretty sure she stopped the lift herself and then released it once she'd got what she wanted. That mildly ruthless streak is a turn-on.

'She's told me a lot about you.' I fill up the kettle and flick it on.

'Did she tell you how I like my coffee?'

Laurie reaches for some mugs out of the cupboard as she speaks, and I hate the reflex that sends my eyes down her body. She's in PJs, more than respectably covered, yet still I observe the fluidity of her movements, the curve of her hip, the navy polish on her toes.

'Erm . . .' I concentrate on hunting down a teaspoon,

and she stretches across to tug out the drawer to show me where they are.

'Got it,' I say, reaching in at the same moment as she does, and she jerks her hand away, laughing to soften the suddenness.

As I start to spoon the granules out she folds herself on to a spindle-backed chair, one foot tucked underneath her backside.

'To answer your question, no, Sarah didn't tell me how you like your coffee, but if I had to guess, I'd say . . .' I turn and lean against the counter to study her. 'I'd say you take it strong. Two spoons.' I narrow my eyes as she watches me without giving any hint. 'Sugar,' I say, passing my hand across the back of my neck. 'None. You want to, but you deny yourself.' What the actual fuck am I saying? I sound like I'm coming on to her. I'm not. I'm really not. The last thing I want her to think is that I'm a player. I mean I've had my share of girlfriends, a couple even edged towards serious, but this thing with Sarah feels different somehow. More . . . I don't know. I just know I don't want it to end any time soon.

She pulls a face, then shakes her head. 'Two sugars.'

'You're kidding me,' I laugh.

She shrugs. 'I'm not. I take two sugars. Two and a half sometimes, if I'm in the mood.'

The mood for what, I wonder. What makes her need more than two sugars? God, I really need to get out of this kitchen and back to bed. I think I've left my brain back there on the pillow.

'Actually,' Laurie says, standing up, 'I don't think I want coffee right now after all.' She backs towards the door as she speaks, and I can't quite read the expression in her tired eyes. Maybe I've offended her. I don't know. Perhaps she's just knackered or maybe she's on the verge of hurling. I've been known to have that effect on women.

Laurie

'Well? What do you think?'

It's just turned four when I slump next to Sarah at the pale-blue Formica kitchen table. We've finally got the place back to something resembling normal and now we're both nursing huge mugs of coffee and the remnants of our hangovers. The Christmas tree we lugged up the stairs between us a couple of days back looks haphazard, as if a gang of cats has attacked it, but aside from that and a few broken wine glasses we're pretty much as we were. I heard Jack leave around midday – okay, I failed miserably in my attempt to be cool about the situation and watched him walk away down the road from behind my bedroom blind like some kind of horror-movie stalker.

'It went well, didn't it?' I say, deliberately misinterpreting Sarah's question to buy myself some thinking time.

She rolls her eyes as if she thinks I'm winding her up on purpose. 'You know what I mean. What do you think of *Jack*?'

And so it begins. A hairline crack has opened up in our relationship that Sarah isn't even aware of, and I have to work out how I stop it from widening, how to prevent it from opening up into a chasm we're both going to tumble headlong into. I'm conscious that this is the one and only chance I'm ever going to get to come clean; this single, solitary opportunity is mine to take, or not take. But because Sarah is looking at me with such hope, and because by now I don't even know if I was imagining the whole thing, I silently promise to for ever hold my peace.

'He seems . . . nice,' I say, deliberately choosing a bland, mundane word for the most exhilarating man I've ever met.

'Nice?' Sarah scoffs. 'Laurie, *nice* is a word you'd use for furry slippers or, I don't know, chocolate eclairs or something.'

I laugh lightly. 'I happen to really like furry slippers.'

'And I happen to really like chocolate eclairs, but Jack isn't a chocolate eclair. He's . . .' She trails off, thinking.

Snowflakes on your tongue, I want to suggest, or the bubbles in vintage champagne. '*Very nice?*' I smile. 'Is that better?'

'Not even close. He's a . . . he's a cream horn.'

She laughs, dirtily, but she's gone all dreamy-eyed on me and I don't think I'm ready to listen to her try to convince me of Jack's merits, so I shrug and wade in before she can speak again. 'Okay, okay. He's . . . well, he seems like fun and he's easy to talk to and he's obviously wrapped round your little finger.'

A snort-laugh escapes Sarah's throat. 'He is, isn't he?' She crooks her little finger and we nod over our coffee mugs. She looks about fourteen; her face is scrubbed clean of make-up and her hair hangs in two long plaits over her 'My Little Pony' T-shirt.

'Is he what you'd imagined?'

Oh God, Sarah, please don't push. I don't think I can for ever hold my peace if you do.

'I'm not sure what I expected, really,' I say, because that much is true.

'Oh, come on, you must have had some image in your head.'

I've had Jack O'Mara's image in my head for twelve clear months. 'Um, yeah. I suppose he's sort of what I'd imagine your perfect man to be.'

Her shoulders sag, as if just thinking about his fabulousness has sapped the small amount of energy from her tank, and she's lapsed into that glassy-eyed state again. I'm relieved we're both still hung-over, it's a ready excuse not to over-enthuse.

'But he's hot, though, right?'

I glance down quickly into my coffee cup while I try to pull the panicked, guilty truth back out of my eyes, and she's looking straight at me when I lift my gaze. Her uncertain expression tells me that she's seeking my approval, and I both understand why and resent her for it in the same breath. Sarah's generally the most striking woman in any given room, a girl accustomed to being the centre of attention. It could have made her precocious or precious or pretentious; it hasn't made her any of those things, but there's no escaping the fact that she's lived her life as the girl who can bag any guy she wants. More often than not that's meant her boyfriends have been outlandishly good-looking, because, well, why wouldn't you?

For the most part it amuses me, and up to now it's meant that our romantic paths haven't crossed. But now . . .

What am I supposed to say? There is no safe answer. If

I say yes, he's hot, I don't think I'll be able to make myself sound un-pervy, and if I say no, he's not hot, then she'll be insulted.

'He's different to your usual type,' I venture.

She nods slowly and bites her bottom lip. 'I know. You can be honest, I won't be offended. He's not the obvious kind of handsome you expected him to be, is that what you're trying to say?'

I shrug. 'I guess. I'm not saying he isn't good-looking or anything, just different to your normal.' I pause and give her a knowing look. 'Your last boyfriend looked more like Matt Damon than Matt Damon does, for God's sake.'

She laughs, because it's true. I even called him Matt to his face once by mistake, which was okay because he only lasted four dates before Sarah decided that, however handsome he was, it didn't make up for the fact that he still called his mum three times a day.

'Jack just seems more grown-up, somehow.' She sighs as she cups her hands round her mug. 'As if all the others were boys, and he's a man. Does that sound ridiculous?'

I shake my head and smile, beyond forlorn. 'No. Not ridiculous to me.'

'I guess he had to grow up early,' Sarah says. 'He lost his dad a few years ago – cancer, I think.' She breaks off, reflective. 'His mum and his younger brother depended on him pretty heavily for a while afterwards.'

My heart breaks a little for him; I don't need telling how devastating that must've been.

'He seems a pretty cool guy.'

Sarah looks relieved by my assessment. 'Yeah. That's

what he is. He's his own kind of cool. He doesn't follow the crowd.'

'Best way.'

She lapses into contemplative silence for a few seconds before she speaks again. 'He likes you.'

'Did he say so?' I intend to sound nonchalant, but I fear I might have hit something closer to desperation. If I did, Sarah doesn't flicker.

'I can just tell. You two are going to be best friends.' She grins as she scrapes her chair back and stands up. 'Just wait and see. You'll love him when you get to know him.'

She ambles from the kitchen, giving my topknot an affectionate waggle as she passes. I fight the urge to jump up and pull her into a fierce hug, both by way of apology and as a plea for understanding. Instead I drag the sugar bowl towards me and stir extra sweetness into my coffee. Thank God I'm heading back home to spend Christmas with my folks soon; I seriously need some time to myself while I work out how the hell to play this.

2010

New Year's Resolutions

Last year, I made two resolutions:

1) Find my first proper job in magazines. Well, I can safely say I've failed spectacularly on that front. Two near misses and a couple of freelance never-got-published articles ranks as neither glittering nor fabulous really, does it? It's both depressing and scary that I'm still working at the hotel; I can see how easy it is for people to get stuck in a rut and let go of their dreams. But I'm not giving up, not yet.

2) Find the boy from the bus stop. Technically, I guess I can tick this one off. I've learned to my peril that you need to be super-specific when you make New Year's Resolutions – but how was I supposed to know I needed to specify that my best friend in the world must not find my soulmate first and fall in love with him too? Thanks for nothing, Universe. You suck big donkey balls.

So my only resolution this year?
To work out how to fall out of love.

18 January

Laurie

It's been a month now since I discovered that Sarah and I have inconveniently fallen for the same guy and, despite my resolution, I don't feel a shred less wretched about it.

It was so much easier when I didn't know who he was; it allowed me the luxury of imagining him, of fantasizing about stumbling into him again in a crowded bar or spotting him drinking coffee in a cafe, of his eyes finding mine and us both remembering and being glad that the stars had finally aligned again.

But now I know exactly who he is. He's Jack O'Mara, and he's Sarah's.

I spent all of Christmas telling myself that it would be easier once I got to know him, that there were bound to be things I didn't like about him in reality, that seeing him with Sarah would somehow reset him in my head as a platonic friend, rather than the man who has broken the beats of my heart. I stuffed myself with food and hung out with Daryl and pretended to everyone that I was okay.

But since we got back to London it's been worse. Because not only am I lying to myself, I'm lying to Sarah too. God knows how people have affairs; even this paper-thin layer of deception has me constantly on edge. I've kept my own counsel. I've heard my own case, I've listened to my own plaintive cries of innocence and mis-understanding, and still I've delivered a damning verdict: *liar.* I've made a liar out of myself by omission, and now every day I look at Sarah through my liar's eyes and speak to her with my forked, serpent tongue. I don't even want to admit it to myself, but every now and then I burn with miserable jealousy. It's an ugly emotion; if I were of a religious bent I'd be spending more than my fair share of time in the confession box. I have moments of a different perspective, times when I know I haven't done anything wrong and try my best to still be a good friend even though I've been backed into a corner, but those moments don't last long. Incidentally, I've also discovered that I'm quite the actress; I'm one hundred per cent sure that Sarah has no idea there's anything amiss, although that's probably because I've found reasons to be somewhere else on the couple of occasions when Jack's been at the flat.

Tonight though, my luck has officially run out. Sarah's asked him over for pizza and a movie, but the subtext is that she really wants me to get to know him better. In fact, she said it, as plain as that, when she handed me a coffee on the way out of the door this morning.

'Please be around, Lu, I really want you to get to know him so we can all hang out together more.'

I couldn't think of a decent excuse off the cuff and, more-over, I realize that avoiding him isn't a long-term solution. What bothers me most of all, though, is that while ninety-five per cent of me is dreading tonight, the other five is sparking with anticipation at the idea of being close to him.

I'm sorry, Sarah, I really and truly am.

*

'Let me take your coat.'

Let me take your coat? What the hell am I, the maid? I'm just glad I didn't call him *sir* for good measure. Jack walked into our flat thirty seconds ago and already I'm acting like a moron. His smile is nervous as he unwinds his scarf and shrugs out of his winter coat, handing them to me almost apologetically even though I asked him for them. I have to work hard not to bury my face in the dark navy wool as I hang it on the already-packed coat hooks beside our front door, almost laying it over my own jacket before pointedly hanging it as far away from it as possible. I'm trying, I really am. But he's half an hour early, and has managed to arrive just as Sarah ran down the fire escape off the kitchen, as if they are theatre actors in a farce.

'Sarah's just nipped to the shop for wine,' I flounder. 'It's round the corner. She'll be back soon. Five minutes, I should think, unless there's a queue. Or anything. It's only round the corner.'

He nods, his smile still hovering despite the fact I've repeated myself at least three times.

'Go through, go through,' I say, bright and overanxious, flapping my hands in the direction of our tiny living room. 'How was your Christmas?'

He perches on the end of the sofa, and I momentarily falter over where to sit before choosing the chair. What else was I going to do? Join him on the sofa? Accidentally press myself against him?

'Yeah, you know.' He smiles, almost bashful. 'Christmassy.' He pauses. 'Turkey. Too much beer.'

I smile too. 'Sounds a lot like mine. Except I'm more of a wine drinker.'

What am I doing – trying to make myself sound sophisticated? He's going to think I'm some kind of pretentious knobber.

Come on, Sarah, I think. Come back and rescue me from myself, I'm not ready to be on my own with him yet. I'm horrified as I find myself wanting to snatch this chance to ask him if he remembers me from the bus. I can feel the question climbing up my windpipe like it's being pushed from behind by a determined colony of worker ants. I swallow hard. My palms are starting to sweat. I don't know what I hope to gain from asking him if he remembers, because I'm ninety-nine per cent certain that the answer would be no. Jack lives in the real world and has a super-hot girlfriend; he'd probably forgotten about me before my bus turned the corner of Camden High Street.

'So, Laurie,' he says, clearly casting around for something to say. I feel the way I sometimes do when I get my hair cut; as if the stylist finds me hard work and I'm shortly going to need to lie about where I'm going on holiday. 'What did you study?'

'Media and Journalism.'

He doesn't look surprised; he must know that Sarah and I were on the same course at Middlesex.

'I'm a words person,' I elaborate. 'Magazines, hopefully, when I can get my foot in the door somewhere. I don't plan on a career in front of the camera.' I stop myself from adding 'unlike Sarah', because I'm sure he already knows that Sarah's life plan involves presenting the local news before moving up the ranks towards the national broadcasters. There's a trite quote I see bandied around on Facebook every now and then, 'Some girls are born with glitter in their veins,' or something similar. Sarah is that, but there's grit mixed in with her glitter; she doesn't stop until she gets what she wants. 'How about you?'

He lifts one shoulder. 'Journalism at uni. Radio's my thing.'

I know this already, because Sarah has tuned the kitchen radio into the station he works at, even though he's only ever on it if the late-night presenter isn't there, which has been next to never. Everyone starts somewhere though, and now I've heard his voice I know that it's only a matter of time before he moves up the ranks. I have a sudden, hideous vision of Sarah and Jack as TV's golden couple, the next Phil and Holly, shining out of my TV at me every day with their in-jokes, finishing each other's sentences and winning every People's Choice award going. It's so realistic that I'm winded, and I'm relieved to hear Sarah's keys clatter in the lock.

'Honey, I'm home,' she calls out, slamming the door so hard she rattles the old wooden sash window frames in the living room.

'Here she is,' I say unnecessarily, springing up. 'I'll just go and help her.'

I meet her in the doorway and take the unchilled wine from her hands. 'Jack's just arrived. You go and say hi, I'll stick this in the freezer to cool down for a bit.'

I withdraw to the kitchen, wishing I could climb into the freezer drawer too as I shoehorn the bottle in beneath the bag of frozen berries we use for smoothies when we feel like we might die from lack of nutrients.

I open the bottle of wine we've already chilled in the fridge and pour out a couple of decent glasses. One for me, one for Sarah. I don't pour one for Jack, because as I already know, he's more of a beer kind of guy. I'm warmed by the fact that I know what he'd prefer without needing to ask, as if this one tiny snippet is a new stitch in the quilt of our intimacy. It's an odd thought, but I run with it, imagining that quilt as I pull out a bottle of beer for Jack and flick the lid off, then close the fridge and lean my back against it with my wine glass in my hand. Our quilt is handmade, carefully constructed from gossamer-thin layers of hushed conversations and snatched looks, stitched together with threads of wishes and dreams, until it's this magnificent, wondrous, weightless thing that keeps us warm and protects us from harm as if it were made of steel. *Us?* Who am I kidding?

I take a second mouthful of wine as I catch hold of my train of thought and try to reroute it along safer tracks. I force myself to see that quilt on Sarah and Jack's king-size bed, in Sarah and Jack's gorgeous house, in Sarah and Jack's perfect life. It's a technique I've been testing out; whenever I think something inappropriate about him, I make myself counter it with a sickly, positive thought about them as a couple. I can't say it's working all that well yet, but I'm trying.

'Come on, Lu, I'm gagging in here!' Sarah's voice runs clear with carefree laughter as she adds, 'Don't bother with a wine glass for Jack, though. He's too unsophisticated for our five-quid plonk.'

I know, I want to say, but I don't. I just shove Jack's beer under my arm and refill my glass before I go back through to join them in the living room.

'Pineapple on pizza is like having, I dunno, ham with custard. They just don't go together.' Sarah shoves two fingers down her throat and rolls her eyes.

Jack picks up the offending piece of pineapple that Sarah has flicked disdainfully into the corner of the box. 'I had banana on pizza, too, once. Trust me, it worked.' He squidges the extra pineapple down on to his slice and grins at me. 'You can have the casting vote, Laurie. Pineapple yay or pineapple nay?'

I feel disloyal, but I can't lie because Sarah already knows the answer.

'Yay. Definitely yay.'

Sarah snorts, making me wish I'd lied. 'I'm starting to think that getting you two together was a bad idea. You're going to gang up on me.'

'Team J-Lu.' Jack winks at me as he laughs, earning himself a good punch on the arm from Sarah that makes him groan and rub it as if she's broken it.

'Easy. That's my drinking arm.'

'That's for trying to split up team Sa-Lu.' She's the one winking at me now, and I nod, keen to show that I'm on her side even if I do like pineapple on my pizza.

'Sorry, Jack,' I say. 'We're wine sisters. It's a stronger bond than pineapple on pizza.' And I have to say, the wine is definitely helping me get through this situation.

Sarah shoots him a 'suck on that' look and high-fives me across the gulf between the mismatched sofa and armchair. She's curled into the end with her feet shoved under Jack's ass, her long red hair plaited round her head like she might nip out the back and milk her herd of goats at any moment.

I've deliberately gone effort-light with my appearance; I've aimed for a 'making a bit of an effort to be sociable' look without obviously looking any different to normal. I'm dressed in leaving-the-house clothes, which definitely isn't a given for a night in front of the TV. Jeans, soft, dove-grey sloppy jumper, slick of lip gloss and a flick of eyeliner. I'm not proud of the fact that I put more than a few minutes' thought into my outfit, but I'm trying to be reasonable with myself about this too. I don't actually own sackcloth and ashes, and I don't want to let Sarah down. Besides, she added her own silver daisy hairslide to my fringe earlier because it kept flopping in my eyes and she knows I covet it, so I reckon she's pleased that I look presentable.

'Which movie are we watching?' I ask, leaning forward to grab a slice of pizza from the box flipped open on the coffee table.

'*Twilight*,' Sarah says, at the exact same time as Jack says, '*Iron Man*.'

I look from one to the other, sensing that once again I'm about to be asked to play adjudicator.

'Remember which team you're on, Lu,' Sarah says, her lips twitching. *Seriously*. I couldn't make this stuff up. I haven't read the books or seen the films yet, but I know enough to know that *Twilight* is about a doomed love triangle.

Jack looks pained, then bats his eyelashes at me like a seven-year-old asking for money for the ice-cream man. Jesus, he's lovely. I want to say *Iron Man*. I want to say *kiss me*.

'Twilight.'

Jack

Fucking *Twilight*?

Everything about this evening screams of awkward. And now we're watching one of the most cringe-worthy films of all time, about some moody-mouthed girl who can't choose between two guys with superpowers. Sarah leans into me, and I kiss the top of her head and train my eyes on the screen, not allowing myself to slide even an occasional glance towards Laurie on the armchair unless she speaks directly to me.

I don't want things between me and Laurie to feel awkward, but they do, and I know it's my fault. She probably thinks I'm some kind of exceptionally dull weirdo, because my conversational skills dry up around her. It's just that I'm trying to establish her place in my head as Sarah's friend rather than the girl I saw once and have thought of often since. All of Christmas – which was terrible, by the way, my mum was so sad, and as usual I didn't know what to do, so I just got drunk – I kept seeing Laurie in her pyjamas in the kitchen, gazing at me with that strange look on her face. Jesus, what a twat I am. I take solace from the fact that it's just the way my blokeish brain stores away a pretty face, and from the fact that she doesn't have a blokeish brain and so hopefully has no awkward memory of me gawking at her from a bus stop. So far I've managed quite successfully by just avoiding spending any time with her, but Sarah came straight out with it yesterday and asked me if I didn't like Laurie, because I seemed to say no every time she invited me over. What the fuck was I supposed to say to that? Sorry, Sarah, I'm currently trying to reprocess your best friend from fantasy sex partner to platonic new friend-in-law? Is that even a phrase? If it isn't, it should be, because if Sarah and I ever split up, she'll spirit Laurie away with her. The thought makes my gut churn.

Of losing Sarah, I mean.

14 February

Laurie

Who was St Valentine anyway and what made him such an expert on romance? I'm willing to bet his full name is St Smugbastard-three's-a-crowd Valentine, and he probably lives on a candle-lit island where everything comes in pairs, even bouts of thrush.

Can you tell that 14 February isn't my favourite date in the calendar? It doesn't help that Sarah is a fully paid-up member of the hearts and balloons brigade this year. To my shame I realize I'd been hoping she'd get bored of Jack or something, but it's quite the opposite. She's already bought three different cards for him because she keeps seeing a new one that sums up how happy he makes her or how ridiculously hot he is, and every time she shows me the latest one my heart shrivels like a dried prune and it takes a good couple of hours for it to plump up again.

Thankfully they're going to the local Italian, where they'll no doubt eat heart-shaped steaks and then lick chocolate mousse off each other's faces, but at least it means I get to commandeer the living room tonight for a pity party for one. Bridget Jones has nothing on me. I'm planning on lying flat out on the sofa, inhaling ice cream and wine at the same time.

'Lu, have you got a sec?'

I close my laptop – yet another job application – lay the reading glasses I don't really need but wear to concentrate on the table, and wander into Sarah's room with my coffee mug. 'What's up?'

She's standing in her jeans and bra, her hands on her hips. 'I'm trying to decide what to wear.' She pauses and picks up the Coca-Cola red chiffon blouse she bought for Christmas dinner with her olds. It's pretty and surprisingly demure until Sarah lays it on the bed beside a black micro-skirt. 'These?'

She looks at me and I nod, because she'll look undeniably fabulous in the outfit.

'Or this?' She pulls her killer LBD out of the wardrobe and holds it against her body.

I glance from one to the other. 'I like both.'

She sighs. 'Me too. Which one says "hot Valentine" more?'

'Has Jack seen the red?'

She shakes her head. 'Not yet.'

'There you go then. Nothing shouts Valentine louder than lipstick red.'

Sartorial decision made, she hangs the dress back in the wardrobe. 'Are you sure you'll be all right on your own tonight?'

I roll my eyes. 'No. Take me with you.' I lean on the door frame and knock back a gulp of too-hot coffee. 'Because that wouldn't look weird at all, would it?'

'Jack'd probably like it,' she laughs. 'Make him look like a stud.'

'You know what, on second thoughts I'll have to take a rain check. I've got a double date tonight with Ben and

Jerry. They're sweet.' I wink as I back out into the hallway. 'We're going to work our way through the Karamel Sutra. It's going to be a thrill a minute.'

Of all the ice creams in all the world, I happen to know that B&J's Karamel Sutra is Sarah's favourite.

'I'm actually jealous, you know,' she calls after me, unbraiding her hair in readiness for the shower.

Me too, I think, miserable as I drop down heavily into the armchair and flip my laptop open again.

Whoever the hell is in charge of TV scheduling needs a bullet between their eyes. Surely they could work out that anyone who needs to resort to watching TV on Valentine's night is single and potentially bitter, so why they thought *The Notebook* would make suitable viewing is beyond me. There's romantic rowing on the lake and there's Ryan Gosling, all wringing wet and shouty and in love. There's even swans, for God's sake. Hang on, I'll just pour some salt in my wounds while I'm at it, shall I? Thank God they've had the good sense to schedule *Con Air* to follow it; I'm going to need a good dose of Nicolas Cage saving the day in a dirty vest to recover from this.

I've made my way through two-thirds of Ryan Gosling, half the tub of ice cream and three-quarters of a bottle of Chardonnay when I hear Sarah's keys in the lock. It's only half past ten; I expected my party for one to still be going strong at midnight, so frankly, this is something of an interruption.

Sitting cross-legged in the corner of the sofa, I look towards the door expectantly, my wine glass in my hand.

Have they fallen out and she's left him to eat his tiramisu alone? I try not to hope so as I call out, 'Grab a glass, Sar, there's enough wine left in the bottle if you're quick.'

She appears swaying in the doorway, but she's not alone. My party for one has segued swiftly into a ménage à trois. That's a thought I don't want to process, so I abandon it in favour of wishing I was wearing something other than black yoga pants and a mint-green vest. I'd optimistically dressed for the Davina workout I knew I wasn't really going to do. It could be worse; I could have gone for the checked flannel PJs my mum gave me because she worries the Delancey Street flat gets too draughty.

'You're early,' I say, stretching my spine and trying to look like a serene yoga guru, if that's at all possible while clutching a glass of wine.

'Free champagne,' Sarah says, or at least that's my best guess at what she says. She's laughing and leaning heavily against Jack; I think his arm round her waist is the only reason she's still standing.

'*Lots* of free champagne,' Jack adds, and his rueful smile tells me that although Sarah has had too much, he hasn't. I meet his eyes and for a moment he holds my gaze.

'Am ver, ver tired,' Sarah slurs, with long, exaggerated blinks. One of her false eyelashes is making a run for it down her cheek; it's usually me that has that problem. I've tried and failed with them twice over the last few months; I look like a drag queen, much to Sarah's amusement.

'I know you are.' Jack laughs and drops a kiss on her forehead. 'Come on. Let's get you into bed.'

She pretends to look shocked. 'Not until we're married, Jack O'Mara. What kind of girl d'you take me for?'

'A very pissed one,' he says, hanging on to her when she sways again.

'Rude,' Sarah murmurs, but she doesn't fight him when he catches her behind the knees and lifts her into his arms. *Shit.* Watch and learn, Ryan Gosling. This man didn't need to wade into a lake to melt the fair lady's heart.

For clarification, I mean Sarah's heart, not mine.

'She's passed out.'

I look up when Jack appears in the living-room doorway again a little later. Ryan Gosling has by now wooed his girl and rowed off into the sunset in favour of Nicolas Cage being all dependable and heroic on screen. Jack's eyes light up and his face cracks into a broad smile.

'Best action movie ever.'

I can't argue. *Con Air* is my go-to movie; when the shit hits the fan in my real life, I invariably opt to watch Cameron Poe have a much worse time of it and still come out on top. However bad my day has been, I can generally be fairly certain that I'm not going to have to crash land a plane full of murderers and rapists on the Las Vegas Strip.

'Everyone needs a hero,' I say, disconcerted by the fact that Jack has decided to flake out on the other end of the sofa rather than leave it to me.

'That's such a girl thing to say,' he mutters, rolling his green-gold eyes.

'Piss off,' I shoot back. 'I'm practising for my long and illustrious career writing greeting card verses.'

'You'll be in great demand,' he says with a grin. 'Tell me another.'

I laugh into my glass; I'm definitely feeling uninhibited by the wine. 'I need to know the occasion, at least.'

He considers the options. I really hope he doesn't go for the obvious and say Valentine's Day.

'My dog died. Cheer me up.'

'Oh, okay. Well,' I pause and cast around for a snappy first line. 'I'm sorry to hear about your dog who passed away, I hope that you remember the way he used to play.' I draw out the last word with an upward inflection for emphasis, impressed with my own wit, before I carry on. 'And how he always liked it when you used to stroke his head, yes, I'm truly very sorry that your precious dog is dead.' I gather pace towards the end, and we both laugh.

'I think I'd probably prefer a beer to any more shite jingles.'

Oh. I feel suddenly rude for being an ungracious hostess, but in my own defence, he's caught me out. I didn't expect him to emerge from Sarah's room again tonight. I'd just pulled the remainder of the ice cream from the freezer for a second sitting and sat back down when he reappeared.

'Go for it, there's some in the fridge.'

I watch him as he leaves the room, all long legs in dark jeans and lean-limbed in an ink-blue shirt. He obviously made the effort for Sarah earlier in the evening, and at some point he's loosened his tie. He drops back down with an open bottle of beer in his hand and holds up a spoon hopefully.

'We didn't get as far as dessert in the restaurant.'

I gaze down into the ice-cream tub and wonder if he's

going to be shocked by the fact that I've already eaten two-thirds of it.

'What flavour is it?' he asks as I hand it over hesitantly.

'Karamel Sutra.' Why couldn't I have just said caramel?

'Is that so?' He raises his eyes to mine, amused. 'Do I need to put my leg behind my head to eat it?'

If I was flirting with him I'd probably suggest he assume the downward dog or something, but as I'm not flirting with him, I just flip my eyes and sigh as if I'm terribly grown-up.

'Only if you think it might aid your digestion.'

'It might, but I'm fairly sure it'd ruin my jeans.'

'Best not then,' I say, my eyes trained on the TV. 'This is one of my favourite bits.'

We both watch as Nic Cage goes into manly overdrive in order to protect the female guard on the plane full of convicts, Jack eating the ice cream, me nursing the last of the wine from the bottle. I'm pleasantly relaxed rather than roaring drunk, because a handy after-effect of student life is that it has given me the drinking capacity of your average rugby player. Sarah's the same, usually.

'There must have been a heck of a lot of free champagne for Sarah to get like that,' I say, recalling the way she'd reeled into the flat earlier.

'I'm not a big fan of the stuff so she had mine,' he says. 'They kept topping us up. She was drinking for two to save me from the embarrassment of saying no.'

I laugh. 'She's all heart, that girl.'

'She's going to have a headache in the morning.'

We lapse into silence again. I cast around for something to say to fill the chasm, because if I don't, I'll do the unthinkable and ask him if he remembers me from the bus stop. I really, really hope that at some point I stop having to consciously fight that particular urge, that it stops being important, or even relevant, to me. It's a work in progress.

'She likes you a lot,' I blurt.

He takes a long, slow slug of his beer. 'I like her a lot too.' He looks at me sideways. 'Are you about to warn me that if I ever hurt her you'll come after me and black my eyes?'

'Don't think I couldn't,' I say, and then I make this ridiculous karate chop motion because I'm all bravado and no conviction, and what I was actually thinking was that I like them *both* a lot and it's giving me the mother of all problems.

My loyalty lies firmly with Sarah, of course; I know where the line is and I'll never cross it, but it's just that sometimes the line feels like it's been drawn with chalk on the grass, like at a school sports day, easily rubbed out and redrawn, but never in quite the same place as before. On nights like tonight, for instance, it has inched forward, and then on mornings like tomorrow, I'll diligently push it back again.

'Your secret ninja skills have been duly noted.'

I nod.

'Not that you're going to need to use them on me,' he goes on. 'I like Sarah more than enough to not want to hurt her.'

I nod again, glad for Sarah that he's kind, sad for me

that he's Sarah's, and mad at the world for being shitty enough to put me in this crap position in the first place.

'Good. Then we understand each other.'

'Spoken like a true mafia moll.' He leans forward to slide his empty beer bottle on to the table. 'A mafia ninja. You're turning out to be a dangerous woman to be around, Laurie.'

Especially when I've had a bottle of wine and I half love you, I think. I really should go to bed now, before I scrub the chalk line out and move it forward again.

Jack

You're turning out to be a dangerous woman to be around, Laurie.

What the bloody hell are these words coming out of my mouth? It sounds like a cheap pick-up line in a naff made-for-TV movie, when all I was trying to do was say we're friends. You stupid Jackass; I berate myself using the nickname I carried through school like a badge of honour. My school reports were littered with variations of the same comment, though more politely put: 'If only Jack applied as much effort to his studies as he does to acting the fool, he'd go a long way.'

I like to think I proved them wrong; when it came to the crunch my grades were just about decent enough to scrape into my first choice of uni. Truth is that I was lucky; I've been gifted with a near photographic memory, so those textbooks and theories only needed to go in once and they stayed there. With that and an ability to talk crap to anyone, I've done okay. Though for some reason my ability to talk doesn't seem to extend to Laurie.

'So, Laurie. What else should I know about you, besides the fact that you'll beat me black and blue if I hurt your best mate?'

She looks startled by my question. I don't blame her. The last time I asked anyone a question like that was my one and only hideous attempt at speed dating. What am I doing, *interviewing* her?

'Umm . . .' She laughs, music-box light. 'There's not really very much to tell.'

I try to bring it back to normal, shooting her a 'try harder' look. 'Come on, throw me a bone here. Sarah wants us to be best buddies. Give me your three most embarrassing facts, and then I'll give you mine.'

She narrows her eyes and her chin comes up a little. 'Can we take it in turns?'

'Go on then. As long as you go first.'

I tell myself that I've suggested this because Sarah is so keen on me and Laurie being friends, and that honestly, genuinely, is partly the reason. *Partly.* But the other part just wants to know more about her, because she intrigues me, and because I'm comfortable here on the other end of the sofa, and because I find myself relaxed in her company. Maybe it's the wine she's drunk, and it's probably the beer I've sunk, but I think I could be good friends with this girl. That's okay, isn't it? I know some people don't believe that platonic friendships can happen between men and women.

I'm going to trade truths with Laurie, and we're going

to become the best of friends. That, ladies and gentlemen, is my grand plan.

She drums her nails against the edge of her glass, thinking, and I find I'm really interested to hear what she's going to say. She looks down into the dregs of her wine, and when she raises her eyes, she's laughing.

'Okay, I was fourteen, fifteen maybe.' She breaks off and presses her hand to her red cheek, shaking her head. 'I can't believe I'm going to tell you this.'

That giddy laugh again, and she lowers her lashes, making me duck down to catch her eye.

'Come on, you've got to tell me now,' I cajole.

She sighs with resignation. 'I was with Alana, my best friend at the time, and we were at the school disco trying to pretend we were super-cool. I think we might even have had a box of cigarettes, although neither of us smoked.'

I nod, wanting to hear more.

'And there was this boy, as there always is, and I really fancied him. Half the school did, in actual fact, but by some miracle he seemed to like me too.'

I want to butt in and tell her that it's not a miracle or even a surprise really, but I don't.

'So he finally asks me to dance at the end, and I nonchalantly accept, and it's all going really well until I look up sharply just as he looks down at me, and I full-on headbutt him in the face and break his nose.' She looks at me, wide-eyed, and then laughter bubbles up in her throat. 'Blood everywhere. They had to call him an ambulance.'

'No way.' I shake my head slowly. 'Wow, you're a really shit date, Laurie.'

'I wasn't even dating him,' she protests. 'I wanted to, but it never got off the ground after that. No surprise, really.' Knocking her knuckles on her skull, she shrugs. 'Iron hard, by all accounts.'

'Okay, so now you're a ninja mafia moll with an exceptionally hard cranium. I can understand what Sarah sees in you.'

She plays it straight. 'I reckon I must make her feel safe.'

'I'll say. You really should think about charging protection money. Pay your student loan off in no time.'

Laurie puts her wine glass on the table and leans back, tucking her dark hair behind her ears as she settles cross-legged, facing towards me. When I was a kid we went on annual family holidays to Cornwall, and my mother had a thing for those tiny little pixies you could buy, usually sitting on toadstools or something equally twee. Something in the neatness of Laurie's lotus position and the point of her chin when she smooths her hair behind her ears reminds me of those pixies now, and for a second I experience a jolt of homesickness out of the blue. As if she is familiar, even though she isn't.

'Your turn.' She grins.

'I don't think I have anything that measures up,' I say. 'I mean, I've never even headbutted a woman.'

'What kind of man are you?'

She feigns disappointment, and even though she is joking, I consider her question seriously.

'A good one, I hope?'

Her laughter dies in her throat. 'I hope so too.'

I know she means for Sarah's sake.

'How about this one . . .' I change the subject abruptly.

'Let me tell you about my sixth birthday party. Imagine a small child who got buried in the ball pit and then got so scared that his dad had to navigate the jungle of slides and scramble nets to find him. I was three foot under the balls and crying so much that I threw up. They had to clear the place.' I have a vivid flashback to the faces of the horrified parents of the kid whose party dress got splattered with my chocolate-cake puke. 'Funnily enough, my party invitation rate dropped off sharply after that.'

'Oh, now that's a sad story,' she says, and I don't even think she's taking the piss.

I shrug. 'I'm a man. I'm made of tough stuff.'

She raps her knuckles on her skull again. 'You forget who you're talking to here.'

I nod, solemn. 'Ironwoman.'

'The very same.'

We fall silent and assimilate what we now know of each other. For my part, I know that she's awkward with men and likely to cause injury. For hers, she knows I scare easily and am liable to throw up over her. She takes the empty ice-cream carton and spoon from me and leans sideways to slide it on to the coffee table, and despite my best efforts, my man brain observes the movement of her limbs, the sliver of breast I can see under her arm, the inward curve at the base of her spine. Why do women have to have all of that going on? It's really not okay. I want to be platonic friends with Laurie, yet my brain is filing away her every movement, storing her up, building a map of her in my head so I can visit her every now and then in my sleep. I don't want to. When I'm awake, I really don't think of

Laurie in that way, but my sleeping brain doesn't seem to have received the memo.

In sleep, I've observed that her skin is creamy pale and that her eyes are the colour of forget-me-nots. Laurie's eyes are a fucking summer hedgerow. And now I can add that pronounced curve at the small of her back, and that she gets giddy after wine, and how she bites her bottom lip when she's thinking. Times like this, my photographic memory becomes more an impediment than advantage. Of course, Laurie's not the only woman I have dreams about, but she seems to warrant a more regular walk-on role than most. Not that I'm dreaming of other women all the time. I'm going to stop now, because I'm making myself sound like a closet sleazebag.

'Right, I guess that makes it my turn again,' she says. I nod, glad that she's derailed my train of thought.

'You're going to have to go some to top the headbutt story.'

'I started too strong,' she agrees, chewing her lip again, struggling to dredge up something suitable.

To help her, I chuck out a few prompts.

'That embarrassing incident when you went out in high winds without knickers?' She smirks but shakes her head. 'Poisoned someone with your cooking? The time you accidentally snogged your sister's boyfriend?'

Her features soften, a sudden study of nostalgia and other emotions I find hard to read as they slide over her face. *Christ*. I must have said something really wrong, because now she's blinking hard, as if she has something in her eyes. Like tears.

'God. Shit, I'm sorry,' she mutters, dashing the backs of her hands furiously across her eyes.

'No, no. I am,' I rush, still not sure what I've said to provoke such a reaction. I want to hold her hand, cover her kneecap with my palm, something, anything to say I'm sorry, but I can't quite make my hand move.

She shakes her head. 'It's really not your fault.'

I wait for her to gather herself. 'Want to talk about it?'

She looks down, pinching the skin on the back of her hand, small repetitive motions; a coping mechanism, using physical pain to detract from emotional upset. My pain-in-the-arse brother, Albie, wears an elastic band round his wrist that he snaps for the same reason.

'My little sister died when she was six years old. I'd just turned eight.'

Shit. I take back that description of my brother. He's four years younger than me and it's true that he can be a right royal pain in the arse, but I love the fucking bones of him. I can't even bear to think of the world without him in it.

'Jesus, Laurie.'

This time I don't think twice. As a tear rolls down her cheek I reach out and swipe it away with my thumb. Then she's properly crying and I'm stroking her hair and shushing her as a mother soothes a child.

'I'm sorry, I shouldn't have blurted that out,' she gulps after a couple of minutes where both of us say nothing, pushing the heels of her palms into her eyes. 'It caught me right out of nowhere. I haven't cried about it for ages. Must be the wine.'

I nod as I lower my hand, feeling hideous for being so unwittingly insensitive.

'I always say I only have a brother whenever anyone asks. I feel disloyal not mentioning her, but it's easier than telling people the truth.' She's calmer now, drawing in slow, shaky breaths.

I have no real clue how to say the right thing in this situation, but I try; I have at least a small idea of how she might be feeling. 'What was her name?'

Laurie's face floods with warmth, and her vulnerability sears straight through me. Piercing, acute longing, bitter-sweet, as if something has been missing from her for too long. She sighs heavily as she turns to lean her back against the sofa beside me, pulling her knees up and wrapping her arms round them. When she speaks again her voice is low and measured, like someone giving a rehearsed speech at a loved one's funeral.

'Ginny was born with a heart condition, but she was bright, and God, was she smart. She ran rings round me. She was my best friend.' She pauses for a brief second, bracing herself for impact, as if she knows that telling the next part of her story is going to physically hurt. 'Pneumonia. She was here one moment and then she was gone. I don't think any of us have ever got over losing her. My poor mum and dad . . .' She trails off, because there aren't really any suitable words; parents should never have to bury their child. She isn't pinching her skin any more; I don't think there's a coping mechanism in the world up to the job of distracting you from something like this.

On TV, Nicolas Cage is crashing around on a motor-bike, all action and brawn, and here in this small living room I put my arm round Laurie's shoulders and squeeze her against me. Her body judders with deep breaths, and she lays her head against my shoulder and closes her eyes. I can't pinpoint the moment she falls asleep, but I'm glad she does because it's what she needs right now. I don't move, even though I probably should. I don't get up and go to bed, even though a wiser man would have. I just sit and keep her company while she sleeps, and it feels . . . I don't even know what it feels. Peaceful.

I don't press my face into her hair.

15 February

Laurie

When I wake up, I know there's something I need to remember but my brain feels as if it's wrapped in fuzzy felt. That'll be the wine, I think groggily, and then I open my eyes and realize I'm not in bed. I'm still on the sofa, but my bed pillow is beneath my head and I'm snuggled under my duvet. A long squint at my watch tells me it's only a little after six in the morning, so I lie back and close my eyes, working my way through the evening from the bit that comes most easily to mind.

Ice cream. Wine. Ryan Gosling rowing a boat. Swans. There were definitely swans. And, oh my God, Sarah had had a skin-full! I'll check on her in a minute, it's a good job Jack brought her home. Jack. Oh shit. *Jack.*

My mind sprints straight into panic mode, convincing myself that I must have said or done something terrible and disloyal and that Sarah is going to hate me. He was talking to me, and we were laughing and watching the movie, and then . . . Oh. And then I remember. *Ginny.* Sliding deep back inside the cocoon of my duvet, I screw my eyes up tight and let myself remember my sweet, beautiful little sister. Slender fingers, her nails so fragile they were almost translucent, the only other person in the world with eyes just like mine. I have to concentrate really hard to pull her childish voice from my memories, the excited joy of her giggle, the shimmer of her poker-straight blonde hair in sunlight. Fractured memories, faded like sun-damaged photographs. I don't allow myself to think of Ginny very often in day-to-day life, or at all, really; it takes me a long time afterwards to reconcile the fact that she simply isn't here any more, to not be furious with everyone else for breathing when she isn't.

I remember last night clearly now. I didn't do anything morally wrong with Jack, nothing that I need to feel compromised over in the traditional sense this morning, at least; I definitely didn't show him my boobs or confess true love. Yet still I can't let myself totally off the hook, because in truth I *did* cross a line, albeit a fine and almost invisible one. I can clearly feel it tangled around my ankles like fishing wire, ready to trip me up and make a liar out of me. I let myself get too close. All it took was a cheap bottle of wine to lower my guard; for one unwittingly misjudged comment to make me crumble like an abandoned sandcastle when the evening tide comes in.

5 June

Laurie

'Happy birthday, old biddy!'

Sarah blows a streamer in my face to wake me up and I struggle on to my elbows as she breaks into a rousing chorus of 'Happy Birthday'.

'Thank you!' I give her a half-hearted round of applause. 'Can I go back to sleep now, please? It's eight o'clock on Saturday morning.'

She frowns. 'You're kidding, right? If you go to sleep now you'll miss out on golden birthday hours.'

She sounds like one of her favourite Disney characters. 'Last time I checked, we weren't American teenagers on some cheesy TV show,' I grumble.

'Stop moaning and get out of bed right now. I've got big plans for you.'

I drop back on my pillow. 'I already have a plan. It involves staying here until midday.'

'You can do that tomorrow.' She nods towards a mug on the side. 'I made you coffee. You've got ten minutes before I come back and *really* wake you up rudely.'

'You're too bossy,' I grumble, flinging my arm across my eyes. 'I'm twenty-three now, and you're still twenty-two. I'm old enough to be your mother. Go and clean your bedroom and do your homework.'

She toots on her streamer again as she leaves, laughing, and I shove my head underneath my pillow. I love that girl.

There are two clothes carriers hanging in the lounge when I emerge exactly nine and a half minutes later, and Sarah is practically hopping on the spot. Even more worryingly, the carriers are emblazoned with a fancy-dress hire company logo.

'Umm, Sar . . . ?' I'm starting to realize she wasn't kidding when she said she had a plan.

'You're going to die when you see,' she says, her fists bunched with excitement like a kid on school-trip day.

I place my coffee down slowly. 'Should I look now?'

'Yes. But first you have to promise me that you'll do exactly as I say for the next few hours, no questions asked.'

'You sound like an undercover spy. Have you and Jack been watching too much James Bond again?'

She holds one of the carriers out towards me, but clutches on to it when I go to take it from her. 'Promise first.'

I laugh and shake my head, intrigued. 'Go on then, I promise.'

She hands it over with a little clap, then flaps her hands for me to hurry up and look inside. Holding it out at arm's length, I give it a shake and then slide the central zipper down a few inches to sneak a glimpse.

'It's pink . . .' I say, and she nods, fast.

I whoosh the zip all the way down and shrug the plastic cover off, revealing an instantly recognizable candyfloss-pink satin bomber jacket and black satin leggings.

'You want me to dress up as a Pink Lady for my birthday?'

She grins and whips her own outfit out. 'Not just you.'

'We're both pink ladies.' I speak slowly, because I'm somewhat confused. 'I mean, I kind of love it already as a birthday theme, but what are we going to do once we're dressed? Because we're going to stick out like sore thumbs down The Castle.'

'We're not going to the pub.' Sarah's eyes gleam with anticipation.

'Can I ask where we *are* going?'

She laughs. 'You can ask, but I won't tell you the truth.'

'How did I know you were going to say that?'

She unzips her jacket and slides her arms into it. 'You have seen the movie, right?'

'Once or twice.' I roll my eyes, because everyone on the planet has seen *Grease* at least a dozen times, usually because it's on TV on New Year's Day and you can't physically bring yourself to move and find the remote.

I hold up my satin leggings doubtfully. The waistband is about six inches across. 'I hope they stretch,' I say.

'They do. I tried them on at about six o'clock this morning.'

Her words make me realize how hard she's trying to give me a fun birthday; and the part of my mind that's constantly feeling guilty at the moment gives me a hefty dig. Whatever it is she has planned for us today, I need to give her my one hundred per cent best.

'Pink Ladies it is then,' I say with a laugh.

She looks at her watch. 'We need to leave at eleven. Go

and jump in the shower, I've already been in. I'll do your flicky eyeliner for you when you're out.'

It's midday and we're on a train out of Waterloo, and it's fair to say we're getting our fair share of odd looks. I'm not surprised. We're the only Pink Ladies on board today, and we definitely have the most fabulous hair and make-up. Sarah's gone with a high, flippy ponytail that seems to swish around independently of her head, and between us we've wrangled mine into bubble curls Olivia Newton-John herself would be envious of. Sarah's thought of everything: gum for us to chew, jaunty black neck scarves, white-rimmed plastic shades perched in our hair and gin-in-a-tin for the train to get us in the mood for wherever it is we're going.

'Should we assume fake names?'

Sarah considers my question seriously. 'What would yours be?'

'Hmm. Tricky. I think it needs to sound kitsch and American and fifties, so how about . . . Lula-May?'

She looks at me thoughtfully. 'I like what you did there. So if you're Lula-May, that must make me Sara-Belle.'

'It sure is nice to meet you.'

'Nice to make your acquaintance too, Lula-May.'

We incline our heads to each other graciously, then clink tins and neck our gin to cement our new friendship.

'Will you tell me where we're going yet?'

'Just trust me, little lady. You're gonna love it.' She attempts a really terrible Deep South drawl.

'You sound more like John Wayne than Sara-Belle,' I laugh. 'I think I might fancy you.'

Sarah stashes our empty tins in the back pockets of the seats in front of us. 'It's my sexual energy. I can't hold it in.' She glances up as the electronic voice-over tells us that we're approaching Barnes. 'Come on. This is our stop.'

The first thing I notice when we get outside the station is that we're not the only people who look like extras in a *Grease* remake. Swing dresses and Teddy boy suits are interspersed amongst the regular sunny Saturday lunchtime shoppers, and the occasional flash of pink satin tells me there's going to be quite a gang of Pink Ladies.

'Sarah!'

Jack's voice rings out and my heart jumps. I've been doing my best to avoid spending any time with him and Sarah lately, and luckily they've both been so busy with work I think they've been quite happy to not have a third wheel on their nights together. And I really feel like I'm starting to think about him less. Perhaps my mind-control efforts are working.

Then I notice who's with Jack – Billy, one of his friends who I've met a few times at various parties. Please God don't let this be a set-up. The boys walk up to us and break into slightly bashful grins as we exclaim over their T-Bird black drainpipes and skinny-fit black T-shirts. They've rolled their sleeves up into shoulder caps to accentuate their biceps and, looking at their quiffs, I shouldn't think there's much hair gel left in the tub.

Wherever we're going, it appears we're going as a foursome. It's not that I mind; I just wasn't expecting them, and Sarah and I have had the best morning in ages.

'Well, if it isn't our dates for the prom.' Sarah laughs

and plants a kiss on Jack's lips, leaving traces of red lipstick on his mouth. He's wearing mirrored aviators that obscure his eyes; he looks more James Dean than John Travolta.

'Billy, you look . . . cool,' I say, and he flexes his muscles obligingly. He's got one of those bodies that looks like he sculpts it carefully in the gym for two hours every day. The kind where you can't help but admire, at the same time as feeling complete disdain.

'Popeye's got nothing on me.' He takes the lollipop stick he's chewing for effect out of his mouth and dips to plant a quick kiss on my cheek. 'Happy birthday.'

I notice Sarah looking at us and roll my eyes at her. Trust her to set me up with someone who's so obviously not my type. He probably loves his women all blonde and toned and docile. I wonder what Jack had to promise him to come along?

'Shall we, ladies?' Jack crooks his elbow for Sarah to take, and after a moment's awkward hesitation, Billy does the same to me.

'We shall,' Sarah grins, slipping her arm through Jack's. 'Laurie still doesn't know what we're doing, so don't say anything.'

I laugh, self-conscious as I take Billy's proffered arm. 'I think I'm getting the picture.'

'Oh, you're really not.' Her eyes sparkle as she looks over her shoulder at me as we move with the throng of people. 'But you will.'

I can't quite believe what I'm seeing.

'What is this place?' I say, fascinated. We're in a zig-zag

queue of people in various *Grease* costumes, everyone buzzing and overexcited. A prim American school radio voice crackles through speakers telling us not to run in the halls, and that heavy petting in the queue will get us detention, and as we reach the entrance we pass beneath a huge, arched college sign welcoming us to Rydell High, poppy-red, lit up with old-fashioned light bulbs.

'Do you like it?'

Sarah has my arm now rather than Jack's, and she half smiles and half grimaces, holding her breath as she waits for my verdict on my big birthday surprise.

'Like it?' I grin, giddy at the scale of the event unfolding before me. 'I don't have a clue what's going on, but I bloody love it!'

Barnes Common, usually home to dog walkers and Sunday cricket matches, has been transformed into a magical wonderland of American fifties kitsch as far as the eye can see. Roller-disco queens serve Coke floats to tables in the open-air marquee and gleaming silver Airstream diners line the edges of the field. All around, people lounge on picnic blankets, girls in frilly dresses and sunglasses basking on their backs in the sunshine, propped up on their elbows blowing bubblegum balloons. Music is everywhere; a live brass band belts out fifties rock and roll for the energetic couples on the wooden dance floor in the marquee, and elsewhere familiar songs from the *Grease* soundtrack ooze from tall speakers set all round the perimeters. I even glimpse a pop-up Beauty School where you can get your nails painted or your eyeliner freshly flicked by girls in fitted pink overalls and matching wigs. People shout and jostle on cherry-red bumper cars, and a huge, glittering Ferris wheel presides over the whole affair, its gleaming ice-cream pink and white seats swinging lightly in the warm breeze.

'If we do nothing else, I want to ride that wheel,' I sigh.

It's the biggest, craziest birthday surprise I've ever had. My heart feels feather-light, as if it's tied to a helium balloon.

Jack

This place is off-the-scale weird. I don't know how Sarah does it; most people buy someone a cake or take them out drinking for their birthday. Not Sarah. She's managed to find this extravaganza, and somehow she's roped Billy and me into being their T-Bird escorts for the day. There aren't many women I'd do this for; I grumbled and almost backed out because, to be honest, it sounded like a bit of a nightmare, but actually it's kind of cool now we're here. Secret Cinema, she said it's called. I expected an open-air cinema with a burger truck or two, and there *is* a huge screen set up for later, but jeez, this place is something else. I feel as if I'm actually *in* the movie rather than at it, and I reckon we've bagged ourselves the two best-looking Pink Ladies at the whole gig.

Sarah . . . Christ. She never does anything by halves. She's walking a little way ahead of me; her legs seem to be twice as long as normal in those spray-on black leggings. I've always got off on the feeling that I'm running to keep up with her, it keeps me on my toes, but lately she's sprinting so fast that sometimes I feel like I lose sight of her altogether. It's disconcerting, a low-level niggle that I stamp down every time I catch up again.

Laurie looks cool too; it's like a magazine article about how the same outfit can look completely different on two different girls. Sarah's high heels and ponytail say most popular girl in class, whereas Laurie's Converse and bouncy curls are more low-key cute. If we *were* high-school kids, Sarah would scare the pants off me and Laurie would be my best mate's sister. I don't even know where I'm going with that thought. They're just different, that's all.

'What do you think? A snog on the cards for me and the birthday girl?' Billy says, strolling beside me. 'Reckon I'll try my luck at the top of that thing.' He nods towards the Ferris wheel.

I flick my eyes towards Laurie briefly and feel a bloom of protectiveness. Billy's one of those guys who will do anything to add a few more notches. I don't really know why I asked him – other than he was the only one of my friends egotistical enough to spend a day playing dress-up.

'No heavy petting, Bill. You heard the rules.'

'This is high school, where rules are made to be broken, my friend.' Billy winks at me as Sarah turns to us and points across the field, interrupting before I can say anything else.

'Come on, you two. I want to go on the bumper cars.'

I'm starting to wish I'd asked anyone other than Billy to come today. So far he's rung the strong-man bell three times when no one else on this whole common could manage it even once, and now he's got his arm round Laurie as he expertly manoeuvres their bumper car around like an F1 driver.

I mimic him, slinging my arm round Sarah as I glance back over my shoulder and reverse right into them, sending them spinning away in a fizz of electric sparks. Sarah screams, laughing beside me as Billy comes straight back at us, jolting our car violently into the wall of tyres, subtly giving me the finger over Laurie's shoulder as he drives away. What would John Travolta do right now, I wonder? And who is Sandra Dee in this scenario? Sarah's too sassy by far; Frenchy all the way. Not that I'm saying Laurie is Sandy to my Danny, because that would be fucked up. Maybe Billy is more Danny anyway, with his Popeye muscles and leader-of-the-pack mentality. I watch him help Laurie clamber out of their car as the engines cut out, the way he hangs on to her hand and spins her against him, a blur of dark curls in pink satin. I hope she isn't fooled by him.

I mean, it's her business, but he can be a bit of a bloke – everything's a lark and a laugh. Maybe that's what she likes. Fuck, what if he decides to come back to Camden with us? Ha! Her mobile's just started to ring in the pocket of her pink jacket. Phonus Interruptus, mate.

Laurie

This is shaping up to be one of my favourite days ever.

I'm squiffy on Pink Lady cocktails, I've laughed until my sides ache, Billy is more fun than I'd anticipated and everyone is in a silly, carnival mood. Even the weather has played ball, bathing us in the best kind of lazy English summer warmth, the sort that always brings freckles out across the bridge of my nose.

If I'd thought the event looked good in daylight, it looks even more razzle-dazzle now that the evening is beginning to draw in. On the T-Birds stand a show plays out; a bendy troupe of male dancers in black leather are bouncing all over the impressive line of imported muscle cars, singing into chrome microphone stands as they dance across the bonnets. Everywhere people dance and loll under the rainbow haze cast by the glittering pastel lights from the fairground rides, and there's a growing sense of anticipation for the movie itself to begin around ten.

Sarah discovered just now that she has a natural talent for rock-and-roll dancing (well of course), and after Jack laughingly backed out, claiming two left feet, Billy has been cajoled into taking part in the master-class competition as her partner.

As Jack and I stand on the fringes of the crowd watching them, I see that glitter-grit crackle through Sarah; it's there in the extra sassy flick of her ponytail and the high jut of her chin. Thank God Billy seems to have hidden snake hips. I don't know if it's all the cocktails I've sunk, but he's starting to look a lot more attractive than he did at the beginning of the day. When we were queuing for the bumper cars he showed me photos of his little brother, Robin, a very unexpected surprise to his forty-something mum. Not that Billy minded going from an only child to a big brother so late in the day; he proudly flashed me a shot of Robin blowing out the birthday candles on the cake Billy had made him with his own bare hands. It was no masterpiece, but any girl wondering if Billy might make a good father himself one day would only need to hear him talk about Robin to know there is marshmallow beneath those muscles. I watch him up there with Sarah, pure concentration on both of their faces. They've got their A-game on for sure; I feel almost sorry for the other contestants.

'Sarah loves this kind of stuff,' I say, sucking lemonade through a red-and-white-striped straw because I'm taking a cocktail break.

'I just hope they win,' Jack laughs. I know what he means. A happy Sarah means a happy all of us.

My phone vibrates; that's the second time Mum's tried me today. I already told her that I was out all day, but I think she finds it difficult now me and Daryl have both left home. I consider calling her back, but I don't want to interrupt this moment.

I look out towards the Ferris wheel. It looks even bigger illuminated. 'I hope there's still time to ride the wheel before the movie starts,' I say.

Jack frowns, checking the time. 'We're cutting it fine.'

I nod. 'Especially if they get through to the dance-off.'

'Which they will.'

He's right. There is not a shred of doubt in my mind that Sarah's dancing shoes will see this thing through to the end.

He pauses for a beat, looks away and then back at me.

'I could take you on it now, if you like.' He half laughs, embarrassed. 'Call it a birthday present, seeing as I forgot to get you one.'

It's curiously old-fashioned of him to offer to take me on it, as if I need to be escorted, but the question works perfectly in this curiously old-fashioned setting. I stand on my tiptoes to catch Sarah's eye to let her know we'll be back in ten but she's fully engaged in listening to the master-class host. I look behind me again at the beautiful Ferris wheel.

'I'd like that very much, Jack. Thank you.'

A guy in white chinos with a Rydell High college sweater knotted casually round his shoulders lowers the chrome bar across our knees, raising his eyebrows at us as he gives it a rattle to make sure we're secured.

'You might want to put your arm round your girl, fella. It can get a little scary up there at the top.'

I'm sure he must say variations of the same to every couple he loads on to the ride, but all the same we both wade in to correct him.

'Oh, we're not . . .' I stammer, at the same time as Jack rushes in with, 'She's not my . . . We're just friends.'

Sweater boy winks knowingly. 'Pity. You look good together.'

The wheel lurches a little to move round one place for the next car to be filled, and I close my eyes for a second because I have no clue what to say next.

'Don't tell me you're a scaredy-cat, Laurie?'

'No, siree!' I laugh. Curling my fingers round the bar, I settle back into the deep raspberry-vinyl padding of the swing seat, my feet resting in the chrome footwell. 'You're not scared of heights, are you?'

He leans into the corner of the car and glances at me sideways, his arms flung out across the top of the seat, hands upturned as if I've asked a stupid question.

'Do I look like someone who scares easily?'

Danny Zuko eat your heart out; but the way he drums his fingers on the top of the car close to my shoulder tell me he's not as relaxed as his outward appearance might suggest. I don't know what it is that's making him uptight; being on the wheel without Sarah, or being on the wheel at all, or being on the wheel with me. I sigh, about to ask him, and then the familiar, swoony opening bars of 'Hopelessly Devoted To You' strike up and the wheel begins to rotate.

I shelve my question. It's my birthday, after all, and I love Ferris wheels, and I'm with Jack, who I can't help but genuinely like more and more each time I see him. And that's good. I mean it, hand on heart, I mean it. It's good, because he and Sarah are undeniably great together, and because I love her like a sister.

For the most part I'm pretty accepting of the situation. It is what it is. Perhaps if things had been different, if I'd found him first maybe, then he'd have his arm round me right now and be about to kiss me stupid as we crest the top of the wheel. Maybe we'd be deliriously loved up. Or maybe we would have been a terrible romantic match, and the very best outcome for all of us is exactly what's come to pass. He's in my life and I'm glad of him. It's enough.

'Wow,' I murmur, distracted by the view as we climb higher. Barnes Common is festooned with bunting and lights: neon writing over the Airstream diners, disco flickers from the dance tent, tea lights on trestle tables as early settlers claim their spots on the grass close to the huge screen. We go higher still, and we can see beyond the common, over the spindly streets of South West London picked out by creamy street lamps.

'Stars,' Jack says, flipping his head back to look up as we near the top. I do the same and stargaze with him, and for a few seconds we hang there right on the brow of the wheel, the only two people in the world.

'Happy birthday, Laurie,' Jack says, quiet and serious when I turn to look at him.

I nod and try to smile but find that my face muscles can't do it, because my mouth is trembling as if I might cry.

'Thank you, Jack,' I say. 'I'm glad I got to spend it with you –' I break off, then add, 'you guys,' for clarity.

'Me too.'

Our car crests the summit and jolts over the brow of the wheel, rocking as the breeze catches it, making me squeal and grab hold of the bar with both hands. Jack laughs easily and puts his arm round me, the side of his body a warm press against mine.

'It's okay, I've got you.'

He gives me a brief, bolstering squeeze, his fingers firm round my shoulder, before he lounges back and lays his arm along the back of the seat again.

My stomach backflips slowly as I sit back too, and I'm ashamed to say it had nothing to do with the fact that we're suspended high in the sky over Barnes Common and everything to do with the feeling of being alone on this beautiful old Ferris wheel with Jack O'Mara. Vintage pink and mint-green bulbs light up the spokes of the wheel as it turns, dancing shadows over his features as we slowly move.

Olivia Newton-John sings her hopelessly devoted heart out. I know how she feels.

My fingers close round my pendant, sliding over the

familiar shape of the flat purple stone for reassurance. I had a five-minute meltdown this morning because I couldn't find it; I cried when Sarah finally spotted it wedged between the cracks of the floorboards in my bedroom. Of all the possessions I own, my necklace is my most precious. Ginny and I both had one; I know it's silly but I feel more connected to her whenever I wear it.

Damn. Another missed call from Mum. I feel like the world's worst daughter as I click open the text message she's just pinged across in lieu of a chat, and I resolve to call her first thing in the morning.

> Laurie darling, I'm so sorry to put this in a text and even more sorry because it's your birthday, but I know you'd want to know as soon as possible. It's Dad – he's in hospital, sweetheart, he's had a heart attack. Give me a call as soon as you can. Love you. Mum xx

And just like that, one of the best days of my life has just become one of my worst.

12 December

Laurie

I feel like someone lined my Uggs with lead. It's been full-on bedlam at work with back-to-back Christmas party bookings over the last few weeks and my feet ache as if I've run a marathon. I'm thoroughly bloody knackered. Dad's recovery has been slower than the doctors hoped; it seems to have been one thing after another with his health ever since. He's gone from being my robust, no-worries dad to looking frail and much too pale, and my mum seems to have followed suit because she's worrying herself to death over him. They've always been quite the glamorous couple; Dad's got ten years on Mum but it's never really shown up till now. I can't say the same of late. My father turned sixty last year but looks ten years older again; every time I see him I want to bundle him on to a plane to sunnier climes and feed him up. Not that my mum isn't doing her best; their lives seem to be one long round of specialist appointments and dietary restrictions, and it's taking its toll on them both. I go home as often as I can, but Mum is inevitably bearing the brunt of it.

Christmas insults my eyeballs everywhere I look; I've been shopping for the last few hours and I'm at that point where I want to bludgeon Rudolph, bump off Mariah Carey and strangle the next person who pushes me with the nearest string of tinsel. I've been waiting in this never-ending, barely moving queue in HMV for the last twenty minutes, clutching a box set I'm not even sure my brother will ever watch, and I could genuinely fall asleep on my feet. For a music store, you'd think they'd manage to come up with something more cutting-edge than Noddy Holder screaming 'It's Christmas!' at the top of his lungs. What kind of name is Noddy, anyway? I find myself wondering if he was born with big ears and his mother was just too whacked out on gas and air to come up with anything else.

'Laurie!'

I twist at the sound of someone calling my name and spot Jack waving his arm over the heads of the queue snaked around me. I smile, relieved by the sight of his familiar face, then roll my eyes to transmit how I feel about being stuck here. I look down at the box set and realize that my brother would prefer a bottle of Jack Daniels anyway, so I turn and push my way out of the queue, annoying pretty much everyone by going against the tide. Jack hangs around by the chart CDs while he waits for me, bundled inside his big winter coat and scarf, and I sigh because I'm caught by the memory of him at the bus stop. It's been a couple of years now, and for the most part I don't think about that day any more; my diligence in my mission to replace all of my errant thoughts about him with safer ones has paid off. They say that the human brain likes to follow repetitive patterns, and I've found that to be quite true. Jack now inhabits an appropriate place in my life as my friend, and as my best friend's boyfriend, and in return I allow myself to enjoy his company and I *like* him. I really do like him so very much. He's funny, and he's incredibly caring towards Sarah. And he was a complete life-saver on my birthday, taking charge of the situation when I went to pieces there in the middle of Barnes Common. We were in the back of a taxi in the blink of an eye, my train tickets home booked before we even reached Delancey Street. Sometimes you just need someone to tell you what to do, and on that day Jack stepped up to the mark.

'You look as impressed with this Christmas shopping malarky as I am,' he says, sliding the CD he was idly looking at back on to the shelf and falling into step beside me as we leave the store. 'Although you've clearly been more successful than I have.' He eyes my bags. 'Here, let me.'

I don't argue when he takes the heavy carriers from me; the handles have bitten red welts into my palm and I flex my sore fingers with relief. There's grey slush underfoot as we step out on to Oxford Street, remnants of the snowfall from a few days ago still hanging around because the arctic wind is blowing straight down from the north. Jack pulls a woolly hat from his pocket and jams it on his head, shivering for effect.

'Have you got much to get?' I ask.

He shrugs. 'Sarah's, mainly. Any bright ideas?' He looks at me sideways as we walk, blending our pace with the bustling crowds. 'Please say yes.'

I rack my brain. She isn't hard to buy for, but her gift from Jack should be something particularly personal. 'A bracelet maybe or a pendant?'

We pass a High Street jeweller and pause to look, but nothing in the window really shouts 'Sarah'.

I wrinkle my nose and sigh as we shelter inside the

doorway. 'It's all a bit too . . . I don't know. Not individual enough.'

Jack nods, then narrows his eyes and looks at his watch. 'Do you need to rush off?'

'Not really,' I say, not looking forward to the trudge home.

'Good.' He grins, threading his arm through mine. 'Come with me, I know just where to go.'

Jack

Shopping is so much easier with Laurie than on my own. We've just hoofed it round the corner from Oxford Street to Chester's antique emporium; a place I vaguely remember and hope is still there.

'Wow,' Laurie murmurs, her violet-blue eyes widening as we step inside the tall terracotta-brick building. I came here years ago as a kid to help my father find something special for my mum's birthday. It's a vivid memory; I think it might have been a special birthday, one to mark. We found her a slender silver bangle set with amber stones, and my dad had them engrave all of our names round the inside. She wore it sometimes when he was still alive, at Christmas and on special days. She wore it to his funeral too, and I don't think I've seen her without it since.

I'm pleased to see the emporium hasn't changed much in the intervening years, that it's still the same Aladdin's cave of vintage stalls.

'This place is amazing! I never even knew it was here.'

'Proper London.' I shove my hat into my coat pocket,

pushing my hand through my hair because it's plastered against my head. 'Where do you want to start?'

Her eyes glitter as she laughs, delighted as she takes it all in. 'I have no idea. I want to see everything.'

'Steady on. We'll be here until Christmas.'

I follow her as she moves amongst the stalls, stroking her fingers over the head of a carved leopard, exclaiming over locked cabinets full of beautiful, top-grade diamonds, and then she's just as excited by the paste and costume jewels at the next store along. She smiles, shy when the owner of a retro hat shop takes one look at her and pulls a heather Harris Tweed baker boy cap out for her to try; the old boy clearly knows his hats because she's transformed into a sixties waif as soon as it's placed on top of her wayward curls. Laurie's hair is only ever sixty per cent tamed at best, and right now she looks like a street urchin from *Oliver Twist*. The lavender shades in the tweed bring out the colour of her eyes, but they also highlight the dark, bruised circles around them. She's tired, I notice with a jolt, and it's not 'I just need an early night' tired; it's 'I've had the shittiest few months of my life' tired, the eyes of someone who's worried and has been for a fair while. I realize I haven't even asked her how she's doing.

She takes the hat off after examining herself from each angle in the gilt hand mirror the shopkeeper obligingly holds up, turning the tiny label over to look at the price before she hands it back and wistfully shakes her head. It's a shame. It was a good look on her.

'How about in here?' she asks a little while later. We've considered and discarded a little water-colour painting and earmarked a 1920s turquoise pendant as a definite maybe, but as soon as we step into the little perfume paraphernalia shop I know this is where we're going to find the perfect thing. Laurie's like a little girl let loose in a sweet shop, ooh-ing and ahh-ing over elaborate gilt bottles and exotic scents, and then she breaks into this sunshine-slash of a smile.

'Jack, over here,' she says, calling me to her side to look at something she's just unearthed from the back of a shelf. I gaze over her shoulder to see what she's holding, and I thank my lucky stars I haven't bought the turquoise pendant already. The golden clamshell powder compact lying in Laurie's hand is so very Sarah that it would be wrong for any other woman in the world to own it. Art deco, I'd say, from my extensive viewing of *Antiques Roadshow*, sizeable enough to comfortably fill Laurie's palm, with an enamelled mermaid inlaid into the lid. There's something of Sarah about the auburn waves cascading over her shoulder and the pronounced, coquette dip of her waist. Laurie hands it over to me with a sparkle-eyed grin.

'Job done.'

I'm pleased by the weight of it. It's Sarah-worthy, something that says *I notice everything about you and you're valuable to me.*

'Call off the search,' I say, praying it's not going to cost more than a small mortgage and breathing out with relief when I flip the tag. I can still afford beer after all. 'Am I glad I bumped into you.'

We browse as the woman who owns the shop packages up the compact, taking her time to find a velvet pouch that fits and encasing the package in tissue and ribbons. I think she probably took one look at me and concluded that, left to my own devices, I'd wrap it in tinfoil or something. I wouldn't, but she's not that far off and I'm bloody glad I haven't got to wrangle with the Sellotape myself.

It's almost dark even though it's barely four when Laurie and I make our way back out on to the street again.

'Celebratory beer? I owe you one for helping me out,' I say. She looks like she needs a good sit-down and a chat. 'God knows what Sarah would have ended up with without you. Petrol station flowers and a dodgy pair of knickers from a sex shop. Or something.' Laurie laughs, pulling her coat sleeve back to check the time as if she has places to be.

'Okay,' she says, surprising me. I was sure she was going to dash off.

'Good girl. There's a place I know just round the corner. A proper pub, not some trendy bar where you can never get a seat.' I duck my head against the beginnings of snow on the bitter wind and spread my hand against her back to steer her down a small side street.

Laurie

As soon as we step inside the stained-glass doors of the pub I'm glad I didn't say no to a drink. There's the reassuring smell of a coal fire and beeswax polish, and the dark-green leather button-back booths are deep and comfortable, built for long, relaxed drinking sessions. An old man and his snoozing Jack Russell are the only other patrons. It's one of those unpretentious, end-of-the-world pubs that you know hasn't changed much in decades, ruddy quarry tiles and a brass surround running the length of the well-stocked bar.

'Glass of red?' Jack asks, and I nod, grateful as I take my shopping bags from him. 'You go and find a seat by the fire, I'll bring the drinks over.'

I bag the best booth in the house, closest to the warmth of the fire. I drop down and stow my bags under the table, shrugging out of my damp winter coat and hanging it on the newel post at the end of the booth to warm through for later. Warmed coats remind me of home; when we were kids my dad fitted an extra radiator behind the coat hooks so we'd always have a warm jacket on winter school mornings.

'Wine for the lady,' Jack jokes, appearing with a glass of deep-ruby wine and a pint. He follows my lead and hangs his coat on the other newel post, as if we've marked our territory, claimed this tiny lounge for two.

'Best thing about winter,' he says, rubbing his hands together briskly in front of the fire before he slides along the leather seat opposite me and pulls his pint towards him. 'God, do I need this.' He drinks deeply, smacking his lips appreciatively.

The wine is blood-warm in my mouth, pepper and rich blackcurrants.

'Thanks for helping me today,' he says. 'I'd never have found anything so perfect without you.'

I smile, because I know how much Sarah is going to treasure the compact. 'She's going to be super-impressed with you.'

'I'll claim it's all my own work, of course.'

'Your secret's safe with me.' I drink a little more, feeling the alcohol begin to work its magic.

'Have you heard from Sarah?'

'Not today.' Jack shakes his head. 'She called yesterday. Sounds like she's having a ball, of course. I could hardly hear her.'

She called me from a bar yesterday too, probably straight after speaking to Jack by the sounds of it. She headed back to her parents' a few days ago to celebrate her sister's eighteenth birthday.

'She put Allie on the phone, sounded drunk as a skunk.' He laughs, halfway down his drink already. 'Have you met her sister? They're like two peas in a pod when they're together. Double bloody trouble.'

I look towards the fire for a second and nod. 'I know. Their mum and dad must have had their hands full over the years.'

Jack pauses, clearing his throat. 'Sorry, Laurie. I didn't mean to . . . well, you know.' He doesn't say Ginny's name but I know that's why he's apologizing, and I wish for the hundredth time that I hadn't told him. This is precisely why I don't talk about her; people feel the need to offer sympathy or platitudes when there really isn't anything helpful to say. It's not a criticism. It's just a shitty fact of life.

'Are you heading back to see your mum for Christmas?' I change the subject on to safer ground and he visibly relaxes.

'Not until after my last shift on Christmas Eve.' He shrugs. 'Winding things up, winding things down. You know how it is.'

A couple more red wines later and I'm finally relaxing. I'd forgotten how nice it was to just sit and chat to Jack.

'Will you stay in radio for ever, do you think?'

'Absolutely. I love it.' His eyes light with interest. 'Plus no one cares if you've brushed your hair or still have yesterday's T-shirt on.'

I laugh softly, because despite his attempts to sound laissez-faire, I know that Jack's fiercely ambitious. Whenever he isn't with Sarah he's either at gigs or working, producing mostly, although he still occasionally gets to fill in for the regular late-night DJ, cutting his presenter teeth. I have no doubt that his voice will be on the airwaves somewhere as I eat my cornflakes or drift off to sleep over the years to come. I find the thought strangely comforting. I, on the other hand, have not got any further with my magazine job. The last few months, it hasn't exactly been my top priority.

We get more drinks, and I can feel the heat in my cheeks from both the alcohol and the fire.

'This is nice,' I say, resting the weight of my chin in my hand as I look at him. 'The fire, the wine. It's what I needed. Thank you for bringing me.'

He nods. 'How are you, Lu? Really, I mean. I know it hasn't been easy on you these last few months.'

Please don't be perceptive, you'll unpick me. It doesn't help that he called me Lu; only Sarah does that, and she doesn't know it but the only other person in the world who ever shortened my name to Lu was Ginny. She couldn't manage 'Laurie' when she was a baby; Lu was easier and it stuck. 'I'm okay,' I shrug, even though I'm anything but. 'Most of the time. Some of the time.' I gaze into the fire and try to keep the lump in my throat down. 'It feels as if someone pulled the rug out from under my family's feet, you know. My dad is our cornerstone, he always has been.'

'Is he getting better?'

I press my lips into a tight line, because the truth is we're not really sure. 'A bit,' I say. 'He's over the heart attack for the most part now, but looking back, that seems to have been just the beginning. He's taking so many pills that he practically rattles, and my poor mum has had to take over everything, really. Therapy appointments, dieticians, consultants, not to mention getting a grip on all of the bills and household things. It just seems endless.' I swallow a large slug of wine. You know how some events turn out to be the big stepping stones between one part of your life and the next? I don't just mean the steps you intend to take, like leaving home or starting a new job or marrying the person you love on a summer's afternoon. I mean the unexpected steps: the middle-of-the-night phone calls, the accidents, the risks that don't pay off. My twenty-third birthday turned out to be one of *my* unexpected stepping stones; a step away from the solid foundations built by my indomitable parents towards quicksand where they are fragile and too human and need me as much as I need them. It's knocked my world off-kilter; I'm sickly nervous every time the phone rings and there's a permanent cesspool of fear sloshing around in the base of my stomach. If I had to sum it up in a sentence, I'd say I feel hunted. I'm caught in the crosshairs, waiting for the bullet that may or may not come, running, looking over my shoulder, braced for impact. I dream of my sister more nights than I don't: Ginny cheering me on from my father's shoulders at my primary school sports day, Ginny holding tight to his hand as they cross a busy road and leave me behind on the other side, Ginny sleeping on Dad's shoulder in the pub garden we used to go to sometimes in the summer when we were kids, her blonde hair half covering her delicate face.

'I just want my big strong dad back to normal, you know?' I hate that I can hear the thickness of tears in my throat. And that Jack must be able to hear it too.

'Oh, Laurie,' he says, low and soothing, and then he slips round the booth and puts his arm round me. 'Poor you, you look so knackered lately.'

I don't even have the energy to act annoyed at that comment. I can't deny it. I'm bone-tired. I don't think I've even registered how low I've been because you have to keep on keeping on, don't you? But right here, sitting in this pub feeling insulated from it all, it hits me like a shovel to the face. I'm so exhausted I feel like I'm disintegrating inside my clothes.

'Life can be really shit sometimes,' he says, his arm still warm and reassuring round my shoulders. 'It'll come good again. It always does.'

'You think so? It sounds so stupid but I just feel like I'm failing at everything. Life here, no proper job. Perhaps I should just go back home. I should be with my parents, help my mum out.'

'Don't say that, Laurie. You're down, but you're not out. Your parents will be okay, and they'd want you to follow your dreams. You'll get there, I know it.'

'Do you think so?'

'Come on. Look at you. You're clever and you're funny; you won't be stuck behind that hotel reception for ever.

I've read some of your freelance stuff, remember? You'll get your break soon, I'm sure of it.'

I appreciate the generosity of his praise, but I know that what he actually means is that he's read the scant couple of articles I've had published because Sarah has pushed them under his nose. She's worse than my mum whenever I place anything, which is barely ever.

Jack's looking at me now, really studying me, as if what he's about to say matters.

'I don't think I've ever met anyone in my life with as much . . . I don't even know what it is that you have. Warmth, I guess, although that isn't exactly it.' He looks pissed off with himself for his inability to find the right words. 'You just have a way about you, Laurie. Being around you makes people feel good.'

I'm surprised enough to stop feeling sorry for myself and look up. 'Do you really mean that?'

'Yes.' His smile is slow, crooked. 'Of course I do. Right from the first time we met.'

I catch my breath, trying to keep my thoughts inside my head, but they seep out, like water through my fingers. 'The first time we met or the very first time?'

Oh fuck, oh fuck, oh fuck.

Jack

Oh fuck, oh fuck, oh fuck. She remembers.

'You mean . . . at Christmas?'

We're sitting closer than we were, almost thigh to thigh, and close up I can clearly see the toll recent months have had on her. Those dark circles, the high set of her shoulders as if she's always got her teeth clenched. She looks in need of a hot bath, chicken soup and her bed for a week.

'On the bus?' she breathes. Her cheeks are pink from the wine, and her eyes more animated than they have been since the summer. 'Do you remember?'

I frown and arrange my features into what I hope suggests puzzlement. If there's one thing I'm sure of, it's that to acknowledge my memory of those few moments at the bus stop would be a monu-fucking-mental mistake. Our entire friendship is built on the dynamics of my position as her best friend's boyfriend. I wait in silence and she withers in front of me. The jittery shimmer in her eyes dims and I know she wishes she could suck those words out of the air between us and back inside her body. If I could, I'd blow them back in there myself rather than have to hurt her with a lie.

'At your party,' I say gently.

'No. Before then,' she says, pressing me. 'I think I saw you sitting at a bus shelter. Months before. A year before.'

Oh, Laurie, why is it never the coward's way out for you? Trust me, it's an easier path. Until you get called on it, that is. I feign complete ignorance, my best Hugh Grant nonplussed impression.

'I think the wine's gone to your head, Lu. We first met at your Christmas party.'

She holds my gaze, silent and unwavering, and right there in front of me I see her slowly reach her limit and raise the white flag of defeat. Ten seconds. Fifteen, maybe. It seems longer, and I feel like the world's biggest cock. Shit, I think she's trying not to cry. I'm a complete fucking bastard. Should I have said I remembered? Would it have been better? For Laurie in this exact moment, probably kinder, but for Laurie next week or next month or next year? I don't think so.

'I'm sorry,' she says, compounding my position as the big bad wolf. 'Ignore me.'

'I'd never do that.' Three pints in and it seems that I'm struggling to maintain the lie too.

She blinks a few times and tears spike her lashes. 'Maybe you should.'

I look at her, really look at her, and I don't want to tell her any more lies today. She's all kinds of vulnerable, and we've both had a drink.

'Maybe I should,' I acknowledge. 'But I don't want to. I like being with you too much.' *Christ*. I know, okay? I shouldn't have said that. It's on the edges of inappropriate, and it's selfish.

'I like being with you too much too,' she whispers, and a single, desolate tear slides down her cheek.

'Don't,' I breathe, my voice rough even to my own ears. 'Please don't cry.'

Only a hard-faced bastard would let a girl cry like this without comforting her, and despite the fact that I've told her lies, I'm not a hard-faced bastard, so I brush her tears away with my fingertips, my other arm still round her shoulders.

'It's okay, honestly it is,' I murmur against her temple. How can she smell of wild summer flowers even in winter? Her skin is delicate under my fingertips, and although every atom of my being knows I should drop my hand, I hold her face instead, following her jawline with my thumb. For a moment we stay like that, until she moves slightly to look up at me and her mouth is suddenly dangerously close to mine.

I don't think she's breathing. I don't think I am either. Jesus, she has the most beautiful mouth this close up. Full and trembling. I can taste the wine on the warm heat of her breath. She moves forward, I think, and I swear there isn't any air between our lips. I'm anguished. Torn.

'I can't kiss you, Laurie. I can't.'

Laurie

I've drunk too much wine, and I'm the shabbiest person in the world, but I couldn't move away from Jack now even if this pub was burning down. We're caught in a tiny capsule of time, this unexpected booth at the end of the world, and there is just his generous mouth and his kind eyes and his warm, comforting hands. If this were a TV show I'd be shouting *stop*, because I'd know that however good they seem together, the shit would hit the fan further down the line. But this isn't make believe, it's real life, and in real life people make mistakes. I raise my head, and if he kisses me I won't have the power to stop myself from kissing him back, because to me he looks exactly as he did that day at the bus stop, and for a second I'm that girl on the bus in 2008 again. My dad isn't sick, and Jack isn't Sarah's boyfriend, and there's tinsel in my hair. I can almost hear the whirl of time turning back, whooshing past my ears like the sound of an old-fashioned tape recorder being rewound or a vinyl record being played backwards. God, I don't think I can stop this from happening.

'I can't kiss you, Laurie. I can't.'

His words land on my heart like hailstones. Shit. What in God's name am I doing? What kind of hideous lowlife am I? I need to get away from him.

'Christ,' I whisper, panicked, pressing my shaking fingers against my lips. I'm on my feet, scrabbling for my bags and half running out of the pub before I really know what I'm going to do, and it's only when the bitter-cold air hits me that I realize I don't have my coat and it's snowing steadily.

'Laurie! Laurie, wait up.'

He's out of breath, my coat clutched in his hands as he catches hold of my sleeve. 'Please, just stop a second, will you?'

I pull away, too hard, spilling the shopping from one of my bags over the quiet backstreet. He helps me to shove it back in and wraps my coat round my shivering shoulders, then he wraps his arms round my coat, holding me until the heat penetrates my clothes and my bones. It's so very, very warm from the fire, and I close my eyes because I'm inexplicably in tears again. I'm not generally a crier, yet today my tear ducts seem to be bursting their banks.

'Laurie,' he whispers, raw, his eyes star-bright in the street lamps. 'The last thing I ever want to do is hurt you.'

'I'm such a fool,' I whisper. 'I don't even know why I'm crying.'

Jack sighs, exasperated, kind. 'Because you're tired, and you're worried, and you feel as if you're always swimming against the tide.'

He rubs my back as he speaks low and steady against my ear, his body sheltering mine from the snow. My back is turned to the wall, and my fight is gone because he's saying such incredibly comforting things and he's holding me close. I'm so very tired of swimming. Most of the time I feel like the tide is going to pull me under, but here in Jack's arms I feel as if he's just reached over the side of a life raft and hauled me to safety. I realize, bleakly, that I don't think there will ever be a time when I don't have feelings for this man.

'I wanted you to kiss me, Jack,' I say, bereft. It's not as if he isn't aware what I wanted back there; to be coy would be pointless. 'I don't like myself for it.'

He strokes my hair, cups my chin, looks me in the eyes. 'If I tell you something, do you promise to never tell another living soul, not even a goldfish?'

I swallow, eye to eye with him as I nod, and he takes my face between both of his hands. Whatever he's about to say, I think it's something I'm going to remember for ever.

'I wanted to kiss you back there in the pub, Laurie, and I want to kiss you even more right now. You're one of the loveliest people I've ever met in my whole life.' He looks away, down the length of the deserted street and then back at me again. 'You're beautiful and kind, and you make me laugh, and when you look at me like that with your summer hedgerow eyes ... only a fucking saint wouldn't kiss you.'

Then he leans me against the wall with the weight of his body, and because he *isn't* a fucking saint, he kisses me. Jack O'Mara dips his head and kisses me in the snow, his lips trembling and then hot and sure, and I'm crying and kissing him back, opening my mouth to let his tongue slide over mine as he makes this low, injured animal noise in his throat. I feel the relief of him in every follicle of my hair, and in every cell of my body, and in the blood in my veins. His breathing is as shallow as mine, and it's so much more than I've ever imagined, and trust me, I used to let my imagination run riot where Jack O'Mara was concerned.

He holds my face as if I'm precious and then pushes his fingers into my hair, cupping my head in his hands when I tip it back.

This is the only time we will ever kiss each other. He knows it, I know it, and it's so achingly melancholy-sexy that I feel tears threaten again.

I cling to the lapels of his winter coat, our kiss salty with my tears, and I open my eyes to look at him because I want to remember this kiss till the day I die. His eyes are closed, his snow-damp lashes a dark sweep on his cheek, all of his attention focused on our once-in-a-lifetime kiss.

We break off at last, the spell broken by the engine of a car crawling slowly past because of the inclement weather. Our breath almost crystallizes on the ice-cold air as it leaves our bodies in sharp, painful bursts.

'Let's be kind to each other about this,' he tells me. I expect he wishes that his voice were more steady than it is. 'We both know it shouldn't have happened, but it doesn't have to mean anything, and it doesn't need to change anything.'

It's such a searing understatement that I almost laugh; the sigh that leaves me as I look away from him is rent with longing and self-loathing, and quiet 'no one will ever kiss me like that again' distress.

'Maybe if we'd met under different circumstances,' I say, looking at him again after a while, and he nods.

'In a heartbeat.'

On cue, a taxi trundles slowly along the side street towards us, and he raises his hand to flag it down. It's a good decision.

'Not a soul,' he reminds me quietly as he opens the door and puts my bags inside.

'Not even a goldfish,' I whisper as I climb in. I don't smile to make light of it, because it's not even slightly funny.

He hands the driver a note. 'Take her home safely,' he says. His eyes hold mine for a few long seconds as he slams my door. I'm reminded of the last time I watched him disappear into the night. I didn't know him then; I had no control. It isn't like that tonight. I know who he is, and how he tastes, and for a split second I long to open the door of the cab, to stop history from repeating itself.

I don't. Of course I don't. Despite the fairy-tale snowstorm out there, this isn't Narnia. This is London, real life, where hearts get kicked and bruised and broken, but somehow they still keep beating. I watch him recede as the taxi lurches cautiously away, and he watches me too, his hands shoved deep in his pockets, his shoulders bunched against the wind. I lay my head against the cold glass as we turn the corner, my heart and my conscience lead heavy in my chest.

I wish I'd never laid eyes on Jack O'Mara.

2011

New Year's Resolutions

I'm not sure I should even write this down in case anyone finds it, even a goldfish.

1) I resolve to never, ever kiss my best friend's boy-friend ever again. In fact, I'm never going to allow even one errant thought about him to enter my head.

2) I'm putting all unplatonic thoughts of Jack O'Mara into a crate, sealing it with bright yellow 'toxic' stickers and chucking it into the hinterland at the back of my head.

Jack

'Happy New Year, mermaid girl.'

Sarah laughs as I pull her into my arms.

'I'm sorry,' I whisper into her hair, making a silent resolution to not kiss anyone other than Sarah this year.

'What for?' She holds me at arm's length, her eyes narrowed slightly.

Shit. 'For eating so much garlic last night. God knows
how you're able to come anywhere near this pong, I can
smell it every time I yawn.'

She looks kind of amused and kind of confused. It's a
good job we're both more than halfway towards being
rat-arsed, because it's exactly the kind of comment that
could land me in all sorts of trouble. Honestly, it's as if the
truth is trying to leak out of me. I'm a petrol can riddled
with holes, an accident waiting to happen.

Laurie

HNY, Lu! Love you!

I trace the letters of Sarah's text with my fingertip as I lie
in bed. The New Year is less than two hours old, but

nonetheless, I kissed Jack last year, not this one. This one is a clean sheet.

Love you too, Sar, hope you're not too drunk! HNY xx

I press send, then click my phone off and lie facing the ceiling in the darkness. I'm grateful that my parents didn't rush to reclaim my room as a study or a spare room when I left for uni; it's pretty much as I left it, comforting and familiar. I've never been one to stick posters on the walls, but my childhood books line the shelf over the desk and the lilac dress I wore to my high school prom still hangs in my wardrobe. I cannot put a value on how much these things mean to me right now. Being in here is like stepping into a time capsule, or into my own protective Tardis, perhaps. Where would I have my personal Tardis fly me to, I wonder? I know the answer. I'd take it back to 21 December 2008 and I'd make myself miss that bloody bus. That way I'd never have seen Jack O'Mara before Sarah introduced us, and everything would have been okay. I don't for a second think that I'd have allowed myself the luxury of anything other than platonic feelings for him then, and I wouldn't be lying here now feeling lower than a snake's belly. Before the kiss, I'd been able to uneasily square things with myself. I'd struggled with my feelings for him and I'd felt like a crap friend because of it, but I'd stayed on the right side of the line.

What I've done now is unconscionable; I can't even attempt to justify it to myself. I haven't seen either Sarah or Jack since that afternoon in London. I know he swore me to secrecy, but he didn't have the right to ask it of me. I'm not blaming him, we carry the burden equally. And I don't know if telling Sarah would be the honourable thing or just a way to make myself feel better and her feel worse. I'd lose her. I know that much. She'd probably ditch Jack too; there would be no winners. I don't feel worried that he's someone who will be a serial strayer, constantly ratting around behind her back; if that were the case I'd tell her without question. Perhaps I'm flattering myself, but what happened felt more personal than that, a few minutes of madness that will weigh heavily on both of our consciences.

I'm not going to tell her. I made myself a promise to for ever hold my peace about my feelings for Jack O'Mara, and there's never been a time when that promise mattered more.

28 January

Jack

Sarah's sleeping, Laurie's working late at the hotel and I'm sat at their kitchen table drinking neat vodka at half past two in the morning. I've never been a big drinker but suddenly I can see its merits. It's been weeks now since I kissed Laurie. Weeks, and I'm making a right royal fuck-up of pretending it didn't happen. Literally every time I look at Sarah I wonder if today's the day I should come clean. Every. Bloody. Day. I've been over it and over it in my head, trying to pinpoint the exact moment I was unfaithful. Was it when I asked Laurie to come for a beer? When I held her when she cried? Or was it way back, the very first time Sarah introduced us and we both made the decision not to mention the fact that we'd actually met before? Not that we had, exactly, but we weren't strangers. I know that much for sure now. It was easier when I could tell myself that Laurie didn't recall those few moments at the bus stop, but now I know that's not the truth. I know for a fact that she remembered me, and *because* she remembered me twelve whole months later, I know that means something else too. Maybe just that she's like me, blessed and cursed with an excellent memory; but I'm not sure. I've been unpicking all of the times we've spent together, examining fragments of remembered conversations, trying to see if I've missed an undercurrent. It's not that I think she's harbouring a crush on me or anything. For fuck's sake. I'm not being conceited; I just feel like I've missed something here.

I mean, it was just a kiss. It's not like I screwed anyone, is it? But I kissed *Laurie*, and somehow that's worse than screwing my way through the whole fucking Playboy mansion, because they'd be forget-me-tomorrow strangers. Laurie isn't a stranger, and I didn't kiss her out of anything as basic and easily explained away as stupid, vacuous lust. But I didn't kiss her to restore her dignity either or because she was fragile and she needed me to make her feel better. I'm not that noble. I kissed her because she looked fucking ethereal under the street lamp with snowflakes clinging to her hair. I kissed her because I'd lied about not seeing her on that bus and I felt like a dick, and I kissed her because the need to know how her soft, vulnerable mouth would feel against mine floored me like a goddamn express train. And now I do know, and I wish I didn't, because you can't un-remember something as spectacular as that.

'Let's be kind to each other about this,' I said to her afterwards. 'It shouldn't have happened and it doesn't have to mean anything.'

Of all of the things I've ever said, that ranks up there amongst the most crass. But what *else* was I supposed to say? That I felt as if she'd just kissed fucking stardust into my mouth; that of course I saw her on that bus after all?

I knock back the contents of my glass and refill it. It's no good. I need to speak to Laurie.

Laurie

I knew I couldn't avoid Jack for ever. God knows I'd like to, but this is my complicated, messed-up life, and I've just come in from a late shift to find him sitting at my kitchen table in the dark.

'Where's Sarah?' I say, dispensing with any form of greeting because I'm knackered and I've lost the art of talking to him about inconsequential things.

'In bed.' He's nursing a tumbler – water or vodka, I'm not sure.

'Shouldn't you be too?' I glance up at the kitchen clock. Three in the morning isn't a healthy time to be drinking alone.

'Couldn't sleep.'

I don't quite believe him. This is only the third time I've seen him since that afternoon we . . . I don't even like to repeat in my own head what we did – and it's the first time I've been alone with him since then, by both of our choices, I think. He scrubs his hand over the stubble on his jawline, backwards and forwards again, a nervous tick. If I had stubble, I'd probably do the same.

I pour myself a glass of water. 'I'm going to call it a night.'

He reaches for my wrist as I pass him. 'Please, Laurie. I need to talk to you.'

I want to tell him that it won't help, but the bleak look in his eyes softens my resolve, so I sit down wearily at the table, taking in his tired face and his rumpled T-shirt.

'Is that what you were doing? Waiting up for me?'

He doesn't do me the disservice of lying.

'I feel like the world's biggest shit, Lu. I don't know how to get past it.'

I cup my hands round my glass. I don't know how to help him. What am I supposed to say, that it gets easier? So trite, and not even especially true. Why is he doing this, anyway? Because he thinks I'm the more practised liar and wants some tips? I've turned our conversation from that day over and over in my head. Jack doesn't remember me from the bus stop. He has no recollection of me before Sarah introduced us to each other. It's crushing, because I've spent months and years being defined by that moment, and yet it's freeing too, because it's as if he's rubber-stamped the fact that I need to let it go now. And that's what I'm trying my hardest to do.

'It was a really awful mistake, Jack,' I whisper, staring at my hands. 'More my fault than yours, if it helps.'

'Fuck that,' he says, sharp, loud enough for me to cast a warning look towards the doorway. 'Don't you dare do that to yourself. I'm the one who's been unfaithful here.'

'Sarah's my best friend,' I say pointedly. 'She's like a sister to me. However unfaithful you feel, trust me, I'm up there with you on the feeling lousy scale.' I swallow a mouthful of water. 'There isn't a pecking order for guilt here. We were both wrong.'

He falls quiet and takes a sip of his drink. From the smell wafting my way, I'm guessing it isn't water.

'Do you know what I hate most of all about what happened, Laurie?'

I don't want him to tell me, because if it's the same thing that I hate about it, then we're both only going to feel worse for acknowledging it.

'I hate that I can't forget it,' he says. 'It wasn't supposed to mean anything. Was it?' I'm glad he doesn't raise his eyes from his drink as he speaks, hollow, too emotional. 'Did it . . . did it mean anything to you?'

His quiet, explosive question hangs there, and I swallow hard. For a while I can't look at him, because he'll see the truth all over my face. I know what I have to do. I've lied to Sarah for two years straight now. Lying to Jack shouldn't be as difficult. It shouldn't be, but it is. Excruciatingly so.

'Look,' I say, finally meeting his troubled, beautiful eyes full on. 'I was upset and horribly low, and you were kind and lovely, because that's who you are. We're friends, aren't we?' I break off to swallow the painful tears in my throat, and he nods, his hand pressed against his mouth as I speak. 'We're really, really good friends, we had too much to drink, and it was Christmas, and we stupidly blurred the lines between friendship and something else. But we stopped and we both knew it was awful, and it's done now and it can't be undone. What good can come of letting it rip Sarah apart too? You're sorry, God knows I'm more sorry than I've ever been about anything in my life, and it'll never, ever happen again. I don't think of you in that way and I'm damn sure you don't harbour secret fantasies about me, either. If we tell Sarah, it'll only be to salve our guilt. And do you think that's a good enough reason?'

He's been shaking his head slowly all the time I've been talking, his hand still over his mouth as if he feels nauseous.

'Nowhere near good enough.'

I nod. 'Just go to bed, Jack. Go to bed, go to sleep, and when we get up in the morning, we're both going to get on with the rest of our lives without ever mentioning this again. Not to Sarah and not to each other.' I take a breath. 'Not even to a goldfish.'

He looks away from me, pushing his hand through his already messed-up hair. I've been flailing around so much in my own guilt that I haven't really stopped to wonder how Jack was handling it. Not all that well, so it seems, and I almost resent him for needing me to teach him how to carry the burden of his guilt.

I sit at the table for a long time after he's gone. I make a coffee and let it go cold as I look out of the dark kitchen window over the rooftops of Delancey Street. I think of Sarah and Jack asleep down the hall, and of my parents back at home, and my brother and Anna, his new wife, tucked up in the smart new house they bought after their wedding in the springtime.

Two, and two, and two, and me. Maybe I'll buy myself a goldfish.

3 May

Laurie

'It's gone by too fast.'

We're slouched next to each other on the sofa, Sarah and me, feet up on the scratched coffee table and wine glasses in our hands. We're all packed up and ready to go, almost prepared to hand our Delancey Street bolthole over to its next lucky inhabitants.

'Five years,' I sigh. 'You're right. I don't know where it's gone.'

Sarah takes a massive gulp of wine and frowns. 'I don't want to leave this place. I wish we could stay for ever.'

We sit in silence and gaze around the living room, the scene of our student parties, our drunken nights, our traded secrets, our late-night laughter. We both know that we can't stay; this phase of our lives is at an end. Sarah has bagged a new, glitzier job at a start-up cable TV station over on the opposite side of the city and commuting from here to there just isn't possible. I've taken this as my cue for a shake-up too. I can't afford to keep this place on on my own, and I'm going nowhere fast career-wise. The hotel is transient, the publishing trade resistant. I'm heading home to see my family for a few weeks, and then onwards to Thailand for a while. I know. How fabulous does that sound? I'm daunted by the idea of going alone, but spurred on by my dad's renewed zeal for getting out there and grabbing life by the balls. My mother was deeply unimpressed when he used that very phrase; they gifted me and Daryl some money at Christmas. It's not something they'd usually do, but they said Dad's heart attack has given them a fresh perspective. They cried, so we did, and we both agreed to do something a bit special with the gift. Daryl and Anna are going to buy their marital bed for the new house, and I'm going to spend mine grabbing life by the balls in Thailand. I wish I could pack Sarah in my suitcase; I don't have a clue how to do life without her next to me. At least I'll have some respite from the malingering guilt.

'You're the best friend I've ever had,' I say.

'Fuck off,' she mutters, starting to cry. 'I told you not to say that.'

'And I told you not to bloody cry,' I say, dragging the end of my sleeve across my eyes. 'Now look what you've done.'

We hold hands, really tightly.

'We'll always be friends, right?' Her voice is small and shot through with vulnerability. 'Even when you go to Thailand and join a hippy commune, or whatever it is you're going to do over there?'

'Even then,' I say, squeezing her fingers. 'How about when you become a big-shot TV presenter? Will you ditch me for your celebrity friends?'

She laughs, pretending she needs a second to think it over. She went to see the new station about a behind-the-scenes role and wound up being asked how she'd feel about taking on maternity cover for their roaming reporter. They obviously took one look at her and saw what we all see: star quality.

'Well . . . I reckon Amanda Holden can hold her drink.'

I thump her on the arm and she sighs, faking disappointment.

'Fine. I won't ditch you, even for Amanda Holden.' She pauses for a second. 'We've had a laugh though, haven't we?' she says, leaning against me.

I close my damp eyelashes and lean my head on hers. 'We have.'

'You know what my favourite memory of you is?'

I don't answer her, because there are tears rolling down my cheeks and my throat is aching.

'It's a recurring memory, actually,' she says. 'I like how you look after me when I'm hung-over. No one will ever hold my hair back like you do when I throw up.'

I laugh despite my tears. 'You've got a lot of bloody hair, too. It's not easy.'

'And how you make my morning coffee just right,' she says. 'Everyone else gets it wrong. Even my mother.'

'You have four grains of coffee, Sar. You can't even classify it as coffee.'

'I know that. But *you* do. You ask me if I want coffee, and then you make it how I like it. Four grains.'

I sigh. 'You've probably made me more cups of coffee than I've made you. And you've *definitely* made the most sandwiches.'

'You always forget about the mayo. You know how crucial it is.' She sags. 'How are you going to survive out there in the big wide world without me, Lu?'

'It's not as if we're never going to see each other,' I say, wiping my face. 'I'll be able to see you on the TV if nowhere else. I'll be waiting for the day they make you slide down a fireman's pole.'

'But I won't be able to see you when you're on the other side of the world.'

I put my arm round her shoulders. 'I'm not going for ever.'

'You better bloody not,' she sniffs. 'Don't go shacking up with some yogic monk and knocking out a dozen Thai babies or anything, will you? I want you back in London by Christmas.'

'I don't think monks are allowed to have babies.' I laugh shakily. 'I'll only be gone a few months. I'll be back in time to spend New Year together.'

'Promise me?' She links her pinky finger with mine like a little girl, and those damn tears threaten again because she reminds me of another little girl from a long time ago.

'I promise I'll come back, Sarah. I promise.'

20 September

Laurie

'You're sure you've got everything? Insect repellant? Disinfectant spray?'

I nod, squeezing Mum as she and Dad prepare to leave me at the airport. Her perfume and the jangle of the bracelet she always wears are so dear and familiar to me; I'm choked up at the thought of being so far from home.

'Torch?' Dad says, ever practical.

'Got it,' I say, and he puts his arms round us both.

'Come on, you daft things. Let's make this a happy send-off. It's an adventure.'

I untangle myself from them and wipe my eyes, half laughing and half crying as Dad lifts my backpack on to my shoulders. 'I know it is!'

'Go on then,' he says, kissing me on the cheek. 'Be off with you.'

I lean in and kiss Mum too, then step back and take a deep breath. 'I'm going now,' I say, my lip wobbling.

They stand together, Dad's arm round Mum's shoulders, and they nod. I'm sure it would feel less of a wrench if I wasn't going alone; I feel about fourteen as I turn round at the gate to give them one final wave before I lose sight of them. Mum blows me a kiss and Dad lifts his hand, and then I turn away and walk determinedly towards the gate. Thailand awaits.

12 October

Laurie

'*Sawatdee kha.*'

I raise my hand in greeting to Nakul, and he grins and throws me a thumbs-up as I take a rickety seat at an equally rickety table at his cafe on Sunrise Beach. It sounds bizarre to say that my time here has been a hectic blur of Buddhist temples, but that's how it feels – a weird juxtaposition of absolute serenity amid happy, noisy chaos. No one could ever call Thailand boring; my head is in a spin and I've got muscles where I never had them before. I travelled north after I arrived in Bangkok, intent on getting my shot of culture in early; I feared that if I headed straight to the south I'd spend my entire trip in a hammock on the beach.

But now I've seen enough to allow myself the luxury of resting, and I've hit the eye-wateringly perfect castaway beaches of southern Thailand. I've set up temporary home in a cheap-as-chips beach shack; it's one room, but it's my room, and there is a veranda to sit and read on overlooking the beach. I don't think I'd realized how much I needed this break from reality. When I first got to Thailand I cried for almost a week straight as I trekked through jungle terrain with a small group of other travellers. I didn't cry because the trek was so strenuous, although it certainly was. I cried with sheer relief, hot, salty tears, releasing my heavy burdens into the earth as I walked. A few weeks before I came out here my mum and I caught *Eat Pray Love* at the local cinema, and though I haven't got anywhere near to finding love, I am having some kind of mini epiphany. I'm like an in-patient in recovery, learning how to forgive myself for the mistakes I've made and acknowledging that I'm still me, still a good person and still a true friend to Sarah, despite what happened with Jack. Perhaps one day I might even deserve to be happy.

'Coffee, Lau-Lau?'

I smile, pleased by Nakul's adulteration of my name as he picks his way across the warm, powder-soft sand to my table. I've been here on each of the four mornings since I arrived on Koh Lipe, and the island is working it's laid-back magic into my skin and bones. It is as if I'm finally standing still for the first time in years.

'*Khop khun kha,*' I say when Nakul places a small white cup down in front of me, still hesitant over my Thai manners. He grins nonetheless, hopefully because my clumsy attempt at his language is better than not at all.

'Your plan for today, Lau-Lau?'

He's asked me the same question each morning, and every time my answer has been the same: 'I don't have a plan at all for today.'

Koh Lipe isn't a place for people with big plans. The entire point of the island is to chill out. He laughs as he walks away to speak to new customers who've just ambled up from the beach.

'No plans on a beautiful day like this?'

I turn towards the distinctly English voice and a guy drops down at the little table on the other side of me. He catches Nakul's eye and raises his hand in greeting, his smile easy and relaxed as he stretches his long legs out in front of him on the sand. The Thai sun has baked my own skin honey gold, but this guy has been more serious altogether on the sun-worshipping stakes. He's chestnut brown, his almost blue-black hair flopping in his dark, amused eyes.

I smile and shrug a little. 'Nothing beyond floating in the sea and reading my book.'

'A fine plan,' he says. 'What are you reading? Please don't say *The Beach*.'

'It's a good book,' I joke. Not that it isn't, but no self-respecting traveller can admit to such an obvious choice. '*The Great Gatsby*, actually.' I don't elaborate and tell him that my reading matter is completely dictated by the small stack of books someone left behind in my shack. Much better that he thinks me educated enough to carry F. Scott Fitzgerald around the world in my backpack.

'Shack find?'

I roll my eyes and laugh. 'Busted.'

'You could have lied and I'd have believed you.'

'I find that lies encumber me.'

He stares at me, as well he might. I sound as if *The Great Gatsby* has gone straight to my head.

'I'm Oscar,' he says, stretching his hand out formally across the space between our tables. 'And my plan for the day is to spend it with you.'

'You look like a starfish.'

Oscar prods me idly with the oar of the kayak, and I let

him spin me slowly on my back with my eyes half closed against the glare of the sunlight. Brilliant blue above me and below me, bath-water warm over my blissed-out skin when he ladles seawater over my belly with the paddle of the oar.

'I *feel* like a starfish.'

True to his word, Oscar has spent his day with me. I wouldn't usually warm to someone who sounded so horribly self-assured, but something in me is determined to do the opposite of what I'd normally do. He's been in Thailand for a couple of months longer than I have, choosing to stay on in Koh Lipe for a while after his travelling companions returned home to the UK. It explains his native tan, at least.

'Have you ever eaten one? They sell them on sticks like lollipops on Walking Street.'

I open my eyes, appalled, and find him laughing.

'Very funny.'

He's lounging in the boat, his chin resting on his forearm as he looks over the side at me, his fingertips trailing in the sea. I flick a little seawater at him, speckling a shimmer of droplets over the bridge of his straight nose. I'll admit it. He's bloody good-looking in a classic, chip-off-the-old-Greek-god kind of way. He has the confident aura of wealth about him, louche and debonair. *I know, I know.* Who uses words like that any more? Me, apparently, after a day spent drinking local beer and reading *The Great Gatsby* in a hammock. There's something about living in a different place that allows you to be whoever you want to be.

'Can I take you to dinner tonight?'

I lay my head back in the water and close my eyes again, floating. 'As long as it isn't starfish.'

'I think I can promise that much.'

I roll on to my front and swim the few strokes to the kayak, curling my wet fingertips over the edge. His face is inches from mine.

'Let's not make each other promises,' I say.

He gives me the same perplexed stare he did when we met at the beach cafe this morning, then leans in and brushes his warm, sea-salt lips over mine. 'I like you, Starfish. You're interesting.'

Laurie

Oscar Ogilvy-Black. It's quite a mouthful, isn't it? I don't think he and I would have crossed each other's paths in the normal course of things back in London, but here in Thailand the dating rulebook has been ripped up. He tells me he's a banker but not a wanker, and I confide my hope of gaining my first foothold in the world of magazine journalism one day soon. I have to admit that I judged him when we first met. But underneath the undeniable poshness, he's funny and self-deprecating, and when he looks at me there's a kindness in his eyes that warms me.

'You're not going to be one of those awful gossip column queens, are you?'

I gasp, mock offended, and then sigh, a little giddy because his fingers lace with mine as we walk along the cool sand after dinner. 'Do I look like I care about worst- and best-dressed celebs?'

He takes in my denim cut-offs and black vest, then the lemon toggles of my bikini top visible around my neck.

'Umm . . . maybe not,' he laughs.

'Cheeky, you're hardly suited and booted.' I raise an eyebrow as he looks comedically down at his ripped shorts and flip-flops.

Laughing, we reach my shack, and I kick my shoes off on the deck. 'Beer?'

He nods, leaving his shoes outside beside mine before he flops down on my huge beanbag, his hands folded behind his head.

'Make yourself at home,' I say, and I drop beside him with the cold beers.

'Are you sure about that?' he asks, rolling on to his side, propped on one elbow to look at me.

'Why? What would you do if you were at home?'

He reaches down and drags his T-shirt over his head, leaving him in just his shorts. The moonlight shades his skin coconut-shell brown. 'I'd get more comfortable.'

I pause for a beat, considering just laughing at him – I mean, what a line – but then I follow suit and pull my vest off. Why not? Oscar is everything that my life is not: light-hearted; uncomplicated.

'Me too.'

He holds out his arm for me to settle in beside him, and when I do his body is warm and vital. I am as free as one of the small, blush-pink birds that wheel through the sky above my shack at dawn.

Through the window I can see the black spindle out-lines of the long-tail boats anchored just off the shore in readiness for the morning, and the pitch-dark sky over-head studded with a myriad of diamond stars.

'I can't remember the last time I felt this peaceful.'

Oscar takes a long drink then puts his beer bottle down on the floor before he replies.

'I think I might be insulted. I was hoping you were outrageously turned on.'

I laugh softly into his chest and prop myself up to look at him. 'I think I could be.'

One arm still bent behind his head, he slides his free hand round the back of my neck and tugs slowly on the string ties of my bikini top. It falls when he lets go, and he doesn't take his eyes from mine as he reaches lower between my shoulder blades to finish the job.

'Now *I'm* outrageously turned on,' he says, tracing one fingertip from the dip between my collarbones to the button on my shorts. He swallows hard as he looks at my bared breasts. A breeze catches the wind chime hanging from the corner of my shack, a soft glitter of bells as he shifts slightly, pressing me back into the beanbag as he draws my nipple inside the heat of his mouth. Jesus. Aching, spiralling lust unfurls octopus-like inside my body, its tentacles licking fast along my limbs, heavy in my abdomen, fast in my chest as I push my hands into the thickness of his hair and hold him to me. I never thought I could feel like this for someone other than Jack, but something about being here with Oscar has freed me.

He reaches for the button of my shorts, lifting his head to look at me before he goes any further. I'm relieved he's that kind of man; even though his breathing is shallow and his eyes are begging me not to stop him, I know that he would, and that's enough.

'Do you have a condom?' I whisper as I stroke his hair, praying he says yes.

He moves over me, his chest on mine, and his kiss is so unhurried and exquisite that I wrap my arms round his shoulders and hold him to me.

'I think so,' he breathes, then laughs shakily. 'I just

hope it's in date.' He reaches into his back pocket, kissing me some more. Laying his wallet on the floor beside the beanbag, he flicks it open and pulls out a silver foil packet, checking it before he presses it into my palm for safekeeping.

He sits up, and this time he doesn't pause over the business of unbuttoning my shorts. His fingers are sure and steady, working them down my hips until I have only my small, yellow bikini bottoms left.

He spreads my thighs and kneels between them, then splays my arms wide and pins me lightly in place. 'Do you know what you are?'

I stare up at him, unsure what he's going to say.

'A fucking sexy starfish.'

I close my eyes and laugh, and then I gasp, because he's lowered his face between my legs and I can feel the heat of his mouth moving over the silky material of my bikini.

There isn't one atom of me that wants him to stop as he discards what's left of his clothes. For a second we hold a silent conversation with just our eyes. I tell him that I know he's running away from the responsibility and stress of the city life awaiting him back in London, and he tells me he can paper over the cracks in my heart and make me better again. We make each other promises even though we pledged that we wouldn't, and then he settles over me and I forget about everything but now.

Later, I wake and find him sitting on the steps of my shack watching the beginnings of another pink and purple dawn.

I sit beside him, an elephant-patterned throw pulled round my shoulders, and he looks at me sideways.

'Marry me, Starfish.'

I laugh softly and get up to make coffee.

Laurie

I'd planned to go home a few weeks ago, yet here I am still in Thailand, still with Oscar.

Oscar, Oscar, Oscar. Who knew? I think we're both living in denial, completely unprepared and unwilling to return to the world we belong to. But who's to say that you have to belong to somewhere for ever, anyway? Why do I have to belong to England, when everything there is grey and confusing and difficult? Were it not for the people I love, and my promise to Sarah, I'd stay here on this beach and have a dozen little babies, though not with a Thai monk. Back in England, Mum reports, the rain has settled in for the long haul, like an unwelcome relative at Christmas, but here when the rain comes it's fast and furious and then gone in a blink, shoved aside by the sun. I don't think I've ever been colder than the day Jack kissed me on a London backstreet nearly twelve months ago, and I don't think I've ever been warmer than I am here on Koh Lipe with Oscar. My blood is warm, my bones are warm and my skin is warm.

Sometimes, when we're lying on our backs on a beach or reading in a hammock or falling asleep in bed, I lie and listen to the gentle rush of the sea meeting the shore and I imagine we're castaways, washed up on a desert island, left to spend the rest of our days eating fish we've caught and having sweat-filmed sex. Every now and then we'd hear the petrol rumble of a plane's engine in the cornflower sky above, and we'd hide in the shelter of the treeline rather than write SOS in the sand.

12 December

G'day from the bottom of the world, lovebirds!

Hope you're not freezing your tits off too much up there, ha ha!

Australia is heaven on a stick. Jack has gone completely native, I'm going to buy him a hat with corks on and call him Crocodile Dundee. He even went and checked out a radio station in Melbourne; seriously, if they offered him a job I don't think he'd ever come home again. Except, ha, get this! He's <u>MORTALLY TERRIFIED</u> of snakes. I didn't know until there was a tiny one on our balcony last week and he practically screamed the place down. I had to coax him down off a chair with a brandy. It's a good job he's got me to protect him.

Oscar! Take care of my girl, can't wait to meet you!

Laurie, let's all get together as soon as we can, dying to see you.

Lots of love and kisses, Sarah xx

PS Jack says to say hi! :)

2012

New Year's Resolutions

1) By hook or by crook, I'm moving back to London this year to start my fantasy job in publishing.

I've let my ambitions simmer on the back-burner for too long now because of Thailand and Oscar, and most of all because I wanted to spend some proper time at home and be around for Mum and Dad. There are lots of reasons and explanations, all excuses; what I've really been doing is avoiding Jack.

I've decided I'm not going to do that any longer. I miss Sarah so much, and I miss the buzz and crackle of London life too. I'm going to hand in my notice at the hotel I've been temping at lately; my CV so far is all hospitality-based, stop-gap jobs and temporary positions to keep money in my pocket while I wait for the rest of my life to kick in. Well, I'm done waiting. I'm going to pull on my boots and kick life's butt, instead.

2) And then there's Oscar. Oscar Ogilvy-Black, the man who found me on a beach in Thailand and jokingly asked me to marry him at sunrise the next morning. He's asked me to marry him dozens of times since, mostly after sex or when we've had a few drinks — it's become our standing joke. At least I think it's a joke.

I don't actually know what my New Year's Resolution is about Oscar. Just to try and keep hold of him, I think, and keep hold of the feelings I have for him now that we're going back to reality.

3) Oh, and I've decided I'm ready to give false eyelashes another go. Because gluing your eyes shut once in a lifetime isn't enough for a woman like me.

Laurie

'I'm so nervous,' I mutter, straightening the collar of my woollen winter coat as we walk hand in hand along the pavement. I'm wearing a *brooch*. I know, who does that? Nobody sane under thirty. I'm just desperate to make a good impression. 'Is this too much?' I touch the little jewelled daisy and look up at Oscar, who just laughs.

'You're being ridiculous. It's my mother, Laurie, not the queen.'

I can't help it. Everything seemed far simpler in Thailand; we got to know each other while stripped back to whatever basics we could fit in a backpack. Here amongst the trappings of our usual lives, our differences seem more stark. I'm back to being socially awkward, doubly so today, and Oscar is far more man-about-town than I imagined.

'Here we are,' he says, leading me towards a patent-black front door in an elegant sweep of townhouses. 'Stop fidgeting, you look fine.'

I swallow hard as we wait for the door to be answered, hoping that Oscar's mother likes the bunch of winter white roses I bought on the way over. God, what if she's allergic? No, Oscar would have said. I tap my foot, nervy, and then the door opens at last.

'Oscar, darling.'

Lucille Ogilvy-Black may not be actual royalty, but there is a definite regal air to her straight back and white, perfectly blow-dried hair. She's dressed all in black, a sharp contrast to the lustrous circlet of pearls round her neck.

'Mum, this is Laurel,' he says as he steps out of her hug, his hand on the small of my back to encourage me forward. Afterwards, I realize that I should have read more into the fact that he called me Laurel rather than Laurie.

I put my best foot forward and smile, and she accepts the flowers with a gracious incline of her head. She doesn't look at all like Oscar, and she certainly exudes none of his natural warmth. I follow them into the immaculate hallway, awkward as we hang our coats. I compliment Lucille on her beautiful home, and then start to worry because that's my small talk quota used up.

She serves us tea in her formal sitting room, and I can't help but feel as if I'm being interviewed for a job I don't stand a chance of getting; as if I'm the Saturday girl going for a managerial role.

'What does your father do, Laurel?'

'He retired recently,' I say, not wishing to go into his health woes. 'He owned a cleaning company; my brother, Daryl, runs it now.' I can't be sure, but I think Lucille just flinched. 'Mum works there too, she keeps the books.'

The expression on Oscar's mother's face is crystal clear; she thinks we're a bunch of Brummie cleaners. I reach for my pendant, following the outline of the purple stone with my fingertip for reassurance. My mum and dad started their company more than twenty-five years ago and employ more than fifty people now, but I don't feel like justifying my family. The more Lucille Ogilvy-Black looks down her nose at me, the less inclined I become to impress her.

She excuses herself from the room momentarily; I wouldn't be surprised if she's gone to hide the good silver in case I slip it in my handbag. The lid of the grand piano in the bay window is covered with photographs, and I can't help but notice (probably because it's been pulled to the front) the large photograph of Oscar and a blonde; they're dressed in ski gear, suntanned and laughing into the camera. I see it for what it is: a gauntlet being silently thrown down by Oscar's mother.

We talked about his family when we were in Thailand, one of our many late-night shack conversations. As a consequence, I probably know a lot more than Lucille would like to think I do.

I know Oscar's father was a bounder; work-shy and handy with his fists towards his wealthy wife every now and then behind closed doors. My heart broke a little when Oscar told me how much he's tried to protect his mum and how close they've been in the years since his parents separated; he was around a lot more than his older brother and as a result he and his mum are incredibly tight-knit. I was, and am, impressed with him for being his mother's rock, and I naively expected her to be warm and, well, motherly. I thought she'd be glad to see Oscar with someone who makes him happy, but if anything she seems hostile to my intrusion. Perhaps she'll warm to me.

10 March

Laurie

'God, I've missed you, Starfish. Come inside and let me do sinful things to you.'

We only get to see each other every few weeks now I'm living back at Mum and Dad's; it's been ages since I was last here. Oscar pulls me over the threshold of his flat, taking my weekend bag from me and slinging it aside so he can haul me into his arms. Yes, we've become one of those loved-up couples who call each other ridiculous names like ickle-pickle and dinky-toes.

We. At last there is a 'we'. And it's amazing. I've never felt this wanted or cared for in my life. Oscar makes no secret of how into me he is. He has this intense way of looking at me that makes me feel the need to glance over my shoulder just to check if Jennifer Lawrence is lurking behind me.

'Let me get my coat off!' I laugh, and he unbuttons it for me and peels it down my arms.

'I was rather hoping you were going to be naked underneath.' He pauses to eye my practical jeans and warm sweater.

'I thought about it. Didn't want to shock the cabbie.'

'This is London, remember?' he grins. 'You're not in the sticks now, Laurie. You could have been naked with

148

four legs and no one would turn a hair.' His eyes glitter. 'Except for me, of course. I'd notice if you were naked.'

'I don't live in the sticks,' I bristle, because he always refers to my home back in Birmingham as if it's some kind of straw-chewing backwater. It's on the very edges of suburbia, a typical greenbelt village. I get it. He's London through and through; the open spaces and lack of black cabs came as a shock to him when I took him home to meet my family over Christmas.

It wasn't the smoothest of 'meet the parents' visits, to be honest. He was perfectly lovely and they were super-polite, but common ground was difficult to find. Dad tried with football, but Oscar's more rugby, and Oscar tried with malt whisky where my dad's more of an ale man. It's early days, but I think we were all relieved when it was over.

'So much green,' he'd muttered, and it hadn't sounded like a compliment.

I shake off the memory; this is our big reunion after six weeks apart, I don't want to feel out of sorts with him for no reason.

'Can I just use the loo?' I ask, and he reaches behind me and pushes a door open.

'*Voilà.*'

'Wait right there. I'll be back in a sec.'

Inside the magazine-perfect bathroom, I throw the lock, strip naked and then belt my coat back on again. The silky lining is slippery against my skin, making me feel suddenly sexy and ready for Oscar to do his worst.

'Come on, Laurie,' he wheedles, and I swing the door wide and look at him, my head on one side. Without a word I walk the length of the hall and step back outside the front door, then after pulling it closed I rap my knuckles lightly against it.

'Who is it?' His voice is low and amused, laced with bad intentions.

'It's me, Laurie,' I say, attempting husky. 'Open the door, I want to show you how much I've missed you.'

He takes his time, leaning on the door frame with his arms crossed even though his eyes tell me he's anything but nonchalant. I let my gaze sweep over him, assessing, taking in his dark jeans and expensive shirt, his bare feet somehow still tanned.

'You're overdressed,' I say. 'Can I come in?'

He doesn't step aside, just reaches out and tugs my belt open. I don't move to stop him when he unbuttons the coat with slow deliberation, his tongue snaking over his top lip, an unconscious tell.

'Promise me you'll always visit me like this?'

I smile. 'We don't make each other promises, remember?'

He tugs me inside by my lapels, then presses me against the back of the door as he slams it and slides his warm, searching hands inside my coat.

'I remember,' he whispers, half laughing, half groaning as he palms my breast. 'Now stop talking and come to bed.'

Jack

'Come on, Sar, we're going to be late at this rate.'

Sarah always does this. She operates on an elastic

timescale, imagining that time will stretch to accommodate however long she feels is necessary to get ready for a night out.

'How do I look?'

When she appears in the lounge doorway I look up from the newspaper her flatmate must have left on the table and give her my full attention. Any man would; she looks incredible.

'New dress?'

I get up and cross the room, running my hands over the soft oxblood leather. It tracks the flow of her body like a second skin, ending mid-thigh. My fingers linger there on her bare leg, slowly rucking her skirt until I skim the silk of her underwear.

A tiny, knowing smile plays over her mouth. 'I'll take that as your approval, shall I?'

I kiss her neck. 'You do that.' When I slide my hand behind her head and press my mouth into the dip between her collarbones, she sighs and takes a step back from me.

'Don't, Jack. We're late enough already.'

I look into her smoky, perfectly made-up eyes. 'I could be really fast.'

'I know you could.' There's an edge to her voice.

'What the hell is that supposed to mean?'

She pauses too, glancing down at her black skyscraper heels and then back at me again. 'Just that – nothing.' She sighs, shaking her head. 'Let's not fight. We're both really busy. Let's just go.'

She can say that again. My life is bloody full-on and Sarah's the same, pulling us three ways at once and usually in the opposite direction. I've had to switch stuff around at work this weekend so we can finally catch up with Laurie and the much-talked-of-but-not-yet-met Oscar Farquhar-Percival-McDougall. Or something like that. And where are we meeting them? At his fucking private members' club, naturally.

'Are you going like that?'

I look down at my clothes as if I don't know what she means. My jeans might look battered but that's purposeful; I paid a lot of money to look this casual. Perhaps it's my T-shirt with 'Star Fucker' emblazoned across the chest that's got up her nose – my attempt at subtle irony. I'm finally gathering a bit of a rep as an up-and-coming radio DJ, and you have to dress the part, though there's a fine line between hipster and wankster.

'Yes, Sarah. I'm going like this.' I reach for the battered vintage leather jacket she gave me last Christmas and shrug it on, just to reinforce the point that I'm not going to change.

She double-checks her immaculate lipstick in the hallway mirror, then picks up her handbag and coat with a shrug. 'Okay.'

I follow her down the stairs and, as I watch her skip down confidently in heels no one should be able to look so comfortable in, I roll my shoulders to shake off my dark mood.

'Hey.' I catch her hand to slow her down as she reaches the pavement. 'Let's not fall out. I've missed you this week.' I trail the back of my hand down the smoothness of her cheek, then hold her delicate jaw. I'd rub my thumb over her full mouth if it wouldn't ruin her lipstick. 'You really do look knockout in this dress. I'm already thinking about peeling you out of it later.'

She softens, as I knew she would. 'Smooth talker.'

'You know it.'

'I do.' She turns her face into my hand and nips my thumb. 'Now flag us a taxi, fool-boy. I'm freezing.'

Laurie

Does it sound crazy to say I'm nervous? It's only Sarah and Jack, for God's sake, my oldest and best friends. I just want them to love Oscar as much as I do, that's all. It's been too long since we saw each other; our pact to meet at New Year fell by the wayside with the advent of Oscar. This is the first date since New Year that we've all been able to make; life is pulling everyone in different directions, it seems. They haven't arrived yet, and he's deep in conversation across the other side of the room with the barman, because he wants to have the perfect first round of drinks ready for them when they come in. He shoots me a smile when he catches me looking his way. His eyes linger on me for longer than is polite, a look that telegraphs that he's remembering our afternoon in bed.

I look away first, my eye drawn to the door by Sarah and Jack's arrival. Joy blooms hot in my chest at the sight of Sarah's familiar red hair, although she's warmed the shade down from fire engine to rich mahogany and it's been styled into lustrous, tumbling waves rather than the Princess Leah plaits of Delancey Street. I touch my own messy bun, self-conscious for a moment, but then her face cracks into a huge grin when she spots me and her gait goes from uncertain to almost skipping across the bar to get to me.

I'm glad, actually, that Oscar isn't beside me right at this moment; it gives me a couple of seconds to just be myself, for it to be me and Sarah, like old times. Her grip is fierce when she hugs me.

'It's so good to see you,' I say, at the same time as she says, 'Bloody hell, Lu. It's been too long.'

We stand back at arm's length and check each other over. I take in her screamingly sexy leather dress and she takes in my standby black dress that she's seen countless times before; I think she may even have worn it herself once or twice. I've jazzed it up with a skinny snakeskin belt and the small gold and diamond starfish pendant Oscar gave me at Christmas, and up to the point of Sarah's entrance I felt pretty glam, in an understated way. She looks like herself after a TV makeover, which, I guess, is effectively what she's had. Her job seems to have transformed her from my beloved potty-mouthed friend into someone who could easily have walked out of a magazine. Until she opens her mouth, and then, thank God, she's still exactly as she always was.

'Fuck,' she says, wiping one fingertip under each eye so her mascara doesn't run. 'I don't get this upset over my own sister. I bloody love you, Laurie James.'

I laugh, squeezing her hand. 'Love you too. I'm so glad you're here.'

Jack steps out from behind her then, and I brace myself for impact. I've no idea if I'll be able to act casual around him. I've put off even thinking about seeing him again, a tactic which has worked right up to this very second where I now find myself wholly unprepared.

He looks right into my eyes, no shifty gazing off over

my shoulder, and for a moment I'm knocked off-centre by that aching, familiar longing. Old habits die hard, it would seem.

'Good to see you, Laurie,' he says. For an awful moment it seems as if he's going to shake my hand, but then he holds it and pulls me close into a hug. The scent of him fills my head, warm spices and lemon, probably something expensive Sarah has given him, underscored with that inimitable essence of him, a smell I can neither describe nor reimagine when he isn't there. But he's here now, and for a second I close my eyes and feel the heat of his body through his inappropriately worded T-shirt as he kisses my forehead. It's a casual embrace, I tell myself. Of no significance to me now I'm with Oscar.

'Happy New Year,' he says into my hair. He sounds self-conscious, and I half laugh as I step away.

'You're three months late, you plonker.'

'Where is he then?' Sarah's excited eyes scan the half-full bar, and Jack stands at her side, one hand resting on her waist. I'm struck by how much they've changed in a relatively short time, or perhaps how they seem to have grown up without me. It's subtle: a gloss on Sarah, a layer of self-assurance on Jack. Oscar has it too, to an extent; he's now firmly entrenched in his role at the bank alongside his brother, and although we speak most days I've become aware of something edging between us. It's an inevitable consequence of living separate lives, I suppose. He's here in London making new friends, eating at cool places, and I am back living with my parents in Birmingham. It's possible that I'm imagining it because I'm anxious about my lack of job. Or maybe I'm just plain old jealous.

Not everyone can make it, can they? Some do, and others settle for less. I think all of this in the split second between greeting Sarah and Jack and catching Oscar's eye as he moves towards us across the bar bearing a tray of impressive-looking cocktails. I wink at him subtly as I step aside so he can deposit them on the table, and Sarah catches my eye and gives me a little thumbs-up behind his back. I don't look at Jack as I catch hold of Oscar's hand when he straightens and steps back. I love that Sarah doesn't stand on ceremony; she lunges straight in and kisses him on the cheek, catching hold of his other hand.

'You must be Sarah,' Oscar says with a laugh, and for a moment they silently size each other up. I wonder if she is what he expected; whether he measures up to her idea of him. No one speaks for a second. I think Sarah, Jack and I are each trying to decide where Oscar fits into our trio. Will he be given equal billing? Or must he be assigned a temporary spot in the corner, holding space while he's assessed for permanent residence?

'And you must be Oscar,' Sarah says, still holding on to his hand. 'Come on then, let me get a good look at you.'

She pretends to scrutinize him, and he obligingly holds his breath and waits for her verdict, solemn-faced, like a schoolboy in front of the headmistress.

'I approve.' She grins, looking from me to him and back again. Belatedly, she turns to Jack and draws him into the circle.

'This is Jack,' she says, presenting them to each other, and now it's my turn to catch my breath. I watch as Oscar is first to hold his hand out and note how Jack allows a deliberate beat to pass before reciprocating.

'Look at you, all big-brother posturing.' Sarah bumps shoulders with Jack to lighten the atmosphere. 'Laurie has her actual brother to do all of that stuff for her so you can stand down, soldier.'

'You're not going to ask me about my intentions towards Laurie, are you?' Oscar deadpans. 'Because they're all very, very bad indeed.'

'Oh, I like you already,' Sarah laughs, delighted, and Oscar rewards her with a champagne cocktail, and the same for me. Jack sniffs the tumbler of iced amber Oscar passes him, practically turning his nose up.

'They call it Penicillin,' Oscar says. 'Whisky. Ginger. Honey.' He grins at Jack. 'Almost a health drink.'

Jack raises his eyebrows. 'I'm more of a beer bloke, to be honest, but I'll give anything a go once.'

Oscar's smile falters a fraction as he raises his glass. We all follow suit.

'What shall we drink to?' he asks.

'Old friends,' Jack says.

'And new ones,' Sarah adds pointedly, her megawatt smile all for Oscar.

We clink glasses and I shoot Jack a micro-look that I hope sends a macro-message. *Don't you fucking dare, Jack O'Mara.*

He appears to receive it, because he turns to Oscar and engages him in a question about Thailand, leaving me and Sarah free to catch up.

'This is fancy,' she whispers, her excited eyes flickering around the private members' bar.

I grin, because I knew she'd get a kick out of it. 'It is a bit, isn't it? Oscar wanted to make a good impression.'

'Any man who orders champagne cocktails and makes my best friend smile gets the thumbs-up from me.'

I flick a glance towards Jack and Oscar as Sarah speaks. They share a similarity in height, but very little else. Jack's sandy hair always looks as if he's been scrubbing his hands through it, whereas Oscar's freshly cut blue-black waves flop perfectly over his eyebrows. He debated for longer than I did over what to wear tonight, wondering whether his striped shirt was too banker, his tweed jacket too headmaster. In the end he settled for a chambray blue linen shirt; it reminds me of our days in Thailand. To be honest, it doesn't really matter what Oscar wears. He comes from wealth; there is an undisguisable whiff of establishment about him that would show through even if he was wearing a hoodie. I find myself wondering again whether I'd even have spoken to him if I'd met him any-where other than on a beach, where all bodies are more or less equal. It certainly came as a culture shock to see him so well-heeled when we met again for the first time in England; it really rammed home the point that we come from two different worlds. I'm hoping Jack will be able to see through the polished exterior. Jack has gone for the 'just tumbled out of bed after shagging a hot model' look that comes off as slightly arrogant. If I didn't want to think better of him, I'd wonder if it was a deliberate move to undermine Oscar. But because I *do* want to think better of him, I let it slide and just absorb the sight of them standing together. So different. Both so important to me. I gulp down a mouthful of cold champagne and refocus on Sarah.

'So am I likely to see you sliding down that fireman's pole anytime soon?'

She laughs. 'I'll have you know they see me as a serious reporter. They only send me to cover the most important stories.' She sips her drink. 'I met Gok Wan last week.'

'No way!'

'Way. *And* he told me he liked my shoes.'

'Were you interviewing him?'

She nods, and then caves and shakes her head, laughing. 'I was behind him in the queue in Pret in Covent Garden. He did really like my shoes, though.'

I grin. 'Lorraine Kelly better watch her back.' I'm only half joking.

'So . . . Oscar.' She leans in and lowers her voice, her eyes lingering on his profile as he bends to catch something Jack said. 'How serious is it?'

'Well, it's early days still,' I say, because although it feels like longer, we've only been together for five months. 'But I like him a whole lot, Sar. I wouldn't have thought he'd be my type, but somehow we just seem to work.'

She nods, watching him with Jack. 'Will they have much in common?' she asks. 'Besides you?'

I'm momentarily blindsided by the thought that she knows about the kiss. She starts to laugh.

'Do I take that as a no?'

I smile, faltering. 'No, of course not. I mean, they're pretty different, but I can't imagine how anyone wouldn't get on with Oscar. He's . . . well, he's pretty easy to like.'

Sarah's smile widens, and she sneaks her arm round my shoulders and squeezes me, her cuff bracelet cool against my skin. 'I'm so happy for you, Lu! You just need your dream job now and then you can move back to the city where you belong.' Her eyes shine. 'You are coming back, right? Because now there's the four of us we can do all that double-dating shit.' She laughs and rolls her eyes, but I know she'd love it.

'I'm not sure. I hope so,' I say. 'But you know . . .' I shrug. 'Rent and all that. It's just so expensive. I need to stay at home until I get a proper job, not waste my time earning money in a crappy job which leaves me no time to get a new one.'

I think again about Oscar's much-repeated suggestion that I move in with him, even if it's just as a practical stop-gap while I find something else. He lives in a flat owned by his mother, rent free of course. But something makes me want to do it myself. Not depend on anyone too much. Mum and Dad always impressed on us the importance of making our own way in life.

'Imagine if we could go back to Delancey Street,' she says wistfully. 'I'm sharing with a woman from work now and she's a right bitch-bag. Fanatical about keeping every-thing separate, even our loo rolls. She's drawn up a rota for when we get to use the lounge. Can you believe that? Says she doesn't like to feel I'm watching her watch the TV.'

It's my turn to slide a supportive arm round Sarah's shoulders. 'What about you and Jack? Will you look for somewhere together soon, do you think?'

Sarah flicks her eyes sideways, the tiniest of eye-rolls, but I don't miss it. 'It's not on the cards yet. He's super-busy at work and he house-shares with Billy and Phil, one of the guys he works with.'

'Snake-hips Billy?' It's been his unofficial nickname since the day he revealed his 'Greased Lightning' dancing skills. Though just the thought of it reminds me sharply of the awful way the day ended.

She nods. 'I'm not sure Jack enjoys it all that much but it's the right side of town for the station and affordable, so he's kind of stuck there for a while.'

She watches Jack lean in to look at something on Oscar's mobile. 'I'm starting to worry about him, Lu. He hasn't seemed himself lately.'

My stomach turns over with dread. 'In what way?'

Sarah folds her arm across her slender, leather-clad midriff and stands closer to me so we can't be overheard. 'I can't put my finger on it. He's . . . distant?' It comes out as a question, as if she's asking herself rather than telling me, and she lifts one shoulder, biting her bottom lip. 'Or maybe it's me. I don't know, Lu, I've asked him if he's happy and he just brushes me off as if I'm going crazy or something.' She half laughs, sounding anything but amused. 'Just busy, I guess.'

I nod, wishing I had something useful to say. I'm massively unsettled by the idea of trouble in their paradise. In the early days of their relationship I selfishly hoped their romance would be short-lived, but over time their love has become an integral part of the map of my life; a bloody massive island I've had to reroute my own path round, yet rely on to locate myself all the same.

'Did you show Sarah these, Laurie?' Oscar says, turning to us with his mobile in his hand. He tilts the screen our way as he steps closer and scrolls through images of our perfect ramshackle beach shack, the endless blue ocean and the pink-and-purple-streaked Thai dawn that I know so well.

'Some of them,' I say quietly, and Oscar's eyes are tender when I look up at him. Can he see that I wish with all of my being that we were back there right now, sitting on the steps of the beach shack, burying our toes in the cool sand? They are my favourite memories, those shoulder-to-shoulder hours, those hushed conversations and languorous kisses. It's unexpected, this stab of longing through the ribs, more so because I'm with Sarah and Jack, who I've never wanted to run from before.

I'm surprised by the heat of my anger towards Jack. I want to yank him out of the bar by the sleeve of his cool leather jacket and tell him: *Be happy, you stupid, stupid man. And let me be too.*

'God, it looks so amazing,' Sarah sighs. 'I'd love to go there.'

Jack drains his cocktail without disguising a mild shudder. 'I'll get the beers in.'

Sarah looks as if she's going to say something, then smiles tightly, catching Jack's hand as she offers to help him. We watch them pick their way across the busy bar and Oscar slips his arm round my waist, his still half-full glass in his other hand.

'Okay?' I ask, hoping he and Jack have hit it off.

He nods. 'Sarah's just how I thought she'd be.'

From this, I deduce that I've given him the impression that Jack is kind and easy-going, and that so far he's coming across as guarded and uptight.

'Did I get it wrong?' Oscar's dark eyes cloud with

consternation as he studies his drink. 'We could have met them somewhere else, you only had to say.'

I'm suddenly furious with Jack for being so unfriendly. What the hell is he trying to prove here, with his offensive T-shirt and lightly veiled disdain at the exclusivity of the bar and Oscar's cocktail choice? That he wins at being cool, even if Oscar is wealthier?

I put my empty glass down and slide my arms round him, relieved when the troubled look in his eyes clears. 'You got it exactly right, Oscar. This is you,' I skim my eyes around the bar, 'and you're lovely, and I want them to know you just as you are. They're going to love you, and you them when you get to know them better.' His hand rubs up and down my arm as I speak. 'Just relax and enjoy the evening.'

I spy Jack and Sarah coming back, two beers in his hand, more champagne cocktails in Sarah's.

'She definitely looks as if she belongs on TV,' Oscar observes. I try to see Sarah through his eyes as she heads our way, all golden tanned legs and Hollywood curls.

'Are you sure you chose the right girl?' I joke. I hate it, but there's always a part of me wondering why – why would this gorgeous man want to be with someone like me?

He shows a mild flash of annoyance, and I wish I'd just kept my mouth shut. 'You're so wrong that I don't know what to say.' He softens and his hand moves to cup the back of my neck. 'You're always the most spectacular woman to me, Laurie. In any room or any bar or on any beach.'

He dips his head and kisses me, gentle but sure. I close

my eyes and for those seconds I feel like the most spec-tacular woman.

'Get a room, kids.' Sarah's laughter spins light and bright, and I open my eyes again and smile.

'Blame me,' Oscar grins. 'I can't keep my hands off her.' He runs his hand from my shoulder down to my hand and catches hold of my fingers.

Behind Sarah, Jack manages to laugh while frowning at the same time, a feat of facial engineering. 'A proper drink to cool you off, mate.'

Oscar accepts the beer, laughing, good-natured despite Jack's inference that Oscar's cocktail hadn't made the cut as a proper drink.

Sarah hands me a glass of champagne, her eyes giddy with delight about me and Oscar.

Jack lounges against the wall, beer in hand. 'So what do you do, Oscar? Besides bum around on Thai beaches picking up girls?' He softens his comment with a wink, but all the same it feels like he's having a dig.

'Living with Billy seems to be rubbing off on you, Jack,' I say, throwing in a none-too-friendly wink of my own. He shoots me a tiny 'not bothered' shrug, then looks away.

'Banking,' Oscar says with a self-deprecating smile. 'I know. Typical posh wanker, right?'

'Whatever floats your boat, mate.'

Okay, now that was rude. Sarah looks at Jack sharply, and quite honestly, I could tip his beer right over his annoying head. Oscar, however, is very used to derision around banking, and it rolls off his back.

'Dull, I know. Not like you, from what I hear? Radio, isn't it?'

Crisis averted. Jack finally finds the grace to pick up the conversational baton that Oscar has passed him, entertaining us with stories about the radio station and telling us about a more high-profile job he's ninety-five per cent certain he's in line for in the summer. He lights up like a flare when he talks about work, more himself, more relaxed, and I'm finally able to relax too. Perhaps the evening might not be a disaster after all.

Jack

Tonight's all about making a point, isn't it? Oscar posh-boy double-barrelled twat face. Let me buy you expensive fucking cocktails in my private members' club, let me drop that I'm a banker casually into conversation, let me stick my tongue down Laurie's throat when I know you're both watching. Well, I'm on to you, posh boy, with your floppy black hair and your deck shoes (because who knows when you might need to step aboard someone's yacht at a moment's notice).

I think all of this with my cock in my hand at the urinal. I've been hiding out in here for the last five minutes, mostly because I know I'm acting like a dick and I don't seem able to reel myself in. Sarah's flashing me daggers; I won't be peeling that dress off her anytime soon. She's more likely to peel my scalp off, and I can't say I blame her. I don't know who's winding me up more tonight, Oscar with his unshakable good nature and refusal to be needled, or Sarah for the way she's practically jumping up and down begging to be his new best friend. I can't help

165

but wonder if she wants to force the same relationship with him that I have with Laurie, and I want to tell her that I'm sorry but you just can't fake that kind of thing. It took me and Lu years. I pause to stare at myself in the mirror over the basins as I wash my hands and think about that for a second. Laurie and I hardly have much of a friendship left these days. I haven't been alone with her since that night back in the kitchen at Delancey Street more than a year ago. Sarah accused me of acting like an over-protective big brother, but she's wrong. I can't claim to feel brotherly towards Laurie, I forfeited that when I – No, I'm not going to think about that now.

I step out of the gents intent on winding my neck in and run smack bang into Laurie. She doesn't waste any time.

'What the hell are you doing, Jack?' I don't think I've ever seen her this angry. Her cheeks are flushed pink and her shoulders are braced.

I glance over my shoulder towards the door I've just come out of. 'Pissing.'

Her violet eyes spark with annoyance. 'Pissing me off, more like.'

'It's good to see you too,' I say, flicking into defensive mode.

'Don't,' she hisses. 'Don't you dare do that, Jack O'Mara.' We're in an upstairs corridor with people milling around us, and she leans in to make herself heard. 'What point are you trying to make out there, exactly? That you're cooler, better, funnier? Is it too much to ask that you just be happy for me?'

I shrug. 'I would be if he wasn't a twat.'

'He isn't a twat. He's good and he's kind and I think he might even love me.'

I hear a sound of derision, and I realize too late that it came from me.

'What?' She shakes her head, her eyes over-bright with fury. 'Is it so improbable that someone might actually love me, Jack?'

'You barely know him.'

She reels as if I've punched her.

'Who made you the expert all of a sudden?' she comes back. 'Who are you to tell me if I can fall in love in a minute or a month or a year?'

We stare each other down, and I realize with a sideways jolt that she isn't the girl from Delancey Street any more. She's a woman with a life that I'm by and large no longer a part of.

'*Do* you love him?'

She looks away, shaking her head because I have no right to ask her. Especially not like this.

'He matters to me, Jack,' she says, softer now, and the vulnerability in her eyes makes me feel like a dick.

'Okay,' I say, and I mean it. I wish I could pull her into my arms and put our friendship back where it should be. But something in me knows that hugging Laurie isn't the right move. Instead I grab her hand and look into her stormy eyes.

'I'm sorry, really sorry, okay?' And I feel as if I'm apologizing to her not just for this evening, but for everything that's gone before. For lying about not seeing her years ago on that damn bus, for kissing her in a snowstorm, for always getting it so fucking wrong.

Finally, after what seems like ten minutes, but is probably about ten seconds, she nods and releases my hand.

I smile. 'Go back downstairs. I'll be right behind you.'

She nods again and walks away without glancing back.

Laurie has grown up when I wasn't looking. It's time for me to do the same.

14 May

Laurie

'Pick up, Oscar, pick up,' I murmur, reading and rereading the letter in my hand as I listen to his mobile ringing out. *This is the voicemail service for* . . . Dammit! I hang up and try again, and once more I get that bloody annoying robot woman telling me that she's terribly sorry but Oscar Ogilvy-Black can't come to the phone right now. I stand in my parents' quiet hallway, my fingers absently wrapped round my purple pendant. I wore it for the job interview last week and haven't taken it off since in an attempt to summon good luck. And it worked! Desperate to tell someone my good news, I scroll through to Sarah's number instead. I don't try to call her because she invariably can't answer at work, so I compromise and send her a text.

> Guess who's FINALLY got herself a proper job? Me! Brace yourself, Sar, I'm coming back to London!

I press send, and it's less than thirty seconds before my mobile vibrates.

> HANG ON! Going to loos to call you. DON'T call anyone else!

Right on cue, my phone starts to ring. It's another thirty seconds before I can speak, because she's shrieking and clapping; I can see her in my mind's eye right now, locked in the cubicle doing her happy dance, bemused colleagues listening outside.

'Come on then, I want to know everything!' she says, and at last I can officially tell someone my news.

'It's that job I told you about, you know, the one on the teen magazine?'

'You mean the Agony Aunt job?'

'Yes! That one! As of three weeks' time, I'm going to be the woman that our nation's teenagers turn to for advice on hair straighteners, spots and dodgy dates!' I'm laughing, borderline hysterical at the prospect of working on a magazine at long last. It won't be *all* of the nation's teenagers of course, just the small percentage who read the not-all-that-prolific magazine, but it's something, isn't it, it's real. It's my much-longed-for stepping stone into the next part of my life. I wasn't at all sure I'd be offered the position. The interview wasn't particularly conventional, two women who couldn't have been more than twenty-one firing make-believe problems at me to see what answers I might give.

'Emma has an awful spot the night before her prom,' one had said, pointing at her own unblemished chin for emphasis. 'What would you suggest?'

Luckily, even at the interview stage, Sarah was my saviour; our Delancey Street bathroom shelf came straight to mind. 'Sudocrem. They sell that stuff for babies' bums, but it's also a secret weapon for spots.'

They'd both written that down really fast; I got the distinct impression they'd be running out to the chemist as soon as the interview was over.

'A run in your tights on an important day?' the other interviewer asked me, her eyes narrowed.

'Clear nail varnish to stop it spreading,' I'd shot straight back. Standard sixth-former tip. By the time they'd finished I felt as if I'd been grilled by the Stasi rather than for a prospective job with a magazine.

'Christ, I hope no one asks you for advice about false eyelashes,' Sarah says. 'You'll get sued.'

'Tell me about it. I'm relying on *you* to be my main research source.'

'Well, you know me, I'm the font of all knowledge on all things false and glittery!' She sounds giddy. 'I can't believe you're finally coming back, Lu, it's the best news I've had all year. Wait till I tell Jack!'

She rings off, and I sit on the bottom step of the stairs and grin like a loon. Is ten in the morning too early to drink gin?

Laurie

Oscar reaches behind the sofa and pulls out a ribboned box. 'I've got something for you.'

He lays the large square gift on my knees and I shoot him a surprised look. 'Oscar, I've only just had my birthday.'

'I know. This is different. It's for the new job.'

It's Saturday night, we're full of Chinese takeaway and halfway down a bottle of champagne, and come Monday, I'll be gainfully employed by Skylark, the publishing house who put out *GlitterGirl* magazine.

'Open it then,' he says, nudging the box. 'You can change it if it's not right.'

I look from his excited eyes to the box, and slowly tug the lime-green ribbons open. He's already made a big fuss of me on my birthday, so this feels like real extravagance. I shake the lid of the smart gift box free and fold back the striped tissue paper to admire the black Kate Spade tote inside.

'Oh, Oscar! It's perfect.' I smile, tracing my finger over the discreet gold logo. I sense Sarah's involvement, seeing as I admired a very similar one on her arm at the restaurant where we celebrated my birthday. 'But you know you shouldn't have. It's too much.'

'Making you happy makes me happy,' he shrugs, as if it's a no-brainer. 'Look in the inside pocket, there's something else.'

I reach into the bag, curious, and unzip the pocket. 'What is it?' I laugh, pushing my fingers in until they touch cool metal. And then I know, and extract the set of keys dangling from a silver Tiffany padlock.

'How will you come and go as you please if you don't have your own set?' he asks, going out of his way to make light of the fact he's giving me the keys to his home. Or to *our* home, as it's going to be for the short-term, at least. It was pretty much the first thing he said after 'Congratulations' when I told him about my new job: 'You'll stay with me for a while, won't you?' I have to admit I'd kind of hoped he'd offer, seeing as I'm starting on not much more than a pauper's wage. We've agreed it's an interim measure while I work something out. But as I look at the shiny set of keys, I see the huge set of expectations that come with it and I falter, wondering if I'm doing the wrong thing. We've only been together for eight months, after all, and I've always been determined to do this my own way.

'I don't want you to think I'm taking advantage of your generosity, Oscar. And you know me – Miss Independent,' I say.

His dark eyes brim with amusement. 'Trust me, I plan on taking advantage of you too.' He takes the keys from my fingers, raising his eyebrows at me. 'Besides, how else will you be able to let yourself in to have dinner ready and waiting for me?'

I punch him on the arm.

'I hope you like baked beans.'

He drops the keys inside my fancy new bag as he sets it down on the floor, then presses me back into the deep leather sofa and kisses me. 'Let's not talk about dull stuff any more. I can think of better things we can do.'

4 August

Jack

I'd rather punch myself in the face than go to a dinner party at Laurie and Oscar's tonight, especially since they've invited his brother as well. Another banker wanker. What are the odds? Sarah's all but tattooed the time I need to be there on my head. *Bring flowers*, she said. *I'll take wine*, she said. I think she's been googling dinner-party etiquette.

She's just sent me a text — Think of some good questions to ask Oscar's brother tonight. I'm tempted to send something pissy back, but I just switched my phone off. I'm at work, I don't have time for this shit.

I'm grateful to have playlists to draw up for the next seven days, and a meeting with the producer tabled for this afternoon to discuss a new quiz we're thinking of introducing. Reaching for a biro, I make a note on my hand of the latest possible time I can leave and still scrape in on time. God knows I don't want to be early.

Laurie

'Are you sure it looks okay?'

I stand back with my hands on my hips and cast a

critical eye over the dining table. Oscar slings his arm over my shoulders.

'Looks fine to me,' he says.

I was hoping for more fulsome praise than that; this is my first ever grown-up three-course dinner party, a far cry from pizza on our knees at Delancey Street. I wish I'd had the chance to just invite Sarah and Jack, a trial run before extending the invite out further. Not that I did, actually; it was only meant to be the four of us, but then Oscar invited his brother, Gerry, and his wife, Fliss, last weekend when we ran into them at Borough Market while buying artisan chocolate for the mousse. *I know*. Could I sound any more like a middle-class twat if I tried? Indulge me, this is my first dinner party and I've watched back-to-back episodes of Nigella snapping artisan chocolate into a pan while batting her eyelashes at the camera for weeks in preparation.

I've only met Oscar's brother once before. All I can recall is that Gerry doesn't seem to be much like his easygoing younger brother, and his poker-thin wife, Felicity, looks as if she exists on fresh air and Chanel No. 5. She reminds me of someone famous, I just can't put my finger on who it is. Anyway, that's how my cosy party of four became a scary party of six, and I've spent the whole day in the kitchen painstakingly following a complicated recipe for coq au vin. It's no ordinary coq, either. This lucky bird was corn-fed and pampered and folded into waxy brown paper by a butcher, and I hope to God this is reflected in the taste because it was triple the cost of its shrink-wrapped supermarket brethren. I've whipped air into the chocolate mousse, tossed the salad, and now I'm gagging for a glass of wine.

'Would it annoy you if I kissed your lipstick off?'

'Yes.'

One of the perks of working on a teen magazine is the plethora of beauty samples that flood the office; teenage girls today clearly spend a hell of a lot more on cosmetics than I did a decade ago. Tonight I'm testing out a trendy new brand of lipstick; the case looked more like a space-age dildo than a lippy and while it doesn't quite give the promised bee-stung look, the product is creamy and rich and makes me feel that tiny bit more confident.

Oscar looks momentarily crestfallen, but the sound of the buzzer cuts the conversation dead.

'Someone's here,' I whisper, staring at him.

'That is the general idea of a dinner party,' he says. 'Shall I get it or do you want to?'

I creep towards the door and peer through the peep-hole, hoping Sarah and Jack are first. I'm out of luck.

'It's your brother,' I mouth, tiptoeing back to Oscar.

'I take it that means I'm answering it?' he asks.

'I'll go in the kitchen and you call me when they're inside as if I didn't know,' I say, heading for the kitchen.

'Can I ask why?' he asks mildly.

I pause in the doorway. 'So I don't look over-eager?' What I'm really thinking is that I want to neck a glass of wine for Dutch courage; my socially awkward streak is suddenly alive and kicking again.

I reach for my mobile as I pull the wine from the fridge and fire off a quick text to Sarah.

Hurry! G&F already here. Back-up required!

I check the coq au vin, and I'm pleased to report it

looks quite a lot like the picture in the recipe book. Hey there, Jamie Oliver, my coq's better than your coq. I'm laughing to myself as my phone vibrates, and I grab it quickly as I hear Oscar calling my name.

On my way, 5 mins max. Jack's running late, be there when he can. Sorry. Don't drink all the wine without me!

Five minutes. I can do that. Bloody Jack, Sarah was practically in tears right here in our kitchen last week after he'd missed another of their dates because he had to work late. And it's going to get worse when he starts the new presenting job in a couple of weeks. Pretty soon the only way we'll be able to keep up with Jack is to tune into his radio show. I shake off my annoyance and plunge the opened wine bottle into the ice bucket as I plaster a smile on my nearly bee-stung lips and head through to the lounge.

'I don't think I can hold off much longer without it drying up,' I say. Sarah and I gaze down at the already slightly less impressive coq, then she looks at the clock and shakes her head.

'I'm really sorry, Lu, he's acting like a complete twat lately. He knows how important this is for you.'

Jack is more than an hour and a half late, and aside from a text to say he'd be here soon, just after Sarah arrived, it's been radio silence.

'Shall I text him too? He might be too scared to open your messages,' I say, filling up her glass.

She shakes her head. 'Don't bother. Come on, let's take this through and eat. It's his loss.'

It might be better all round if Jack decides to swerve

coming tonight; he's already late enough to look horribly rude, and there's every chance Sarah will knock his head off his shoulders.

It's after ten, the coq was a triumph and Gerry isn't so bad after a couple of drinks. Fliss is hideous – teetotal and a fucking vegetarian (not that I would have minded, but she never bloody said until I put a great big chicken limb in front of her! And it's come to me who she reminds me of – Wallis Simpson, proper waspish). And Jack still isn't here. Not only that, he hasn't even called. Sarah's so pissed off that she's started to refer to him only as shitface while swigging more than her normal helping of wine, and poor Oscar is doing his best to defend him, even though Jack's done nothing to earn such loyalty.

'Chocolate mousse, anyone?' I say loudly, to change the subject.

'God, yes,' Gerry groans as if I've offered him a blow job, at the same time as Fliss makes a hissing sound similar to the cry of the Wicked Witch of the West when Dorothy doused her in water. I look from one to the other, unsure what to do, when Sarah's mobile starts to trill and we all stare at it expectantly. Over the course of the dinner Sarah's gone from having it tucked under her bum for a sneaky check every now and then to having it in full view on Jack's empty dinner plate. I think she might be making a point.

'There we go,' Oscar breathes, relieved. 'Tell him it's fine, Sarah, there's food left if he hasn't eaten.'

Her mobile rattles and bounces on Jack's white china plate.

'Personally, I wouldn't dream of answering that.' Fliss looks down her nose, full of haughty disdain. 'Bloody cheek.'

Sarah looks at me, wavering and uncertain. 'What shall I do?'

'Get it,' I say, mostly to piss Fliss off, and after a second Sarah grabs it and stabs at the button.

'Balls. Missed it,' she says, disappointment in her eyes even as she adds, 'Serves him right, shitty shitface,' and lays the phone back on Jack's plate. 'Let's have dessert.'

As I push my chair back, Sarah's phone rattles again to alert her to the fact that Jack has left her a message.

'Odds-on he's in a pub somewhere,' Fliss says, even though she has no right to an opinion having never even met Jack.

'He'll be stuck at work.' Gerry bats for Team Jack, God knows why – perhaps he dislikes his wife as much as I do.

Sarah picks up her phone. 'Let's see, shall we.'

A hush falls around the table and we can all hear the tinny voice informing Sarah that she has one new message in her inbox. She huffs and clicks again, and I cross my fingers under the table that Gerry's on the money.

'Hello, this is a message for Sarah,' someone says, fast and loud, traces of an Australian accent. Sarah raises her eyes to mine, frowning at the unknown male voice. 'I'm calling because this phone has fallen out of the pocket of a guy who's just been involved in a serious road accident on Vauxhall Bridge Road. Your number comes up as the one he dials most often – we're just waiting with him for the ambulance crew now. I thought you'd want to know as soon as possible. My name's Luke, by the way. Let me know what to do with his phone when you can.'

Sarah's already crying hot, panicked tears before the end of the message, and I drop to my knees beside her chair and take the phone from her shaking hands before she drops it.

'What do I do, Laurie?' She's breathing too fast, clutching my hand. All of the colour has drained from her face; she can't keep a limb still.

'We go to him,' I say, trying to keep my voice steady. 'I'm calling a cab now, we'll be there in a few minutes.'

'What if he's . . .' She's shaking so violently that her teeth chatter.

'Don't,' I cut across her, my eyes nailed to hers because I need her to listen to me. 'Don't say it. Don't even think it. It's going to be okay. Let's just get there first, you and me together, one step at a time.'

She nods, still dithering, trying to get a hold of herself. 'You and me. One step at a time.'

I hug her, fast and fierce, and Oscar's bleak eyes meet mine over her shoulder. I look away.

5 August

Laurie

He's alive. Thank God, thank God, thank God.

We're huddled on nailed-down metal chairs drinking something lukewarm Oscar got from the vending machine. I can't tell if it's tea or coffee. The doctor came to see us a couple of hours back; we can't see Jack yet. He's in theatre, she said, in a quiet, reassuring voice that actually frightened the hell out of me. Head injury. Broken ribs. Fractured left shoulder. I can handle broken bones, because I know bones can mend. It's the head injury that terrifies me; they're going to get him scanned, or whatever it is they do, then they should know more. I couldn't digest everything she said because my red-alert panic button was screaming inside my brain. Head injury. People die from head injuries. Don't die, Jack. Don't you dare die on us. On me.

We sit on either side of his bed, Sarah and I. We tried to get hold of his mum in the confusing minutes after we located him at St Pancras Hospital, but then Sarah remembered that she's in Spain with Albie, Jack's brother. I left the message rather than Sarah, so we didn't frighten the life out of her.

And so we watch over him together, and we wait,

182

because we've been told that's all we can do for now. He's out of theatre, out of immediate danger, but they won't know the extent of his head injury until he's conscious. He's shirtless and pale and absolutely still aside from the rise and fall of his chest. A mess of bandages and tubes cover him, hooked up to all kinds of machines and drips. I've never been this frightened. He looks too fragile, and I find myself worrying about what happens in here if there's a power cut. They have back-up, right? Because I don't think Jack's keeping himself alive right now, he's beholden to the national grid. How ridiculous. Across London people are boiling their kettles and nonchalantly charging their phones, using up precious energy when it should all be saved up and sent here to keep Jack alive. Please stay alive, my lovely Jack. Don't leave us. Don't leave me.

Intensive Care is a strange place of quiet industry laced with panic; the constant soft footfall of the nurses, the clatter of patient notes against the metal bed-ends, a background symphony of bleeps and alarms.

I watch Sarah re-secure the plastic fingertip peg monitoring his oxygen levels as a nurse writes Jack's name on a whiteboard over his bedside cabinet, bright blue capitals. I close my eyes and, though I've never been remotely religious, I pray.

10 August

Laurie

'Don't try to move, I'll call the nurse.'

I look over my shoulder for help as Jack struggles to pull himself up in bed, even though he's been told in no uncertain terms by the ward sister to press his buzzer if he needs help.

'For fuck's sake, Lu, stop fussing. I can do it.'

He wouldn't pull this kind of stunt if Sarah was here; she'd kick his sorry ass. He's only trying his luck today because it's Friday and I got off work early to come and visit on my own. He regained consciousness a couple of days ago and the doctors were, thank God, able to confirm no lasting brain injury, although they're still running tests because he's struggling with his hearing on one side. Since then it's become apparent that he's the patient from hell. His streak of independence is generally one of his better qualities, but his refusal to ask for help is borderline dangerous in his condition. He's catheterized, and he has a cannula in his hand administering pain relief; every time he acts up and tries to do stuff for himself he sets off a furious series of alarms and high-pitched wails that bring nurses running.

I sit down as the staff nurse stalks down the ward and hoicks him into position against his pillows.

'Your pretty face is starting to get on my nerves, O'Mara,' she says, in that no-nonsense way experienced medical staff have.

He grins, apologetic. 'Thank you, Eva. Sorry. Can I offer you a grape?' He nods towards the fruit basket on the side, a gift from his colleagues.

'Can you imagine how many grapes I get offered in here?' She looks at him over her glasses. 'If you want to do something for me, just press the buzzer next time you need help.'

She doesn't hang around, leaving us alone again. I'm sitting in one of those fake leather, wipe-clean armchairs next to Jack's bed in the corner of a ward of six beds, mostly older men. It's afternoon visiting time, although you wouldn't know it from the fact that most of them are snoozing in their pyjamas on top of their rumpled white sheets, no relatives to be seen. The window behind me is pushed up as far as it'll go, and fans whir on some of the bedside cabinets, yet still there's hardly a breath of air.

'Hot out there today,' I say. I've taken care to sit on the side that he can still hear properly from.

He sighs. 'Is that what our friendship has come to? We're reduced to talking about the weather?'

'What else do you want to talk about?'

He shrugs his unbroken shoulder, then winces. 'You're the agony aunt. Tell me what the youth of today are worrying about.'

I unsnap a hairband from round my wrist and pull my hair back into a ponytail. 'Okay. Well, it's mostly girls who write in, so I get a lot of period-related questions.'

He rolls his eyes. 'What else?'

'Spots. They have a lot of spot issues. Someone asked me last week if dog saliva was good for acne.'

He brightens at the absurdity. 'What did you tell them?'

'Cat saliva is better.'

'You didn't.'

'Of course I bloody didn't.'

'Should've.'

I pour him a glass of iced water from the jug an orderly has just deposited on his side table and stick a fresh straw in.

'Here, have a drink.' It's difficult for him to lift the cup with one shoulder broken and his other hand tethered by the cannula, so I hold it in place while he sucks from the straw.

'Thank you,' he says, laying his head back on the pillow, closing his eyes with a huff of self-annoyance at the effort and the fact he has to ask for help with something as basic as a drink of water. 'Tell me some more.'

I cast around for something that might catch his imagination. 'Oh, I know. A boy wrote in a couple of weeks ago because the girl he's mad about is moving to Ireland. He's fifteen and she's from a strict Catholic family who don't approve. He wanted advice on how old he had to be before he could legally move there alone.'

'Love's young dream,' Jack says, his eyes still closed. 'What did you tell him?'

I look at his too-pale face, the pronounced hollows of his cheeks. He's never carried any spare weight, and the toll of nearly a week of barely any solid food is apparent.

'I said that I know how painful it can be letting someone you think you love go, but that I don't believe there's

186

only one person in the world for each of us. It's too fanciful, too limiting. I said he should give it some time and see how he feels, and he'll probably find that he stops thinking about her so much, because that's just how it goes, especially when you're fifteen. I told him that there comes a point where you have to make the choice to be happy, because being sad for too long is exhausting. And that one day, you'll look back, and you'll not be able to remember exactly what it was you loved about that person.'

Jack nods, his eyes closed.

'But I also said that sometimes, rarely, people can come back into your life. And if that happens, you should keep those people close to you for ever.'

I lapse into silence. He's sleeping. I hope his dreams are good ones.

15 September

Jack

Fuckers. I chuck my mobile on top of the mess of dirty mugs and food detritus on the coffee table and sink back into the lumpy sofa. The weather can piss right off too, the bloody sun's right in my eyes. I'd get up and close the curtains if I could be arsed. I can't though, so I just shut my eyes. I may as well go back to sleep, seeing as I'm now officially unemployed. That's what happens when you get too cocksure and hand in your notice at your old job before starting your new one, then get blindsided by a bloke who has a stroke at the wheel of his Volvo. At least I'm alive, everyone keeps telling me, look on the bright side, or some other equally trite shit. Where is the bright side of not being able to take up the job you've been working towards for your entire bloody career? I went through endless meetings and interviews, had the handshake, all but signed on the dotted line, appointment to be announced in the press within days. My dream contract was in the post for me to sign, and then bang, I'm busted up in a hospital bed and Jonny Fucking Nobody can't wait to jump into my shoes instead. I've fallen between the gaps, and now *I'm* the nobody, and the way it's going I won't even be able to pay my rent in a couple of months' time. The doctors can't even tell me if I'll get my hearing back in my right ear. I don't think they'll be queuing round the block to employ a DJ who can't fucking hear. What happens then? I move in with Sarah and that cow-bag of a woman she works with? That's not even an option. Cow-bag would be right on to the landlord about illegal subletting; she already begrudges the fact she has to share with one person, and she seems to especially detest me. I'm sure there's nothing she'd like better than to see me in a cardboard box by the Thames. I don't think she'd even toss me the money for a cup of tea.

Oh, deep joy, I can hear keys rattling in the front door. I wish to God I'd had the forethought to stay in bed and put the bolt on. Billy's away at a family wedding some-where up north, and Phil, a sound technician from my now *ex*-workplace, is in Goa, which means there's only one person it can be. Sarah. Sarah, with her ever-present smile and undiluted zeal for life, when all I want to do is plough my way through an out-of-date ready meal and watch the Saturday afternoon football. And I don't even like football.

'Jack? I'm back. Where are you?'

'In here,' I say, as grouchily as possible. She appears in the doorway, all legs in a pink summer dress, and some-where in the back of my head I feel ashamed at being slouched on the sofa in three-day-old joggers with curry stains. She's been down in Exeter or somewhere on an assignment for a couple of days; if I'm honest, I didn't think she was home until tomorrow. Bloody painkillers have fried my brain. I'd have changed my trousers, at least.

'You look as if you've been on an all-night drugs binge,'

she says, trying for funny. 'That or you're reliving your student days. Which is it?'

Great, remind me of what I'm missing, Sarah. 'Neither. It's just me, the remote control and a chicken vindaloo,' I say, not looking at her.

'Sounds like the title of an arty film,' she laughs lightly, gathering up the dirty coffee mugs.

'Leave that stuff, I'll do it.'

'It's no trouble.'

'All the same.'

She looks at me, that sunshine smile fading fast. 'Let me take care of you every now and then? Please?'

Resigned, I close my eyes and lay my head back against the sofa as she clears up my mess, feeling like a resentful teenager whose mum just rocked up in his bedroom when he'd been about to knock one out. Jesus, I'm a dick. I can smell Sarah's perfume, distinct and exotic, and it reminds me of nights out on the town, and even later nights in bed together. We haven't had sex since the accident. In truth, we weren't having all that much of it before it happened, either. I open my eyes as I hear her clatter the plates and cups into the kitchen sink. Her perfume lingers, layering over the smell of last night's curry and my stale sweat. It's not a good combination.

'I thought we could head out in a while,' she calls through, flicking the kitchen radio on. 'It's gorgeous out there today.'

I sigh, though not loud enough for her to hear. I feel rancid, and too worn out to bother doing anything about it. I don't think I have any clean boxers left. My shoulder still hurts and my ribs still ache, probably because I've been neglecting the exercises given to me at the weekly physio appointments I sometimes attend. God knows why. My bones broke. They'll mend. There isn't any physio for my ear; the only thing I really care about them mending is the one thing that's damaged for good. Oh, there's talk of hearing aids and such stuff, but to be honest what's the bloody point? The real problem is that my career broke, and there's nothing the doctors can do to mend it.

'What do you think?' Sarah appears in the doorway again wearing the mint-green Marigolds she bought a few weeks back.

'That you look like a fifties housewife?'

She rolls her eyes. 'About going out, Jack. Just for a walk to the park or something, get some lunch at that new cafe on the Broadway, maybe. Someone said it's very Californian.'

What the fuck is that supposed to mean? Wheat juice and kale? 'Maybe.'

'Shall I put the shower on for you?'

Irritation streaks through me. 'What are you, my fucking mother?'

She doesn't answer me, but I see the hurt settle in her eyes and feel like a cock again. I'm just sick of everyone fussing over me. If it's not Sarah, it's my mum turning up twice a week with food I don't feel like eating.

'Sorry,' I mumble. 'Off day.'

She nods slowly. If I could see inside her head, I expect she'd be having a good old rant, calling me all kinds of well-deserved names. I can clearly hear her shouting 'selfish bastard' even though she hasn't said a thing.

'Just go and take a shower,' she says eventually, turning

back towards the kitchen. I get up to do as she's asked, and as I pass by the kitchen I consider wrapping my arms round her where she stands at the sink, kissing her neck, saying sorry properly. Then I hear the perky radio jingle, someone I used to consider a rival, and the acrid burn of jealousy wipes out any passing desire to be civil. *Fuckers*.

24 October

Laurie

'I don't know what to do, Laurie.' Sarah swills her wine around in her glass, looking thoroughly miserable. She texted earlier to see if there was any chance of meeting up for a drink after work; although I still had a bunch of emails to get through, I could tell from the tone of the message that she needed to get something off her chest, so I dropped them and went to meet her. I wasn't wrong. I knew that life with Jack hadn't been a bed of roses since his accident but from what she's told me over the last hour or so it sounds as if lately he's making things almost intolerable.

'And now he's decided that he's not going to take any more painkillers,' she says. 'Flushed them all down the loo last night. He said they were making him numb, but I think he'd rather be in pain so he can moan about it.'

If she sounds uncharitable, don't judge her harshly. She's been trying her best to put a cheerful face on ever since the accident, and I know for a fact there's been precious little coming back from Jack in the way of gratitude. It's been almost three months now, and every time I've seen Jack since he got out of hospital he's been borderline rude, particularly to Oscar. It's got to the point where I'm almost avoiding him.

'I take it he's not had any joy on the job front?' I know

the answer to the question before I ask it. Although he's well enough now physically, emotionally he's far from out of the woods. Of all of the injuries he could have sustained, partial hearing loss seems particularly cruel given his career.

She shakes her head. 'I don't know if he's even been looking and I'm damn sure he hasn't been in contact with any stations.' She eats a cashew from the bag open on the table between us. 'I'm worried, Lu. He just seems so bloody angry all the time. And he doesn't want to do anything; it's a massive palaver to get him to even leave the house.' She sighs. 'I'm worried he's becoming a recluse or something.'

I try to choose my words carefully. 'He's been through a big trauma. I guess it's his coping mechanism?'

'But that's just it. He *isn't* coping. He's sitting and staring at the wall and growing a fucking beard that doesn't suit him.'

I top our glasses up from the half-empty bottle of white in the cooler beside our table. 'You could try talking to his doctor?'

'Jack says I'm smothering him.' She frowns into her glass. 'He'll be lucky if I don't, the way he's going. He never calls or texts me any more. I've had more texts from Luke than Jack since the accident. That's how bad it's gotten.'

Sarah has stayed in loose contact with Luke, the good-natured Aussie who found Jack's phone on the night of the accident.

'Is it bad that I can't wait to go away next week?'

I shake my head. 'Not bad at all. You must be desperate for a break.' Her sister's hen party in the Canaries couldn't have been more timely. 'It might do Jack good to stew on things without you there to jolly him up. He'll have to fend for himself a bit more.'

She sighs, shrugging. 'You're so lucky with Oscar. I don't think I've ever seen him in a bad mood.'

I have to think really hard to remember the last time we clashed. 'Yeah. He's a pretty steady guy.'

'I don't suppose you'd call in on Jack while I'm away, would you?' She looks at me as if I'm her last hope. 'He might open up to you. God knows he won't talk to me.'

What am I supposed to say? No isn't an option. 'Do you think he'd talk to Oscar? Maybe he'd be better with a man?' Even before I say it I know it's a ridiculous idea.

She shakes her head, downcast. 'Please don't be offended, Lu, and don't repeat this to Oscar, but I don't know if he and Jack are on the same wavelength. I mean, he likes him, but I think he struggles to know what to say around him sometimes.'

I don't really know how to respond to that, so I just nod and knock back a mouthful of wine. Because I'm left with no other choice, I reach down into my Kate Spade bag and pull my diary out.

'Okay.' I flip it open and run my finger down next week's page until I get to Saturday. 'Looks like Oscar's going shooting in the morning.'

I laugh when Sarah raises her eyebrows. 'Don't ask. One of those gift experience things someone gave his brother, I think. I could call round to see Jack while he's off doing that?'

Sarah's shoulders sag with relief. 'I don't know how to get through to him; I'm at the point now where everything I say pisses him off. He might not think he can get away with being so rude to you.'

My mobile goes off on the table between us, and I feel almost guilty as a loved-up image of me and Oscar in Thailand flashes up.

'It's just Oscar checking about dinner,' I say, scanning his text quickly. I'm terrified of ignoring messages in case there's anything wrong; not surprising really given what happened to Jack.

'Very domesticated,' Sarah says. I can't deny it. I've made no headway at all with looking for somewhere else to live, partly because of what happened to Jack, but if I'm honest mostly because I'm enjoying playing house without the onerous responsibility of a mortgage or bills. It's a ridiculous way to live, I know, but for Oscar it's just how life has always been, and I have to admit it's amazing to feel so safe. Every now and then I wonder if it's *too* safe, too steady, but sitting here listening to Sarah, I know I should thank my lucky stars.

'Right then.' Sarah nods towards my phone, where a picture of the Bolognese Oscar's just made is flashing up. 'Looks like you need to make tracks.'

I pause to hug her tightly as I get up to leave. 'He'll come good again, Sar, I know he will. He's been through a lot. Just give him time.'

'It's all I seem to do,' she says, shrugging into her jacket. The weather has been getting colder for the last few days. Winter coats suddenly fill the streets of London.

'Enjoy a bit of sunshine.' I'm hit by an intense longing to go with her, to dance, to laugh, to be carefree and silly the way we used to in Delancey Street.

'I'll have a cocktail for you,' she grins.

3 November

Jack

'Visitor for you in the living room, Jack m'lad,' Billy shouts through from the hallway. I'm in the bathroom, half-heartedly brushing my teeth. I know it can't be Sarah, because she's off sunning herself in Tenerife. And I know it's no one from work, because, oh yeah, I don't have a job. And I hope to God it's not my bloody mother again, because if it is and Billy has let her in on his way out to the footie with Phil then I'm going to fucking kill him. I should have accepted their invitation to go with them. Oh, wait. They didn't ask me. I don't blame them, to be honest. They've pretty much stopped asking me to do anything any more because they already know the answer will be no. Maybe it's Mila Kunis. She's in luck, I've had a shower.

'Laurie,' I say, surprised enough to come to a halt in the doorway of the living room. She's perched on the arm of the chair, still buttoned into her red woollen coat, her bobble hat in her hand.

'Jack.' Her smile is hesitant and doesn't quite make it as far as her eyes.

I look over my shoulder towards the kitchen suddenly, struck by the possibility that she hasn't come alone. 'Where's posh boy?'

197

'His name is Oscar,' she says, testy.

I shrug. I don't really want to pass the time of day talking about that tosser, so I change the subject. 'Coffee?'

She shakes her head.

'Wine? A beer?'

Another refusal as she takes off her coat and I go to the kitchen and grab myself a beer.

'It's good to see you,' she says as I head back through and drop down on the sofa. 'How's things?'

'Peachy.' I raise my bottle. 'Down the hatch.'

She sits quietly as I swallow half the beer.

'You sure you don't want one?'

'It's half past ten in the morning, Jack.'

I'm hoping the beer will be hair of the dog for my hangover. I'm starting to regret ditching all the painkillers in one go and using vodka instead to medicate. I know this can't go on; I'm still half-cut from last night.

'Did you come round here just to tell me what time it is? Because I have a watch to do that for me.' I look at my bare wrist and belatedly realize it's been a while since I last saw my watch. Probably somewhere amongst the piles of stuff in my room; Billy and Phil insist on being neat freaks out here, so my room is the dumping ground for all things Jack. Laurie looks thrown by my question. God knows why. She started it with her pious observations about my drinking.

'No, I came because I'm worried about you,' she says, sliding from the arm of the sofa on to the seat, her knees angled towards me.

'Well, as you can see, there's no need to be.' I gesture grandly down at my fortuitously clean T-shirt. 'Contrary to what Sarah has no doubt told you, I'm not wallowing in a stinking cesspit of my own self-pity. I've showered and I've eaten breakfast, so you can stand down from your suicide watch or whatever this is supposed to be.'

'A clean T-shirt isn't enough to convince me that you're fine,' she says. 'I'm always here if you need someone to talk to, okay?'

I laugh. 'Go and volunteer at the Samaritans if you want to listen to someone's problems.'

'Just stop, will you?' she says, staring at me. 'That's enough.'

'That's enough?' I hope the razor-sharp derision is enough to cut. 'Enough?'

Her chin comes up, her round, wary eyes watching me. 'Yes, Jack. Enough. I haven't come here to fight with you. There's no reason for you to be so damn rude.'

I glance at her. 'How's work?'

She looks for a second as if she's having trouble keeping up with my swift change of direction. 'Umm, yeah,' she says. 'It's fine. I like it.'

'Good for you,' I nod, pointing at her with my beer bottle. 'Although I always imagined you'd find something a bit more, you know, grown-up.' I'm not proud of myself right now. I know how much landing that job meant to Laurie, and that she'll be damn good at it. I can't think of another person more full-hearted and kind to answer teenage problems without belittling their worries. I see how my offensive remark hurts her. It would be better for both of us if she just left.

'Is that so?'

I nod. 'Everybody has to start somewhere though.'

'Yes, I suppose they do,' she says. 'How's the job hunt going?'

Oh, clever. Just when I was already feeling like a tosser, she throws that one in. 'Oh, you know how it is. They're queuing round the block but I'm keeping my options open.'

'You should probably buy yourself a new razor if you get called in for any interviews.'

I run my hand defensively over my stubble. Okay, so maybe it's gone past stubble into minor beard territory. I think I can carry it off. 'Did you come here for a row? Because you'll get one.'

'No, of course not,' she says, exasperated. 'Look, Jack. Everybody is worried about you. Sarah. Your mum . . . I know the accident must have been incredibly tough, and that losing out on your job was really crappy, but you can't just sit here and rot. That's not who you are.'

I watch her as she speaks; the way her mouth moves, the even line of her teeth. The beer must be going to my head. 'You've barely changed at all over the years,' I surprise myself by saying, and her expression slides from concerned to wrong-footed. 'You still remind me of a street urchin or a Parisian waif.'

She looks startled, as if she's going to say one thing and then rejects it in favour of something else. 'Sarah said you've thrown your painkillers away.'

'They were numbing me.'

'That's what they're supposed to do, Jack. Numb the pain.'

I huff, because it wasn't just my pain they were numbing. It was my brain, too. I've been walking like a man in lead boots, too tired to raise my bones from my bed, too fuddled to think any further ahead than my next meal and how long it is until I can go back to bed again. A small part of me acknowledges that the booze is doing pretty much the same thing.

'I miss you.' The words don't register as my own, so much so that I almost look behind me to see if there is someone else here.

Her demeanour changes, and she drops to her knees in front of me, her hands over mine. 'Look at me. Jack, listen. Please let us help you. Let *me* help you. Let me be your friend again.'

She's looking at me sincerely with those big violet eyes of hers, as her fingers squeeze mine.

'It's always been like this with us, hasn't it?' I don't have any control over the words spilling from my mouth. 'When you look at me, I know that you really see me. I don't think anyone ever has, Lu. Not the way you do.'

She swallows and looks down, frowning and confused by the direction our conversation has taken. I am too.

'How can I help?' she says, meeting my eyes again, staying doggedly on message. 'Shall we make a list of all of the stuff on your mind and work through it?'

The only thing on my mind right now is Laurie. 'You always smell like summer flowers. It's my favourite smell in the fucking world.' What am I doing?

'Jack . . .'

I can't not do this. This is the first time I've felt like a man in as long as I can remember, and it feels so damn good, like waking up from a coma. Her hand is warm and fragile in mine, and I do the only thing I can do, or perhaps the one thing I can't not do. I lower my mouth over hers and kiss her, my mouth trembling, or perhaps it's hers. I catch her off guard, and for just a second it's perfect, my hand on her face, her lips warm under mine. And then it isn't perfect any more, because she wrenches back and away from me, stumbling to her feet.

'Jesus, Jack, what are you doing?' She's breathing fast, one hand on her hip, bending a little as if she's just stopped running.

'Isn't this what you came for?' I say, spiteful in my shame, wiping the back of my hand across my mouth as if she tastes rancid. 'While the cat's away and all that?'

She gasps and presses her hands to her flushed cheeks, horrified by my implication. 'We've been friends for a long time, Jack O'Mara, but if you ever say anything like that to me again, we're done. Is that clear?'

'Oh, so high and mighty, Laurie,' I mock, getting to my feet and pacing because the room suddenly feels claustrophobic. I've been cooped up in here for months, and now all I want is to open the door and get out. I'd walk to the edges of our island, and then I'd walk into the sea, and not stop until it's over. 'It hasn't always been like that though, has it? Everything was different when it was you who needed comforting, wasn't it? When you were sad, bonetired and wallowing in your own misery?'

She's shaking her head slowly and her eyes have filled with tears. 'Please don't say any more, Jack. It's not the same and you know it.'

'Yeah,' I spit. 'It was different because it was you who needed me back then, and I wasn't so fucking high and mighty as to turn you down.' I jab my finger towards her in the space between us. 'I took pity on you, and now the tables have turned and you can't lower yourself to return the fucking favour.' It's not true. Not a word of it. I don't recognize the vicious loser I've become. I take a step towards her, to do I don't know what, and she backs away from me, horrified. I see the person I've become in her eyes and it makes me sick. But then, as she moves, that bloody starfish pendant catches my eye and I reach out to grab it. I don't know why, it's irrational, I just want to do *something* to make her stop, but she jerks away from me and it snaps from round her neck. I stare at it for a moment, then throw it to the floor, and we stand stock-still and glare at each other. Her chest is heaving and I can hear my blood rushing in my veins like water crashing against rocks.

Slowly, warily, she stoops down and retrieves her neck-lace, never taking her eyes off me, as if I am an animal about to attack.

'Run on home, Starfish, and don't come back,' I say, choking on the pathetic endearment I've heard Oscar use when he thinks no one's listening. She sobs, full-on sobs, then she turns and runs, out of the door, out of the flat, out of my life. I watch her go from my window, and then I lie down on the floor and stay there.

Laurie

Jack scared me this morning. No, he horrified me. I don't know what I'm going to tell Sarah when she asks how my visit went. I'd no idea the state he was in, he's dangerously low. God knows he's not a man given to violence or vicious words under normal circumstances; it scared me to see him like that.

I tie my hair up in the bathroom and twist to look at the back of my neck. As I thought, there's a mark, a small red graze where the catch on my necklace dug into my skin before it snapped. I place a cold flannel on it and then I sink down and sit on the edge of the bath. I don't care about my neck; I know Jack well enough to know he would never hurt me intentionally; the chain was delicate enough to snap easily. But it was what it meant. And his words. *Don't come back.*

12 November

Jack

'I need to order some, er, flowers,' I say. I've been loitering in the florist's for the last few minutes, waiting for everyone else to leave. It's fully Christmassed up in here already, decked out with ribbons and holly wreaths, and one whole wall of shelves is covered with those huge red plants that everyone sticks on the fireplace and battles to keep alive until New Year.

The forty-something florist is bundled into a puffa jacket, her fingers red and chapped. It's cold enough in here to see my breath.

'Any idea what kind you want?' she asks, still scribbling on the previous customer's order slip.

'The kind that say I'm sorry I've been an idiot?'

Her pencil stops moving, and the look she gives me tells me she's been here before. 'Red roses?'

I shake my head. 'No, no. Nothing, you know, romantic.'

She narrows her eyes. 'Chrysanths go down well with more mature ladies . . . mums, for instance?'

Jesus, what is she, a florist or a therapist? 'They're not for my mum. I just want something that says I'm genuinely sorry. To a friend.'

She disappears into the back and comes back carrying a glass bowl brimming with fat peonies, creamy-white and lavender blue. 'Something like this?'

I study them. They're almost the exact same colour as Laurie's eyes.

'Just the white ones,' I say. I don't want the flowers to carry a jot of unintended meaning. 'Do you have a card I can write to send with them?'

She hands me a shoebox that's been divided by hand-written labels. One of the biggest sections, tellingly, is 'I'm sorry'; clearly I'm not the first and won't be the last guy in here who's been a shmuck. I flick through the designs for the simplest, make a snap decision and pull out two.

'I need to order two of those please,' I say, nodding towards the peonies she's placed down on the floor behind the counter.

'Two?' She raises her eyebrows.

I nod, and this time her look suggests that she's distinctly unimpressed. 'You don't want me to vary them even slightly?'

'No, exactly like that, please.' She can think what she wants to think, I don't care. If I order the same then I can't get it wrong when Sarah mentions them.

She shrugs and attempts to look neutral. 'I just deliver the flowers,' she says. 'Your business is your business.' She hands me a biro and walks away to help another customer who's just come in with a 'Santa Stop Here' sign and a bunch of mistletoe from outside.

I look down at the tiny card and wonder how on earth I'm supposed to say enough in such a small space. I've acted like a headcase for weeks. Laurie's visit was the final straw; I lay on the floor after she left and it occurred to me that all of the people I love are in danger of giving up on me. It's frightening how easily your life can spiral out of control;

one day I was on the up and up, the next I'm face down on the carpet dribbling. I haven't had another drink since, and I've seen the doctor for some milder pills to manage the pain. He suggested counselling; it's early days – I'm not sure I'm quite ready to get all touchy-feely yet.

'Sarah,' I write, '*I'm sorry I've been such a twat lately. You're an angel for putting up with me. I'll change. J xx*'. I seal it inside its envelope before Judge Judy can read it over my shoulder, writing Sarah's name and address on the front.

The other card stares up at me, blank and intimidating.

Dear Laurie? Laurie? Lu? I don't know what note to strike. I hesitate, pen poised, and then I think to hell with it and write without thinking too much, in the hope that it's going to come out right. The worst that can happen is I'll need to spend another 20p on a fresh card.

'*Hey Laurie. I'm sorry for the way I behaved. I didn't mean a word of it. Not one. Except that I miss you. I'm so sorry I fucked our friendship up. Jack (shithead) x*'

It's not perfect, but it's going to have to do because the florist is all keen-eyed as she slides behind the counter to finish serving me. I put the card in the envelope and fill out the front, then push them both across the counter towards her.

She doesn't say a word as she rings up my bill, but as she hands my credit card back she smiles. An acid smile that says you're a very, very bad person, and I'll take your money but that doesn't mean I approve of you.

'I'll take care not to mix the deliveries up,' she says, sarcastic.

'You do that,' I say. I'm all out of smart comebacks, because she's right. I'm a very, very bad person, and I don't deserve forgiveness from either of them.

Laurie

'There's another man sending you flowers? Tell me who he is and I'll challenge him to a duel.'

Oscar's just come in from work and is hanging up his overcoat when he notices the bowl of peonies on the hall table. I seriously considered binning them when they arrived earlier, because he was bound to ask who'd sent them and I didn't want to tell him a lie. I didn't chuck them in the end. They're so beautiful, they deserve to be admired; it's not the flowers' fault they were sent by Jack O'Mara. I smile at Oscar's light-hearted comment; I don't know if he's just so secure in our relationship that he isn't concerned or if he's too damn nice for his own good and always ready to jump to the benign conclusion. Though I wouldn't be surprised if he owned a duelling pistol.

'Jack sent them,' I say, fiddling with the starfish pendant I had mended without mentioning anything to Oscar.

He pauses as he lays his keys down beside the bowl, a fractional frown, the tiniest of double-takes.

'We had a bit of a falling-out a few days ago,' I say. I've been struggling to decide what to tell Oscar ever since the day at Jack's flat; how much information constitutes the truth, how much omission constitutes lying. Now I wish I'd just come out with it.

He follows me into the kitchen and sits on one of the breakfast stools as I pour us both a glass of red. It's a pattern we've fallen into on the evenings when he's not dining out with clients; it's a little 'fifties housewife' I know, but he works late so often that I normally have dinner ready and a bottle open by the time he gets home. It feels like the least I can do when I'm staying here for free. Still. Anyway, I don't really mind; as long as he doesn't ask me to warm his slippers or stuff his pipe, I'm good. There's something soothing about coming in and chopping vegetables, especially after long days like today. Being a teen agony aunt isn't all prom dress stress and period advice. My inbox has been particularly heavy-going this afternoon; I've been researching bulimia to try to help a fifteen-year-old boy who wrote to me about the struggle he's hiding from his family. I just wish I could do more; sometimes I feel hopelessly underqualified for this job.

'What did you and Jack argue over?'

'He was upsetting Sarah,' I say. 'His self-destructive behaviour had reached a point where he'd crossed the line into wallowing. She asked me if I'd mind trying to get through to him, and it didn't go so well.'

My speech pattern sounds unnaturally fast, as if I'm a child on stage, rushing to get my rehearsed line out before I forget it and screw up the play. It strikes me that I've been lying about Jack O'Mara to different people for different reasons for almost as long as I've known him. Even if only by omission.

Oscar tastes his wine as he watches me pull the stew I've prepared out of the oven.

'Perhaps a change of scene would do him good,' he says, his voice unreadable.

I nod. 'A holiday might be an idea.'

He loosens his tie and pops his top button. 'I was thinking of something a bit more long term. A new start.' He breaks off, watching me carefully. 'A new city. I mean, everywhere has a local radio station, right?'

What's the collective noun for bats, I wonder? A hoard? A plague? And then it comes to me. A colony. I have a colony of bats behind my ribcage, their claws hooked over my bones as they hang upside down, and the mention of Jack making a fresh start somewhere outside of London has them fussing and stretching their eerie paper-thin wings. It makes me queasy. Would it be for the best if Jack were to leave? Where would he go? And would Sarah go with him? The thought of losing them makes me swallow a mouthful of wine rather than the sip I'd intended.

'It'd be too tricky for Sarah to leave London with her job,' I say mildly, pulling bowls from the cupboard.

He watches me, sipping his wine. 'There're trains. She could stay in London.'

Oscar has never voiced an overtly negative opinion of Jack, and I sense that he's stopping himself short of it now. I know full well there are trains, and they could commute to see each other if they lived in different cities. I just don't want them to.

'It's a thought,' I say, hoping it's a thought neither of them ever has. Is that selfish? I can see merit in the idea of Jack kick-starting his life somewhere without any of the negative connotations dogging him here: the accident, his stalled career. These days I think I'm one of those negatives too. Our friendship is brittle, fire-damaged; as I look back on it I can't discern if it's ever been as genuine as I thought it was. It appears real, but it's been built for purpose because we both love Sarah. Oscar holds his tongue; there's an unusual atmosphere between us tonight, a weight in the air, a storm warning.

'How was your day?' I ask, smiling, at least on the outside.

'Noisy,' he sighs. 'Pressured. Peter's still away so I'm doing most of his job as well as my own.'

I sometimes wonder if banking is Oscar's true vocation. There's a cut and thrust to it that isn't his natural vibe, although perhaps I underestimate his chameleon-like ability to switch character the moment he snaps his red braces over his shoulders in the mornings. Who is the real Oscar? My bare-chested Thai love or the starched city shirt? If you'd asked me a year ago, I'd have said the former without hesitation, but now I'm not so sure. Despite the pressures, there's no doubt he enjoys what he does. He starts early and stays late, and he's never happier than on the nights when he's landed a deal. What will I say in five years or ten? Will he have been so sucked in and chewed up by the corporate world that I can no longer see my Robinson Crusoe? I hope not, for him even more so than for myself.

'Why don't you go and jump in the shower?' I take the lid off the stew and add a little more wine, then slide it back in the oven for a few more minutes. 'This can wait a bit longer.'

*

At the end of the evening, I walk through the flat and turn out the lights before I join Oscar in bed. I linger in the hallway, my finger on the switch of the table lamp that bathes the bowl of peonies in a creamy glow. They're stunning, but already a petal has fallen from one of the blooms and landed on the wooden floorboards. That's the thing about flowers, isn't it? They're lush and extravagant and demand your attention, and you think they're the most exquisite thing, but then in the shortest time they're not very lovely at all. They wilt and they turn the water brown, and soon you can't hold on to them any longer.

I head into the bedroom and slide naked between the covers and into Oscar's open arms, pressing my lips against his chest.

2013

New Year's Resolutions

For the last few years I've started my resolutions with a wish for my first job in publishing.

Officially, I don't need to put that this year, although I will secretly express a desire to move into something slightly more taxing than replying to teenage girls about boys and how to plait their hair like Katniss Everdeen. It's not that I don't enjoy it; it's more that our readership is relatively modest and I can't see how I'm ever going to progress there. Plus I don't even like Justin Bieber.

Technically, I should write down finding somewhere else to live as a resolution, because I've been living with Oscar for six months now and it was only ever supposed to be a temporary arrangement. But I don't want to live anywhere else, and he doesn't want me to go, so I'm not going to. We seem to have leapfrogged several conventional stages in our relationship, but it's been that way for us from the very first moment he spoke to me in Thailand. Who's to say what's right and wrong with love, anyway? This isn't romance by numbers, it's real life. Yes, I find his adoration overwhelming sometimes; he wears his heart on his sleeve with my name scored through it. He still asks me to marry him at least once a week, and although I know he's ninety per cent kidding, I think he'd book the church if I shocked him and said yes. He's a gift giver and a considerate lover and a steady ship.

So I don't really know what my New Year's resolution is. Just try not to fall overboard, I guess.

Laurie

'Are you sure the recipe said to put the whole bottle of rum in?' I splutter a little into the glass teacup of punch Sarah has just passed me to taste. 'I think it's taken the roof off my mouth.'

She laughs wickedly. 'I might have adulterated it a tiny bit.'

'Well, at least everyone will be too pissed to notice if it's not a very good party,' I say, surveying the flat. Oscar has been away in Brussels for most of this week with work, which has left me free to spend my evenings getting everything surprise-birthday-party perfect. He's twenty-nine tomorrow. I've carefully packed away anything of his mother's that looks expensive or breakable, cooked and frozen Delia-worthy canapés, and Sarah and I have spent most of this afternoon rearranging the furniture to maximize on space. We're lucky to live in the garden flat; we can always let people spill out there if it gets too full. Hopefully not though, as it's freezing and the weather forecast mentioned the possibility of snow later.

'It'll be brilliant,' she says over her shoulder as she heads for the loo. 'You've bagged the coolest DJ in town, after all.' I can't quite tell if she's being sarcastic or not.

It's been three months since that hideous Saturday-morning showdown at Jack's house, and thank God it seems as if he's finally getting himself back on track, including agreeing to DJ at my boyfriend's birthday party. And much more importantly than that, his old station have taken him back on, albeit in a slightly less prestigious slot than the one he had before, and Sarah mentioned earlier that he's already scouting around for something better. I've only seen him once or twice since Christmas, and never alone. The first time, back in January, was incredibly awkward; despite the beautiful flowers he sent me, I hadn't really found it in myself to properly forgive him. But when Sarah went to the loo he grabbed my hand and apologized, begged me, almost, and the intense, broken way he looked at me put a crack in my heart. I knew he meant it. He'd hurt me, but he'd hurt himself more.

I'm heartened to report that his beard has finally bitten the dust and the spark is returning to his green-gold eyes. I cannot tell you how relieved I am; for a while I wasn't certain how he'd find the strength to pull himself back from the edge.

Sarah's left her mobile on the kitchen work surface while she's in the loo, and when it bleeps I look at it out of habit. The message is from Luke.

> Don't suppose you're at a loose end tonight? Last minute plan fail,
> am Billy no mates. Save me, Sazzle!

I look at it for a few moments, my mind whirring, then walk away and stand gazing into the fridge. I don't want Sarah to think I was snooping. It was an innocent-enough text; friendly, not flirty. I've only met Luke once when I bumped into them in a cafe close to where Sarah works, and he's not Sarah's usual type at all; he's huge, all muscles and floppy surfer hair. But Sazzle? She's told me that they've chatted, of course, and that he's super-easy to talk to about things. Is there any more to it than that? I watch her out of the corner of my eye as she comes into the kitchen and picks up her phone, then laughs softly and slides it into the back pocket of her jeans without comment. It takes me by surprise, but then I don't tell her about every text I get, either. Not to mention the other things I've never told her.

'This is a long way from our Delancey Street parties, isn't it?' she says, pouring us both a glass of wine as we admire the smart, gleaming kitchen. 'You've changed, Lu.'

I laugh at her sarcasm. 'We both have.'

'You know who I genuinely had a drink with last week?' She slants her eyes at me, up to no good. 'Amanda Holden.'

'No!' I clutch my stomach as if she's stabbed me. 'I knew it.'

She brushes her shoulders off with her fingertips and arches her eyebrows at me, then relents and starts to laugh. 'We were in the same bar, anyway.'

I roll my eyes. 'One day.' And I mean it. She was promoted over New Year to a regular spot on the lunchtime news bulletin; she's becoming someone who people know they've seen before but can't think where. Give her a few years and she'll need to wear a baseball cap and dark glasses to meet me for coffee.

'What did you get Oscar for his birthday?'

A flicker of excitement licks through me. I can't wait for him to see his gift. 'I'll show you,' I say. 'Come on.' I lead her down the hallway towards our bedroom and push the door open. 'There. What do you think?' Hanging in pride of place over our bed is a large canvas painting. 'Carly, one of the girls at work, painted it for me from a photograph I gave her.'

'Wow.' Sarah's soft exclamation tells me that she's as blown away as I am by the way Carly has managed to capture so much more than just the dawn colours and the dimensions of our little shack on the beach in Thailand. The painting vibrates with life and serenity; as I look at it I can almost hear the gentle rush of the sea and smell the strong-but-sweet black coffee as we sit on the front step and watch the sun come up. I nearly cried the first time I saw it.

'I know,' I say, not wanting to take my eyes away from it. 'God knows why she works at the magazine. People would queue round the block if they knew how good she is.'

'I wish I had a talent like that,' Sarah sighs.

'You're kidding me, right?' I say, ushering her from the bedroom and clicking the door closed. 'I have to shade my eyes when you're on TV.'

'Piss off,' she says, but I can hear in her voice that she's bolstered by my words. Sarah's always been a funny mix of brilliant and insecure; one second she'll be prancing around the room like an overexcited show horse and the next she'll be agonizing over a word she got wrong in her last broadcast.

'What time is Oscar coming home?'

I look at the clock, working out how long I have to get everything and everyone in place. 'His plane touches down just after six,' I say. 'So around half seven? I've asked everyone to be here for seven just to be sure.'

She grimaces. 'I really hope Jack remembers.'

She doesn't add 'this time'. But I think both of our thoughts turn back to that other night a few months back, and I send up a silent hope that tonight will be memorable for all the right reasons.

Jack

I'm pretty sure Sarah is expecting me to be late. I can't seem to win with her any more, despite my almost-constant apologies. She banged on and on about me finding a job, and now I have one again she's on at me because I'm always at work. It's not as if it matters whether or not I'm there for the big jazz-hands surprise when Oscar arrives at his party. Who has those anyway? I thought they were the domain of American sit-coms. Sarah's perfectly able to manage the Spotify playlist without me, and I'm pretty certain I don't feature on Oscar's 'it's not a party until you're here' list. That's okay. He wouldn't feature on mine, either.

But despite all that, for some reason I'm here just about on time. I can see the gracious terraced house they live in as I turn the corner on to their road. My breath mists on the cold air in front of me, but still I drag my feet to make the most of the last few minutes before I have to go inside and pretend to like his braying friends. Or *their* braying friends, I suppose I should call them, seeing as he and Laurie are joined at the hip these days. I sometimes think she would have been better off hooking up with Billy. At least he's a laugh, and he doesn't pretend to be something he's not. Every now and then Sarah and Laurie drag us into the hell of a double date, where they laugh like sisters and we make civil chat like neighbours who don't especially care for each other. Not that we could ever be neighbours, because he lives in Wankerville and I live in Stockwell. And whatever world we live in, we're just not similar enough to be friends. The only thing we have in common is Laurie, and she's becoming more like him and less like us by the day.

I'm outside the house now. I consider walking straight past, but Laurie is framed in the open doorway welcoming someone I don't recognize, and she spots me and half raises her hand in greeting. I loiter until her guest's gone inside, then I saunter up and try for a grin.

'Lu.'

'Jack. You made it.'

She heroically resists looking at her watch, and I try, and fail, not to look at the starfish nestled between her collarbones. Her fingers move to cover it, as if she fears I might fly into a hulk-rage and rip it from her neck again.

'You look nice,' I say.

She glances down at her dress as if she hasn't seen it before. It's an unusual style on her; black and vintage-looking with blue piping and a skirt that flips around her knees. It takes me back to Barnes Common, to drinking beer in the sunshine and riding the Ferris wheel.

'Thank you,' she says, a wavering, uncertain smile on her lips as she brushes a kiss against my cheek. 'Come through. Sarah's in the kitchen.' She leads me across the tiled lobby to their door. 'She's made rum punch.'

'Has she put too much rum in?'

Her laughter over her shoulder jolts me; it's the first time she has genuinely laughed at anything I've said in a long time. 'Of course she has.'

We pass through groups of people I mostly don't recognize and a few I do, including Oscar's florid brother, whose name escapes me, and his wife, who looks like she sucks whole lemons for breakfast, lunch and dinner. Sarah and I met them on Boxing Day at a pub not far from here. True to form, Oscar had hired a room for a Christmas get-together – because why mix with the riff-raff in the bar when you can kill the mood by putting too few people in too large a room?

Oscar's brother pumps my hand as I pass. 'Good to see you looking well, fella,' he says, and to give him his due I recall that he's not all that grim. I can't say the same for his wife. She looks as if her pencil-thin smile actually hurts her face and her narrowed eyes tell me to keep on moving along. Fine. I wasn't planning on talking to her anyway; I don't know anything about quinoa or how to perfectly poach a quail's egg.

'Jack, in here.'

Sarah. My saviour. Perhaps she'll be nice to me now we're in company. Laurie lays her hand on my arm and excuses herself, and I head into the relative safety of the kitchen. Sarah looks her usual knockout self in a dress I haven't seen before; it's yellow and tight and contrasts with her hair.

'What happened to the music?' I say, cocking my head to listen as she hands me a beer from the fridge. This definitely isn't the playlist I painstakingly curated.

'One of Oscar's friends has commandeered my phone.' She grimaces, just as an Oscar lookalike swaggers in. 'This one.'

'Boyf's messaging you again,' he says, holding her phone out.

Boyf? I reach out and intercept it. 'Cheers, mate. I'll sort the music from here.'

The lookalike glances at Sarah, and she takes his empty glass and ladles punch into it. 'He's in charge now,' she says, smiling to remove the sting as she nods in my direction.

I shake his hand because it's dangling limply in the air between us, but behind him Sarah looks panicked.

'Boyf?' I say quietly, passing her phone back when we're alone. There's a message lighting up the screen. It's from Luke.

'He wants you to know he wishes he could see you tonight.'

She meets my eyes and opens her mouth to answer just as Laurie claps and calls everyone through. Apparently Oscar has been sighted getting out of a cab.

'We should . . .' Sarah looks towards the kitchen doorway, apologetic.

Someone reaches a hand round the door frame and flicks the light off, plunging the kitchen into darkness, and she slips from the room. I stay where I am, processing what just happened.

Laurie

'Surprise!'

We all wave and clap as Oscar comes through the front door and switches the light on. His expression goes from concerned to shocked to incredulous as he looks around at the unexpected collection of people in his lounge. Everyone crowds in to wish him many happy returns, but I hang back and watch, smiling as he starts hugging his friends and air-kissing their girlfriends. Keeping a surprise party a surprise is no mean feat these days, what with mobile phones and emails ready to trip you up at any moment. He'd have been within his rights to wonder if I was having an affair over the last few weeks; I've been jumpy and grabbing for my phone every time the message alert has gone off. I have his trusting nature to thank for the fact that he hasn't thought to question me, and I'm glad of it tonight because it's allowed me to pull off this surprise. He's so very good to me; unstintingly generous and thoughtful. I can't repay him with expensive gifts, but I hope that gathering together people he's fond of to help kick off his birthday weekend in style goes some way towards showing him how much I appreciate him.

'Is this your doing?' he says laughingly, when he finally makes it out the other side of the scrum.

'Might be,' I grin, standing on tiptoe to kiss him. 'Did we surprise you?'

He nods, surveying our crowded living room. 'You certainly did.'

'Punch?' Sarah asks, appearing beside us with two brimming cups. Oscar kisses her cheek and relieves her of one of the glasses.

'I'm guessing you made this?' he says, sniffing it.

'It's a special gift from me to you.'

She gestures for him to drink up, and to his credit he does, opening his eyes wide and nodding.

'It's, er, certainly punchy,' he says, amused. I sip mine and wonder how anyone is going to be able to walk out of here later if they have more than two cups of it.

'I might just go and get out of this. I feel like a stuffed shirt amongst you all.' He looks down at his business suit. I hang on to his hand; I hadn't thought about the fact that he'd want to get changed. He'll see the new painting as soon as he goes in the bedroom.

'I'll come with you,' I say, catching Sarah's eye, feeling flustered.

He looks down at me, surprised. 'Saucy.' He squeezes my waist. 'You should probably stay out here though, hostess with the mostest and all that.'

Sarah wades in to help, on the ball as ever. 'You two sneak off for five minutes, no one'll notice. I'll create a punch-related diversion if anyone asks where you are.'

I don't give Oscar time to say anything else, just tug him round the edge of the room and into the hallway. Before I open the door I whisper, 'Close your eyes.' Hero-ically, he just goes with it, probably expecting some kind of sultry surprise. I lead him by the hand into the bed-room. 'Keep them closed,' I warn, shutting the door and edging round him so I can see his face when he opens his eyes. 'Okay, you can open them now.'

He blinks, looking at me first, shocked perhaps that I'm still fully clothed. God, I hope he's not disappointed. I smooth my hands down my heavy skirt. I fell in love at first sight with this dress, it makes me feel like Audrey Hepburn.

'Not me,' I say, nodding my head towards the painting as he starts pulling off his tie. 'That.'

He turns to stand at the end of the bed and his eyes settle on the vivid scene in pride of place. It's like looking through a window to the other side of the world, and for a few seconds we stand together, hand in hand, and gaze at it. He squeezes my fingers, and then he climbs on to the bed so he can study it closer.

'Who did this?' he asks.

'A friend.' I kneel alongside him. 'Do you like it?'

He doesn't answer me straight away, just stares at the painting, then runs his fingertip over the raised oils.

'Let's go back,' he whispers.

'Okay.' I smile, wistful. 'We could be there by this time tomorrow.'

I slide my hand inside his unbuttoned shirt and lay it flat over his heart. 'You make me so happy, Oscar,' I tell him, and he puts his arm round my shoulders and kisses my hair.

'I mean to,' he says. 'This is the second-best gift you could ever have given me.'

I look up at him. 'What's the first?' Maybe I should have gone for racy underwear instead.

He puffs a breath out, and out of nowhere I feel nervous, because his eyes are intense and he's moved from kneeling beside me to facing me.

'I know I've asked you this a hundred times before, Laurie, but this time I'm not joking or laughing or messing around.' His dark eyes are damp as he holds my hands. 'I want to take you back there. But this time I want it to be with you as my wife. I don't want to wait any longer. I love you and I want you with me for ever. Will you marry me?'

'Oscar . . .' I'm reeling. He kisses the backs of my hands and then looks at me fearfully.

'Say yes, Laurie. Please say yes.'

I look at him, and there in front of me, on his knees, I see my next stepping stone. Oscar Ogilvy-Black, my husband-to-be.

'Yes. I say yes.'

Jack

'Why did he think Luke was your "boyf"?' I make twatty air quotes round the last word, my back against the fridge.

Sarah shrugs it off. 'I don't know. It was just a mistake, Jack. Forget it.'

I look away from her, nodding. 'Maybe it was. But let's face it, Sarah, you and my Aussie hero have become pretty pally of late, haven't you?'

She sighs and looks at the floor. 'Not now, okay?'

'Not now?' I half laugh as I parrot her words, turning them over out loud for consideration. '*What* not now, Sarah? Let's not argue at Oscar's party or let's not talk about the fact that you're spending so much time with some random bloke who picked my phone up while I was unconscious?'

I'm not proud of how ungrateful that made me sound or how seedy it probably made Sarah feel.

'I'm not.' Her chin comes up, but her eyes tell me she's not being completely honest, with me or with herself. 'Get down off your high horse, will you?' she says. 'I haven't done anything with Luke or with anyone else and you damn well know it. I wouldn't do that to you. But, Jack . . .' Her eyes fill suddenly, unexpectedly, with tears.

'This isn't the time or place for this conversation. It's too important.'

'Sure,' I say, but I'm not ready to let it go, because that text did not sound innocent. 'Would you like me to leave the room so you can reply?'

I know I should leave it, but we've been tip-toeing around the truth for a long time now and, for whatever reason, tonight seems to be the moment it's finally going to trip us up. It's not just about the text, it's everything.

'You know something, Jack? I will reply to him. I'll reply because, unlike you, he actually takes the time to message me.'

'I message you,' I say, although I know I'm on shaky ground.

'Once in a blue moon if you want a shag or you've forgotten something at work,' she says.

'What do you expect, love notes?'

I know I sound like a cock, but surely she realizes I don't have time at the moment? She's hardly much better.

'You know what? Fine. You want me to be honest, I'll be honest. I've thought about it, about Luke, in that way. He makes me laugh and he listens to me. He notices me, Jack. You don't, and you haven't for a long time now. All you notice is yourself.'

Luke's a fucking hyena, I want to say, *waiting to pick over the bones of our relationship.*

'I notice you.' I'm suddenly breathless, because one careless comment from a stranger at a party has turned out to be the lit flame to the last thread tethering us together. Slow, threatening slicks of realization that this is it slide through the soles of my boots, up my legs, into my body, freezing me to the spot when I know I should reach out and hold her. This has been coming for a long time, hovering on the seat beside us when we watch a movie, at an empty chair at the next table when we go out for dinner, standing in the corner of the bedroom as we sleep.

'You need to actually *be* there, to listen,' she says. 'You haven't been there for a long time, Jack. Not before the accident, and certainly not after.'

We stare at each other across Oscar's fancy kitchen, afraid of what happens next, and then Oscar's brother rolls in waving his empty punch cup in Sarah's direction.

Ever the trained professional, she switches her smile on and says something chirpy to him as she reaches for the ladle. I press pause, watch her in action, and then let myself out into the garden for some air.

'You shouldn't be out here without a coat.'

Sarah sits down beside me on the garden bench ten minutes later and hands me a beer. She's right. It's bitter tonight and I'll know about it in my shoulder tomorrow, but right now it's preferable to the heat and forced bonhomie inside the flat.

'We could just forget all about our conversation back there,' she says, her knee touching mine on the bench as she sips her red wine. That's my girl. She might be plying everyone else with punch, but she's sticking to the good stuff. She's one of the most stylish women I've ever known, and one of the very, very best.

'But do you *want* to, Sar?' I ask her. Something in me can't help it. I don't want to ask her – and yet I have to. 'Do you want to pretend?'

She stays silent for a while, looking into her wine glass. Then she closes her eyes and I study her profile; so dear to me, so familiar. Tears glitter on her lashes.

'Sarah, it's okay to say it,' I say, gentle now because this is going to hurt us both. You don't throw yourself over a cliff and walk away uninjured.

'How will it ever be okay?' she says. She sounds about twelve years old. I put my beer down on the floor and turn to face her.

'Because you're you.' Her hair falls over her face and I smooth it back behind her ear. 'You're marvellous, beautiful you.'

Tears run down her face. 'And you're you. Stubborn, gorgeous you.'

For a long time now I haven't felt like a good man; this might be the most decent thing I've done for Sarah in months. I just wish it didn't hurt so damn much.

'We were good though, weren't we?' She reaches out for my hand, her cold fingers wrapped round mine.

I can see her now, leaning on that stop button in the lift until I'd agreed to ask her out to lunch.

'Really good, Sar. Close to perfect, for a while.'

'Close is enough for some people,' she says, 'for a lot of people. The world is full of close-to-perfect couples.' She's wavering, searching my face. I get that. I'm wavering too. I can't imagine what my life will be like without her in it. Who I will be.

'Is it enough for you?' I ask, and I swear if she says yes then I'm going to take her home, take her to bed and let it be enough for me too.

She can't answer me. Not because she doesn't know

what to say, but because she knows that once the words are out there they can't be unsaid.

She leans against me and rests her head on my shoulder. 'I always thought we'd love each other for ever, Jack.'

'We will,' I tell her, and I feel her nod.

'I don't want to say goodbye,' she whispers.

'Let's not do it yet,' I say. 'Just sit here with me for a bit longer.' I hold her for the last time. 'I'll always be proud of you, Sar. I'll see you on the news, and I'll think there she is, that dazzling girl who changed my life.' I'm not too proud to say I'm crying too.

'And I'll hear you talking on the radio, and I'll think there he is again, that brilliant man who changed my life,' she says.

'See?' I wipe her eyes with my thumb. 'We can't leave each other, not even if we try. I'll always be in the background of your life, and you'll always be in mine. We've been friends for too long to stop now.'

We sit there for a while longer, huddled together, watching as the first flakes of snow drift down from the midnight sky. There are no rings to give back, no possessions to tussle over, no kids to hand over in blustery car parks. Just two people, about to part ways.

One of us has to be the one to do it – be the one who gets up and leaves – and I know it needs to be me. She's been the strong one for too long; I have to leave her here under Laurie's protection. For a second I hug her to me, feeling the absolute impossibility of it. Every part of my body wants to stay here. Then I kiss her hair, and I get up and walk away.

16 February

Laurie

'I made us some sandwiches.'

It's been a week since the night of the party. Since Oscar proposed, and Sarah and Jack split up.

The party was a roaring success, much aided by Sarah's punch of course. Even Fliss had a cup for the birthday toast, then half an hour later she shook her hair out of its neat chignon and asked if anyone had a cigarette. Gerry almost broke his leg in his haste to fetch her another cup of punch. I hadn't intended to tell everyone about our engagement until we'd told our parents, but as soon as we stepped out of the bedroom, someone called 'We know what *you've* been doing!' and Oscar couldn't hold it in. 'Yes. Proposing!' he shouted, and everyone clapped and kissed us.

Sarah was the first person I wanted to tell, of course. She cried; at the time I thought they were happy tears, punch-induced emotion. Even the fact that Jack had left the party early wasn't alarm bell enough, probably because I was too caught up in my own happy bubble to realize the devastation that had occurred out in the garden. Heroically, Sarah didn't mention that she had some big, devastating news of her own. In fact, she didn't tell me at all. Jack did. He called me yesterday to find out how she was because she hadn't been answering his calls and when

I asked why he had to tell me. I waited for her until she stumbled out of work, brought her home with me, and now she's here huddled on our sofa under a blanket.

'Delancey Street Special,' I say, handing her the plate of sandwiches while I slide under the blanket next to her. Oscar has tactfully made himself scarce for the weekend, leaving us free to watch rubbish movies, drink restorative red wine and talk, if she wants to. She looked as if she'd barely eaten all week when she came out of work yesterday; a ghost Sarah.

'It's been a long time since we had these.'

'Years,' I say. She's right. All our dates in London seem to have been rushed meetings in fancy restaurants or cocktail bars – I miss our cosy nights in. 'I haven't forgotten how to make them though.'

She opens one and peers inside. 'You remembered the mayo,' she says in a small voice. I wish she'd pick one up to eat. 'Jack never really liked them. Not a blue cheese fan.'

I nod, unsure what to say because I'm more than a tiny bit furious with Jack O'Mara. He didn't make a great job of explaining to me what happened with Sarah, something about realizing that good enough is not enough, that they were each other's ninety per cent. I was probably sharper than I should have been; I said that holding out for one hundred per cent was unrealistic, a dangerous and childish experiment which was highly likely to result in a lifetime of meal deals for one. Sarah still hasn't told me exactly what happened, but I'm trying to let her tell me in her own time.

'All the more for us.' I take the plate from her, but hold it towards her so she can help herself before I do the same and put it down on the sofa next to me. She slants me a 'don't think I don't know what you're doing' look.

'I'm not going to stop eating and wither away,' she says, even though she doesn't take a bite. 'You don't need to worry about me.'

'You know that's one of the dumbest things you've ever said, right?' I eat and nod towards her sandwich that she should too. She rolls her eyes like a teenager, but obliges me all the same by taking a tiny bite.

'There. Happy now?'

I sigh and give up on the sandwiches in favour of wine. Alcohol is more useful than cheese in a situation like this anyway.

'You should probably speak to Jack. Or text him at least,' I say, because for the past hour he's been lighting my phone up with endless messages to see if she's okay. 'I've told him you're with me. He's worried about you.'

'I don't know what to say to him.' She puts her head back against the sofa and tucks the blanket underneath her armpits as if she's in bed. Given that Oscar's sofas are the reclining type and we're close to full tilt, we pretty much are. 'More than three years together, and I have no clue what to say.'

'You don't have to talk to him. Just text him. Let him know you're okay.' Though I realize I don't know the full story yet; he might deserve to wallow in it instead.

'I will,' she says. 'I'll do it later.' She sighs, then asks me how he seemed.

'Worried?' I say. 'He didn't tell me very much, probably thought it was up to you.'

'I don't want you to feel stuck in the middle, Lu. You don't have to cut him out of your life too.'

The irony of her words isn't lost on me. I've been stuck in the middle of Sarah and Jack for years.

'Are you going to cut him out?'

She picks at a loose thread of cotton on the blanket. 'I think I have to. For a while, at least. I don't know how to be with him as anything other than us, you know? I seem to have spent the last twelve months resenting him for one thing or another, and now I don't have to do that any more and I don't know what to do with myself.'

'Twelve months is a long time to be miserable,' I say, surprised that she's been unhappy for a whole year without me realizing. I mean, I knew they were both busy and stressed before Jack's accident, and that Jack had been a jerk at times, but don't all couples go through a bad patch? I feel like a crappy friend, floating around obliviously in my own love bubble.

'I've blamed him in my head for everything that's gone wrong, Lu. For the fact that we saw less and less of each other, for how much we'd grown apart or been pushed apart by our different lives, perhaps. The accident should have been a wake-up call, but it just made everything worse. And then I blamed him for that too – for wallowing, for not bouncing back.' She looks so downcast. 'Easier than blaming myself, I guess. But I've hardly been around much either. I wish I'd tried harder to get through to him.'

I realize I've lumped the blame squarely on Jack's shoulders myself since he called; he said nothing to suggest the break-up was in any way Sarah's choice. I mean, I know these things are never black and white, but he left me with the impression that he'd called time because she didn't quite measure up to his mythical one hundred per cent. I'm both relieved and disquieted to know it wasn't exactly like that.

'I don't suppose blame is really what's needed right

now,' I say. 'You just need to look after yourself, make sure you're okay.'

'I miss him already.'

I nod and swallow, because I miss him too. It's odd because I don't see him all that much these days, but he's always been there in the background. Sarah and Jack. Jack and Sarah. It's become part of my vocabulary, forced at first, inevitable in the end. And now it's just Sarah or Jack. The idea of him drifting away now they are no longer together makes me sadder than I know how to articulate.

'Maybe after a while you'll both feel differently? Maybe you just need a bit of a break?' I say, feeling like a kid whose parents are divorcing.

She half smiles, far away, as if she knows it's fanciful. 'We won't. Or I won't, anyway.' She swirls her wine before drinking some. 'Do you know how I know?'

I shake my head. 'No.'

'Because there's a part of me that's relieved.' She doesn't look relieved. She looks more bereft than I've ever seen her. 'Don't get me wrong, I feel as if someone literally cut my heart out of my body. I don't even know how life works without Jack in it, but there's this bit of me –' she breaks off and looks at her hands – 'this bit of me that feels relieved. Relieved, because being in love with Jack has always been, to one degree or another, bloody hard work.'

I don't know what to say, so I just let her talk.

'Oh, he's so lovely and, God, he's good-looking, but when I think back our entire relationship has been a million tiny compromises, his or mine, so our differences weren't big enough to pull us apart. It's been a constant effort, and I don't know if love should feel like that, you know? I don't mean making an effort for each other ... I mean making an effort to be someone ever so slightly different to who we really are. I watch you and Oscar together, and it seems to come so naturally to you both, as if you don't have to try because you just fit.'

It's in that moment I know there's no going back for Jack and Sarah. I never realized – they made their love look so easy. And I'm quietly devastated; for them, mostly, but for me too. It feels as if part of my life is splintering away, floating off into space.

'What can I do?' I ask her.

Her eyes fill with tears. 'I don't know.'

I wait and let her cry it out on my shoulder, stroking her hair.

'You c-could d-do one thing.'

'Yes, anything.' I'm desperate to do anything I can; I hate this feeling of powerlessness.

'Will you still be his friend, Lu? Please? I'm scared he's going to shut everyone out again.'

'Of course,' I say. 'You're my best friend, but I care for him too. I'll keep an eye on him. If that's what you want.'

I put my arms round her and she rests her head on my shoulder. I hear her breathing slow as she falls asleep. As I close my eyes too, I remember the first day I met Sarah, and the first time I saw Jack, and how very tangled and complicated our lives have become over the years. We are a triangle, but our sides have kept changing length. Nothing has ever quite been equal. Perhaps it's time to learn how to stand on our own, rather than lean on each other.

20 April

Laurie

'You have to be on my side in here,' I say, clutching Sarah's arm before we push the door open at the bridal boutique in Pimlico. 'My mum is all over the meringue dresses and I just want something simple. It's a small church. Don't let her bully me into something that won't fit down the aisle.'

Sarah grins. 'I'm quite partial to those big sparkly numbers. I think you could pull it off.'

'I mean it, Sar. She's one step away from ringing up that woman off *Gypsy Weddings* to see if she can fit me in at short notice. Don't encourage her, for God's sake.'

We step inside the boutique, still laughing, and I spy my mum already deep in conversation with the sales assistant, a glamorous fifty-something with a tape measure slung round her tanned neck.

'Here she is now.' Mum beams at me as we approach and I see the assistant's eyes light up at the sight of Sarah, and then dim a little when she realizes that I'm the bride. I'm sure she has a million dresses in here that would suit someone tall and curvy like Sarah, whereas my shorter, more regular-girl body needs more skilful dressing to make the best of it. The assistant's glasses are balanced on top of her auburn up-do, and she reaches for them and slides them on to study me as I hang my coat on the hanger she's holding out.

'So, *you're* my bride!' She says it as if she's the one I'm getting hitched to, all panto over-emphasis. 'I'm Gwenda, otherwise known around here as the fairy godmother!'

My smile is thin; if there's one thing I've come to realize about weddings, it's that pretty much everyone who works in the industry has perfected a false air of perpetual excitement, like nothing delights them more than making your every wedding wish come true. I get it. More gushing equals more money spent. The mere fact that something is wedding related seems to make it instantly three times more expensive than it might otherwise be. You want a couple of bay trees to put either side of your front door? Sure. These beauties are fifty pound a pair. Wait, you want them for your wedding reception? Ah, well, in that case let me tie ribbons round the pots and charge you double! But I've got their number now. I try not to throw the bridal bomb in until the very last minute, if at all. Not that Oscar is interested in cutting corners; he and his mother have gone into a full-scale wedding mania. I'm having a hard time reining them in. What I'd really love, if they cared to listen to me, is a small wedding – and unlike most people who say that, I really mean it; something intimate and special, just for us and our very dearest. The only people I really want there from my side are my immediate family, Jack and Sarah, and the couple of old school friends I've stayed in touch with. As for my colleagues, I like them well enough, but not well enough to want them at my nuptials. Not that it matters a great deal what I think. It seems I'm going to end up with something lavish and public. I mean, I don't have a religious bone in my body, but apparently a church wedding is non-negotiable, preferably the same church Oscar's parents married in. A family tradition to uphold, even though Lucille's own marriage was hardly one to aspire to.

I'm just glad I've managed to ring-fence choosing my own wedding dress and Sarah's maid of honour dress – believe me when I say that it wasn't a given. My mother-in-law-to-be has been sending me dress links for weeks, all of them suitable for Kate Middleton, or perhaps more accurately, Oscar's previous girlfriend, Cressida. Oscar rarely mentions her. I wish the same could be said for his mother; she keeps their photo in a frame in their sitting room, on the piano, naturally. I say naturally, because Cressida was – is – a concert pianist. She has long, skinny fingers. She has long, skinny everything, to be honest.

'I find that a sweetheart neckline makes the most of a more modest cleavage,' Gwenda says, eyeing my chest with something like pity.

Sarah turns away into the wall of dresses because she's laughing. This is the second time today I've been made to feel as if my boobs leave something to be desired; we've just come from an equally depressing shopping experience being measured for a bridal bra, which of course was twice the cost of the non-bridal underwear beside it. I'm now wedged into this eight-way basque one-piece that I'm not sure I'll ever be able to get off or have a wee in, so Gwenda's unimpressed reaction to my assets riles me. My mother, bless her, steps in.

'I quite agree, Gwenda,' she smiles. 'Laurie takes after me in that department.' Mum rolls her eyes down towards her own chest. 'Perhaps if we could have a bit of a glance around first and then come and find you?'

Gwenda smarts a little, fast flutters of her eyelashes behind her horn-rimmed spectacles. 'As you wish, ladies. Your appointment is for the whole hour, so take your time.' She steps behind her counter, then looks up again. 'Just so you know, we do all of our adjustments in-house, no sleepless nights for you worrying your dress might get misplaced while it's away being shortened.'

Lovely. Now I'm flat-chested *and* short. Some fairy godmother she's turning out to be.

'How are you doing after all that business, Sarah, my love?' I hear my mum whisper her question as she puts an arm round Sarah's shoulders over by the rack of meringue dresses I'm purposefully avoiding. Mum's met Sarah several times over the years, and they share a sense of humour — mostly at my expense — that bonded them from the outset.

'Not too bad, Helen, thank you. I'm just trying to get on with things, keep myself busy.' Sarah chucks in a small, grateful smile to reinforce her words. Me and Sarah have drunk more wine together than is healthy over the weeks since it happened, but all things considered she's holding it together. Jack, I'm not so sure about. We've met up a couple of times for coffee; Sarah knows, of course. I promised her I'd tell her whenever I saw him. I didn't tell her the nitty-gritty — that the first time we met he looked like hell, the second time even worse, as if he'd done the walk of shame to get to the coffee house. I guess everyone has their own way of coping, but seeing him like that left me feeling uneasy.

I'm wondering how to get my mum away from the five-foot-wide frocks when Gwenda comes unexpectedly to my rescue.

'Mum,' she calls loudly, peering over her specs. 'I find that the fuller skirt can swamp my more petite brides.'

It's my turn to put my face into the nearest wall of dresses to hide my smile. Gwenda calling her 'mum' is another symptom of the wedding industry. Everyone is referred to by their role in the proceedings. Bride, groom, mother of the bride.

Sarah puts her head on one side and nods slowly. 'You know, I think Gwenda's right there. We don't want Laurie to be all skirt, do we? She'd be unbalanced, like one of those toilet-roll-holder dolls.' She laughs breezily and links arms with my mum, throwing me a wink as she steers her towards me. I smile, but shoot her a few tiny daggers too. It's not that I'm ungrateful for the intervention, but a toilet-roll holder? Anyone else want to chuck a few insults my way today? The wedding magazines assured me this would be one of the most memorable shopping trips of my life. I'm sure they mentioned tears and champagne. Given the way this day's shaping up, I'm not too hopeful, although there may well be tears of pain and the need for a very stiff drink.

'How about something like this?' Sarah says, holding up a silvery white shimmer of art deco material. It's beautiful, but very detailed and looks like it fishtails at the bottom. On Sarah, it would be stunning. It's on the tip of my tongue to say how fantastic she'd look in it herself, like a mermaid-bride, but then I remember the compact Jack and I found for her that Christmas and I hold my tongue.

To be honest, that afternoon is the last day I want to think about either. I'm proud of how she's refused to sink into self-pity since she and Jack split; she's out there putting her best foot forward as always, and I know she's been out a couple of times with Luke, though she doesn't talk about it much. I think neither of them are in any hurry to put a label on what's happening between them, it's too early – but all the same, I'm glad he's there in her life.

'I was thinking something more simple,' I say, slowly sliding the dresses along on the rail to look at them. We spend a happy ten minutes pulling them all out and laying aside the ones I like, or they like so much I agree to try on. Although it's not my favourite experience ever, I can't think of anyone I'd rather do this with than Mum and Sarah. I was a little bit low last night, imagining how it would have been to have Ginny with me for this, but Sarah somehow makes it all okay.

Gwenda glides over and claps lightly. 'Looks like we're going great guns here,' she says, her eyes moving over the dresses we've hung on the special gold rail she ceremonially wheeled across to us earlier. 'Mum, matron of honour, this way.' She grasps their elbows and ushers them through a curtain with the steely force of a prison officer. I stand on the spot for a sec, then my curiosity gets the better of me and I poke my head through to see what's happening. Oh, I see. *This* is where the champagne happens. Mum and Sarah are sitting on dusky-pink velvet thrones being handed chilled champagne flutes by a younger assistant.

'Chloe will be here if you need a top-up, ladies,' Gwenda twinkles. Sarah catches my eye, and the unadulterated humour in her eyes makes the insults I've endured up to now worthwhile. This is the happiest I've seen her in weeks. I'd dithered over whether to even ask her in case it upset her, but in the end she invited herself, as she does. Looking at her now with her legs crossed, swigging champagne, I'm glad she did.

Gwenda does a little bow, as if we're actors about to pop back behind the curtain. 'I'm going to spirit the bride away now and create some magic! We'll be back anon.' She glances at her assistant. 'Tissues at the ready, Chloe!'

I sense a well-oiled performance as Chloe picks up a floral padded box of tissues and lays them ceremonially on the glass table between Mum and Sarah. I cast a slightly panicked glance over my shoulder at them as I'm steered away and they both raise their glasses in toast and do absolutely nothing to help me.

Gwenda has chosen the dress my mum picked out for me to try first. I don't argue; this is her rodeo. She's made me strip down to my eight-way one piece, and she's standing behind me in the changing room with the dress over her arm. When I say changing room, I don't mean a cubicle at the back of the shop with an ill-fitting curtain to pull across. I mean an actual room surrounded with mirrors. I'm like a ballerina in one of those mirror-lined music boxes.

'This one is called the *Vivienne*,' she says, pronouncing the name in a French accent and shaking the dress out so the sequins send shivers of light around the room. It's fussier than I'd choose, with a heavily beaded bodice and layers of netted skirt. I follow her instructions, stepping into it carefully as she unbuttons it. I watch my reflection as she fastens me in, fixing all kinds of clips along the back so that it pinches in at the waist, then fanning out the layers of netting.

As I stare into the mirror, the weirdest thing happens. I slowly turn into a bride in front of my own eyes. It's a shock. I've been swept along with the tide of Oscar and his mother's enthusiasm, and somewhere along the line I've forgotten that this is my wedding day we're planning, my once in a lifetime.

Gwenda is watching me, shrewd blue eyes over my shoulder.

'Your mother was right, perhaps,' she says, suddenly more serious.

'It's not that,' I say, still staring at myself as if I'm looking into one of those magic mirrors where a different you is reflected in the glass. I half expect the bride in the mirror to wink at me, she's so alien. 'It's me . . . I'm . . .'

'A bride?' She smiles sagely. 'A lot of women feel a bit of a shock when they put their first wedding dress on. It's certainly a special moment, isn't it?'

I'm not sure Gwenda totally understands, but then I can't quite articulate it either, so I just nod.

'My goodness! If it has this effect on *you*, imagine how your groom is going to feel,' she coos, probably as she has to many other brides standing in this exact spot. 'There he'll be, the man you've always dreamed of waiting for you at the altar, about to turn round and get his first glimpse of his blushing bride.' She sighs, pure theatre. 'It's a precious moment.'

I stand completely still, her words swirling around my head so clearly it's a wonder I can't see them in the mirror.

I see myself as Oscar and all our guests will see me as I walk up the aisle.

'I don't like it,' I say, suddenly breathless. 'Please, Gwenda, just get me out of it. It's too tight.'

She looks at me, shell-shocked; she obviously thought she had me wrapped round her heavily jewelled finger. And she sort of did, right up to the moment she mentioned 'the man you've always dreamed of'.

Back at home, hours later, I strip off in the bathroom and turn the power shower up to full-on assault. What a bloody disaster. I managed to pull myself together in the bridal boutique enough to try the other dresses on, but none of them were the mythical 'one' all of the magazines bang on about. Gwenda tried to coerce me back into the first dress at the end of the session, but that wasn't going on my back again for love nor money.

I turn the water temperature up to a tiny bit hotter than is comfortable and stand there with it raining down over my head. I'm so achingly disappointed with myself. It's not that I don't love Oscar or that I don't want to marry him. It's nothing like that. It's just crushing to know that it's still there, like a muscle reflex.

That when someone says 'the man you've always dreamed of', I think of Jack O'Mara.

23 April

Jack

She's standing looking into a shop window when I see her. I'm not here by coincidence, I've been hanging around close to where she works for a while now hoping to catch her coming out for lunch, and there she is, her black-and-pink-striped brolly sheltering her from the rain. I move quickly in case I lose sight of her on the bustling street. She turns up a side street and I hurry after, nearly bumping into her as I round the corner.

'Laurie.'

She turns, frowning at the unexpectedness of my being here, then smiles and half laughs.

'Jack,' she says, bobbing up on tiptoe to kiss my cheek. 'What are you . . . ?' She trails off, looking at me. Belatedly, I realize that we're standing in front of a vintage clothes shop, and the dressmaker's dummy in the middle of the window is being used to display a wedding dress.

'Were you . . .' I nod towards it, aware that for some reason we're only able to talk in half-finished sentences.

'No,' she says, shaking her head as she looks back at the dress again. 'Well, yes, kind of. It caught my eye.'

'You're going to need one,' I say. 'Have you set a date yet?'

She nods as she looks back at the window. 'December.'

'Wow, this Christmas,' I say softly. 'That's great, Lu. It's really . . . great.' Where are my words when I need them? *Great?* How come I can talk for hours on my show, but find myself dumb-struck now? 'Have you got time to grab a coffee somewhere, get out of the rain for a bit?'

As we stand there, someone inside the shop leans into the window and turns over the price tag on the wedding dress to get a look at it. I see Laurie flinch and I realize she wasn't idly gazing in the shop window; she really loves that dress. I'm no expert on these things, but even I can see that it's very Laurie. There's something unique about it; it's nothing like the Disney princess dresses most girls seem to go for.

'Unless you were going inside?' I nod towards the shop door. She looks at it too, her teeth sunk into her bottom lip, undecided. 'I can wait for you, if you like?'

She looks from me to the dress again, a tiny frown tugging her brows together. 'It's stupid really. I've tried loads on already and none of them look right. This one just seems different somehow.' As she speaks, the customer looking at the dress gets her phone out and takes a photo of it.

'I think I will just go and have a quick look,' Laurie decides. 'Have you got time to hang around?'

Because the most pressing thing on my list today is to speak with her, I say yes. I loiter, unsure what to do as she folds her umbrella down and pushes the shop door open. She looks back at me and then up at the dark skies.

'You should come inside. This rain isn't going to stop.'

She's right, of course. It just seems an odd thing for me of all people to be doing with her. I hold the door open for the woman who'd been looking at the wedding dress, and relief flashes through Laurie's eyes as she steps into the shop. I follow her gingerly. It's not what I expected. Forties swing music plays unobtrusively in the background, as if someone has their wireless on. Wireless? I've slipped back in time too, it would seem. The yesteryear clothes are arranged in huge old open wardrobes, and jewellery spills carelessly from drawers tugged open on dressing-table tops. It's like walking into a wartime dressing room abandoned mid air-raid.

Laurie is over by the dress now, her fingers turning the label over to read it. I hang back as the assistant approaches her, and after a moment lifts the dummy carefully out of the window and sets it down for Laurie to take a better look. She circles slowly round it, a tiny, wistful smile on her lips. I don't have a shred of doubt in my mind; she's going to buy that dress. The assistant must have asked if she'd like to try it on, because she looks suddenly nervous and turns to me.

'Are you okay for time?' she asks when I make my way over.

This isn't the kind of shop where anything is hurried, but we're the only customers in here on this grey, wet afternoon, so I nod. 'Go for it. You can hardly buy a wedding dress without trying it on, can you?'

The assistant directs Laurie towards the changing room at the back of the shop while she cautiously removes the dress from the dummy, and I wander away to look around. Italian suits fill one mahogany wardrobe, sombre colours and sharp, old-school cuts. They shout Frank Sinatra and Dean Martin. I turn from them and look through the hat collection, trying on a Fedora for size in the mirror.

'You should probably head outside now,' the assistant smiles, slowing to straighten a gleaming pair of patent brogues. 'It's bad luck for the groom to see the bride in her dress before the big day.'

I'm reminded of Laurie's birthday years ago when the Ferris wheel attendant made the assumption that we were together. 'I'm not the groom,' I say. 'We're just friends.'

'Ah.' Her expression clears, although her eyes linger on me. She's pretty, in a bold kind of way. 'She's lucky to have a male friend willing to go dress shopping with her. Most men would run a mile.'

I shrug. 'It's not just any dress, though, is it?'

'I guess not. That one is lovely, from the twenties I think.'

'Cool.' I get the feeling she'd like to chat, but I'm well out of my depth with wedding dresses.

'You should take the hat. It looks good on you.'

I laugh and touch the brim of the Fedora. 'You reckon?' She nods. 'It says "man about town".'

'You're selling it well.' I grin.

'Sorry.' She smiles. 'Pushy sales women annoy me. I'll stop.'

'You weren't pushy,' I say. 'I think I'll take the hat.'

'Good choice.' She moves to refold shirts, then looks up at me, hesitant. 'Look, I honestly don't do this kind of thing usually, but would you . . . I mean, do you fancy meeting for a drink sometime?'

I could say yes. She's definitely attractive, and I'm single. 'That's an offer only a madman would say no to . . . or one who's moving out of town tomorrow.' I smile ruefully.

She smiles too, and I hope that she's not offended. 'Pity,' she says, moving away.

'You're leaving?'

Laurie's voice is quiet behind me, and I turn slowly towards her, taking the Fedora off. She's standing in front of me in the wedding dress, wide-eyed and beautiful. More beautiful than I've ever seen her, or anyone else. The dress has come to life around her, turning her into a barefoot wood-nymph bride. But her eyes are glistening, and I'm not sure if it's happiness or sadness.

'You don't look that bad, Lu.' I try for humour, because no one should cry in their wedding dress.

'You said you're moving away.'

I am. I'm leaving for Edinburgh on the overnight train tomorrow.

I glance over my shoulder to make sure the assistant is out of earshot, the Fedora in my hands in front of me like a prop. 'Let's talk later, Lu, it's not that big a deal, honestly. For now, you have to get this dress. You look like the fucking fairy queen,' I say.

She's watching me with those big, vulnerable eyes of hers. 'Are you lying to me, Jack?'

I shake my head. 'No. If all brides looked like you, there'd be no single men left in the world.' I know that wasn't what she was asking.

She shakes her head and turns away from me to look at the dress in the full-length mirror. I'm glad of the chance to compose myself, and perhaps she's doing the same thing. I watch as she turns to consider it from all angles.

'It's your dress, Laurie. It looks as if it's been waiting for you to find it.'

She nods, because she knows it too. As she steps back inside the changing room, I resolve that I won't ruin this day for her. I want her to have only happy memories of the day she found that dress.

Laurie

We're in a coffee shop a few doors down. I can't believe I've stumbled upon my dream dress by accident; Jack's right, it's as if it was waiting patiently for me. When I was standing there looking at myself I knew that Oscar would love it, and that I would love him loving it. It's the most special dress I've ever seen, slim fitting with tiny capped sleeves and a scooped neckline. I imagine it's the kind of dress Elizabeth Bennet would have worn when she married Mr Darcy.

There's a tag included in the box, scraps of information about its previous owners. I know it was made from parachute silk and French lace in the 1920s, and worn first by a girl called Edith, who married an American businessman. In the sixties, someone named Carole wore it for her barefoot wedding, and they held their reception in the park because they couldn't afford a venue. There must have been others too, but now it's mine, for a while at least. I've already decided that I'll return it to the shop after our honeymoon, adding our name and wedding date to the tag. It's a dress with a history, and though I'm its latest custodian, it's journey doesn't stop here.

'What's going on, Jack?' I don't beat around the bush when he sits down opposite me with two mugs of coffee. I realize that I've been caught up in the wedding plans, and in being a good friend to Sarah, and somewhere along the line I've relegated Jack to the subs bench.

He stirs sugar into his cup slowly. 'I wanted to tell you myself.'

'So it's true? You *are* leaving?'

He hands me a slim paper tube of sugar, and then a second one just in case. 'I've got a new job,' he says.

I nod. 'Where?'

'Edinburgh.'

Scotland. He's moving away, to a different country. 'Wow,' is all I can think to say.

'It's a promotion. Too good a chance to pass up,' he says. 'My own evening talk show.' He sounds excited.

I realize it's the first time I've heard him sound positive in a long time, so I'm furious when my eyes well with tears.

'It's good news, Jack, it really is. I'm thrilled for you.' I know that my face doesn't look thrilled. I expect I look as if I'm being tortured, as if someone is drilling holes in my kneecaps beneath the table. 'I don't want you to go.' The words blurt from me.

He reaches across the table and covers my hands with his own, warm and real and soon to move miles away.

'You're one of the best friends I've ever had,' he says. 'Don't cry or I will.'

Around us, the cafe is bustling with office workers grabbing takeaway lunches and mothers bouncing babies, and we sit amongst them, letting each other go. He asks me to let Sarah know because he can't do it, and he tells me that he needs to do this, to start again somewhere where the past isn't all around him.

'I have something for you,' he says, letting go of my hands to reach inside his coat, pushing a brown paper parcel towards me. It's soft, and I pick open the taped edges and fold the crumpled paper back to look inside. It's a hat, folded in half. A heather-purple tweed baker boy cap. I smooth out the paper with my fingertips, reading the familiar Chester's stamp embossed inside it, remembering when I tried it on.

'I've had it for years and never really found the right time to give it to you,' he says. 'It was for Christmas, really.'

I shake my head, half laughing. It's always been like this for me and Jack. 'Thank you. I'll think of you when I wear it,' I say, aiming for decisive and hitting desolate. 'You're doing the right thing,' I tell him. 'Be happy, Jack. You deserve to be. And don't forget us – we're only a phone call away.'

He rubs his hand across his eyes. 'I could never forget about you,' he says. 'But don't worry if it's not for a while, okay? It might be a good idea to find my feet for a bit.'

I try to smile but it's a struggle. I understand what he's saying; he needs time to start over, to build his new life without us in it.

He picks up the hat and puts it on my head. 'Just as perfect as I remember,' he smiles. I realize too late that he's leaving; he's on his feet before I've gathered my things together.

'No, don't come out with me,' he says, laying his hand

on my shoulder. 'Finish your coffee, then go back and tell Oscar you've found your wedding dress.' He leans down and kisses my cheek, and I catch hold of him, an awkward half-hug because I don't even know if I'll ever see him again. He doesn't push me away. He sighs, his hand gentle on the back of my head, and then he says, 'Love you, Lu,' as if he's exhausted.

I watch him shoulder his way out through the cafe, and when he's gone I take the hat off and clutch it. 'Love you too,' I whisper. I sit there for a while, the hat in my hands, my wedding dress at my feet.

12 December

Laurie

In two days' time I'll become Mrs Laurel Ogilvy-Black, which is going to take a lot of getting used to after twenty-six years as Laurie James. I can't even say it without sliding into the Queen's English, all plummy and clipped.

Oscar left for his mum's this afternoon and my parents are arriving here tomorrow. They're staying with me in the flat, and then we'll be going together to the church from here on Saturday morning. Once they arrive it's going to be all systems go, so tonight is officially the calm before the storm. Sarah's coming over any time now, and we're having a mani-pedi and movie night with champagne cocktails to celebrate. I don't have the kind of nails that grow; only women with the same kind of nails will understand. They get to the end of my finger and consider their work done, flaking and breaking. I've tried all of the oils, serums and creams known to man in the run-up to the wedding, because all the bridal forums tell me it's essential that my hands are in tip-top condition. Well, I'm forty-eight hours away from the altar and they're as good as they're going to get; Sarah's going to French polish them for me.

Everything about this wedding is planned, controlled and listed on Lucille's spreadsheet. For someone who thinks her son is marrying beneath him, she sure has invested a lot of her time in dictating how it's going to happen. To be honest I realized quite early on that she was going to steamroller her way through proceedings whether I liked it or not, so I've gone for the path of least resistance. By that, I mean I've agreed graciously to eighty per cent of her decisions, and held the other twenty per cent close to my chest and refused to be moved on them. My dress. My bouquet. My matron of honour. Our rings. They're the only things that really matter to me anyway. I don't mind which champagne is served for the toast, and though I'm not a huge fan of salmon mousse as a first course we're having it anyway. Oscar has been grateful for my unterritorial approach; as he and his mum are so close, it would have made waves if I'd been difficult about things.

Thankfully, Sarah's been there the whole way, allowing me to vent.

'Let me in, Lu! I've got no hands to knock!'

Sarah's voice rings down the hall, and I jump up to let her in. When I open the door, I see what she means. She's dragging a hard silver suitcase behind her, has two bags hanging off her arms and a large cardboard box in her hands. She peers at me over the top of it and puffs her fringe out of her eyes.

'Travelling light?' I laugh, taking the box from her.

'This *is* light for me.' She smacks my hand when I try to peak under the flap of the box. 'That's my box of surprises. Wine first?'

'No arguments here.' I shut the door with my foot before I follow her down the hall. I didn't want a traditional hen night, it's just not my thing, but this is perfect.

'Are we alone?' she whispers, looking for Oscar.

'Yes.'

She busts out a disco chest pump and then falls flat on her back on the sofa with her arms spread out wide and her feet in the air.

'You're getting married in the morning, ding-dong the bells are gonna chime!' she sings out of tune.

'You're a day early.'

'Better than a day late.' She sits up and gazes around. 'Are we having a seance?'

I've lit scented candles everywhere to create a calm, Zen-like atmosphere. 'It's supposed to be spa-ish,' I say. 'Go on, sniff.'

She smells the air. 'I think my nose would work better if I had a glass of wine in my hand.'

I take the hint and head into the kitchen. 'Wine . . . or Oscar's mother's champagne?' I call through.

'Oh, HRH's champagne, please.' Sarah comes into the kitchen and perches on one of the breakfast stools. Is it disloyal that I've grumbled to Sarah on numerous occasions about my mother-in-law-to-be? Everyone needs to unload to someone, don't they, and Sarah is as good as a sister. Which reminds me . . . I spin round and pull a small, wrapped parcel from the cupboard.

'I'm going to give you this now before we get too drunk and I forget, or before we get too drunk and I can't do it because I'm crying big snotty tears.'

I uncage the champagne as she looks at the gift bag, her eyes narrowed.

'What is it?'

'You'll have to open it to find out.'

She tugs the grey ribbons as I pop the cork on the bottle of Oscar's mum's expensive champagne. I wanted to give Sarah something really special, and after hours of fruitless internet searching I realized that I already owned the perfect thing.

'I'm nervous in case I don't like it,' she says, making light. 'You know I'm a terrible liar, you'll know straight away.'

I push a glass towards her and lean against the breakfast bar, facing her. 'I'm pretty confident.'

She has the threadbare velvet box in her palm as she reaches for the stem of her glass and takes a sip for courage. As she goes to open it, I reach out and lay my hand over hers.

'Before you do, I want to say something.' Shit. I didn't need a drink to get over-emotional about this after all. Tears are already pricking my eyes.

'Fucking hell,' she says, drinking a good half of her wine and topping her glass up. 'Don't start already, you're not getting married for two days. Pace yourself, woman.'

I laugh, pulling myself together. 'Okay, I've got this.' I drink a little more and then set my glass down.

'It's to say thank you,' I say, looking at the box and then at Sarah. 'Thank you for . . . I don't know, Sar, everything. For letting me have the biggest bedroom in Delancey Street, and for always being next to me on Saturday nights out and groggy Sunday mornings, and for inventing our signature sandwich. I don't know where I'd be without you.'

Now she's choked up. 'It's a bloody good sandwich,'

she says, and then she opens the box. For a few seconds she's uncharacteristically silent.

'This is yours,' she says quietly.

'And now it's yours,' I say. I've had my wafer-thin purple agate pendant reset into rose gold and refashioned, now set on a slender bangle.

'I can't take it, Lu. It's too precious.'

Right. 'I'm going to cry when I say this and then we're going to get drunk and laugh, okay?'

She bites the inside of her already shaky bottom lip.

'I lost my sister a long time ago, Sar, and I miss her. Every single day, I miss her.' I wasn't exaggerating. Big fat tears roll down my face. I know Sarah understands, because she dotes on her own younger sister. 'That stone reminds me of Ginny's eyes, and how they were like looking into my own eyes, and my grandma's eyes. It's part of my family, and I'm giving it to you because you're my family too. I think of you as my sister, Sarah. Please have it, and wear it, and keep it safe.'

'Jesus bloody God,' she says, coming round the breakfast bar and hugging me. 'Shut up, will you! If that's what it'll take you to stop talking, then of course I'll keep it.'

I squeeze her, half laughing, half crying.

'I'll wear it on Saturday,' she says.

'I'd really like that.' I could tell her what's in my heart; that it will feel as if she's representing Ginny on my special day. I don't though, because it'll set us both off again, and she knows it anyway. So I tell her instead that it'll be perfect with her dress – an understated sea-foam green gown that makes her red hair come alive – and she agrees and then puts it carefully down before topping up our champagne.

We've made our way merrily through two bottles of Lucille's expensive champagne, and I can hazily report that it gets you just as tipsy as its less expensive shelf-buddies.

'I can't believe you're beating me down the aisle,' Sarah says. The credits to *Bridesmaids* are rolling on Oscar's massive flat screen (I still think of everything here as his, as if I am the lodger – I wonder if after we marry that will finally change), and we have foam toe separators on our feet.

'Me neither,' I say.

She reaches down into her box of tricks and pulls out a pack of cards. She wasn't kidding when she said it was full of surprises; so far tonight she's pulled out a succession of silly presents for me, from a pot of cinnamon which is meant to increase virility, to flip-flops with my new name on. We're now on to a card game designed to embarrass and advise potential brides before they walk down the aisle.

'How do we play?'

She takes the deck out of the box and reads the instructions on the back. 'Deal everyone three cards, and then going in an anti-clockwise direction, read the question to the person two places to your left, blah blah blah.' She starts to laugh and chucks the empty box over the back of the sofa. 'Okay, let's just take it in turns.' She puts the deck down on the sofa between us. 'You go first.'

I pick up the top card and read the question aloud to her. 'What percentage of UK marriages end up in divorce (2012 figures used for representation)?'

'Bloody hell, I'm taking these back,' Sarah yelps. 'The

last thing you want to think about is divorce.' But she breaks off to think. 'Twenty-nine?'

I turn the card over to read the answer. 'Forty-two per cent. God, that's a bit depressing, isn't it?'

I put the card down and she takes one. 'Ah, this is better. What's the first thing most women notice about a man?' She reads the answer on the other side and laughs under her breath. 'You can have three guesses.'

'His car?' I say, wasting one of my guesses.

'Nope, not that.'

'I don't know . . . if he looks the spitting image of Richard Osman?'

He isn't a random choice. He's Sarah's celebrity crush. 'Don't even joke,' she says, glassy-eyed. She met him once at an award ceremony she was covering and only just refrained from whipping her top up and asking him to sign her boobs. 'No one looks like Richard Osman except Richard Osman. Last chance.'

I take the question more seriously now it's my last chance. 'Eyes?'

'Yes!' She high-fives me. 'Eyes. Have you seen Luke's eyes? I've never seen bluer eyes in my life.'

I nod. She's been loosely dating Luke since the summer; he's her date at the wedding. She's asked me not to mention it to Jack until she's had time to tell him herself, although I don't know if she's done it yet. He left for Edinburgh the day after I bought my wedding dress, and aside from a text to let me know he could make the wedding, I haven't heard from him. I stumbled over a photo on the internet of him at an event a few weeks ago, some music launch with a tiny blonde on his arm, so at least I know he's alive.

I pick up the next card and squint at it. 'Most popular bridal flower?'

Sarah rolls her eyes. 'Roses. Too easy. One all.'

I let her have the point without bothering to check if she's right.

'This one better be more interesting or we'll give up,' she says, flipping the top card. 'How many times does the average person fall in love in their lifetime?'

I pull a face. 'How can that be averaged? Everyone's different.'

'Go on your own experience. You know how hard you fell for all those guys I set you up with at uni.' She laughs. 'What was his name in the shorts again?'

I don't dignify the question with an answer, because my champagne-soaked brain can't drag up anything beyond his hairy legs.

'Twice, maybe?' I take a stab at the answer.

Sarah puts the card down in favour of reaching for our wine glasses.

'I think more. Five.'

'Five? You reckon? That's a lot.'

She shrugs. 'You know me. I like to spread it around.'

We both laugh, and she rolls her head sideways against the sofa to look at me.

'So the two loves of your life have been Oscar and who? Bus boy?'

It's been years since she mentioned him. I was sure she'd forgotten all about him. I shake my head. 'Oscar, obviously, and my college boyfriend.'

'Then your magic number is three, Lu, because you totally fell in love with bus boy. Hook, line and sinker.

We spent an entire year looking for him. You were obsessed.'

I feel a bit cornered, so I swill my wine around and try to think of a quick change of subject. I'm too slow.

'I wonder what would have happened if you'd ever found him. Maybe you'd have been married now with a baby. Imagine that!'

Because I've had too much wine, I do imagine it. I see a little boy with green-gold eyes, grubby knees and a gap-toothed smile, and the reality of him winds me. Is that what might have happened in another version of our lives, one where I found Jack first? Or one where he'd just got on that damn bus? I close my eyes and sigh, trying to send the make-believe child back on his way to never-never land.

'Did you ever stop looking for him?'

Her softly spoken question knocks me off guard. 'Yes.'

She's staring at me oddly, probably because that sounded more heavy and resigned than it should have.

Her sharp intake of breath is the only warning I get of impending danger.

'Laurie, did you find him and not tell me?' she breathes, her eyes round.

I struggle to lie convincingly or fast enough. 'What, no! Of course I didn't! I mean, God, you'd know if I had and you don't know so I can't have.'

She narrows her eyes, and I start to panic because she's like a dog with a bone. A sniffer dog with a T-bone. 'I think you're holding out on me. Tell me or I'll flash my knickers at Oscar's family in the church.'

I shake my head. 'There's nothing to tell.' I try to

muster up a light-hearted laugh, but I misjudge it and it comes out with too much force.

'Oh my *God*! There *is* something,' she says, sitting bolt upright. 'Laurie James, you bloody well tell me this minute or I swear I'll flash the bloody vicar as well!'

How I wish she didn't know me so well or that I hadn't drunk too much champagne. 'No,' is all I can manage. I daren't look her in the eye yet.

'Why won't you tell me?'

She's starting to sound hurt and I feel hideous, so I reach for her hand. 'Let's just talk about something else.'

'I don't understand,' she says, then she falls quiet and slowly, slowly extracts her hand from under mine. 'Shit. Lu.'

I still can't look at her. I want to; I want to fall around laughing and say something smart that stops us going from where we're heading, but I'm a champagne-soaked rabbit in the headlights.

'It was Jack.'

She doesn't phrase it as a question. She enunciates every word as if she's sober as a judge, as if she's known forever. Then she gasps, a delayed reaction, slapping her hand over her mouth. I shake my head, but I can't force the lie out of my trembling lips.

'Jack was bus boy.'

'Stop saying it,' I whisper, and a hot tear runs down my cheek.

She holds her head in her hands.

'Sar . . .' I struggle upright and put my wine glass on the table. When I lay my hand on her shoulder, she shrugs me off. I feel as if she slapped me. I almost want her to. I sit and wait, agonized, and then she gets up sharply to her feet.

'I always knew there was something. I – I think I'm going to be sick.' She lurches for the bathroom.

I think of Delancey Street, of the times I used to hold her hair for her after a big night out. Knowing that I'm the one who's made her feel like this is the worst feeling in the world. I find myself automatically following her, but can only hover silently outside the door, hearing her retch. After a moment I sit back down. When she comes out again a few minutes later, white and drawn, she sits down on the chair opposite me rather than alongside me on the sofa.

'Did you recognize him straight away?'

'Please don't,' I say. I don't know how to deal with this. I thought it was history, I've made it so in my head, but now it's all coming out.

'We've been friends for a fucking long time, Laurie. Tell me the truth.'

She's right, of course. Our friendship deserves to be honoured with honesty.

'Yes,' I say, flat. 'I recognized him the second you introduced us. Of course I did.' I can't get the words out at much above a whisper. They're razor blades in my throat.

'Why didn't you tell me? You could have told me there and then, or the next morning at least, or any other *damn day.*' Her voice rises as she speaks. 'You should have told me.'

'Should I?' I say. 'Should I, Sarah? When? When you brought him home and told me he was the man you were going to marry? What should I have said? Oh dear, there's been some silly mix-up, you've inadvertently gone and fallen in love with the same man as me?' I swipe my hands across my tearful face. 'Don't you think I wanted to? Don't you think I thought about it every day?'

We stare at each other.

'2009,' she says, counting the years up on shaky fingers. 'Four years, and all of that time you were secretly in love with my boyfriend and didn't think it was important enough to tell me?'

I have no defence, and I can't expect her to understand. I doubt if I would if the boot were on the other foot.

'I didn't secretly love him,' I say, wretched. 'It was an impossible situation and I hated it. I can't tell you how much I hated it.'

She's not really listening to me. I don't think she can, the shock is still sinking in. 'All those stupid nights we spent together in Delancey Street . . .' She's shaking her head slowly, throwing all the pieces of our lives in the air and putting them back together in a different and terrible pattern. 'Were you just waiting for your moment to pounce?'

She's being cruel because she's hurt, but I can't help it, I bite back. 'Of course I wasn't,' I say, louder, clearer, harsher. 'You know me better than that. I tried my best every damn day not to feel anything at all for him.'

'Am I supposed to say thank you?' She slow claps me. 'Well done, Laurie! You're a pal.'

'You could at least try to understand. I was horrified when you introduced us.'

'I very much doubt that,' she spits. 'At least you'd found him.'

'No. *You'd* found him. I wish I'd never laid eyes on him.'

We fall into silence, and then she makes a sound that's horribly like a hiss.

'Did he know too? Were you both laughing about it behind my back?'

I'm mortified that she could imagine either Jack or I could do that. 'God, Sarah, no!'

'Were you snogging in doorways, shagging in our flat when my back was turned?'

I get to my feet. 'That isn't fair. You know full well I'd never do that.'

She stands too, facing me down across the coffee table. 'You swear on my life you never so much as kissed him?'

It's in that moment I realize I'm about to lose my best friend for ever.

I can't lie. 'Once. I kissed him once. It was –' I break off because she holds her hands up in front of her, as if my words are bullets.

'Don't you dare. Don't you dare make excuses for yourself, I don't want to hear them.' Her face crumples. 'It hurts right here,' she says, banging her fingers against her chest, vicious. She bends and grabs her discarded shoes and her suitcase, then makes a dash for the hall. I follow her, begging her to stay, and when she spins round by the door her face is a study of disgust.

'Good luck for Saturday, because I won't be there. You know who I feel sorry for? Oscar. Poor fuck doesn't even know he's second best.' She's saying things I know we'll never come back from. 'Keep your precious bracelet. I don't want it. Keep your bracelet and your secrets and your fake friendship. I'm done here.'

I stand and stare at the door after she's slammed it, rooted to the spot. I'm paralysed; I don't know what to do. She obviously can't stand the sight of me. But how will I do this without her? My family are arriving tomorrow. Our guests are coming. Even bloody Jack is coming, probably with his new girlfriend in tow.

I stuff everything – the cards, her dress, the box of surprises, into the cupboard – then go to bed and curl into a ball with my arms round my head. I've never felt so alone in the world as I do right now.

14 December

Jack

I know already what she's going to look like. I've seen her dress, I've felt the sucker punch. So I should feel prepared for today. But as I sit here in the packed-out church with Verity beside me, I realize I am anything but. I shiver. You'd think they'd put heating in these places; maybe they feel that a bit of discomfort is part of the experience, a way of showing commitment to your faith. I'm just itching to get the whole thing over with, to get out of this suit, to get a beer inside me, and then get back to Edinburgh as soon as I can without looking rude. My life there is fast and full-on; the show is gaining a bit of a cult rep and I'm working hard to build good relationships with everyone at the station. It's still early days, but I think this might be my place. I've made some friends, I can even afford to rent a flat on my own there. Brick by brick, I'm building myself a new life, and it feels good.

I still don't know if bringing Verity was the best idea. She was keen to come and meet my old friends, and in truth I imagined that having her here would put on a bit of a 'look how well I'm doing' show, because she's an eye-catcher. To be honest, she fits this crowd better than I do; she's even double-barrelled. We met at a charity social thing. She presented a colleague with an award in her capacity as local gentry and took me home as her own reward at the end of the night. The girl owns a horse. Do I need to say more?

I haven't seen Sarah yet. I'm hoping we can all be polite and grown-up about things. She texted me for the first time since our break-up to say she was looking forward to catching up, and casually mentioned that she's bringing Luke. I got the feeling she was telling me in advance so I didn't land one on him in church, not that I ever would. I told her it was cool and that I was bringing Verity down to meet everyone, and after that she didn't text back. It's bloody awkward all round. God, suddenly I'm really hot. This damned shirt is sticking to my back. I wonder if it's grossly inappropriate to take my jacket off? Oh, hang on, here we go. The organist has started up, way too loud, and everyone's roused out of their botoxed skin and is craning their necks towards the door.

Verity is on the end of the pew nearest the aisle, and it's only when she leans back in for a second that I get to glimpse Laurie. I was definitely wrong about being prepared. I feel that sucker punch again in my solar plexus as I look at her, serenely beautiful, white flowers and jewels threaded into her curls and yet more flowers in her hands. She isn't one of those perfectly coiffed and primped brides. She looks bohemian, beautifully undone, herself on her best day; she shines. As she draws level with me, her summer hedgerow eyes find mine and settle. She's walking slowly beside her dad, and for a second I feel as if she's the only other person in the church. If I were on the end of the pew, I think I'd reach out and squeeze her hand and tell her that she looks like a goddess, but as it is, she shoots me this tiny, barely there trace of a smile and I nod, fierce in my wish to convey my feelings. I try to say all the things I want to say with my eyes. Go and marry the man waiting at the altar for you, Laurie, and then live the glorious life that's waiting for you. Be happy. You deserve it.

And as she walks past me, her eyes on Oscar, I feel something in me break.

Laurie

I woke up at five yesterday morning with a jolt. I could barely believe what had happened. That my best friend hates me; that I have to get married without her by my side. I've told Oscar and anyone else who has asked that Sarah had a family emergency and was needed urgently back at home in Bath, that she feels wretched about it but there was nothing she could do. I'm not convinced Mum fully bought the lie, but I'm grateful that she chose not to push me on it because I'd have broken down in tears and blurted out the whole sorry truth.

On the surface I put on a good show, but inside I'm dying. I'm haemorrhaging the people I love and I don't know how to stop it. Is this just a fact of life? You have to grow up and shed your old friends like papery snakeskin to make room for the new? I sat propped up against the bed pillows in the shadowed hours before dawn yesterday and looked at Oscar's painting, wishing I could snap my fingers and be there again. He's moved it from my original hanging place so he can look at it when he lies in bed. It soothed me to see it yesterday; it reminded me that there are other places, and there will be other times. I knew as I lay there that Sarah wouldn't change her mind about coming to the wedding. I can't expect her to. I've lived with my secret for four years, she's had less than twenty-four hours to get used to it. It's too soon. I don't know if there will ever be a time when it isn't. I'm on my own now, and because there was no choice but to focus on the wedding, I decided to shut down all other thoughts.

So here I am, standing in the entrance of the church, the same church Oscar's mother's parents married in. I couldn't argue; I was hardly going to drag everyone back to the suburbs of Birmingham, was I? Besides, this place is ridiculously pretty, especially given the sprinkle of frost on the ground. It looked like something out of a fairy tale when the Rolls-Royce – one of Oscar's choices – pulled up in the picture-perfect village a few minutes ago, and I had a bit of a moment when I wasn't sure I could breathe. Dad was a trooper; he just patted my hand and let me take my time, steady as a rock.

'You're sure this is what you want?' he asked, and I nodded. I'm as sure as anyone can be.

'Thank God for that,' he said. 'Because, to be perfectly honest, I'm terrified of Oscar's mother. I had a whisky earlier to be on the safe side.'

We both laughed, and then I choked up a bit so he told me to pack it in and helped me out of the car, wrapping my gran's fur wedding stole round my shoulders for the walk to the church.

And now we're in position at the head of the aisle, arm

in arm, me in my beloved vintage dress, him splendid in his morning suit. He's not much of a fan of the top hat, but he's promised he'll don it dutifully for the photographs later. Mum phoned me last week to talk about the wedding, and she let it slip that he's been practising his speech every evening before dinner because he's terrified he's going to let me down. I give his arm an extra little squeeze and we share a last 'let's do this' look; I've always been a daddy's girl, and losing Ginny brought us closer still. We're quite similar, both a bit reserved until we trust someone, both slow to anger and quick to forgive.

Inside the church is a riot of fragrant, tumbling white flowers, all stunning and slightly less tamed than Lucille would have liked. That's my doing, inadvertently. I've been in to see the florist on several occasions about my own flowers and we've become quite pally. She could obviously see the gulf between my own informal choice of bouquet and the far more regimented pieces ordered for the church and reception venue. I didn't expressly ask her to change anything, but I was truthful when she quizzed me on how I'd really like it to look and she's worked a little magic to give us both something we approve of. I take a deep breath, and we're off.

Either side of the aisle I see faces, some I know and some I don't. My family have made the journey; aunts, uncles and cousins keen to get a look at Oscar and the fancy London high-life my mum has no doubt been regaling them with tales of. My colleagues, Oscar's friends, his ex, Cressida, in a black dress and pearls (Black! What is she, in mourning?), his brother, Gerry, with strait-laced Fliss, tasteful in teal organza. And then I catch sight of

Jack. I'm halfway down the aisle, and there he is, shockingly real and smarter than I think I've ever seen him. He's even brushed his hair. I'm not sure what I think of Jack in a suit. But then I can't think about that any more because his familiar eyes find mine, and I wish I could grip his hand for even a fleeting second before I become Oscar's wife. With no Sarah here he feels like the only person who knows the real me. Perhaps it's as well that he's too far away from me. For a second I wonder whether Sarah told him anything about our fall-out. But they've barely spoken since their break-up, and he doesn't look like he knows a thing. I shoot him the smallest of smiles, and he nods, and thank God my dad keeps walking because it leaves me no choice but to do the same thing.

We haven't written our own vows. Lucille looked as if I'd asked for naked karaoke when I suggested it, and to be honest Oscar wasn't very far behind her. I didn't push it. I'd been half joking anyway, but the look on their faces told me the joke was in poor taste. What did I think this wedding was? Some kind of *modern* affair?

Oscar still has his back to me as we'd agreed, straight and proud. His mum thinks it looks unseemly if the groom gawks as the bride walks down the aisle, and I'm happy to go along with it so I can be beside him when we first see each other. It's more tender, more us. We've both been so caught up in work and the wedding whirlwind lately, it feels as if we've barely had any proper time together; I can't wait to see him today, to spend all of my time with him again. I hope on our honeymoon we can recapture the magic of those precious weeks in Thailand.

I'm there at last, and as I draw level with him he finally

turns to look at me. His mum said he should lift my veil at this point; tricky, because I'm not wearing one. I should have told them, but I didn't want to be railroaded into something that isn't me for the sake of convention. I've opted instead for a delicate 1920s hair vine that the hairdresser has wound into my hair along with tiny fresh flowers, a serendipitous find in the same shop as the dress came from. It's the prettiest thing, fine gold wire scattered with jewelled sea creatures: a seahorse, shells and, of course, a starfish. To the untrained eye it just looks suitably bridal, but I hope Oscar will see it as an intimate nod towards our history.

Regardless of the fact that I don't have a veil, Oscar's hands move to lift it; he's practised every step of today in his head, and he looks momentarily wrong-footed that there's nothing there until I smile and shake my head a tiny bit. 'No veil,' I mouth, and he laughs softly.

'You're beautiful,' he whispers back.

'Thank you,' I smile, and his dark eyes flood me with love. He's a world away from cut-off jeans and T-shirt right now, but that's what I see when I look at him. My Robinson Crusoe, my rescuer, my love. I don't think he's even noticed that Sarah isn't behind me. I don't think he'd notice if the reverend flung off his cassock and performed an Irish jig around the altar, because he has eyes only for me, and those eyes are full of wonder and joy and love. However hard Lucille has tried to plan our wedding like a military operation, she hasn't counted on these moments, and they are the ones I'll remember long after my brain jettisons the salmon mousse for taking up too much space. He looks so dashing, every inch the groom.

Everything about him is perfect: the artful flop of his hair, his shiny black wedding shoes, his dark, intense eyes as he looks at me for the first time. Has any man ever made a more picture-perfect groom? It's as if all of those tiny grooms perched on top of wedding cakes across the country were modelled on him.

I wonder what HRH Lucille is making of my veil-free attire; she's probably got a spare one in a bag in the vestry just in case. No doubt she'll try to force it on me the second we get out of here.

When the priest asks whether anyone has knowledge of any lawful impediment I wonder, fleetingly, about Sarah; will she crash through the church door and tell everyone what I've done?

This doesn't happen, of course. In what seems like a few seconds I find myself walking back down the aisle wearing Oscar's diamond and platinum band on the third finger of my left hand, the church bells ringing out. We walk hand in hand and everyone applauds. Just before we step out into the pale winter sunshine, Oscar carefully ties the ribbons of my fur stole, then kisses me.

'My wife,' he whispers, cupping my face.

'My husband,' I say, then turn my face and kiss his palm.

My heart is full to bursting and I feel a pure joy at the simple truth of it; he's my husband and I'm his wife.

The photographer has had his work cut out gathering our two families together for the pictures. Oscar's mum seems determined to be art director; my lovely mum even took me aside at one point to tell me she might throttle

Lucille before the day is out. We had a little laugh about it and mimed choking her, and then straightened our faces and went back inside to pose for the pictures.

My family have been the only thing keeping me sane. Oscar's ex, Cressida, mistook my brother for a waiter and complained that her champagne wasn't chilled enough. So he remedied it with ice cubes fished from a nearby water jug. When she caught him doing it and threatened to have him sacked he took great delight in telling her he was my brother, in his strongest Midlands accent of course. He's still in 'wet the baby's head' mode after the recent birth of my gorgeous baby nephew, Thomas, who looks so angelic today that he's almost upstaged me as the centre of attention. Daryl took me aside for a little heart to heart earlier and asked if I'd like to be Tom's godmother next summer – talk about making a girl cry on her wedding day! I love my family so much, never more so than today when we're so badly outnumbered by Oscar's side.

'Ladies and gentlemen, it's time for the speeches.'

Oh God! I completely forgot that Sarah was going to make a speech. She had it specially time-tabled in as the first one, and her absence is going to screw up Queen Lucille's carefully scheduled programme. It would have helped if I'd remembered to tell her but I didn't, and now the red-faced toastmaster has just asked everyone to give the Matron of Honour a hearty round of applause. People are clapping, but it's that slow, scrappy, confused kind of clap when the crowd know that something is amiss and aren't quite sure what to do. Christ, don't the staff in this place communicate? You'd think the fact that the top table had to be hastily rearranged when we arrived would have alerted them to the fact of Sarah's absence, but no, he's calling her name again now and looking towards us expectantly. Oscar, bless him, looks horrified, as if he knows he should do something but has no idea what, and Lucille leans forward and gives me a 'do something right now' stare. I look out at the sea of faces in front of me and start to get to my feet, wondering what the hell is going to come out of my mouth. Lying to people one by one about Sarah's absence was excruciating enough. I'm not sure I've got the bare-faced cheek to lie to all of these people in one go. But what else am I supposed to tell them? That Sarah discovered I once loved her boyfriend and now she can't stand the sight of me? My heart starts to race and I feel my face going red. Then there's the sound of someone scraping their chair back on the parquet and clearing their throat to speak.

It's *Jack*.

A murmur ripples around the room, a low buzz of anticipation that this might be about to get juicy.

'As Sarah isn't able to be here, Laurie's asked me to say a few words instead.' He looks at me, a question in his eyes. 'I was lucky enough to play third wheel to Sarah and Laurie for a fair few years, so I've got a good idea of what she'd have liked to say if she were here.'

I very much doubt he has any idea what Sarah would say if she was here right now, but I nod my head at him quickly and take my seat again. I don't know why I'm even surprised that Jack's role in my wedding just became more significant; he seems to have been there at every important event in my life, one way or another.

'You see, me and Sarah were together for a while – until

quite recently in fact – sorry, you don't need to know that, erm . . .' He looks at the woman sitting next to him as a couple of titters start up from the far corners of the room.

'And when I say I was the third wheel, I mean it in the loosest sense, obviously. I mean we were close, but not *that* close . . .' He trails off again as people start to laugh. 'Sorry,' he says, glancing at me and pulling a bit of a grimace.

'Okay,' he says. I only realize that he's nervous when he rubs his palms down his thighs. 'What might Sarah have wanted to say about Laurie? Well, that she's a good friend, obviously, that goes without saying. I know Sarah always said she'd won the roommate lottery at university – you two have a once-in-a-lifetime kind of friendship. You're the gin in her tonic, Laurie. Sarah loves you very much.'

A few people clap, and my mum dabs her eyes. Oh God. I hold myself together and pinch the skin on the back of my hand. Pinch, release. Pinch, release. Pinch, release. I daren't let even a single tear slide out, because if I start crying I don't think I'll be able to stop it from developing into full-on body-racking sobs. I've missed Sarah so very much today. My precision-planned wedding has a Sarah-shaped hole in it, and I'm scared to death that the rest of my life will too.

Jack sighs, taking a breath. You could hear a pin drop in here.

'You know, even if I'd known I was going to speak today I think I'd still have struggled over what to say, because there aren't really any words to explain what it is that's special about Laurie James.'

'Ogilvy-Black,' someone heckles. Gerry, I think.

Jack laughs, pushing his hand through his hair, and I'm sure I hear the entire female contingent of the wedding party sigh. 'Sorry. Laurie Ogilvy-Black.'

Beside me, Oscar reaches for my hand and I shoot him a reassuring little smile, even though my new name sounds clunky and strange on Jack's lips.

'Laurie and I have been friends for a few years now, good friends even, and right under my nose you've turned from Sarah's clever, unassuming friend who once forced me to watch *Twilight* into –' he pauses and holds his hands out towards me, even though he's three tables back – 'into the woman you are today, someone with such incredible poise, someone spectacularly kind; you have a way of making every single person feel like the most important person in the world.' He looks down, shaking his head. 'It's no exaggeration to say you once saved my life, Laurie. You saw me at my very worst and you didn't turn your back on me, even though you had every reason to. I was revolting and you were lovely. I'd lost sight of who I was, and you made me remember. I don't think I ever said thank you, so I'm saying it now. Thank you. You tread lightly through life, but you leave deep footprints that are hard for other people to fill.'

He stops and takes a slug from his wine glass, because he's speaking as if we're the only people here and I think he realizes that he's veering close to too personal.

'So there you have it. You're bloody wonderful, Laurie. I miss you now we're on opposite sides of the border, but I'm glad to know you're safe in Oscar's capable hands.' He raises his glass. 'To you, Laurie, and you too of course,

Oscar.' He pauses and then adds, 'You lucky bastard,' making everyone laugh, and making me cry.

Jack

'Jesus Christ, Jack. You may as well have just shagged her over the top table and been done with.'

I stare at Verity, who right this second resembles an angry feral kitten. Pretty, but she wants to scrape my eyes out. We're in a corridor of the hotel, and I gather that she didn't appreciate my impromptu speech.

'What the hell was I supposed to do? Let Laurie die on her arse at her own wedding?'

She fires bullets at me with her eyes. 'No, but you didn't need to make her out to be fucking Wonder Woman, either.'

'She doesn't wear her knickers over her jeans.' I know it's a mistake as soon as it leaves my lips, but I've had three glasses of toast champagne and I don't like being mauled on my home turf.

'You're clearly on intimate fucking terms with her knickers,' Verity snarks, her arms crossed over her chest.

I relent, because she's here as my guest and I can see that it must have been slightly irksome hearing your new boyfriend praise another woman quite so fulsomely. 'Look, I'm sorry, okay? But you're wrong, Laurie and me truly are just friends. It's never been anything more than that, I promise you.'

She isn't ready to soften yet. 'What was that crock of shit about big footprints?'

'I was being metaphorical.'

'You said she was wonderful.'

I check there's no one else in the corridor, then press Verity against the wall. 'You're more wonderful.'

Her hand snakes round and grabs my backside. She doesn't mess about, Verity. 'Don't you forget it.'

I kiss her, if only in an attempt to stop that conversation going where it was heading. In response she bites my lip and starts tugging my shirt out of my trousers.

Laurie

'It was good of Jack to step up for Sarah.'

I smile at Oscar, even though his words have sharp edges. 'It was.'

We've retired to our suite to freshen up in that lull between the wedding breakfast and the evening reception. I think 'freshen up' is supposed to be a polite term for having sex, but that isn't what Oscar and I are doing. He's been tense since the speeches, and I'm desperate to work out how to clear the air because we should remember today for ever for the right reasons.

'Where's Sarah again?' Oscar frowns and pinches the bridge of his nose, as if he's struggling to remember the details of her absence. That's probably because I didn't provide him with many, a bad attempt to minimize the lie.

'Back in Bath.' My tone is deliberately flat, and I turn away because my cheeks are flaming. I don't want to argue, so I cast around for something to distract us and spot a gift bag standing on the hearth of the grand fireplace. Everything about our honeymoon suite is grand, from the size of the sunken bathtub to the four-poster bed that has a boarding-step beside it because it's so 'Princess and the Pea'-like.

'What's this?' I read the tag on the gift bag aloud. 'To the happy couple, with love and gratitude from Angela and all of the wedding team. We hope you've had the day of your dreams.' I turn back to Oscar. 'Ah, that's lovely, isn't it?'

He nods as I take a seat in one of the armchairs in the window and unpick the ribbons. 'Come and look?' I say, trying to ask him other things with my eyes too: *Please don't push the issue about Sarah. Please don't overanalyse Jack's speech. Please let's concentrate on what's important today, each other.* His eyes hold mine for a few seconds from across the room, and then his expression softens and he comes to kneel beside me.

'Open it then.'

I run my hand lightly over his glossy blue-black hair and smile. 'Okay.'

Inside the paper and tissue, we find a delicate glass Christmas bauble, hand-blown and engraved with our names and the wedding date.

'Isn't that gorgeous?' I say, swallowing the lump in my throat as I place it carefully down.

'You deserve gorgeous,' he says, kissing the back of my fingers. Then he draws in a breath. 'Are you happy, Laurie?'

I'm surprised by his quietly spoken question. He's never asked me before. 'Do you even need to ask?'

'Just once.' All of a sudden he looks deadly serious.

I take a breath too and look into his eyes. I know that our marriage hinges on my answer to this question.

'I'm so very, incredibly happy to be your wife, Oscar. I thank my lucky stars you walked into my life.'

He looks up at me, silent and impossibly handsome, and his eyes tell me there are things he'd like to say but isn't going to because today is our wedding day.

He stands and tugs me to my feet. 'And I thank mine for you.'

He kisses me slowly, deeply, his arm round my waist, his hand on my jawline, and I allow myself to melt into it, into him. I hope and pray that we'll always be able to find each other like this, like we did in Thailand, like we do in bed at night. My love for him is distinct from everything else in my life, clear and simple and straightforward. I cling to it, to the idea of us on the steps of the beach shack. Oscar's lips are sealed about where we're going on honeymoon, but I hope with all of my newly promised heart that it's Thailand.

We stand in front of the tastefully decorated Christmas tree that has been placed in our suite, and I hook our bauble over one of the empty branches. Oscar is close behind me, his mouth warm on my neck as we watch the bauble spin and catch the light.

'Jack was right,' he whispers. 'I am a lucky bastard.'

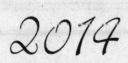

2014

New Year's Resolutions

1) *Sarah.* Just writing her name fills me with shame and desolation. I need to find a way to make her believe that I'm sorry. That I was in an impossible situation, that I didn't just allow myself to fall in love with her boyfriend. That I tried as hard as I possibly could *not* to. Somehow I need to make her forgive me because I can't imagine life without her.

2) *Oscar.* My husband! I just want us to stay as happy as we are now and enjoy our first year as smug marrieds. Not that I think we're smug. But there is a security to being Mrs Ogilvy-Black, especially when all the other rocks in my life seem to have disappeared. My resolution is that he'll never again have to ask me whether I'm happy with him.

3) *Work.* I'm in desperate need of a career change. Since the wedding I feel as if I've outgrown answering teen questions on love and heartache; after all, I'm officially no longer the world expert on unrequited love. Now the wedding mania is over I find I'm craving a new challenge; perhaps I will find something more in line with my life now. *Good Housekeeping* or *The Lady*, maybe. Ha! If nothing else, seeing my name in her favourite

magazines would give Lucille something new to dislike me for.

4) *Which brings me to ... HRH Lucille.* I must try harder to make her like me.

5) *Mum & Dad.* I must try harder to see more of them. Life here is busier than ever, but that's no excuse. The wedding made me realize how much I miss them. I'm glad my brother and his family live close by them – Mum is always posting pictures of them all with Tom, the new baby. I love seeing the photos, but a tiny bit of my heart aches too because they're all together while I'm miles away.

16 March

Laurie

'What's all this?' I struggle awake and sit up because Oscar is standing beside the bed with a tray.

'Breakfast in bed to celebrate our anniversary.' He places the tray down on my knees, and I go into silent panic mode in case I've forgotten a special date. 'We've been married for three whole months,' he says, putting me out of my misery. 'Well, three months and two days, actually, but it's better to wait for Sunday, isn't it?'

'I suppose it is,' I laugh. 'Come back to bed?'

I hold the tray steady as he climbs back in and relaxes back, still beach brown against the pillows. His skin tone is naturally pre-disposed towards tanning, so he's managed to hang on to traces of his honeymoon tan long after mine has faded under the assault of a British winter. It wasn't Thailand, in the end. We spent three loved-up weeks island hopping in the Maldives, total barefoot paradise. It's probably as well that we didn't return to Koh Lipe and try to recreate the magic of our first stay; the memories are too precious to risk. Does it sound ridiculously prima donna of me to say that I would have preferred Thailand to the Maldives? It's probably not even true, really, it's just that I'd have loved Oscar to have wanted to take us back there, or perhaps to have guessed that my romantic heart belonged there. I felt like the world's most ungrateful wife at Heathrow when my heart secretly plummeted as we joined the Maldives check-in queue. The luxurious resorts Oscar had booked for our honeymoon itinerary were a long way from the simplicity of the Thai beach shack – we dined like royals in water bungalows, lazed in double hammocks on our own secluded beach, and a butler – yes, a butler! – took care of our every whim. Now we're back in Oscar's – I mean *our* – flat, and Oscar seems determined to never let the honeymoon end.

'Coffee?'

'Please.' I line the cups up ready and spoon sugar into mine. Oscar doesn't take sugar. He doesn't have a sweet tooth at all, really, so I'm trying to curb mine because eating cake or pudding on my own makes me feel a bit of a scoffer, which I'm sure isn't Oscar's intention but still. I used to indulge my sweet tooth with coffee and cake binges with Sarah a couple of times a month, but we still haven't spoken since our fall-out. Whenever I think about it my heart feels too heavy in my chest. While we were on honeymoon I shoved it all to the back of my mind, telling myself I shouldn't ruin even a little part of Oscar's amazing trip. And since we've been back I've maintained the same approach – every day that goes by I bury my head deeper in the sand. The only positive to draw from it, if there is one, is that I'm no longer burdened by the weight of my secret. The worst happened, Sarah knows, and in a strange way I feel purged and more able to love Oscar without ambiguity. I've paid a high price for a clean conscience, though.

'You poach a good egg, Mr O,' I say, giving my egg a little exploratory poke with the very tip of my knife. 'I never get it right.'

'I phoned Mum and she told me how to do it.'

Heroically, I don't throw him a 'you did what?' look, even though I can well imagine Lucille's face when Oscar told her that I was lazing around in bed while he slaved in the kitchen. It's barely eight on a weekend morning, but all the same, I know she'll have filed it in the 'Laurie is a lazy layabout sponger' dossier in her head. She might need to start a second one soon, I expect it's stuffed to busting after the wedding.

'Well, you made a marvellous job of it.' I watch with satisfaction as the yolk spills all over the English muffin. 'I could get used to this.'

'I like treating you.'

'Being married to you is one long treat.'

He smiles, pleased at the compliment. 'Will we always feel like this?'

'I don't know. If we want to?' I say.

'People keep telling me to give it a few years, that the glow wears off.'

'Do they?' People have said similar things to me, of course, that our relationship has been a whirlwind, that when reality bites all the romance will disappear.

He nods. I don't ask him if by people he means Lucille.

'Well. What do they know.' I lower the finished-with tray carefully down to the floor and settle into the crook of Oscar's arm against the pillows.

'They don't know us,' he says, lowering the strap of my slip to reveal my breast.

I lift my face to his kiss as his fingers close round my nipple. 'My wife,' he whispers, as he so often does. I love it, but I sometimes wish he'd say Starfish instead, like he used to.

I wrap myself round him when he rolls me on to my back, and we make love. Afterwards, I haul the quilt up over our shoulders and snooze with my cheek against his chest. I wish it could be just us, that life was always just like this.

Later, over roast lamb (cooked by me, without having to consult my mother), Oscar looks at me as he tops up our wine glasses.

'I've got a bit of news,' he says, replacing the bottle in our new metal stand that tilts the bottle just so. Don't ask me why. It was a wedding gift from Gerry and Fliss.

I pause. We've been together all weekend, and news generally isn't something that steals up on you on Sunday evening, is it? If I've got news, I can't help but burst out with it at the first opportunity. What news can Oscar have that he's chosen this moment to drop it casually into conversation? I smile and try to look pleasantly inquisitive, but I can't shake the feeling that someone just drew an ice-cold fingernail down my spine.

'I've been promoted at the bank.'

Relief washes through me. 'That's great news. What will you be doing?' I don't know why I've asked this, because I don't especially understand what he does there now.

'Kapur's moving over to the States at the end of the month so they need someone to take over the Brussels account.'

I've met Kapur a couple of times; he's my idea of an archetypal banker – pinstripe suit, pink shirt and a big mouth. I don't like him very much.

'It's a decent step up?' I phrase it as a question, smiling to show I'm pleased even if I don't completely understand the hierarchy.

'Quite a big one really,' he says. 'VP. I'll be over four staff.' Oscar wouldn't even know how to be boastful, it's one of his many endearing qualities. 'I wanted to talk to you about it first though, because it's probably going to mean spending part of the week over there.'

'In Brussels?'

He nods, and his eyes flicker with something.

'Part of *every* week?' I try, and fail, to keep the note of alarm from my voice.

'Probably. Kapur usually goes out three days a week.'

'Oh.' I flounder, because I don't want to be a buzzkill; he's earned this and I want him to know I'm proud of him.

'I can pass on it if you think it's going to be too much,' he offers, and I feel like a bitch.

'God, no!' I get up and round the table, sliding into his lap. 'My clever husband.' I wrap my arms about his neck. 'It's just that I'll miss you, that's all. I couldn't be prouder.' I kiss him to show I mean it. 'Well done. I'm thrilled. Honestly, I am.'

'I promise not to be a part-time husband.' His dark eyes search mine as if he needs reassurance.

'And I won't be a part-time wife.' I say it, but I worry how it can be true in either of our cases. He's increasingly ambitious and clearly excited by the prospect of the promotion, and I'm going to have to find new ways to fill half of every week. I can't help but compare us to my parents, who always make a big thing of the fact they've never spent so much as a night apart, other than when Mum was in hospital having us kids, and when Dad was poorly. Being together all of the time is part of the marriage deal, isn't it?

Oscar unbuttons the top couple of buttons of my shirt and I pull back to look at him. 'I know your game, mister,' I say. 'But this table's digging in my back and I haven't finished my dinner yet, so you're fresh out of luck.'

He looks downcast, then lifts one eyebrow, amused. 'The lamb *is* bloody good.'

And that's that. Three months into wedded bliss, and we're about to live apart for half of our lives. The lamb doesn't taste quite so good when I pick my cutlery up again.

Laurie

Lucille knows perfectly well that Tuesday is one of Oscar's Brussels days, so why she's pressing our door buzzer is anyone's guess. For a second I consider pretending I'm not home. I don't though, because she probably watched me come in a few minutes ago; or more likely has a spy-cam in here watching my every move.

'Lucille,' I say, my face wreathed in welcoming smiles when I open the door – at least I hope it is. 'Come in.'

Instantly I feel crass for inviting her into her own flat. After all, it's her name on the deeds. She's far too polite to say it though, even if the haughty look as she passes me suggests otherwise. I sweep the empty coffee cup up off the table, glad I ran the hoover round before work this morning. Oscar keeps trying to get me to agree to a cleaner, but I just couldn't imagine telling Mum that I was paying someone to clean up after me. HRH Lucille flicks her critical eye around as she takes a seat. God, what do I say to her?

'Oscar isn't home today, I'm afraid,' I say, and her face falls.

'Oh.' Her fingers flutter to the fat, buttery pearls she always wears. 'I didn't realize.'

Sure. She has his engagements in her organizer written

with a special green pen she uses just for him. 'Cup of tea?'

She nods. 'Darjeeling, please, if you have it?'

Normally I wouldn't possess such a thing, but someone gave us a selection of different teas as a wedding gift so I just smile and leave her to her own devices for a moment while I check. Ha! Yes, I could punch the air, I have Darjeeling. I know full well that she only asked for it because she thought she'd catch me out, and the sense of victory I feel is unbecoming. I wish it wasn't this way between us; perhaps now is a good time for me to try and make some headway. While I wait for the tea to brew, I put the sugar bowl and milk jug – more wedding presents – on a tray with two teacups and add a plate of shortbread.

'Here we go,' I say, bright as a button as I take the tray through. 'Milk, sugar and biscuits. I think I've covered everything.'

'No, no and no, but thank you for the effort.' Lucille's eyes are a different shade of brown to Oscar's, more amber. More snake-like.

'This is nice,' I say, sitting on my hands so I don't fidget. 'Did you need Oscar for anything special?'

She shakes her head. 'I was just passing this way.'

I find myself wondering how often she's just passing; I know she has a key. It wouldn't surprise me if she let herself in when there's no one home. The thought disconcerts me. Does she search for proof that I'm a gold-digger? Go through our mail looking for maxed-out credit-card statements or search my drawers for evidence of a shady past? She must be spitting tacks that I'm clean.

'I imagine you find it lonely here during the week?'

I nod. 'I miss him when he isn't here.' I feel a wicked urge to tell her I throw wild parties to fill my time. 'I just try to keep busy.' As if to prove my point, I pour her tea. No milk, no sugar.

She takes a ladylike sip and winces as if I've given her battery acid. 'A little less time in the pot next time, I think.'

'Sorry,' I murmur, privately thinking that the most alarming part of that sentence was 'next time'.

'Admin, isn't it? For a magazine? Sorry, you'll have to remind me what you do.'

I sigh inwardly at her abruptness. She knows exactly what I do, and for whom. I've no doubt she's checked it all out online. 'Not exactly. I'm a journalist on a teen magazine.' I know, I know. I'm hardly at the cutting edge of journalism.

'Have you spoken with Oscar today?'

I shake my head and glance up at the clock. 'He normally calls after nine.' I pause, and then in the spirit of offering an olive branch, I add, 'I can ask him to call you tomorrow, if you'd like?'

'Don't trouble yourself, dear. I'm sure it's burden enough having to call home every day without adding to his list.' She puts a little peal of laughter at the end, as if I'm some harpy wife who needs to learn her place.

'I don't think it's any trouble to him,' I say, offended despite myself. 'It's hard on us both being apart, but I'm proud of him.'

'Yes, I expect you must be. It's a pressured job, especially managing an overseas team.' She smiles. 'Although Cressida tells me he's marvellous to work under.'

Cressida works out there? She wants me to ask her what she's talking about. I swallow the question, even though it burns in my throat. To mask it, I pick up my teacup and sip the wretched tea. It tastes of cat piss. We assess each other across the glass coffee table, and then she sighs and looks at her watch.

'Goodness, is that the time?' She gets to her feet. 'I should be on my way.'

I jump to my feet too and see her out. As I kiss her papery cheek by the door, I dig deep and finally find my balls. 'Well, this has been an unexpected pleasure, *Mum*. We should do this more often.'

I don't think she could look more horrified if I'd called her a whore. I genuinely think she's going to slap me.

'Laurel.' She inclines her head formally and glides out of the door.

Once she's definitely gone, I dump the piss-tea in the sink and pour myself a large glass of wine instead. How such a bitter woman raised such a sweet man is a mystery to me.

I sit down on the sofa, feeling very alone. Lucille came here for one reason and one reason only: to make sure I'm aware that Oscar is spending half the week in Brussels with his far more suitable ex-girlfriend. His ex-girlfriend who he didn't think to mention was now working *under* him.

The one person I'd love to pick the phone up and talk to now is Sarah. I almost try her number, but what am I going to say if she actually answers? *Hi, Sarah, I need someone to talk to because I've discovered that my husband is spending too much time with his ex?* I somehow doubt she'd be a sympathetic ear. Instead I reach for my laptop and open Facebook. I'm not friends on there with Cressida, but Oscar is, and it's a moment's work to hop on to her page from his. Much of it's set to private, aside from the few posts she wants the world to see, shots of her sophisticated lifestyle in Brussels. I click through until I find one of her in a group outside a bar, Oscar laughing beside her at the table.

Oh, Oscar.

10 June

Jack

Edinburgh in the sunshine is bloody cracking. I've been here for a little more than a year now and it's really starting to feel like home. I know the streets without asking for directions – well, most of them – and I've got muscles in my calves I never had before because the whole place seems to be built on one huge sodding mountain. When I first arrived I found the looming granite buildings austere, but perhaps it was more a reflection of my state of mind than the gothic architecture. I see the city now for what it is: vibrant, buzzing, welcoming. I'm still not keen on bagpipes though.

'Got you one in, Jack.' Lorne, my huge, bearded producer spots me and raises a pint glass towards me across the beer garden. We're having our team meeting in the pub, because that's the way we roll.

'No Verity today?' Haley, my assistant, raises her eyebrows at me as I flop down at the table.

'Nope,' I say. 'We've amicably parted ways.'

There's six of us round the table in all, and the others make an *oooooh* noise in unison. I flick them the Vs.

'Children.'

Haley tries to be grown-up, which is ironic given that she's the youngest member of the team.

'Sorry, didn't mean to pry.'

I shrug. 'You didn't.'

'Shit, man,' Lorne says, doleful. 'Sorry we took the piss.'

I shrug again. In truth, I'm not overly upset. It's been on the cards for a while; Verity has been getting more and more demanding in every sense of the word. She wanted more of everything than I have to give her: my time, my energy, my emotions. I don't think either of us will find the separation too hard to get past; she was constantly hung up on Sarah and Laurie anyway, always pushing me to say she's prettier, more successful, more fun than them. The competitiveness wearied me; it was more about being the best than being the best for me. I wasn't the best for her, either. Our interests were wildly different; I don't understand the rules of polo and I'm not especially keen on learning. I know that makes me sound like an ass; in truth I don't have it in me for a relationship right now, with Verity or anyone else.

I lift my pint. 'To freedom.'

Beside me, Lorne laughs and mutters something sarcastic about *Braveheart*.

25 June

Laurie

'Laurie . . .'

I've just been for a job interview, and I'm rewarding myself with a coffee in the sunshine outside a cafe in Borough Market when someone pauses beside my table.

It's her.

'Sarah.' I stand, shocked to see her unexpectedly, even more shocked that she's stopped to speak to me. 'How've you been?'

She nods. 'Yeah, you know. Same old same old. You?'

It's so painfully stilted, I could cry. 'I've just had an interview for a new job.'

'Oh.'

I want her to press me for the details, but she doesn't. 'Can you stay for coffee?'

She looks at my cup, deliberating. 'I can't, I'm expected somewhere.'

The joy of speaking to her is so searing, so absolute, that I want to hang on to the edge of her jacket to stop her from leaving. My disappointment must be written all over my face, because the smallest of smiles crosses her lips.

'Another time though, Lu, yes?'

I nod. 'Shall I call you?'

'Or I'll call you. Either way.'

She lifts her hand in farewell, and then melts into the bustle of the market crowd. A few seconds later, my phone buzzes.

Fingers crossed for the job. S x

I can't stop the gulp of tears. I was sickly nervous all morning about the interview for a job on the features desk of a glossy women's mag, and now I couldn't care less if I get it or not because I just got something far more precious. I think I might have got my best friend back – some small part of her, at least. I feel like chucking the coffee in the nearest plant pot and ordering a cocktail.

12 October

Laurie

'Happy birthday, dear Thomas,
  Happy birthday to you!'

We all clap, and the baby laughs like a contented loon.

'I can't believe he's one already,' I say, bouncing him on my hip as I've watched Anna do for most of the weekend. My sister-in-law is fully immersed in parenthood, never knowingly seen without a muslin cloth over her shoulder or the hip rest slung round her waist in readiness for Tom's chubby little behind to land on it. I'll give it to him: he's super-cute. All blond curls and pudge, with a couple of tiny white bottom teeth and peaches in his cheeks. For one so tiny, he's completely dominated the weekend; everything is geared around being compatible with a baby.

'He looks good on you, Laurie.'

'Don't say another word.' I shoot my mum a warning look.

She shrugs, laughing. 'I was just thinking . . .'

What everyone else is thinking, I think but don't say. When are we likely to hear the patter of tiny feet is pretty much the first thing most people ask us now that we're married, with the notable exception of Lucille, who probably falls to her knees beside her bed every night and prays that I'm barren. It's 2014 not 1420, I want to yell when yet another colleague asks me if we're thinking of kids. What if I want a career first?

Daryl puts his arm round my shoulders in welcome solidarity, and straight away the baby fusses to be handed over to his dad. 'Put it off for as long as possible, sis. Your life will never be the same again afterwards.'

I'm relieved that Oscar has already left for home, thus avoiding this entire conversation. He left the party early because he's flying out to Brussels tonight in readiness for a prolonged five-day stretch; they're in the middle of crucial takeover negotiations and he needs to be there to oversee things. I haven't allowed myself to quiz him over whether or not Cressida will be there for the duration too; he's promised me there's nothing for me to worry about where she's concerned and I'm choosing to wholeheartedly believe him. He was right after all – I knew that Cressida worked for the same company – I just didn't know they worked in such close proximity. But Oscar assures me that they didn't, right up until the week before Lucille visited me to crow about it. Thankfully, I'm not the jealous type, and he's never given me any reason to think he still harbours feelings for her. They have to work together – it happens. They have to work together in a different country – to be fair, that probably happens less often, but I trust Oscar, and that's that. So with him on his way to Brussels, I've decided to stay over with my folks until tomorrow afternoon. I'm trying my best to stick to my New Year's resolution where they're concerned, if not where Lucille is.

Is it terrible to say I feel slightly more relaxed since I waved him off? He's never anything but complimentary about my parents, yet still I always feel slightly awkward when we're all together, as if without me there'd just be three strangers in a room. I spent a chunk of our train journey pretending to sleep, when actually what I was doing was assembling a small selection of subjects I could bring up. Holidays, work (mine more than Oscar's, for obvious reasons), the new colour we're painting the bathroom, that kind of thing. I hadn't counted on baby Tom, of course. There's no conversational lulls with a baby around, so all in all it's been a pleasant family weekend. I find that I almost don't want to go back to London tomorrow, back to our lonely, quiet flat.

'Take this through to your dad, will you, love?' Mum rolls her eyes as she hands me a mug of tea. 'He's in the den watching football.'

Dad's an avid Aston Villa fan; if they're on screen he's watching it, even on his grandson's birthday, it would seem. I take the mug and escape down the hall, glad of an excuse to get out of the 'when will Laurie have a baby' conversation. The answer is when – and if – Laurie is ready.

'Dad?' I push the den door, startled when it won't open. It can't be locked; it doesn't even have a lock on it. I push again. There's something wedged behind it. 'Dad?' I call out again. My heart starts to race when he doesn't answer. Panicked, I shoulder the door, slopping tea on to Mum's new beige carpet, and this time it opens an inch or so. Then everything seems to stop, and I hear someone who sounds like me, but can't possibly be, yelling out for help again and again.

13 October

Laurie

'I've given her something to help her sleep, she's exhausted.'

I try to smile at the doctor when he comes downstairs but my face won't do it. 'Thank you.'

Dr Freeman lives across the street from my mum and dad, and over the years he's been in and out of our house for both social and medical reasons. Christmas parties, broken bones. He came the second Daryl banged on his front door yesterday, yelling for help, and he's here again now to see how things are.

'I'm so sorry, Laurie.' He squeezes my shoulder. 'If there's anything I can do, just pick up the phone, day or night.'

Daryl sees him out, and then we sit together at the dining table in our parents' too-quiet house. Anna has taken the baby home, and Oscar is stuck in Brussels until tomorrow afternoon at least. He feels desperate about it, but to be honest there isn't anything he, or anyone else, can do or say.

My dad died yesterday. Here one minute, and then gone, with no one at his side to hold his hand or kiss him goodbye. I'm plagued by the thought that we might have been able to do something to help if only we'd been with him. If Daryl or I had taken the time to watch the game with him like we used to as kids, even though neither of us are big into football. If Mum had made his tea ten minutes earlier. If, if, if. The ambulance crew who arrived and declared him dead tried their best to assure us otherwise, that it bore all the hallmarks of a massive heart attack and it would have taken him regardless. But what if he called out and no one heard him? Daryl pushes the tissues towards me and I realize I'm crying again. I don't think I've stopped today. Don't they say that human beings are seventy per cent water or something crazy like that? It must be true, because it's flooding from me like a tap left on in an abandoned house.

'We need to make funeral arrangements.' Daryl's voice is hollow.

'I don't know how,' I say.

He squeezes my hand until his knuckles are white. 'Me neither, but we'll sort it out, you and me. Mum needs us to do it.'

I nod, still seeping tears. He's right, of course; Mum is in bits, there's no way she's going to be able to do anything. I'll never forget as long as I live the sight of her scrabbling on her knees to get to Dad. She came running, panic-stricken, as soon as I yelled, as if some sixth sense had alerted her to the fact that the love of her life was in trouble. They've been together since they were fifteen years old. I can still hear it now: the sound of her screaming his name when she couldn't rouse him, the low wail of grief as the ambulance crew recorded the time of his death and gently moved her away from his body. And since then, nothing. She's barely talking, she won't eat, she hasn't slept. It's as if she's shut down, as if she can't be here now that he isn't. Dr Freeman said it's okay that she's reacted this way, that everyone reacts differently and to just give her time. But I don't honestly know if she'll ever get over this. If any of us will.

'We'll go tomorrow,' Daryl says. 'Anna will come and sit with Mum.'

'Okay.'

We fall back into silence in the immaculate, quiet room. This is the house where we grew up, and this is the room where we always ate dinner together, always in our same places round the table. Our family of five barely survived becoming a family of four after Ginny died; always an empty chair. I look towards my dad's empty chair now, crying again. I can't fathom how we can go on as a family of three. It's too few.

Jack

'Whoever you are, fuck off.'

They don't, so I fling my arm out of bed and grope around on the floor for my mobile. People know full well I work nights, they can bloody hear me on the radio, so God only knows why someone is insisting on calling me before lunchtime. My fingers close round my phone just as it stops; typical. I bring it up close to my face and squint at it, my head already back on the pillow. Missed call from Laurie. *Shit.* I eye Amanda's straight, naked back turned towards me and weigh up whether it's crass to call Laurie back while my girlfriend sleeps beside me. On balance, I think it probably is, so I click it off. It can't be that urgent.

'Who was it?'

Amanda turns to me, all honey skin and blue eyes and stiff nipples. We're still in the 'shag like rabbits' stage of our relationship, and the sight of her no-tan-lines body does freaky things to my brain.

'Cold call.'

I lean in and close my lips over one of her nipples, and behind me on the bedside table my phone rattles loudly to indicate a new message. Laurie doesn't call very often. We mostly email or chat on Facebook every now and then like civilized adults these days. If she's left a message, she must want something particular.

'Fuck, sorry.' I roll away and pick my phone up. 'I better just check it. Hold that thought.'

She watches me idly as I click to listen, and as the automated voice tells me I have one new message, she slides her hand under the sheet and down my stomach. Christ, she's good. I close my eyes, breathless as the message begins. I've pretty much forgotten who's called me.

'Hey, Jack. It's me. Laurie.' I want to tell Amanda to stop, because it suddenly feels all kinds of wrong listening to Laurie's quiet voice with another woman's hand wrapped round my cock. 'I wanted to talk to you. Hear your voice.' Christ, I feel as if I'm hallucinating. Even now I sometimes still dream about Laurie, and often the dreams go pretty much like this. She calls me, she wants me, she needs me. I'm rock hard.

'I'm sorry for calling when you're probably sleeping. It's just that my dad died yesterday. I thought you might be around.'

Somewhere in the middle of listening to that sentence

I realized she was crying and pushed Amanda away. I sit bolt upright in bed. *Laurie's dad's died.* Fucking hell, hang on, Lu. I stumble out of bed, dragging my jeans on as I stab the buttons on my mobile and mumble an apology at Amanda. I lock myself in the bathroom and sit on the closed loo so I can speak to Laurie without being overheard. She answers on the third ring.

'Lu, I just got your message.'

'Jack.'

She doesn't get beyond my name before she's sobbing too hard to get her words out, so I do the talking instead.

'Hey, hey, hey.' I speak as softly as I can. 'I know, sweetie, I know.' I wish with all of my heart that I could hold her. 'It's okay, Laurie, it's all right, sweetheart.' I close my eyes, because her grief is so raw it hurts me to hear it. 'I wish I was where you are,' I whisper. 'I'm wrapping my arms tight round you. Can you feel me, Lu?' The sound of Laurie crying is the worst thing in the world. 'I'm stroking your hair, and I'm holding you, and I'm telling you everything's going to be okay,' I say, quiet words as her sobs slow. 'I'm telling you that I've got you, and I'm here.'

'I wish you were,' she says after a while, ragged words.

'I could be. I'll get the next train.'

She sighs, her voice steadier at last. 'No, I'm okay, honestly I am. Daryl's here, and Mum, of course, and Oscar should be here tomorrow night.'

Oscar should be there right now, I think but don't say.

'I don't know what I'm supposed to do,' she says. 'I don't know what to do, Jack.'

'Lu, there isn't anything you can do. Believe me, I know.'

'I know you do,' she says softly.

'You don't need to rush or do anything at all today,' I tell her, because I remember those dark, difficult days all too well. 'It's going to be confusing, just do whatever you feel is right – don't beat yourself up for crying too much or for not crying when you think you should or for not knowing how to help your mum. Just be, Laurie. It's all you can do right now. Hang in there, okay? Wait for Oscar to come to do the official things, let him get in touch with the right people for you. Trust me, he'll be glad of a practical way to help.'

'Okay.' She sounds relieved, as if she just needs someone to walk through this with her. How I wish it could be me.

27 October

Laurie

'Alice at number three asked me to bring this in. Said she'll be at the church later.'

Aunt Susan, my mum's sister, hands me a large Victoria sponge. She's been staying for the last few days and has been an absolute rock; having her here has helped Mum get through the emotional meeting with the celebrant to talk about the funeral, to plan what she's going to wear and to realize that the world still has to keep turning without my dad in it. Aunt Susan lost her own husband, my uncle Bob, four years ago; she can empathize with Mum in a way that neither Daryl nor I am able to. We've lost our dad, but she's lost her soulmate, and today she has to face up to that fact at his funeral.

I go through to the kitchen with the cake stand in my hands just as Sarah appears at the back window, her hand poised to tap. Everyone comes round the back at Mum and Dad's, it's that kind of home. I flinch at the idea that one day soon I'll have to get used to calling it just Mum's. I can't stand the thought of her rattling around here on her own.

'Hey,' Sarah says when I unlock the door. And then, 'Wow,' when she takes in the spread of food across the kitchen counters. I doubt if the local M&S have much left on the shelves. Aunt Susan has ordered everything online, right down to napkins and disposable crockery.

'It can all just get swept into the bin at the end,' she told me, brisk as she clicked through the order screens. 'The last thing anyone feels like doing after a funeral is clearing up.'

Added to the half a dozen or so cakes that have appeared over the course of the morning from various neighbours and friends, it's a sure fact that no one will leave here hungry.

I was so glad to have someone who knew what they were doing take charge, though Oscar, Daryl and I made the basic arrangements with the funeral directors when Oscar arrived back from Brussels. Is there anything worse in the world than having to choose coffin options? Who really cares whether it's ash or pine, or if the handles are brass or silver? We fumbled our way through, and somehow whichever casket we selected is going to be here shortly bearing my lovely dad. It feels unreal, too cruel to possibly be true.

Sarah turns to me and puts her arm round my shoulders. 'Okay?'

I nod, blinking away the tears that are always just behind my lashes. I haven't told her that I called Jack first when it happened. But I tell myself that he's the only person I know who's lost a parent; I needed someone who knew what it felt like. But when it got to the end of the day and I found myself sitting alone in my childhood bedroom, all I wanted was to call my best friend. We've been texting and meeting up for coffee and cake every couple of weeks since that day in the market, wine sometimes too, slowly gluing our friendship back together. Within seconds of hearing her familiar voice, any last shreds of distance in our friendship disappeared. She arrived on the doorstep the next evening without being asked. And though she had to go back to London for a few days to work, she came back again yesterday in time for the funeral.

'I think so.' I shrug and give her a helpless look. 'There's nothing to do really, just wait.'

She hangs her coat over the back of one of the kitchen chairs and puts the kettle on. 'How's your mum?'

I shake my head, passing Sarah a couple of mugs. 'Coping, I guess.' It's the most positive word I can muster. She's coping. She wakes up and she goes to sleep, and in between she answers if someone speaks to her, but most of the time she just sits and looks a million miles away. I don't know what to say to her; it's like suddenly I'm the parent but I have no idea how to do it, how to comfort her.

'Perhaps today will be a turning point,' Sarah offers. She isn't the first person to say that, that sometimes the funeral is the point where it sinks in that someone has actually gone. It seems like after the funeral everyone else just gets on with their lives and you have to find a way to get on with yours.

'Maybe,' I say, uncertain how any of us will ever be able to do that. 'You look nice.'

Her low ponytail swishes as she glances down at her Jackie O-style black dress. 'Perk of the job,' she smiles. She's a regular face on the rolling news channel now, as she was always destined to be. We sit down at the kitchen table, coffees in hand. I add sugar to mine, watching the grains as they spiral into the liquid.

'This reminds me of Delancey Street,' she says.

Suddenly I'm hit by a pang of longing and regret. 'I wish we could go back.'

'I know, honey.'

'Sarah, I'm so sorry . . .' I find myself desperate to apologize, to get it all into the open. Because despite her being here, we still haven't said a word about our argument; about Jack.

'Let's not talk about that now. A lot of water has gone under the bridge since then.' She clasps my hand and squeezes.

But it sits between us, unresolved, as if we shrouded it in a dustsheet and repainted around it, and I know that one day we're going to have to take the sheet off and see what's left underneath.

'One day though,' I say.

'Yeah,' she says. 'Not today, but one day.'

Jack

'Beer?'

I'm grabbing a quiet five minutes on a bench next to the brook that runs across the bottom of Laurie's parents' rambling garden when Oscar finds me and hands me a beer.

'Thanks.' I look at him sideways as he sits down alongside me, elbows on his knees. 'Long day.'

He nods. 'Do you think she'll be all right?'

It's such an unexpected question that I have to ask him to qualify it. 'Laurie?'

'Yeah.' He drinks from whatever it is in his glass, whisky by the look of it. Over the years we've established that I'm the beer drinker and he's a single malt man. 'I don't know what I'm supposed to do or what to say to her.'

Is he asking for my advice? I dig deep, because even though he's never going to be someone I feel any affinity with, he cares about Laurie. We have that much in common.

'In my experience, she's tougher than she looks, but not so tough that she doesn't break sometimes.' I remember back to the day I saw her break, when I kissed her in a snowstorm. 'Ask her how she's feeling, don't let her bottle it up.'

'But I don't know what to say.'

'Nobody does, Oscar. But something, *anything*, is better than nothing.'

'You always seem to know what to say.' He sighs and shakes his head, thinking. 'That speech you made at our wedding, for example.' He pauses, watching me, and I think, oh fuck, because this isn't something he and I should ever talk about.

'What about it?' I look at him sharply.

He leans back and drapes his arm along the back of the bench. 'I'll level with you, Jack. I've sometimes wondered if your feelings for Laurie are entirely platonic.'

I laugh as I look away and drain the beer in one. 'Of all the days, you choose the day she buried her father to talk about this?'

'It's a simple enough question,' he says, reasonable as always. 'I'm asking you if you have feelings for my wife, Jack. And I think I've been patient long enough.'

A simple enough question? Patient long enough? I don't think he even realizes how patronizing he sounds. If this wasn't Laurie's dad's funeral, then this would probably be the day when Oscar and I finally stopped pretending to like each other. As it is, I dignify his simple enough question with a simple enough answer.

'Yes.'

'Beer?'

I look up at Sarah half an hour later. 'What are you people trying to do, get me drunk? First Oscar, now you.'

She looks upset. 'Sorry. I can leave you alone if you'd prefer?'

'No,' I sigh, accepting the beer from her outstretched hand. 'Sorry, Sar, that was rude. Sit down. Come and talk to me a while.'

She slides in next to me, warm in black fake fur. 'What's the matter?' she asks, sipping red wine. 'Beside the obvious.'

It takes me a moment to understand that by 'the obvious', she means the fact that we're at a wake.

'Just the obvious,' I say. 'It gets to me, makes me remember stuff I'd rather not think about, you know.'

'I do,' she says. 'You're probably the most qualified of all of us to talk to Laurie.'

I drop my arm round her shoulders and steal her warmth. 'I don't think it'll make it easier for her to hear I miss my dad every damn day.'

She leans into me. 'I'm sorry if I didn't ask you enough about him.'

'You don't need to be sorry for anything,' I say. 'You were marvellous and I was a shit.'

She laughs softly. 'Well, I'm glad we finally got that straight.'

'Damn straight.'

We sit in contemplative silence, the clink and hubbub of glasses coming from the house behind us, the low babble of the brook in front of us.

'Are you ever going to tell me what happened between you and Lu? Tell me I'm wrong if you like, but I'm pretty sure it wasn't a family emergency that kept you from her wedding.'

Her mouth twists as she considers my question. 'I don't think there's much point in dragging it all up. It's in the past.'

I don't push the point. 'Still with Luke?'

She can't keep the light from her eyes as she nods. She tries, but I see it.

'Is he good to you?'

She laughs under her breath. 'He definitely isn't a shit.'

'Good.'

'I think he might be my one hundred per cent.'

I look at her, so bright, so vibrant, and I feel nothing but love and gladness for her. It's proof enough that we did the right thing, even if it ripped our hearts out at the time. She takes my hand. 'He's asked me to go out to Australia with him.'

'To live?'

She swallows, nods, then kind of shrugs. 'It's a big decision.'

'I'll bet.' I can't imagine her leaving all she's worked for here to start again in Oz. 'Is he worth upheaving your whole life for?'

'If I have to choose between him and here, I'd choose him.'

Wow. 'I'm really happy for you, Sar.' It's true. I think of her now on the first day we met, and then again on that awful freezing night in Laurie and Oscar's garden, and on all of our days in between. We were each other's chrysalis love, we grew together until we couldn't grow together any more. 'Laurie tells me he flies search and rescue helicopters.'

She smiles, and it's the loveliest thing I've seen all day. 'Yes.'

'Proper fucking hero,' I mutter, but I sort of mean it. I clink my beer against her wine glass, and we drink to them.

'What about you and Amanda?'

I'm impressed she's remembered Amanda's name from the occasional texts we've swapped; it's taken me a while to work my way through to a woman I can stick with.

'I like her.'

'Like isn't much of a word,' she says.

'She's nice.'

'Jesus, Jack. Like? Nice? Just put her out of her misery and dump her already.'

I frown. 'Just because I'm not rushing in and pinning a gold star on her chest and awarding her full marks?'

'Yes.' She looks at me, incredulous. 'Or what's it all been for?'

What's it all been for? Her question renders me momentarily silent. 'I guess I'm trying to work out if people need to start out at one hundred per cent or if they can start at, I don't know, seventy, and work their way up.'

She shakes her head and sighs as if I ought to know the answer to that by now.

'If I ask you a question, do you promise to answer honestly?'

Jesus. It really is 'put Jack on the spot' day. I get the feeling she's going to ask me a question I'd rather not answer. 'Go on then.'

She opens her mouth to speak, and then closes it again as if she's deciding how to phrase it. 'If you'd met Laurie instead of me, do you think she might have been your one hundred per cent?'

'Whoa. Where the hell did that come from?'

'I heard about your speech at the wedding.'

Ah. That damn speech again. 'Someone had to step in, Sarah. I was just there.'

She nods, as if it's a perfectly reasonable answer. 'Way I heard it, you made every other woman in the room wish you were talking about her.'

I laugh softly. 'You know me. I can talk myself out of anything.'

'Not this time.' Her voice cracks; I can't look at her. 'You stupid, stupid man. I wish I'd known. I wish I'd realized. I think a small part of me did, but I just didn't want to. Why didn't you tell me?'

I could pretend not to understand what she means, but what would be the point? 'There would've been no use, Sar. And she's married now. She's happy. She stopped loving me years ago.'

'Did you love her?'

I don't know what to say to her. We sit side by side in silence. 'I don't know. Maybe for a second. I don't know. This isn't the movies, Sar.'

She sighs and leans against me.

'But what if it was? If Oscar left, what would you do?'

I press a kiss against her hair. Some things are best left unsaid. 'Let's go inside. It's too cold out here.'

We walk back towards the house hand in hand, then I make my excuses and head for the train station. It's obvious that my presence is only doing damage here; I need to go home. Perhaps while I'm on the long train ride back to Edinburgh, I can work out if seventy can ever become a hundred.

2015

New Year's Resolutions

I just read back over my resolutions from last year. I can't believe how much I took for granted: *spend more time with Mum and Dad*. How I wish I could write that again this year. I miss my dad with indescribable ferocity.

I'm not in the mood to make any new resolutions for the year ahead. Instead, I'm just going to try to concentrate on looking after what's really important. The people I love.

6 May

Laurie

'But, Oscar, you know how important tonight is.'

I can't keep the plaintive note from my voice. Oscar promised he'd come back a day early from Brussels this week to attend Sarah's leaving dinner. I so rarely impact on his travel plans; I'm well aware that his diary is full and difficult to rearrange, but I thought just this once he'd be able to do what I needed him to do.

'I know I did, and I wish there was something I could do, but my hands are tied,' he says. 'Brantman flew over this morning out of the blue, and between you and me I think there might be another promotion in the pipeline. How's it going to look if I duck out early to go to a party?'

I sigh. Brantman is Oscar's boss, the big cheese. 'I see. It's okay.' I don't especially see and it's not really okay, but there's nothing to achieve from arguing with him – I know he won't change his mind. The huge commitment Oscar puts in for the bank compromises our marriage in a million ways, and it isn't just any old party tonight. It's a farewell dinner; the night I have to hug my best friend in the world goodbye and wish her well with her new life on the other side of the globe.

'Maybe we could look at planning a trip out there to see her next year.' He casts around for something mollifying to say, even though we both know there's not even a chance of him taking a few weeks off to accommodate such a break, especially if this promotion happens. With the exception of our honeymoon, our holidays have been more like long weekends fitted around his working week in Belgium: a couple of days in Paris, a flying visit to Rome. On both occasions we've separated at the airport on Sunday evening and flown to different countries for work on Monday morning. Despite our best efforts to the contrary, our marriage is becoming exactly what we said it wouldn't be – part-time.

'I'll see you tomorrow night, then,' I say despondently.

'You will,' he says softly. 'Sorry, Laurie.'

He rings off with an 'I love you' before I can say anything else.

'I'm so glad you're here!' Sarah hugs me and twirls us round, laughing as she glances towards the hotel doors. 'Where's Oscar?'

'Brussels. Sorry, Sar, he got stuck.'

She frowns, and then it clears. 'No worries. You're here, that's the main thing.'

Our heels click against the marble floor as she leads me towards the bar. She's chosen to have a farewell dinner with friends tonight before she and Luke head over to Bath tomorrow to spend their final few days with her family. I still can't believe she's going to live in Australia. I feel as if I'm losing her all over again. I'm thrilled for her of course, but I couldn't help crying when she told me, and then crying again when I told Oscar at home later. I seem to have done a lot of crying lately.

'This is nice,' I say, trying to distract myself. I've not been to this hotel before; it's got that intimate boutique thing going on, all warm greys and chandeliers with tall vases of flowers everywhere. 'Very grown-up.'

She grins. 'I had to do it some time, Lu.'

'Moving across the world to be with the man you love certainly counts as grown-up in my book.'

She squeezes my hand. 'Mine too. I'm bloody terrified.'

'I don't know why,' I say. 'Australia's not going to know what's hit it.'

If there's one thing I know, it's that Sarah is going to rock it over there. She's already secured a job with one of the leading TV networks; all hail Australia's sparkling new showbiz correspondent.

Before we go through the glass doors into the bar, she catches hold of my hand to stop me.

'Listen, Lu, there's something I need to say.' We stand close together and she squeezes my fingers. 'I can't fly to the other side of the world without saying sorry for the way I was about . . . well, you know, everything.'

'Oh God, Sar, you don't need to apologize,' I say, choking back tears already. I don't think our argument is something we'll ever talk about without being emotional. 'Or maybe let me apologize too. I hated so much about what happened that day.'

She nods, her lip trembling. 'I said some horrible things to you. I didn't mean them. Missing your wedding day is the worst thing I've ever done.'

'I hurt you. I never wanted to, Sar.'

She dashes her hand over her eyes. 'I should have accepted your bracelet. It was the loveliest thing anyone has ever given me. I love you like a sister, Lu, you're my best friend in the entire bloody world.'

I'm wearing the bracelet right now, and I do exactly as I've planned to. I open the clasp and slip it off, then fasten it around her wrist. We both look at it and she grips my hand really tight.

'There,' I say, my voice shaky. 'It's where it belongs.'

'I'll always treasure it.' Her voice catches in her throat.

I smile through my tears. 'I know you will. Now come on.' I pull her into a hug. 'Dry your eyes. Tonight's supposed to be a happy night.'

We hang on tight to each other; it's an 'I'm sorry' hug, and an 'I love you' hug, and a 'what am I going to do without you' hug.

Luke pulls me into a headlock as soon as he spots me in the bar.

'*Now* we can start the party,' he says with a grin. 'She's been watching the door for you.'

He's adorable. Built like a rugby player, loud and full of sunshine, he only has eyes for Sarah. When she and Jack were together, I thought I saw love. And perhaps it *was* love, of sorts, but not of this sort, and certainly not on this scale. Sarah and Luke ooze love from their bones.

'Laurie.'

I turn as someone touches my arm.

'Jack! Sarah didn't know if you'd be able to make it.' Pleasure and relief wash through me at the unexpected sight of him.

He dips and kisses my cheek, his hand warm on my back. 'I wasn't sure we could come until this morning,' he says. 'It's really good to see you.'

We. I look at him, and for a few seconds we say nothing at all. Then he looks away, towards a woman in a cerise dress who's just appeared beside him with a couple of glasses of champagne in her hand. He smiles as he accepts one, slinging his arm loosely round her waist.

'Laurie, this is Amanda.'

'Oh,' I say, and then catch myself and overcompensate. 'Hi! It's good to meet you at last, I've heard so much about you!' I haven't really; Jack's mentioned her in passing in emails and I've seen her on his Facebook page, but somehow it hadn't quite prepared me for seeing them together in the flesh. She's quite beautiful, in a gilded blonde kind of way. Her chin-length flapper-girl waves look as if they've been set by one of those super-cool celebrity stylists, and she's wearing her dress with a black leather jacket and ankle boots. She's glamorous in an edgy way, and the watchful look in her blue eyes doesn't quite marry up with the warmth of her voice.

'Laurie,' she smiles, air-kissing me on both cheeks. 'We meet at last.'

I try not to overanalyse her words. *At last?* What does she mean by that? Her eyes linger on me, as if she wants to say something else.

We're saved from the need for further immediate conversation by Sarah clapping her hands and ushering us all through into the restaurant. There's fifteen or so of us, a mix of Sarah and Luke's friends and closest colleagues. I glance at the two circular tables and see Oscar's place card beside mine, with Jack on my other side, and then Amanda. I sigh and wonder if it's too late to mess around with the cards, because without Oscar to balance us out, this is going to be testing. I don't recognize any of the other names on the table. *Joy*.

'Looks like I bagged the best seat in the house,' Jack says with a grin, coming to stand beside me as he surveys the table.

My smile is so tight I wonder how my teeth don't ping out and bounce off the walls. I doubt there's enough wine in this hotel to make tonight bearable. I'm losing my best friend, my husband hasn't turned up, and now I'm to spend the next couple of hours making polite conversation with Jack's beautiful new girlfriend.

I take my seat and catch the waiter's eye as he circulates with the wine. I think we're going to be seeing a lot of each other tonight.

Jack

Bloody Oscar. The one time I actually wouldn't mind him being here and he can't be arsed to even be in the same country. Although from what I gather, he's practically emigrated of late. Poor Laurie, it must be pretty lonely for her.

'Great,' Amanda sighs as she scans the set menu card. I sigh inwardly too, because eating out with her is always a bit of a gamble. She's pescatarian and sugar-free, although the sugar in wine gets some kind of special pass because she says the alcohol neutralizes it. I'm pretty sure she's made that up right off the top of her head, something I routinely tease her about. Tonight, though, I really want us to make a good impression on everyone, which is tricky, because the starter is duck liver pâté and the main course is chicken, and it's my fault no one knows that my girlfriend doesn't eat either. Sarah sent an email a while ago asking if anyone was vegetarian and I never answered.

'I'll sort it,' I murmur.

She looks at me as the wine waiter fills up her glass. 'Don't worry about it, I'm sure they'll have other things.' She catches Laurie's eye. 'Pescatarian.' She chucks in an apologetic smile. 'I hate having to make a scene.'

I try to catch Laurie's attention, but she's studying her menu again.

'So what do you do, Mandy?'

I smart on her behalf; the Australian guy – I presume one of Luke's friends – seated across the table couldn't know it, but if there's one other thing Amanda's a bit of a stickler about it's not being called Mandy.

'Amanda,' she corrects him, smiling to soften it. 'I'm an actress.'

'Bonza!' The guy seems like he's already had one too many. 'Anything I'd have seen you in?'

This guy seems to have some kind of sixth sense for all the wrong questions. Amanda's doing pretty well; she's been in a couple of programmes local to Scotland and has a minor recurring role on a soap, but it's highly unlikely this guy's going to have heard of them.

'Amanda's on a soap up in Scotland,' I say.

'It's just a small part,' she amends, laughing.

The guy loses interest, and I lean in and speak quietly so only she can hear me. 'You okay? Sorry if it's a bit weird.'

She smiles gamely. 'Nothing I can't handle.'

She turns and strikes up polite conversation with the guy on her other side, leaving me and Laurie eating awkwardly next to each other. I'm not sure bringing Amanda today was my smartest move; she seems fine, but I'm starting to realize that I'm not.

'It's good,' Laurie says, gesturing towards the pâté with her knife.

I nod. 'How're things?'

She pushes her salad around the plate. 'Work's interesting. I'm covering women's health features mainly, so lots to learn.'

'I'll bet.'

'You?'

'Love it, yeah. Late nights, but I like that.'

Laurie lays down her cutlery. 'Edinburgh looks lovely from your photographs.'

'It is. You should come up sometime, I'll give you the guided tour.' I can feel Amanda stiffen slightly beside me, and on my other side Laurie looks uncertain. 'You and Oscar, I mean, obviously,' I add, to make it better. Then I make it worse again by tagging on, 'If he can take the time off.' What am I doing? Having the two of them visit is my idea of perfect hell.

I'm relieved when the waiting staff clear the plates and Laurie excuses herself from the table. I smile at the wine waitress to come and fill me up again. There's only one way to deal with this level of social horror.

Laurie

What an evening. Every time I get a couple of minutes with Sarah we set each other off crying, Oscar's a no-show and Jack's girlfriend is annoyingly nice, even if she is a pescatarian. I took myself to the ladies to give myself a stern talking to after our first course, and told my reflection that she's Jack's choice of partner, and he's my friend, so I need to try to be hers. In fact, it must have taken a lot of balls for her to come today. Since then I've asked her more about her job and Edinburgh, and she actually seems like an interesting person.

'Are you from London originally, Amanda?' I asked, because her cockney twang placed her as clearly as if she'd been wearing a pearly queen jacket.

'Through and through,' she grinned. 'Although you wouldn't know it when I'm on set. My character, Daisy, is as Scottish as heather and shortbread, hen.' She slipped seamlessly into a thick Scottish burr, convincing enough to make me laugh despite myself.

'Wow, that's really good,' I said.

'Practice makes perfect,' she said with a shrug. She went on to tell me about some of the auditions she's been on recently – I never realized it was such hard work to be an actress. Perhaps she'll be good for Jack. She clearly has an idea of what she wants, and isn't afraid to work hard to get it.

Up to today I hadn't really registered her as being all that important in Jack's life. But now that I've met her, I'm finding her harder to dismiss. Not that I want to; it's just a jolt to see him with someone like her. Someone who might actually be relevant to his future. It's just . . . I don't know. It's something I can't quite put into words; like I never imagined his life in Scotland becoming his life for ever. I want him to be happy, of course I do, it's just a bit of a surprise. That's the word. She's surprised me.

I smile at the pink-cheeked waitress who appears and places my main course down in front of me. 'Thank you, it looks delicious.'

Jack does the same, and while we wait for someone to appear with the salmon they're hastily preparing for Amanda, he nods across the room to the wine waitress to swing back his way.

Jack

I feel a bit bad for saying yes to dessert when Amanda is so tough on herself about being sugar-free, but it's some kind of chocolate-three-ways thing and I've had too much wine to summon the willpower to refuse. She excuses herself from the table for a breath of air, leaving me and Laurie to stuff our faces.

'Amanda seems nice,' she says.

I nod. 'She's a good girl.'

Laurie doesn't seem as impressed with her pudding as I am. She's eating around the edges, picking at it. 'You've been together for a while now, haven't you?'

'Six months or so.' It's probably a few more than that; I still haven't quite forgiven myself for listening to Laurie's distressed message about her dad with Amanda's hand around my cock. We met at a friend of a friend's engagement party – there tends to be an overlap between TV and radio, the circles are surprisingly small, especially in Edinburgh. She looked as if she wanted to be there as much as I did and we got talking, and one thing led to another. I wasn't expecting it to be anything more than casual, but somehow she seems to have become part of my life.

'Is it serious?'

I stop eating and look at Laurie. 'You sound like my mother.'

She rolls her eyes. 'I was only asking.'

'I like her a lot. She knows what she wants, and we have fun together.'

We lapse into silence, and I wash my pudding down with wine.

'How's married life?'

She pushes her dessert plate away half eaten and draws her wine glass towards her. 'Good. Frustrating sometimes with Oscar being away so much, but yeah.' She laughs lightly and shrugs. 'Sorry. Smug marrieds.'

'They'll be next,' I say to change the subject, nodding towards Sarah and Luke at the next table. Laurie follows my gaze, thoughtful.

'Do you ever regret not staying together?'

I don't have to think twice. 'God, no. Look at her. She can't keep the smile off her face. She never looked like that when she was with me.'

Laurie's eyes are still on Sarah. 'I just wish they'd stay here. I'm going to miss her so much.' She drains her glass. 'Where's the waitress? I need another.'

I think I might have had a glass too many. I'm not falling-down drunk, but I'm definitely not sober either. We moved into the function room a while back; there's a band on, playing the usual slightly too loud party covers. I reach up and adjust the small hearing aid I was fitted with when I finally got my act together and saw a specialist. I hadn't been in Scotland all that long; moving away was the right thing for my health, both physical and mental.

Amanda's disappeared off to take a call outside, and Laurie's dancing with Luke a few feet away. I say dancing, but it's closer to acrobatics; he's throwing her around until she's breathless with laughter.

'Hey, Fred Astaire,' I say, ambling over when the band finally change tack to something more mellow. 'I can see now why Sarah's so smitten.'

'That woman is my heart,' he says emphatically. I'm sure it's the several beers he's had, but his eyes definitely well up. I shake his hand; there will always be a strange link between us. He was the first person on the scene of my accident, and even though I can't recall events clearly, I have a memory of him crouching beside me. And now he's with Sarah, and it might have been odd but it isn't, because they're so obviously made for each other. I don't know him all that well, but it seems like he's solid gold.

'Take good care of her for us,' I say. 'Mind if I cut in?'

He twirls Laurie round one last time and dips her over his arm. 'She's all yours, mate.'

She raises her eyebrows at Luke. 'Do I get any say in this?'

He winks and kisses her cheek. 'Sorry, Laurie; I should go and check on the wife anyway.' He grins at me as he walks away.

Laurie stands in front of me. She's bright-eyed and flushed. She looks more like she used to, happy and carefree.

'Dance with me, Lu? For old times' sake?'

I don't know what to say, because I want to say yes. Or rather, a small part of me wants to. The greater, more sensible part of me knows that Jack is a place I shouldn't go. Especially when I've lost count of the glasses of wine I've drunk.

'Please?'

I glance around. 'Where's Amanda?'

He scrubs his hand over his hair and shrugs. 'She went outside to make a call.' He frowns. 'Or take a call. She won't mind.'

'Sure?'

He laughs, as if it's a stupid question. 'She's not a jealous psycho, Lu, she knows you're one of my oldest friends.'

I can't help smiling because his laugh has been missing from my life for so long. It's late and the lights are low, and his green-gold eyes are the same green-gold eyes I looked into one December night from the top deck of a bus on Camden High Street. It seems like a lifetime ago. For that girl, I can't say no.

'Okay.'

He draws me against him, one hand warm round my waist, the other holding mine.

'I can't believe she's actually leaving,' I say. 'It's too far away.'

'It'll be okay,' he says, quiet by my ear. 'Nowhere's that far away these days.'

'But I can't call Australia every day, and she'll be so busy.'

'Call me sometimes instead, then.' He rests his chin on the top of my head.

This isn't going to plan. I came here determined to be polite and civil to Jack if he was here tonight, nothing more and nothing less. Yet somehow I'm dancing with him, his hand rubbing up and down my spine, and time seems to have done something strange, because I'm not the Laurie I was a couple of hours ago. I'm the Laurie I was seven years ago. Oh, Oscar, why didn't you come?

'I remember you telling me once about the boy you danced with at the school disco,' he says, low laughter in his throat. 'Don't go and headbutt me.'

I lay my cheek against his chest. 'We've shared a lot over the years, haven't we?'

'Too much?'

I can't answer him honestly, because what I'd have to say is yes, too much. You take up too much of my heart and it's not fair on my husband.

'Did you tell Sarah that I kissed you? Is that why she wasn't at your wedding?'

I've always known he'd ask me this one day or another. There are very few good reasons why Sarah would miss my wedding, and he probably sussed that she didn't have any family emergency.

'Yes, but I didn't say you did it, just that it happened.' We turn slowly under the glittering low lights, pressed together from shoulder to hip. 'I couldn't lie to her face when she asked me.'

'I lost you for a while afterwards.' His breath warms my ear. 'I hated it.'

'Me too.'

He looks down at me, and then he lays his forehead against mine. There's no one else in this room any more for me. He's Jack O'Mara, and I'm Laurie James, and I close my eyes and remember us.

'Do you think we were always destined to know each other?' I say.

In my head I'm cresting the Ferris wheel with Jack beside me, our heads tipped back to look at the stars. Perhaps it's the wine, but my stomach flips slowly as he laughs quietly against my ear.

'I don't know if I believe in all that destiny stuff, Lu, but I'll always be glad you're in my life.'

He looks down into my eyes and his mouth is so close I can feel his breath on my lips. I ache.

'Me too,' I whisper. 'Even though being with you is hard on my heart sometimes.'

It's difficult to read the look in his eyes. Regret, maybe?

'Don't,' he says. 'Don't say any more.' He brushes my hair behind my ear, probably so I can hear him more clearly, but what it actually does is bring his lips heart-stoppingly close to my skin. 'We've both got too much to lose.'

'I know,' I say, and I do. God knows I do. I'm lonely so much of the time, but Oscar's continued absences are no justification for crossing lines that should never be crossed with a wedding ring on your hand.

'We're not kids any more,' Jack says, his thumb circling slowly on the base of my back. 'You're Oscar's wife. I watched you marry him, Laurie.'

I try to recapture the feeling of my wedding day, but all my treacherous heart can conjure up is Jack's speech.

'Do you ever think what if . . .' I stop, because his lips brush briefly against the skin beneath my ear as he bends his head to shush me. I'm shamed by the sharp twist of lust that stabs through me, all the way from my ear to the pit of my stomach. It takes my breath; I want him with a force that frightens me.

'Of course I've wondered what if,' he says, so low and intimate that his words slide straight into my veins. 'But we know what if, Lu. We tried it once before, remember? We kissed and it made everything worse for both of us.'

'Of course I remember,' I breathe. I'll remember to the day I die.

He adjusts our hands, his fingers warm around mine.

And then he looks down at me, and his eyes say all the things he cannot. His gaze holds mine as we dance slowly, and I silently tell him that I'll always carry him in my heart, and he silently tells me that in another place, another time, we'd have been pretty damn close to perfect.

'For what it's worth –' his hand slips into my hair and he strokes his thumb along my jaw – 'and because we're finally being honest with each other, you're just about my favourite person in the world, and it was the single most spectacular kiss of my whole life.'

I'm lost. Lost in his words, and his arms, and in what might have been.

'We could . . .' I start, but I don't say more, because we both know we can't.

'Don't,' he says. 'We're all where we should be.'

I start to cry; too much wine, too much emotion, too much of my life walking out the door tonight. He gathers me close and presses his lips to my ear.

'Don't cry,' he says. 'I love you, Laurie James.'

I look up, unsure how to read his words, and he looks away.

'Jack?'

I turn at the sound of Amanda's voice as she weaves towards us through the dancers.

'Okay?' She looks from Jack to me, eyebrows raised in enquiry, and I dash my hands across my wet cheeks.

'Sorry. Emotional wreck,' I gulp, shaky. 'Ignore me, it's the wine. I'm just upset about Sarah leaving.' I glance quickly at Jack, not quite meeting his eyes. 'Sorry about your damp shirt. Send me the dry-cleaning bill.'

Wearily, I let myself into the flat and strip off for bed. Considering the amount of wine I've had, I'm suddenly as sober as a judge. I've been over and over the things we said tonight, and I'm shamed by how easily the bedrock of my marriage crumbled under pressure. The truth is that I've walked around the edge of being in love with Jack for too many years. It's made me realize something inevitable, something that's been a long time coming: he and I would be better off without each other.

I need to unwind the roots of Jack O'Mara from my life. He's too much a part of who I am, and me a part of him. The problem with uprooting things is that sometimes it kills them altogether, but that's a risk I have to take. For the sake of my marriage; for the sake of all of us.

12 September

Laurie

'You're sure there's not some specific reason for this get-together?' I ask Oscar as the cab turns into Lucille's road.

Oscar frowns and shakes his head without answering. I'm not surprised; I've asked him the same question several times already since we were summoned a week ago for 'casual summer drinks' at his mother's. Lucille never has casual summer drinks. I'm glad Oscar's been able to clear his diary for his mother, even if he finds it difficult to do the same thing for me.

'Perhaps she's going to make a surprise announcement,' I suggest. 'Retiring to Spain?'

He rolls his eyes. It's selfish of me really; I of all people should be able to appreciate the fact that having your parents around is important. And, truth be told, she's not quite so overbearing these days. She's softened towards me a lot since Dad died. She'll never think I'm quite good enough for her precious youngest boy, but I don't think anyone could be.

'So who's going to be here?' I accept his hand as he helps me down on to the pavement and pays the driver.

'No clue.' He links his arm through mine as we walk towards Lucille's shiny black front door in the balmy evening sunshine. 'Family. A few friends. I think Mum's been feeling quite isolated since the op.'

Lucille had a knee operation in July, and although it was routine, she's had Oscar doing her bidding more than ever. It's uncharitable of me to think she's hamming it up to keep him concerned, but I think she's hamming it up to keep him concerned. I can say it inside my head, at least.

'You'll have to ring the bell,' I say, looking down at the expensive bunch of flowers I have in one hand and the fancy bottle of red in the other.

He obliges, and moments later Gerry swings the door open to let us in. I'm pleased to see him; he's the closest thing I've got to an ally amongst Oscar's family.

'People! Enter,' he booms, kissing me as I pass. 'Everyone's in the garden.'

Lucille has a gorgeous orangery on the back of her house, and we find it already full with neighbours, distant relations and her fellow ladies who lunch.

'Darlings, you're here!' Lucille appears, sailing across the room when she spots us. Oscar hugs her, and I hand the gifts over as she turns to me. It's a practised move, one I've perfected to get past the 'hello' moment; give someone flowers, no need for awkward air kisses. But Lucille only looks at them and smiles politely, then shoves them back towards me.

'Be a darling and go and pop them in some water in the kitchen, would you, dear?'

Darling? Dear? She may still be treating me like the kitchen maid, but these are new and encouraging words in her vocabulary as far as I'm concerned. We might actually be getting somewhere. Lucille makes a beeline for the garden with Oscar on her arm, leaving me to do as I've been asked.

*

I'm arranging the flowers in a vase I found under the sink when Cressida slinks in. *Fabulous. Thank you, Lucille.* I've somehow managed to never exchange more than a word or two with her; even at our wedding I got away with just thanking her for coming. Until now, I thought she was as keen to avoid contact as I was.

'Hello, Laurie, how nice to see you here.'

'It's lovely to see you again, Cressida,' I lie. 'How are you finding Brussels?'

Her dentist poster smile falters; I can only imagine that she wanted to drop her presence over there into conversation herself. 'Fantastic!' she gushes. 'I mean, we're busy, but we work hard, play hard, yah?'

'Yah,' I murmur. Why is it I always find myself imitating posh people? 'I can imagine.'

'Have you ever been to Brussels?'

I shake my head. You'd think I'd have been out there by now, but Oscar always says he prefers to come home. I turn to look around the kitchen for a likely spot to deposit the flowers. As I move to place them in the centre of the table, Cressida lunges.

'Not there. Lucille doesn't like flowers on the kitchen table.'

I smile and try to take the vase back but she clings to it and the water slops all over her floaty coral shirt. We both look down as the sodden material clings to her lean frame, and the look in her eye when she releases the vase and raises her face is unmistakable. The woman detests me.

'You did that on purpose.'

'What? No . . .' I almost laugh, shocked at her audacity.

'Everything okay?' Oscar appears in the doorway as if on cue, his eyes darting nervously between us.

'Just marvellous,' Cressida says. 'Your wife spilt water over me.' She gestures down at her drenched clothes. 'Accidentally, I'm sure.' She shoots me a magnanimous smile and looks at him under her lashes, theatre that suggests she's covering for my mean streak.

'What?' He looks at her wet shirt and then at the vase in my hands, perplexed. 'Why would you do that, Laurie?'

The fact that he didn't stop to wonder whether she was lying is a red flag; I file it away to think about later.

'I didn't,' I say, and she huffs imperceptibly and folds her arms lightly across her chest.

I'm trying to read between the lines to see what is really happening here. Something is clearly eating Cressida up from the inside out.

'I'm going to the bathroom to try and sort this out.' She turns on her heel and huffs off down the hallway, leaving us to stare at each other across the table.

I attempt to put the flowers down on it again, but he reaches out and takes them from me.

'Mum has a thing about flowers on the kitchen table. I'll find somewhere for them in the hall.'

We're finally home. All the way back in the cab we were furiously silent, and now we lie in bed, inches apart, both staring at the darkened ceiling.

'I'm sorry I believed Cress so easily,' Oscar says quietly, finally breaking through the wall of silence. 'I should have taken your side.'

Under the safety of darkness I roll my eyes at his shortening of her name.

'It surprised me,' I say. 'You know me well enough to know I don't go around throwing water over people.'

He pauses for a moment. 'She was soaked through. It sounded plausible for a second, that was all.'

It's my turn to pause. Why would he think it plausible for me to hurl water at Cressida? There's something here I'm missing. 'Is it?'

'Is it what?'

'Plausible. You said it sounded plausible that I might have thrown water over Cressida. Now, either you think I have the maturity of a sixteen-year-old and can't stand the idea of you being friends with your ex, which is categorically untrue by the way, or there's some other reason why you think I might have tossed water at her. So which is it?'

It might be dark, but I hear his sigh all the same.

'Three days a week is a long time, Laurie.'

I swallow. I don't know what I expected, but it wasn't that.

'What do you mean?' Since Sarah left for Australia, I've put all my energy into being the best wife ever. I could win awards. And now he's telling me what? That he's been shagging his ex all along?

'That I miss you when I'm there,' he says. 'And Cress is making it increasingly bloody obvious that she'd be happy for us to have an arrangement.'

'An *arrangement*? How frightfully fucking *Parisian*,' I say, almost laughing at the absurdity, aware that I'm on the edge of yelling. 'And do you *want* that arrangement?'

'I haven't done anything,' he says, heated. 'I swear I haven't, Laurie.'

'Do you want to?'

'No,' he says. 'Not really.'

'Not really? What does that mean?' I'm nearly yelling again.

He doesn't answer me, which is telling in itself. After a minute or two's silence, I speak again. I don't want to go to sleep on an argument, but I need to say this.

'Maybe it's time to ask about transferring back to London full-time. Brussels was only meant to be temporary.'

My suggestion sits between us in the dark. I know for a fact that he doesn't want to transfer back, that he's relishing the work out there. Is it unfair of me to even ask it of him? Or is it unfair of him to ask me to tolerate him working with someone who is blatantly making a play for him? And not just anyone, but his ex?

'Or maybe you'd rather me just lie here every time you're away from now on and wonder if this is the night Cressida's going to catch you at a weak moment?'

'That's never going to happen,' he says as if I'm being ludicrous.

'You said "not really",' I spit. 'I asked you if you wanted to, and you said "not really". It's not the same as "no", Oscar.'

'And it's a bloody long way from saying I'd ever do anything, either,' he says, riled. He so rarely shouts, it sounds harsher than it should in the quiet room.

We're both hurt now. 'We said that we wouldn't let our marriage suffer for this job,' I say, more softly.

He rolls on his side towards me, conciliatory. 'I don't want Cress, or anyone else but you, Laurie.'

I don't move. My jaw's so stiff it feels as if it's locked in place. 'We can't do this for ever, Oscar.'

'There might be opportunities in a few months to come back to the London office,' he says. 'I'll put the feelers out, okay? Trust me, Laurie, there's nothing I'd like more than not to have to kiss you goodbye on Sunday evening every week.'

I roll towards him, accepting his olive branch even though I'm not sure I absolutely believe him. Not just because of Cressida; he just seems more wedded to his job than to me sometimes. It's as if he's living two lives. One here with me as my husband and another that's separate from me: vibrant meetings and city bars, sharp dressers, clandestine deals and celebratory dinners. He shares pieces of it with me of course, snippets and the occasional photo message, but by and large I can't shake the feeling that he's content with this 'have his cake and eat it' lifestyle. He's a long way removed from my laid-back Thai lover; the painting on our bedroom wall seems more fantasy than memory. I sometimes think he married me as a way to try to hang on to the person he was back there in Koh Lipe; the more entrenched he becomes in his life in Brussels, the more he seems to realize that Thailand was only ever a temporary escape. His real life was always here, waiting in the wings for him to return and play his role. I'm just not sure I was ever cast in the same production.

'Look. We're married, Oscar, but that doesn't mean we can just flick a switch and reroute all of our romantic thoughts and feelings along one single track. Sometimes we get tested. Let's not be naive.'

We lie facing each other in the dark room.

'Have you been tested?'

I close my eyes for a second, then decide not to answer that. 'The important thing is the choices we make when we are tested. Being married isn't just a legally binding contract, it's a choice. It's saying I choose you. Every single day, I wake up and I choose you. I choose you, Oscar.'

'I choose you too,' he whispers, wrapping his arms round me. I hold him, and I feel as if we're wrapping our arms round our marriage; cradling this precious, fragile thing between our bodies.

But it feels like a tenuous pact, and I lie awake for a long time after he falls asleep, troubled.

Laurie

'Laurie.'

Oscar spoons round me in bed, waking me from strange mixed-up dreams that cling on even as I surface. The glowing red numbers on the bedside clock tell me it's half past five in the morning.

'Laurie.' He kisses my shoulder and slides his arms round me under the covers. 'Are you awake?'

'A little bit,' I whisper, still in that fuzzy space between sleep and wakefulness. 'It's early.'

'I know,' he says, his hand flat and warm over my stomach. 'Let's have a baby.'

I open my eyes wide at the unexpectedness of his words. 'Oscar . . .' I twist round until we're face to face, and he groans and kisses away anything I might have been about to say, hooking his leg over my thigh. Our sex is sudden and urgent, both of us still emotional from the tumultuous night before. We rowed again; or rather, we had words over dinner, as Oscar would probably phrase it. My fault – I asked him if he'd enquired any further about moving back to London full-time. It's fast becoming a taboo subject.

Afterwards, we sprawl in the tangled sheets, reconnected, choosing each other again for another new day. I don't know if he really meant it or not about the baby, but at least for now I know it's me he's thinking of.

2016

New Year's Resolutions

1) A baby! Yes, Oscar and I have decided that this is the year we're going to try. We've talked about it on and off for the last couple of months, and as of 1 January we've agreed I'm no longer going to take the pill. It feels like a huge leap into the unknown.

I don't think I need to make any other resolutions. That one is monumentally life-changing enough for one year, isn't it? Oscar has promised me that he'll talk to his boss again about moving back to the UK. We stand a much better chance of falling pregnant if he's home more, and when I do have a baby, it stands to reason that he's not going to want to be absent so much.

2) Oh, shit, I forgot. It pains me to write this, but there is another – I'm going on the wagon. It increases the odds of conception, apparently.

Laurie

'Did you definitely remember to take your folic acid every morning?'

I'm sitting on the edge of the bed, my mobile on speakerphone on the bedside table.

'Of course I did,' I say. 'But I doubt it's all down to whether or not I ingest enough nutrients. It's more to do with, you know, eggs and sperm meeting up at the right moment.' I'm sure Oscar didn't mean to make his question sound like an accusation; he's just disappointed.

He doesn't reply.

'Very few couples fall pregnant on the first cycle,' I say more seriously. I spend my days writing women's health features, and I've covered pregnancy-related issues dozens of times. If it were left up to me I'd just get on with life and try not to obsess over whether or not we were getting pregnant. But Oscar's results-driven nature seems to have taken over, and I don't quite know how to tell him to calm down without hurting his feelings. It's quite sweet, really.

'I know, I just thought maybe we'd ace it first time round, you know?' He sighs.

'I know. We'll just have to give it an extra effort next time you're back, hey?'

'You're right. I mean, it's not like it's a chore or anything. Let's book a whole night in, just you and me.'

23 February

Laurie

'Laurie, you've been in there a while.'

Oscar has actually delayed going to Brussels today to see if I'm pregnant. I'm not. I'm sitting on the loo holding a negative pregnancy test and trying to work out how to let him down gently.

'I'll be out in a sec,' I call, flushing the toilet.

He's loitering in the hallway waiting for me when I open the bathroom door. I shake my head, and he can't keep the disappointment from his eyes as he hugs me.

'Early days,' I say. Only two months in and the shine of trying to get pregnant has already well and truly worn off. Who knew it would be so stressful? I'd like it if we could just take our foot off the gas and relax, but it's not in Oscar's nature to be so laissez-faire. He's used to being able to make things happen; it's clearly a huge frustration to him that he can't dictate this so easily.

'Third time lucky.' He presses a kiss against my forehead and picks up his briefcase. 'See you in a few days, love.'

14 March

Jack

'Are you cold?'

Amanda looks at me as if I'm an idiot. 'We're in the Arctic, Jack.'

She's right of course, but we're also underneath several layers of fur hides and drinking rum. We've escaped to Norway for a few days and it genuinely feels as if we've landed in wonderland. I've never seen so much snow; we're currently watching it fall from the comfort of our huge bed beneath the glass dome of our igloo. If she'd had her way we'd have made a run for the sun, but we made a bet and she lost, so we're here scratching my itch to go aurora hunting. We've been unlucky so far; tonight's our final night here, so it's all or nothing.

'What's been your favourite thing so far?' I say, kissing Amanda's forehead. She's naked and nestled in the crook of my arm on the pillows, and she wrinkles her nose as she thinks.

'Probably the reindeer sleigh ride,' she says. 'Too romantic for words.'

'More romantic than this?' I say, my hand cupped possessively over her breast. '*Game of Thrones* has got nothing on us.'

'I thought . . .' She trails off and sighs heavily.

'What?' I say, taking her glass from her before I roll over and pin her beneath me.

'Nothing,' she says. 'Forget I said anything.'

'What is it?'

She looks to the side and kisses my shoulder. 'It's silly,' she says, pink-cheeked. 'I thought you might be bringing me here to propose.'

I hope my shock doesn't show on my face. I thought she'd been acting a bit weird this evening. 'You did? Shit, Amanda, I'm sorry. It's just that we've never really talked about, you know, marriage.' I don't know what to say. We've never talked about anything so serious – marriage just isn't in my head when it comes to us. When it comes to *anyone*, really. She's looking up at me, and I'm gazing down at her, and I know that what I say next matters.

'You're very lovely.'

Her smile is too small as she shakes her head. 'Shut up.'

I kiss her, because it's safer than trying to let her know how I feel with words, and then I nudge her knee wide with my own and watch her close her eyes as she lets go of her thoughts and gives in to her feelings instead.

Afterwards, she clings to me, her mouth on my neck.

'Look up,' she whispers. 'Look up, Jack.'

I slide from her body and lie beside her, and gasp. Above us the skies are flooded green and azure and purple, rolling swathes of glorious colour.

'It's breath-taking,' Amanda whispers.

We lie on our backs beneath the majesty, naked and spent, and I wonder what the fuck I'm waiting for.

23 March

Laurie

The third time isn't a charm in our case. My regular-as-clockwork period keeps me waiting until nine in the evening to bother showing up, by which time Oscar has called me five times and I've been to the loo at least fifty times. I ring him and we console each other, and then I break my no-drinking rule and pour myself a huge glass of red. I briefly consider calling Sian, my friend from the office. We sometimes grab a drink after work or go to the movies on the days Oscar's in Brussels, but the ins and outs of my monthly cycle feel too intimate to burden her with. I speak to Mum most days too, but obviously I haven't told her we're trying for a baby; if I tell her, it's someone else to let down. I don't think it would be nearly this disappointing if Oscar was here, but being apart gives everything this sense of urgency, of make or break.

Miserable, I take myself to bed with my laptop and lie propped up, flicking through all the fabulous things everyone but me is doing on Facebook. As predicted, Australia is all over Sarah like a rash. They can't get enough of her British accent or her sunshine smile. I reach out and touch the screen as I watch a video she's posted on her page of an interview she and Luke gave together on morning TV over there about Anglo-Aussie love matches. She's my Super Sarah: super-loved, super-successful, just super. God, I wish she was here. Our Monday-night Skype sessions are one of the highlights of my week, but it's not the same as having her actual shoulder to lean on.

I feel stupid for crying, and click from her page on to Jack's. Our friendship has effectively ended since the night of Sarah's farewell dinner. The furthest our friendship goes is me liking his photos on Facebook, and him occasionally commenting on mine. From what I see on his page it looks like he's on one long holiday with Amanda. From mine it must look like I have absolutely no social life at all. Just a long, blank post-less space. Perhaps I should unfriend him and be done with it.

Laurie

'Close your eyes!'

I'm in the kitchen making dinner (Tuna Niçoise) when Oscar comes home after his usual three-night run to Brussels. He sounds cheerful for once, and I feel a wave of relief crash through me. Things have grown progressively more tense between us; there's still no sign of Oscar's promised full-time return to London, and we've been trying for a baby for almost six months now without success. Not that that's so massively unusual, especially when you throw in the fact that we're sometimes in different countries at the optimum time for conception. Yes, I know all about these things now.

'Are you sure? I'm holding a kitchen knife,' I laugh, laying it down and doing as he's asked.

'You can open them again now.'

I do, and he's standing there with a bouquet so large he can barely see over the top of it.

'Should I be worried?' I smile, taking it from him.

He shakes his head. 'I'd have bought champagne, if we weren't off the hard stuff,' he says. He's been really good about the not-drinking thing, doing it too out of solidarity.

A knot of dread ties itself in my gut. It's four days until

my period is due or not due. It seems a bit premature to be celebrating.

'Ask me then,' he says, and I realize there's something else. I stop searching for a vase big enough to hold such a generous amount of roses and lay them down.

'What is it?' Already I'm second-guessing what he might be about to tell me. Could this be it? His Brussels run coming to an end? We can be a full-time couple again at last.

'Come and sit down,' he says, prolonging the moment as he takes my hand and leads me through to the sofa in the sitting room.

'You're making me nervous,' I say, half laughing, half worried.

He sits next to me, his body angled towards mine. 'Brantman turned up and called me in for a meeting this morning.'

I knew it! 'And?' I smile.

'You're looking at the bank's newest director!'

His face is wreathed in smiles like a child whose Christmases have all come at once. I catch the whiff of alcohol about him when I lean in and hug him – our drinking ban must have fallen by the wayside today.

'Wow, that's brilliant!' I say. 'And very deserved too, you work really hard for them. I'm glad they see that. Have they given you a date to move back to London?' I squeeze his hand.

'Well, it's not exactly less time in Brussels.' His smile falters. 'Or not at all, actually.'

I go still, filled with a sudden sense of foreboding that there's more to come and I'm not going to like it.

'I'm not leaving Brussels, Laurie,' he says, holding on to my hand. 'In fact, the job will be based there full-time.'

I stare at him, aware that I'm blinking too fast. 'I don't . . .'

He reaches for my other hand and looks at me imploringly. 'Don't say no straight away. I know it's out of the blue, but I've been thinking about this all day and it's the right thing for us to move out there, I'm sure of it. You, me and the baby too, soon. Brussels is a gorgeous city, Laurie, you'll love it, I promise.'

I stare at him, shell-shocked. 'But my job . . .'

He nods. 'I know, I know. But you'd have to give up work for the baby, anyway; this way you get to take your pregnancy off too.'

'Would I? What if I wanted to go back to work?' I don't know yet that I do, but how dare he just decide for me? How typically old school of him to assume that I'll be a stay-at-home mum. And how silly of me, I realize, to not have talked to him about this before.

He frowns, as if I'm throwing up unnecessary obstacles. 'Well, there are plenty of jobs out there too. But honestly, Laurie, I'll be earning so much you won't need to . . . Think about it, please,' he says, pressing on without giving me a chance to speak. 'You can drink coffee – well, mint tea – in the square, and wander by the river. We can get to know the city before he or she is born, it'll be like when we first met. There's loads of expats, you'd make tons of friends.'

I feel completely railroaded, and furious that I don't seem to hold any of the cards. I'm well aware that his earnings are more than enough to support a family, whereas mine are barely enough to support myself, but he seems to have made all of his assumptions without any thought for my wishes, as if my job is a hobby rather than a career. I don't know what to say or what to think. I'm truly glad for Oscar that his hard work and long hours are being recognized, but I don't want to leave my job or London or my life. It's not fair that his success should mean I lose so much I hold dear.

'Did you genuinely expect me to say yes just like that?' I say, incredulous. He's not a man given to thoughtlessness; I can only imagine that his excitement overrode his usual common sense.

'I expected you to consider it, at least,' he says, stung. 'You must know how much it means to me.'

'And I thought you knew how much my job means to me, too, how much I want to be around for my mum,' I shoot back. 'Isn't there a position they can offer you here in London? Why does it have to be in Brussels? It's unreasonable to ask it of you. Of us.'

'I think they see it as a reward rather than a penalty.' Petulance creeps into his voice as he sighs and shakes his head, impatient. 'Can't you see that too?'

I flick my eyes away from him, because he's making me feel like I'm being unreasonable and without good reason.

'Don't you think our families would miss us?' I change tack. 'Your mum would hate seeing so much less of you, and what happens when there's a baby in the mix too?' I can't keep the note of defiance from my voice. The more I think about it, the more annoyed I am by his flowers and celebrations approach. We're married, we need to make these decisions together, regardless of who the main earner is. 'I don't want to be in a different country to my mum when I have a baby, Oscar. She loves being a gran, I want her to be involved.'

We stare at each other, at an impasse. We never used to argue; now it's all we seem to do.

'It's not fair to just drop it on me like this and expect me to be thrilled,' I say. 'I need some time to think about it.'

He sets his jaw, his dark eyes full of consternation. 'I don't have more time. This is banking, Laurie, you know how fast things move. Brantman wants an answer on Monday morning, and the only possible answer I can give him is yes, because if I say no, then what's the fucking point of me working there at all?' He throws his hands up, a helpless gesture. 'My career at the bank will be done for; you don't last in a place like that by being complacent and unambitious.'

I shake my head, reeling at the injustice of being cast as the bad guy.

'I'm going to have a shower,' he says, jerking his chair back. He pauses for a moment, as if he expects me to offer an apology, and I sigh and look away until he leaves the room. It's becoming painfully clear that it's wishful thinking to believe Oscar ever hoped to stay true to the man I met on a beach in Thailand. Perhaps he didn't realize it himself back then, but this hectic commuter life of deals, dinners and boardrooms is exactly where he belongs. But more than that. It's where he wants to be.

13 June

Laurie

It's one minute past midnight, which means my period is one day late. Oscar left for Belgium on a particularly sour note yesterday, after spending the entire weekend trying to railroad me, which only made me dig my heels in more.

It's now officially Monday, and he's no doubt officially a director, and I'm officially late. I curl into a ball on my side and screw my eyes shut. I'm officially deeply lonely.

16 June

Laurie

'I've bought a pregnancy test.'

'Have you done it yet?' It's five in the evening here and two in the morning in Perth, but Sarah's wide awake. I'm an unheard of four days late now, and she was the first person I told.

I dump my keys and bag on the hall table, my mobile tucked under my ear. 'No. I'm too scared of what it might say.' What I don't tell her is that I think I'd be more scared if it were to say yes.

'Oscar's not home yet then?'

I sigh in the empty flat. 'He should be back in a couple of hours.'

'Hang on,' she says, muffled. I can hear her moving around, and then she's back and clear again. 'Sorry, just getting out of bed. Right, I have wine and I'm not going anywhere. Get the test out, Lu.'

'What, now?' My voice is unnaturally high.

'Yes, now. Or would you rather leave it until Oscar's home?'

She's right, of course. Given the way we are just now, it'd be much better if I do it with her and know for sure one way or the other before he comes in.

'Okay,' I whisper, shaking the test out of the chemist's paper bag.

I turn the box over and scan it, reading the by now familiar instructions aloud as I kick off my shoes and lock myself in the loo. Why, I don't know, seeing as I'm the only one home. 'I'm in the bathroom.'

'Good. Open the test.'

I struggle as always with the fiddly packaging, finally releasing the white plastic stick from its foil seal. 'There. Got it.'

I look at the stick and then at the loo, and then I sigh and get on with it.

'I can hear you peeing,' Sarah's voice floats out of my phone on the floor.

'Just be glad we're not on Facetime,' I mutter, wrangling the stick into the right place, managing to pee on my own fingers in the process. 'Why do they make these things so bloody difficult?'

'Don't drench it!' she shouts, unhelpfully.

I sigh as I extract the stick. Straight away I can see something happening in the windows, so I snap the lid on quick smart and put the stick on the edge of the sink.

'Start the clock,' I say, washing my hands.

'Done.'

I sit down on the floor and lean my back against the wall, my legs stretched in front of me, the phone against my ear again.

I close my eyes. 'Tell me something about your life there, Sar. Distract me.'

'Okay. Well, I'm at the kitchen table. It's supposed to be winter but we're having a heat wave, and our air-con is a lazy bastard. I'm mopping up my sweat as I talk to you.' I can almost see her; they live in a gorgeous low-slung beach house. She sent me the particulars when they went to view it and I needed to go and lie down in a dark room to get over my envy. It looks like something out of a seventies *House Beautiful* magazine, all sunken seating areas and double-height ceilings. She pauses, and then says, 'Oh, and I proposed to Luke.'

'What? Oh my God! Sarah!' I shriek, properly shocked. It's so Sarah not to wait around when she knows what she wants. 'When? What did you say? And what did he say?'

'He said yes, of course,' she laughs. 'And he cried like a baby.'

I laugh too. I can believe it; Luke's a big softie.

'Time's up, Lu,' she says, quiet and serious again. 'Three minutes.'

I hold the stick in my hands, the cap still in place. 'I'm scared, Sar,' I whisper.

'Don't be. Whatever happens, you'll be okay, I promise.'

I don't reply, just stare at the stick. I don't know if I can do this.

'For God's sake, Laurie, take the fucking cap off!'

So I do. I pull it off fast and hold my breath as I stare at it. 'Well?'

'One blue line.' I gasp down a huge lungful of air, shaking. 'Just one. That means I'm not pregnant, doesn't it?'

'Oh, Lu, I'm sorry,' she says, gentle now. 'It'll happen soon, I'm sure it will.'

I dash my hands across my eyes and put the stick down on the floor. 'Yeah, I know.'

*

When Oscar comes home just after eight, I'm in my pyjamas drinking a glass of wine at the kitchen table. He eyes the wine, then raises his eyebrows. 'Is that wise?'

The coolness to his tone suggests he's still in the same frame of mind as when he left on Sunday.

I shake my head. 'I thought I might be pregnant, but I'm not. I did a test. I must just be late, it happens.'

His expression softens as his eyes search mine. 'Are you okay?'

I'm not sure how to best answer his question truthfully. 'I don't think I am, no.'

I wait while he pours himself a glass of wine and sits down at the table. He looks done in; I wish I could just make him some dinner and offer to run him a bath, but my heart won't let me back out of the decisions I reached on the bathroom floor after Sarah rang off.

'Did you accept the job?'

He stares into his wine glass. 'You always knew I was going to.'

'Yes.' I nod slowly. 'It was the right thing for you.'

'But not for you?' he asks. He doesn't sound angry or cool any more. I think he's starting to realize that this conversation has the potential to devastate us both.

I sigh, and a tear slides down my face. 'No.' I swallow hard, hating everything about this situation. 'I've spent the last couple of days thinking I might be pregnant, and trying to work out what to do if I was.'

He watches me, silent.

'And then I did the test, and I wasn't pregnant, and all I could think was thank God. Thank God I haven't had all of my choices taken away from me.'

I've shocked him. I hate the words falling from my mouth, but honesty is all I have. 'I don't want to move to Belgium, Oscar.'

He's scanning my face, as if he's looking for traces of the woman he loves. He hadn't truly considered saying no to the job before this conversation, I realize. He's banked on me falling into step in the end.

'We can't love each other from different countries, and what happens if I do fall pregnant? I don't want to be here on my own with a baby five nights out of seven.'

'It could work.' He drags his chair round the table until his knees touch mine. 'I know it's not ideal but we can make it okay, Laurie.'

'Oscar, it isn't just about the job, it's about so much more than geography,' I say, being as gentle as I know how to be. I look at his beloved face, and I can't quite believe we're falling apart like this. He's been my safe harbour for a long time. 'God, you're such a lovely man. I've never met anyone like you and I know I never will again.'

'We made vows,' he says, frustrated. 'For better, for worse. We promised each other.'

'Our lives are headed in two different directions,' I say, holding his hands in mine. 'Yours is leading you along a path I can't follow, Oscar. And that isn't your fault or mine.'

'But I love you,' he says, as if it's a magic phrase that trumps any other.

I don't know how to express myself without hurting him more. 'Oscar, you're the best husband anyone could wish for. You're kind and you're funny and you've given me so much more than I can ever give you back.'

'I never expected you to.'

'No. But you *do* expect me to move to Belgium, or else live here on my own most of the time,' I say.

Consternation furrows his brow. 'I hoped you'd realize it's for the best,' he says. 'I thought I'd come home tonight and you'd have come round.'

I sigh, because I know he hasn't even entertained the idea of saying no to the job. It's a done deal, and all of the decisions are now mine.

'I'm not going to come round,' I say. 'I'm not just being obstinate. I don't want to move to Brussels.'

'But you know that turning the job down isn't an option for me,' he says, and a part of me is glad. I don't want him to offer to give up the promotion he's earned. Not that he's offering, and in a way that makes the next thing I need to say a little easier.

'I didn't realize how unhappy I've become until I looked at that blue line,' I say, bereft. 'I didn't know.'

He's got his face in his hands, and I feel like the most stupid, wretched, ungrateful woman in the world.

'So that's it? You won't come and I can't stay?'

'Or I can't come and you won't stay,' I say, challenging his blinkered viewpoint even though I know he'll never try to see it my way. His life is firmly on track and that track now leads to Brussels, with or without me. He finds it utterly unfathomable that I'm not cock-a-hoop to jump aboard the train, and it serves only to make me even more certain that we've come to the end of the line. No more living life at half-mast; the lights have gone out on our marriage. Back in Koh Lipe, our love blossomed beneath a string of flickering fairy lights wrapped around the railings of the beach shack. Here in London, the life has been slowly choked out of it under the glare of Lucille's oh-so-sophisticated lamps and the relentless weekly monotony of Heathrow's runway lights. I realize now that Oscar hasn't changed at all. He was always this man, but Thailand, and me, for a while maybe, made him feel like he could be someone else. He tried a different life on for size, but in the end he's gone full circle, because *this* life, the one he's living right now, is the one that fits him best.

'I'm so sorry, Oscar, I really am.'

'Me too,' he whispers. 'I'm sorry too, Starfish.'

I look away, upset because I know that's the last time I'll ever hear him call me that.

A sigh racks his body, as if it's wrenched from him. 'If you'd been pregnant, do you think you might have come with me?'

I genuinely don't know what to tell him. Perhaps that I'd have felt trapped into it and forced to give it a go. I don't say it; it's too bleak.

I lean forward and hold his head in my hands, my lips pressed to his hair. He wraps his arms round me too, and the familiar smell of him makes me cry uncontrollably; the cologne he's always worn, the shampoo he uses, the scent of his days and my nights and our love.

2 July

Jack

I follow Amanda silently through her apartment; I say silently because I've just removed my Converse – this is a strictly no-outdoor-shoes kind of place. There's even a trite sign and rack just inside the front door in case you forget. I don't mind, exactly. No, that's a lie. It gets right up my nose; I find it pompous when people insist you take off your shoes. It's not an Amanda-centric complaint though. It sets my teeth on edge whoever does it.

'You cooked?'

We're in her sleek white kitchen, which as a general rule sees very little in the way of food preparation. Amanda has many wonderful points, but her cooking skills aren't legendary. She freely admits it: she's a master of the micro-wave, a mistress of sushi home delivery and the queen of the Edinburgh restaurant scene – so why would she want to peel onions herself?

'I have,' she says, opening the fridge to pour me a glass of white.

'Should I be scared?'

She arches her eyebrows at me. 'You should be terribly complimentary and grateful, Jack. I've burned my finger for you.'

I watch her as she moves around the kitchen, holding

378

the pre-prepared pack of green beans at arm's length so she can read the microwave instructions on the back.

'What's on the menu?'

I don't know why I've asked, because I know the answer is fish.

'Cod,' she says. 'I'm baking it with lemon and parsley.'

'Did you blow the dust off the oven before you used it?'

She rolls her eyes at me and I laugh.

'I'm only looking out for you, it's a fire hazard.'

'Complimentary and grateful,' she reminds me, and I get up and take the green beans from her.

'Complimentary, huh?' I kiss her bare shoulder. She's wearing a strapless sundress with an apron over the top. 'You look sexy in a pinny.'

'The food, Jack,' she says, turning her face to mine.

'Okay. I'm grateful that you've cooked for me.' I kiss her briefly. 'And I'm grateful that you look like a blonde Swedish princess while you do it. I fancy thee rotten, Princess Amanda of Ikea.'

She turns into my arms and kisses me properly, her tongue in my mouth.

'That was most unladylike,' I say when she's finished, pulling on the ties of her apron until she slaps my hand away.

'Make yourself useful,' she says. 'Go and lay the table out on the balcony.'

The table looks holiday-brochure perfect on Amanda's holiday-brochure-perfect balcony. It's typical of her mind-set; Grassmarket commands the best views of the castle in the city, so she made sure she rented here.

I'm about to head back inside when my phone buzzes. I glance at it, hoping it's not Lorne calling me in to cover for someone. I'm in luck; Sarah's name flashes up. I click on the message, and lean on the balcony railings to read it.

Have you spoken to Laurie recently?

Well, that's fucking cryptic. I check my watch. Surely it's the middle of the night where she is? Probably pissed up at a beach party. I text back.

Not in a while. Go to bed!

Grassmarket reels out down below, bright and thronged with Saturday-night party people. My mobile buzzes again.

Call her, Jack. She and Oscar split up a couple of weeks ago, I wasn't meant to tell you, but she needs her friends. I'm too far away to be any bloody use!

I stare at the screen, reading and rereading Sarah's message as I slide down hard on to one of Amanda's outdoor dining chairs.

Laurie and Oscar have split up. How can that be? I watched her marry him. She stood there in that church and told me and the rest of the world that he was the man she wanted to spend her life with.

What the hell happened? I send back, wondering if I've got time to call Sarah before dinner.

Stuff. Talk to her. It's complicated.

Frustration rattles through me; Sarah's words tell me nothing. Why's she being so vague? Complicated? I'll tell you what's complicated. Standing on your girlfriend's balcony reading a message from your ex about someone else you once kissed.

'Jack?' Amanda's voice jolts me. 'Can you fetch this please?'

I stare at my phone, my head full of questions, and then I make a snap decision and turn it off. *This* is my life now. I've got something here; my show is gaining fans, I care about the people I work with, and Amanda is ... she's everything any man could want.

I shove my phone in my pocket and go inside.

3 July

Jack

I stare at Sarah's message again now I'm home. I've known for a whole night and day that Laurie's in trouble and I haven't been in touch. I don't know if that makes me a good boyfriend or a shit friend.

I keep tossing it backwards and forwards, trying to decide the right thing to do. What's right for me might not be right for Laurie, and not right for Amanda either. I don't want to fuck up.

I look at the open screen. I've typed and deleted a message twice already. The first one, Hey, Lu, how's tricks? was too cheery and out of the blue, and my second attempt, I'm always here if you need me was too intense. My fingers hover over the buttons, and then I try again.

Hey, Lu, Sarah told me your news. Can I call you?

I press send before I can deliberate, and then fling my phone down and grab a beer from the kitchen.

It's half an hour before she replies. My heart does its old familiar flip at the sight of her name on the screen.

Would you mind not? I'm not really feeling ready to talk to people yet.
Thanks though. I'll call you when I can. Sorry. X

Christ. I've been relegated to *people*, outside of her most trusted circle. I slump and close my eyes, wondering if there will ever be a time when it feels like all the pieces of my life are in the right place.

Laurie

Only a rookie singleton would book a package holiday to Majorca at half-term. Rather than finding myself barefoot on deserted beaches I've become an unpaid nanny for a bunch of badly behaved children whose parents are too exhausted or lazy to watch them themselves. I daren't make eye contact with anyone else, in case they ask me to just keep a five-minute eye on little Astrid or Toby or Boden. No, I don't want to hold their child. I don't want to hear about school fees or food allergies. And I definitely don't want to admit that, yes, I have a husband (technically), but no, he isn't here on holiday with me. Anyone would think I'd sprouted a third eye or something. The only safe place seems to be the hotel bar.

'Mind if I sit here?'

I look at the woman hovering close to the empty stool beside me at the bar. She's older than I am, mid-forties at a guess, and she has that well-put-together look, from her perfectly applied coral lipstick to her diamond tennis bracelet.

'Be my guest,' I say, wishing I'd just gone up to my room to read after dinner.

She orders a glass of wine, then looks at me and my almost-empty glass.

'Another?'

The hotel is all-inclusive, so this is hardly the offer of the century. I smile. 'Why not. I'll have the most ridiculous cocktail on the list, please.'

My new neighbour looks at me with fresh appreciation. 'Scrap the wine. I'll have what she's having.'

The bartender nods, as if this is all pretty standard. It probably is.

'Vanessa,' she says, even though I didn't ask her name. Her accent places her up north. Newcastle, I think.

'Laurie.'

'On your own?'

Reflexively, I twist my wedding ring round on my finger. 'Yes.'

We break off as the bartender places two tall, lurid blue and green cocktails in front of us. My neighbour looks at them, then shakes her head sadly. 'They're missing something.'

I put my head on one side. 'I think you're right. They need pimping up.'

The bartender turns away with a sigh, and returns with cocktail umbrellas and straws adorned with wrap-around parrots, rather like those paper Christmas decorations that concertina round themselves to make a bell. Only these are, well, parrots.

'Now that's more like it,' I say, once he's shoved so many accessories into our glasses that there's hardly any room to take a drink.

'What do you reckon it's called?' my drinking partner asks.

We stare at the drinks.

'Sex on the parrot-infested beach?' I suggest.

She considers my suggestion, then wrinkles her nose. 'Not bad. Although I'd probably have gone for something more along the lines of, "Don't ask me for sex, I'm not over my ex".'

I look at her properly then, and I notice she's also wearing a wedding ring that she keeps twisting round on her finger too. It's like a secret signal no one teaches you to read.

'Ten years married. He left me nine months ago,' she says glumly. 'For the woman who lives three doors down.'

'Does she still live three doors down?' I ask, interested despite myself.

'Aye, with my husband.'

'God.'

'Apparently they bonded over the community garden.'

We start to laugh at the absurdity of it.

'He said their eyes met over the compost heap and that was that.'

We laugh so hard that tears roll down my face, and she pats my hand.

'How long for you?'

I swallow. 'Five months. My choice though. We weren't married all that long.'

I don't add how shell-shocked we both are or how horrified my mother-in-law was. The only thing worse than my marrying Oscar is my divorcing him. My own mum's at a bit of a loss; she keeps sending me texts to see if I've eaten breakfast, but whenever I try to talk properly to her she doesn't seem to know what to say.

I've been renting a colleague's spare room for the last

few months; Oscar tried to insist I stay on in the flat, but there was no way I could.

'Not because of anyone else,' I add. 'It just didn't work out.'

We pick up our drinks and do our worst. 'Fucking awful,' she says as we slam them down. I'm not sure if she means the drink or our predicament. She splays her left hand flat on the bar and pokes her wedding ring with the end of a straw. 'Time to take it off, really.'

I do the same, placing my hand alongside hers on the bar. 'Me too.'

We stare at our fingers, and then she looks at me. 'Ready?'

'I don't know.'

'Are you ever going back to him?'

Not long after we separated, I wavered late one night and called Oscar in Brussels. I don't even know what I wanted to say, I was just overwhelmingly sad without him. Perhaps it's as well that Cressida answered his phone in a loud bar; I hung up and he didn't call back. I don't need a crystal ball to know that, in time, she will be the one who picks up his broken heart and pieces it back together. It's as it should be; perhaps she's always held on to a piece of it anyway. I'm embarrassed by how often I publicly cried in the aftermath of our marriage break-up. I cried silently on the bus going to work and again on the way home to my empty bed. Sometimes I didn't even realize tears were rolling down my cheeks until I caught sight of my reflection in the dark bus windows. I recognize it now for what it was: a grieving process – for him, and for me, and for us.

I shake my head at Vanessa, downcast. No, I'm never going back to Oscar.

'Then you're ready. We both are,' she says.

My ring hasn't left my finger since Oscar placed it there on our wedding day. I can't imagine ever feeling ready to take it off, but this bizarre moment has presented itself to me, and I can't wear the ring for ever. I nod, then feel sick.

She reaches for her wedding band, pausing to look pointedly at mine.

I take a big swig of my disgusting cocktail. 'Let's get it over with.'

We watch each other and keep pace, turning our rings a couple of times to free them. Mine's looser than usual anyway; my appetite has disappeared of late. The diamond-set ring slides up over my knuckle and I take it off slowly, because once it's off I can never put it back on again. Tears prick my eyes, and beside me Vanessa slips her ring all the way off and lays it on the bar.

I take her bravery for my own and follow suit, my mouth trembling. I can't hide a sob, and she puts an arm of solidarity round my shoulders as we sit side by side and stare at the two wedding bands.

I've cried more tears than I ever thought possible over the last year. Perhaps it's time to dry my eyes.

17 December

Jack

Amanda's angling for a ring for Christmas. She's dropped every hint in the book, from leaving magazines open on the pertinent pages to studiously watching *Don't Tell the Bride* every Thursday, and now we're walking through town on the coldest Saturday afternoon of the year and she's stopped to gaze into a jeweller's window.

It's become a difficult subject since she first mooted the idea of marriage in Norway, and I'm not really sure how to address it.

Now she's pointing out one with a massive diamond – fuck, is that really the price! It looks like a weapon, not a piece of jewellery.

'Shall we go and get drunk?' I say, looking at the pub across the road.

She frowns. 'Is the thought of marrying me so bad you need a drink?'

'No, but shopping is,' I say, and hate myself when she looks wounded. I don't look directly at the rings, because I don't want to have this conversation today.

'Okay,' she sighs. 'Beer it is.'

*

'Another?'

I should say no. We've been in here for three hours now and we're really quite pissed.

'Go on,' Amanda says. 'You said you wanted to get drunk.'

Maybe I'm getting too old for this game, but I've had enough.

'Let's go home instead,' I say, swaying a bit as I stand up.

'*We* don't have a home,' she says. 'It's your flat or mine.'

'You sound sexy when you put it like that.'

She doesn't get up. She folds her arms across her silvery metallic jumper and crosses her long, denim-clad legs, a dangerous glitter in her vodka-bold eyes.

'Propose to me.'

I blink a few times to focus. 'Amanda . . .'

'Go on. Do it now, I'm ready.'

Clearly those diamonds are still on her mind. She's laughing as if she's larking around, but there's a steely edge to her voice that warns me of incoming trouble.

'Come on,' I wheedle. 'Let's get out of here.' I'm aware that the couple at the next table overheard her and are trying not to make it obvious that they're watching. She's a vaguely recognizable face from TV; the last thing either of us need is a public row.

'You said that to me the very first time I met you,' she says. 'At that party. *Let's get out of here.*'

I nod, remembering. 'I did say that.' I sit back down on the stool, my elbows on my knees as I lean in to make our conversation more private. I'm struggling to hear her properly in here.

'No, *I* did,' Amanda says, contradicting herself. 'I did as you asked, and I've been doing whatever you ask ever since. And now I'm asking *you* to ask *me* something instead.' She frowns, tripping up over her confusing speech.

'That's a lot of asking for one woman.' I smile, going for light-hearted, aware I'm probably grimacing more than smiling.

'Ask me now or we're done.' She's not going to let it go, and I'm feeling increasingly backed into a corner.

'Don't be daft.'

'I'm deadly fucking serious, Jack,' she says, too sharp, and I fall quiet because it's clear that I'm not going to cajole her out of this pub. 'Last Christmas' starts up on the jukebox and Amanda's mouth twists at the irony.

'This isn't the place,' I say, my hand on her knee.

'Probably not,' she says, shaking me off. 'But then there isn't a good place to propose to someone you don't love, is there?'

Fucking hell. 'Please . . .' I start, not even knowing what I'm going to say next. This isn't going to be okay.

'Oh, please yourself, you usually do. You know what, Jack? Forget it.' She's angry now, tears on her lashes. 'Forget the whole fucking thing. I'm done with waiting for you to decide if you'll ever love me enough.' A tear runs down her cheek and she dashes it away. She stands up, wobbling on her high boots. 'This is officially the last time you get to say no to me.'

I wish we hadn't had a drink. She's saying things, I'm saying things, and they're the kind of things that stay unspoken for a reason. I stand, picking up our coats. 'Come on,' I say, because all I want is to get out of here.

'No.' She lays her hand flat on the centre of my chest. It's not a loving gesture; it's a 'stay there'. 'I'm leaving and you're not. I'm leaving you because you don't deserve me. Because I won't be your girl in reserve any more. Because you can't love someone if you're already in love with someone else.'

We stare at each other, knowing there's no coming back from this. I feel winded. Is that what I've done to her?

'I'm sorry,' I say. 'I –' I stop, because she's already turned away and is pushing a path through the busy Christmas drinking crowd.

I sit back down again with my head in my hands, and a few minutes later the bloke from the next table lays a whisky down in front of me.

I nod, try to say thanks, but the words clog in my throat. Someone puts 'Lonely This Christmas' on the jukebox, and I close my eyes and feel like a fool for a million different reasons.

2017

New Year's Resolutions

My life feels so far removed from the person I was twelve months ago; I can barely stand to look at those hopeful resolutions of last year. Where would I be now if Oscar and I had fallen pregnant on our first or second attempt? Pushing a stroller around Brussels? Would I have been happy? It feels too far away from the reality of my life to visualize.

Anyway, enough looking back. It's time to look forward.

1) I need to sort out my living accommodation. I'm thirty this summer – too old to be renting someone's spare room.

2) Work. I don't mind my job, but it feels stale. It covers the bills, just, but I don't think that's enough any more. I'm treading water. In fact, that's how I'd sum up my whole life right now. It's strange – you'd think that in the upheaval of separation, the stability of work would be welcome. It's actually had the opposite effect; it's made me want to throw all my cards up in the air and see where they land. I'm treading water, but what I want is to swim.

There. That's my resolution for the year ahead in one word.

3) Swim.

Jack

'Happy birthday.'

Martique (I know, it's a stage name; she won't answer to her actual name, which is Tara – I saw her passport) has just strolled into my apartment on heels higher than some people's kneecaps, and now she's unbuttoning her dress.

'I didn't know what to get you, so I bought myself some new underwear instead.'

Her dress pools around her ankles and she dips one knee, her hand on her hip. She's filthy hot and she knows it. She reminds me of a young Sophia Loren; all delicious curves and smoky eyes. 'Well?' she pouts. 'Do you like it, Jack?'

No red-blooded man could resist. She's a temptress; I wouldn't be surprised if she produced an apple out of nowhere and asked me if I'd like a bite.

'I like it,' I say, crossing the room.

'Then show me.'

Her perfume is pure bordello, sending a message straight to my groin, and her mouth tastes of lipstick and one of the ten million cigarettes she smokes a day. Her teeth are tugging on my bottom lip, her hands working my jeans open. We've been doing this on and off for a few weeks now. It's an arrangement that suits us both. She's on the way up, one of the many starlet singers who pass through the radio station. I'm her ideal man, she told me when we first met. By that, I know she means I'm her ideal step up on the route to stardom, someone slightly less good-looking than her who she can shag without any emotional complications and no fear of exposure.

I don't think we even like each other very much; my personal life has hit the buffers. Even as she steps out of her underwear, I'm thinking that this is going to be the last time.

We sink on to the sofa, her astride me, and as we fuck I admire the way even the mess of smeared lipstick somehow looks sexy on her. She leans in, saying all the right words in the right order, and I close my eyes and try not to feel bad.

'Happy birthday,' she murmurs when we're done, biting my earlobe before she climbs off me and checks her phone. 'There's somewhere I need to be.'

I watch her get dressed, my jeans round my ankles. I rub my ear, checking if she's drawn blood. I'm not sorry she's leaving.

Later, at the station, I pick up a text from Sarah and Luke, who bizarrely has turned out to be one of my favourite Aussies – not that I know that many. He likes a beer and he loves Sarah in a clear and uncomplicated way that he doesn't even try to hide. They've sent me a picture of them holding up a 'Happy Birthday Jack' sign, both of them pissing about laughing. They're on a beach and the words have come out backwards, which only seems to have amused them more. It amuses me too, and I send them back a quick Thank you, you pair of idiots.

Laurie has texted too. All her message says is Happy Birthday x. It's so brief that there's nothing to read into it. All the same, I study it, wondering if she puts a kiss at the end of every text she sends.

That's when I decide. I don't want to be the type of person who shags the type of person like Martique. I want what Sarah and Luke have. I may not be worthy of someone as good as Laurie, but I want to try to be that person.

I read her message over one last time, and then reply.

Thanks x

Laurie

'You live in paradise.'

Sarah and I are sitting outside a cafe overlooking the impossibly white sands of Cottesloe beach. It's winter here, but still a million times sunnier than the grey skies I left behind a couple of weeks ago. We've spent a gorgeous two weeks catching up; Skype is all well and good but it's not a patch on being in the same room or on the same beach or laughing over a movie together. We ceremonially recreated our Delancey Street signature sandwich a few days ago; Luke declared it disgusting, but we put our feet up and savoured the moment. I don't think either of us would make that sandwich without the other one being there; the fact that it's ours is the whole point of it. We're refilling our friendship with new memories, and I'm loving every minute of being here.

'Come and live out here. We can be neighbours.'

I laugh softly. She's said the same thing a dozen times or more since I arrived. 'Okay. I'll ring work and tell them I'm never coming back.'

'Fancy us getting to thirty,' Sarah says. She's sitting in the shade sipping some health-juice thing on account of the fact that she's four months pregnant; she and Luke have put their wedding plans on ice for a while in favour of welcoming the baby. It's all just so easy between them; they live in each other's pockets in their gorgeous beach house with their windows and doors flung open to the world.

There was always a part of me that used to envy her, but I know life hasn't just dropped good things in her lap; she made all of this happen for herself. She was brave enough to take chances – she always has been.

'I know you think I'm kidding, but what's holding you there?'

I sip the champagne Sarah insisted I have. 'It's her birthday,' she told the waitress as soon as we arrived. 'Bring her the good stuff.'

'Imagine what my mum would say if I told her I was leaving England?'

She nods, her face turned towards the ocean. 'She'd adjust though. Everyone does. And she's got your brother and his family.' She sucks more of the green gunk up the straw and pulls a face. 'What else is holding you there?'

'Well, my job, for starters,' I say.

'Which you could do from anywhere,' she counters. I moved on from the health desk a couple of months ago; ironically enough I've returned to my old stomping ground as an agony aunt. This time, though, it's troubled adults who write to me rather than teenage girls; clearly I'm qualified to dish out advice on the stuff that matters these days. Divorce, grief, love, loss. I've been there, and I have the drawer full of T-shirts to prove it. I've turned out to be so much of a hit with readers that I've been asked to do something similar for one of the magazines in a Sunday paper. I'm as surprised as anyone. I've returned to studying recently too; a psychology degree to deepen my understanding of the human condition – at least, that's how I described it when I was convincing my boss to help fund it shortly after I started there. I'm quietly loving it; the industry of study, the organization, the stationery even. It's not a direction I'd ever imagined I'd go in, but that's okay. Life does that, doesn't it? Reroutes you as it goes along. But Sarah's right, I *could* work and study from anywhere – as long as I have my laptop and a Wi-Fi connection, I'm good.

Could I live here? I look at Sarah in her wide-brimmed red sun hat and glamorous sunglasses, and I can see the advantages.

'This place is beautiful, Sar, but it's your place in the world, not mine.'

'Where's yours?' she says. 'Because I'll tell you what I think. Your place isn't some*where*. It's some*one*. I'm here because it's where Luke is. You'd have gone to Brussels if Oscar was your place.'

I nod, and she pushes her glasses up her nose.

Now that Oscar and I have been apart for some time, I'm starting to understand that we didn't have what it takes to stay together for a lifetime. I thought we did, for a while; he was a safe and secure interlude in the tumult of my life, but in the end we weren't a forever fit. We were just too different. I'm sure that doesn't matter sometimes if the love is strong enough; opposites attract, as they say. Perhaps we just didn't love each other enough? I don't like that thought, though. I prefer to think we had something wonderful for a while, and that we shouldn't regret anything about the time we gave to each other.

I never see him; I don't run into him in bars or spot him out walking and cross the street – a positive side effect of living in different countries. Not that I'm spending my time in bars. I seem to have gone into hibernation.

He mailed our painting to my mum's house at Christmas. The accompanying note said that he finds it too difficult having it around. I don't know what I'll do with it; I feel as if I have no right to it. I looked at it for a long time after it arrived. I lay on the single bed I slept in as a child and I thought of all the moments leading up to now. My childhood with Mum and Dad, Daryl and Ginny. School and college boyfriends. Delancey Street. Sarah. The top deck of a packed bus. A kiss in the snow. A beach in Thailand. A proposal in front of this very picture. Our beautiful wedding.

I hope Oscar is okay. It's strange, but you never stop caring about someone, even if you don't want to be with them any more. I think I'll always love him a little. And it's hard not to feel an element of failure at becoming a divorce statistic.

It seems inevitable that, sooner or later, Cressida will step into my shoes. I bet his bloody mother never did take that photo of them down from her piano.

'I think you know where your place is, Lu.'

Sarah and I look at each other, and then we don't say anything else because Luke appears from the beach and drops into the spare seat at the table.

'Looking good, ladies,' he grins. 'What did I miss?'

1 August

Jack

Lorne looks like the hulk's smaller, un-green brother, a fact that comes in handy when he's trying to get served at the bar. It's packed in here tonight, but he's only been gone a couple of minutes before he's already shouldering his way back across the pub bearing a couple of pints, a bag of crisps hanging from his teeth.

'You bought dinner,' I say, swiping them when he reaches me.

'Closest thing you'll get to a date tonight,' he grins. 'Although the woman at the table behind you is making a bad job of pretending not to check you out.'

I open the crisps and lay the bag out between us without turning round. 'Piss off.'

'I'm serious. She's pretty hot too.' He winks at her over my shoulder, and I thump him on the leg.

'What are you doing, man? Kerry's at home about to have your baby.' Lorne's very lovely wife is eight months pregnant; we're out for a couple of pints tonight at her insistence because he's driving her half crazy with his fussing.

'It's for you, twat,' he mutters, shoving a handful of crisps in his mouth.

I sigh, adjusting my hearing aid because we're next to a

speaker. 'I've told you. I'm off the dating merry-go-round for a while.'

'You said that.' He drinks deeply. 'I just don't believe you.'

He should. It's been more than four months since Martique and I decided to knock things on the head, a separation that meant little to either of us. That was why we split, in essence; it was going nowhere, and I'm kind of over sex for sex's sake. I don't tell Lorne that though.

'I'm thinking of becoming a monk,' I joke. 'I look good in orange.'

He looks at me. 'You're sure? Because she really is a looker.' He nods towards the woman behind us. 'Bit like Holly Willoughby.'

Time was that would have been enough to have me twisting round in my seat, but I just drink my pint and finish off the crisps. She may well look like Holly Willoughby and perhaps I could buy her a drink and take things further, but the fact is I don't want Holly Willoughby or Martique or anyone else.

I wear myself out walking Edinburgh's fascinating, steep streets, immersing myself in the city's culture; I even bought a pushbike last week. I came to Scotland to escape and it worked better than I could have hoped.

I jumped in feet first when I arrived and lost myself in the work and the women, and now at last I've surfaced and I'm sucking down fresh, sweet air into my lungs. At first it seemed that I was gasping for breath; it burned my chest. Now, though, I breathe easy and I sleep through the night.

It's just me and, for now, I'm good with that.

Laurie

'Night night. Miss you too,' I say, waiting for Mum to ring off before I hang up. She's in Tenerife with Aunt Susan; they're both still in mourning, I think, but helping each other through it. In this case with sangria and sun. I don't blame them; I seriously contemplated their offer to tag along, but in the end the pull of a dreary, cold London Christmas on my own was just too tempting to pass up. I'm kidding. Half kidding. I do at least have the house to myself for a couple of weeks though; my flatmate and her clan have all decamped to Wales until New Year. My plan, such as it is, is to just chill out, stuff my face and see a couple of friends here and there. Anna and Daryl have insisted I go to them for New Year, but aside from that, I'm as free as a bird. I wander into the kitchen and flick the kettle on, trying hard to feel urban and cool rather than lonely girl in London at Christmas.

An hour later, and I'm making a cake. I know, totally out of character, but the bottle of Baileys Mum sent me was next to a pile of cookbooks in the kitchen and I was suddenly overcome by the urge for cake. I'm on my second generous Baileys, and I couldn't care less that it's nearly ten at night and it's taken me nearly an hour to mash up a load of unripe bananas. I'm even humming along to Christmas songs on the radio. Is it sad that I tune in to Jack's station most nights? His late show is one of those where people can call in to talk about anything they fancy, sometimes funny, sometimes sad. He's not on yet though, and I'm having a full-on croon to Nat King Cole. I'm reminiscing; he was my dad's favourite.

I sit down at the kitchen table and close my eyes, and I'm back in my mum's kitchen, the same smells of cake batter and Christmas songs, old-fashioned fairy lights pinned under the wall cupboards. We're all there. I'm probably five or six, Daryl a year or so older, Ginny about three. Mum and Dad are there too, of course. No one's doing anything in particular, no schmaltzy dancing or profound speeches. We're all just *there*, and it's so heart-warming and perfect that I don't want to open my eyes and see all the empty chairs round the table. And then the music stops and Jack's voice washes over me, and I'm okay again because his company stops me from feeling so alone.

I follow the recipe, weighing out the rest of the ingredients as he takes a couple of calls, one from a guy who wants to tell him about the fight he got into today with the Santa at his local garden centre, and another from a woman whose decree absolute arrived in the mail this morning; she feels like the luckiest woman alive because her husband had been the very definition of The Grinch. It's all very light-hearted; Jack is an old hand at keeping the tone just right.

I scrape the cake batter into the tin I've lined, licking my finger to test it as the next caller comes on.

'I want to tell my girlfriend that I love her, but I can't,' he says. From his voice, I'd say he isn't much more than a teenager.

'What do you mean, can't?' says Jack. '*Do* you love her?'

The guy doesn't miss a beat. 'Oh yes. I nearly told her today after college. I was looking at her, and she asked me why I was looking at her oddly, but then the words got stuck in my throat. I can't get it out.'

Jack laughs softly, and the sound is so familiar that I can see him clearly in my head, that amused glow that lights his eyes. 'Look, if there's one bit of advice I can give you, it's for the love of God, man, just say it. You won't die, I promise. What's the worst that can happen?'

'She might laugh?'

'And she might not. The way I see it is you've got two choices here. Take the risk and tell her you love her or wait until it's too late and someone else tells her they love her. How will you feel then?'

'Like a fool?'

I stand there with the cake tin in my hands, ready to put it in the oven.

'For the rest of your life, mate. Trust me, I know, because it happened to me. It's Christmas – take the risk. You'll always regret it if you don't.'

I stare at the radio, and then I put the cake tin back down on the table and reach for my phone.

I've lied to the radio show producer about my name. I'm Rhona, and I'm up next.

'Hi, Rhona,' Jack says. 'What would you like to talk about?'

I've turned my radio off because of feedback, so it's just me and Jack chatting on the phone, like always.

'Hi, Jack,' I say. 'I was listening to your earlier caller and I wanted to say how much your advice rang true with me.'

'It did? Why's that?'

I can't gauge whether he's realized it's me or not yet. I don't think so.

'Because I know what it's like to miss your chance and to spend the rest of your life waiting to feel that way again.'

He pauses for a beat. 'Want to tell everyone your story, Rhona?'

'It's pretty long,' I say.

'That's okay. I'm not going anywhere. Take your time.'

'Okay,' I say. 'Well, it started on a snowy December day almost a decade ago.'

'Fitting,' he murmurs. 'Go on.'

'I was on the bus home from work. I'd had a God-awful day and I was done in, and then all of a sudden I looked out of the window and saw the most beautiful man – or boy as I thought of him then – sitting at the bus stop. I looked right at him, and he looked right at me, and I've never in my life felt anything like it. Not before and not afterwards,' I say, letting it all out in a rush. 'I spent a whole year looking for him in bars and cafes, but I didn't find him.'

Jack's breath is uneven in my ear. 'You never found him?'

'Not until my best friend found him first and fell in love with him too.'

'Wow . . . Rhona,' he says slowly. 'That must have been tough.'

'Unimaginably,' I say. I'm done, and I have no idea what to say next.

'Can I tell you something you probably don't know?' he

asks after a second of silence. 'I bet it was as tough for him as it was for you.'

'Oh, I don't think so,' I say. 'I asked him once, stupidly, if he remembered me from the bus, and he said no.'

I hear him swallow. 'He lied to you. Of course he saw you sitting there. He saw you there with tinsel in your hair, and he felt the exact same way, and he wished like hell that he'd got on that damn bus before it was too late.'

'Do you really think so?' I ask, my eyes closed, remembering. I'm that girl again.

'Yes,' he breathes. 'But he didn't know what to do. So he did nothing, like a mug, and then he stood on the sidelines and watched you fall in love with someone else, and *still* he didn't say it. He had his chances and he missed them all.'

'Sometimes you just meet the right person at the wrong time,' I say softly.

'Yeah,' he says. 'And then you spend every day afterwards wishing that time could be rearranged.'

I can't speak; tears clog my throat.

'Did you ever tell him how you feel?'

'No.' Tears spill down my cheeks. 'He told me a while back that he loved me, and I didn't say it back.'

'No,' he says, low, fractured. 'You didn't.'

'I should've.'

'Is it too late?'

I take a second to get my breath and hope his listeners will bear with me.

'I don't know,' I whisper.

'I think you should tell him. Perhaps he's still there, waiting for you to say it. What have you got to lose?'

*

I'm trending on Twitter. Or rather Rhona is.

#FindRhona #WhereIsRhona #JackAndRhona

It seems that David Tennant heard my late-night radio conversation with Jack, tweeted #findRhona, and in doing so caught the imagination of the entire nation. I'm now one half of a Christmas love story that the twittersphere is determined to give its happy ending. I scroll through the hundreds of tweets that have popped up in the minutes since the call, wide-eyed. Thank God I used a fake name, I think, listening to the snippets of our conversation shared all over the net.

I jump as my mobile rings. *Sarah.* Of course. She always listens to his shows too.

'Oh my GOD!' she shouts. I can hear the baby crying in the background. 'You're Rhona!'

I put my phone on the table in front of me and hold my head in my hands. 'I'm sorry, Sar, I didn't mean to tell everyone like that.'

'Christ, Laurie, I'm not angry, I'm bloody crying buckets here! Get your sorry ass up there to him this minute or I'm getting on a plane to drag you up there myself!'

'What if . . .'

She cuts in. 'Check your emails. I've just sent your Christmas present.'

'Hang on,' I say, dragging my laptop over and opening my inbox to see Sarah's new email.

'Ah! I need to go, Lu, the baby's just piddled all over me without his nappy on,' she says, laughing. 'I'll be watching Twitter for Rhona updates. Don't screw this up!'

She rings off as I click open her gift: a one-way train ticket to Edinburgh.

23 December

Jack

Shit. There's press outside my flat and my mobile has been ringing non-stop since I got home last night. Everyone wants to know who Rhona is, because it was pretty damn clear from our conversation that we know each other very, very well. Unbelievably, it's just scrolled across the rolling TV news tickertape – have they got nothing else to talk about? This wouldn't happen at any other time of the year. Scotland has officially gone into a Christmas love story meltdown, and unlikely as it would seem, I'm playing Hugh Grant.

My mobile rings yet again, and this time I answer it because it's my boss.

'O'Mara!' he barks. 'What's all this then?'

I struggle to answer. 'It's all a bit crazy, Al. Sorry, man.'

'The switchboard's flashing brighter than the bloody Christmas tree, son! The whole damn country will be tuning in to see if Rhona calls back again. You'd better get your scrawny backside in here pronto and make sure she does!'

As usual, he dispenses with the social niceties, hanging up without a goodbye. I stand in the middle of my lounge and rub my hands through my hair. What the hell am I supposed to do next? I don't think I can even get out of here without being mobbed. I look at my mobile and finally pluck up the courage to ring the one person I really need to speak to.

'*Hi, this is Laurie. I can't pick up right now. Please leave a message and I'll call you soon.*'

I chuck my phone on the side and sit down out of view of the windows.

I've never been in through the back entrance of the studio before; we save that for the celebrity guests who sometimes rock up for the breakfast show.

'Big for your boots now, fella,' Ron, our sixty-something security guard, jokes as he lets me in. He's usually posted out in reception doing the crossword at this time of night. 'Go on up.'

I take the lift to the top floor, and as I step out, I get a little ripple of applause from the handful of staff on duty.

'Very funny.' I shrug out of my coat, sticking my thumb up to Lena through the studio glass. She's on air before me every night, and she waves like a loon then makes a heart symbol with her hands. Great. I don't think there's a single person in Scotland who doesn't know about me and Laurie now. Or Rhona. I've tried her a dozen more times, and she still isn't picking up; this whole circus must have freaked her out. I almost tried her mum last night, but common sense kicked in; I'm sure the last thing she needs is a late-night call because I can't find her daughter. Laurie's gone to ground, and the whole country is waiting for me to find her.

Laurie

I had to lie to the cab driver just now. All I knew was the name of Jack's radio station, and the first thing he said when I told him where I wanted to go was, 'Here, you're no' that Rhona, eh?' He was joking around, but my stomach was in knots every time he glanced at me in the rear-view mirror as we slipped through the busy, Christmas-bright city streets. I'm here. I'm actually here. I've been on the train since four o'clock this afternoon; I thought the long journey would give me some valuable thinking time. What am I going to say to Jack? What am I going to do when I get to Edinburgh? But in the end I just laid my head against the cold glass and watched the scenery change as we moved northwards.

It's a much more beautiful city than I'd imagined, soaring grey buildings and grand, imposing architecture. Perhaps it's the fact that the streets glitter with frost and there are snowflakes blowing in the air, but there's a magical edge to it. It's Christmas in two days; revellers spill on to the cobbled pavements from the bars and pubs, and it's wall-to-wall festive music on the cab radio.

'There you are, doll.' The driver pulls over into a bus stop to let me out. 'It's just there.' He nods across the street towards a glass-fronted building. 'Good luck with getting in *there* tonight.' I follow his line of vision and my heart clenches at the sight of the gaggle of press photographers hanging around on the stone steps outside. I look back at the cab driver, uncertain.

'How much is it please?' My voice sounds thin and wavering.

He looks across the street, shaking his head. 'You're her, eh?'

I nod, terrified. I don't know if I can trust him, but at this point, I don't have any better options. 'I don't know what I'm going to do.'

He drums his fingers against the steering wheel, thinking. 'Stay there.' Then he flicks the hazards on and gets out of the cab, dodging the traffic as he jogs towards the radio station building.

Jack

Every caller so far has been someone asking about Rhona or giving me some kind of tip about how to win her back, and I've tried to fend them off as vaguely as I can. I'm almost done for the night and I'm just about to treat the listeners to 'Fairytale of New York' when Lorne shakes his head at me from his booth and tells me there's one last caller on line one. I flick the red flashing light and wait.

'Hey, Jack. It's me again. Rhona.'

At last.

'Hey, you,' I say, and I think I hear the whole country sigh with relief.

'It's so good to talk to you again. I wasn't sure you'd call back.'

'I missed you,' she says. There's a soft, husky note to her voice that makes me wish I was the only one who could hear her.

'I've missed you for the last nine years.' My voice cracks;

the truth is the only thing I have to give Laurie now, and I don't care who else is listening.

I hear her intake of breath, and outside in the office, Haley, my assistant, stands up at her desk and smiles at me through the glass with tears running down her cheeks.

'I love you, Jack,' Laurie says, and I can hear she's crying too.

'Don't be sad,' I say, gentle. 'I've spent nearly a decade wishing I'd got on that damn bus.' Suddenly I realize: I need to be wherever she is, right now. 'I need to see you,' I murmur, and Haley clasps her hands and kind of punches the air.

'I'm here, Jack,' Laurie says, half laughing. Confused, I swing towards Lorne in his booth, and she's there. *Laurie.* Laurie's really there, smiling at me like that first time we ever saw each other. She's here, she's smiling, and she has tinsel in her hair. Lorne grins behind her and throws his hands up in the air, then thank God he cuts to the next track.

'I'll take over now,' he says, smooth in my ear. 'Get in here. This girl's come a long way to see you.'

Laurie

If I needed any reassurance that coming to Scotland was the right thing to do, the look on Jack's face when he sees me is it. My guardian angel/taxi driver and the radio station security guard cooked up a plan between them to sneak me in through the back door, ably assisted by Haley, Jack's assistant. She met me downstairs, thoroughly overexcited, and when we stepped out of the lift she gave me a quick hug.

'I'm really glad you came,' she said, shiny-eyed. I thought for a second she was going to cry. 'I've always thought there was someone . . . he's never seemed properly settled,' she added. As we passed the office Christmas tree, she stopped and grabbed my hand.

'Wait,' she said. 'Let me just . . .'

And then she tugged a strand of silver tinsel from the branches and wound it in my hair.

'There. Perfect.'

And now, finally, it's just me and Jack. He laughingly closed the blinds on his cheering colleagues, giving us some privacy in the tiny glass booth.

'How did you . . . ?'

He reaches out and holds my face in his hands, looking at me as if he can't believe I'm really here.

'I had help,' I laugh, giddy. 'The taxi driver and —'

He stops my words with his kiss, making me gasp, his hands in my hair, his mouth full of longing and sweetness and relief.

After a long, breathless minute he stops kissing me, and his eyes lock with mine. 'Why did we wait this long?'

'I'd wait a lifetime for you,' I say. 'I love you, Jack O'Mara.'

'And I love you, Laurie James,' he breathes. 'Stay with me?'

'Always.'

He kisses me again and I melt, because his kisses have been forbidden for so long. Finally I pull back in his arms and look up.

'Do you ever wonder what might have happened if you'd just got on the bus?'

He half shrugs, laughing as he unwinds the tinsel from my hair. 'Boy sees girl. Girl sees boy. Boy gets on the bus, snogs girl's face off, and they live happily ever after.'

I laugh softly. 'It's a pretty dull story when you put it like that.'

'We got there in the end,' he says, pressing a kiss against my forehead.

I hold him, and he holds me, and for the first time in years, there's nothing missing at all.

Acknowledgements

Huge thanks to Katy Loftus, my clever, kind and wise editor. Your instinct and insight have been my unerring guide throughout this book, from conception to The End. I honestly couldn't have written it without you, you're properly brilliant.

Wider thanks to Karen Whitlock, Emma Brown and everyone at Viking – it's been a pleasure and a thrill to work with you all.

Much appreciation to Sarah Scarlett and all on the brilliant and terrifyingly glamorous rights team.

To Jess Hart – I cannot tell you how much I love and adore the cover! Thank you, it's for ever on my office wall.

Many thanks as always to my agent Jemima Forrester and all at David Higham.

On a personal note, love and thanks to the Bob ladies and the minxes – there seems to be nothing I could ask that one of you doesn't know the answer to! You're my secret weapons.

Thank you as always to all of my lovely family and friends for your unstinting support and encouragement.

Lastly and most of all, thank you to my beloved James, Ed and Alex. You're my for ever favourites.

Loved *One Day in December*? Then
look out for Josie's new novel in 2020

Available now for pre-order online and
at all good bookshops

Read on for an exclusive extract
from Josie's new novel

the
two lives
of
Lydia
Bird

Thursday 10 May, awake

Freddie Hunter, otherwise known as the great big love of my life, died fifty-six days ago.

One moment I'm cursing him for running late and ruining my birthday dinner, the next I'm trying to make sense of the two uniformed policewomen in my living room, one of them holding my hand as she speaks. I stare at her wedding ring and then at my engagement ring.

'Freddie can't be dead,' I say. 'We're getting married next year.'

It's probably a self-preservation thing that I struggle to recall exactly what happened afterwards. I remember being blue-lighted to A&E in the police car and my sister holding me up when my legs buckled at the hospital. I remember turning my back on Jonah Jones when he appeared in the waiting room with barely a scratch on him, just his hand bandaged and a wound dressing over one eye. How is that fair? Two get into the car, only one gets out again. I remember what I was wearing, a new green blouse I'd bought especially for the dinner. I've given it away to a charity shop; I never want it on my body again.

Since that awful day I've wracked my brain countless times to try to recall every word of my last conversation with Freddie, and all I can remember is grumbling at him about cutting it fine for the restaurant. And then come the other thoughts. Was he rushing to please me? Was the accident my fault? God, I wish I'd told him that I love him. Had I known that it was the last time I'd ever speak to him, I would have, of course I would. Since it happened I've sometimes wished he'd lived just long enough for us to have one more conversation – but then I'm not sure my heart could have withstood it. It's probably for the best if the last time you do something momentous passes you by unheralded: the last time my mother collected me at the school gate, her hand reassuring around my smaller one; the last time my father remembered my birthday. The last time I spoke to Freddie Hunter as he dashed back to see me on my twenty-eighth birthday. Do you know what the last words he said to me were? Over and out. It was a habit, something he'd done for years, silly words that have now become one of the most significant phrases of my life.

I guess it was just so Freddie, though, to go out on a phrase like that. He had this insatiable lust for life, a lightness of attitude coupled with a killer competitive streak – fun but lethal, if you like. I've never met anyone with such a gift for always knowing what to say. He has – he had – a knack of making other people think they'd won when in fact he'd got exactly what he wanted; he walked into his advertising career and shot up the ranks like a meteor, eyes always on the next prize. He is – he was – the bright spark amongst us, the one who was always going to be someone or do something that made people remember his name long after he'd gone.

And now he bloody well *has* gone, his car concertinaed against an oak tree, and I feel as if someone has sliced me through and tied a knot in my windpipe. It's as if can't quite get enough air into my lungs — I'm breathless and perpetually on the edge of panic.

The doctor has finally given me something to help me sleep after my mum yelled at him yesterday in the living room, a month's supply of some new pill that he wasn't at all sure about prescribing because he thinks grief needs to be 'passed through sentiently in order to emerge'. I'm not making this shit up; he said those actual words to me a couple of weeks ago, before leaving me empty-handed to go home to his very-much-alive wife and children.

Living around the corner from my mother is a blessing and a curse in varying measures. When she makes her champion chicken stew and brings a pan round for us still hot off the stove, for instance, or when she's waiting for me at the end of the road on a cold November morning to give me a lift into work — those times our proximity is a blessing. Other times, like when I'm in bed seeing double with a hangover and she appears in my bedroom as if I'm still seventeen, or when I haven't tidied up for a couple of days and she looks down her nose as if I'm one of those extreme hoarders in need of a reality-TV intervention, those times our proximity is a curse. Ditto when I'm trying to grieve in private with the living-room curtains still closed at three in the afternoon and the same PJs on as when she visited me yesterday and the day before; making me tea I'll forget to drink and sandwiches I'll bury in the back of the fridge when she's upstairs cleaning the bathroom or outside pulling the bins down.

I understand, of course. She's fiercely protective of me, especially at the moment; she had the doctor practically shaking with fear when he wavered over the idea of pre-scribing sleeping tablets. I'm not all that sure about popping pills either, as it happens, although God knows the idea of oblivion is appealing. I don't know why I'm bringing God into this; Freddie is, was and would have always been a strident atheist, and I'm ambivalent at best, so I don't expect God has had much to do with my being placed on a clinical trial for the recently bereaved. The doctor recommended joining the drug trial, probably because my mother was demanding maximum-strength Valium and these new pills are being touted as a milder, more holistic option. To be perfectly honest I don't really care what they are; I'm officially the world's saddest, most tired guinea pig.

Freddie and I have this fabulous bed, you see. It sounds unlikely, but the Savoy were auctioning off hotel beds to make way for new ones for hardly anything, and sweet heaven, this bed is a fantasy island of epic proportions. People raised eyebrows at first: you're buying a second-hand bed? Why on earth would you do that, my mother said, as aghast as if we were buying a camp bed discarded by the local homeless shelter. Clearly those doubters had never stayed at the Savoy. I hadn't either, in truth, but I'd seen something on TV about their handmade beds and I knew exactly what I was getting. And that's how we came to be in possession of the most comfortable bed in a hundred-mile radius, in which Freddie and I have demol-ished countless Sunday-morning breakfasts, laughed and cried and made heart-achingly sweet love.

When my mother told me she'd changed the sheets for me a few days after the accident, she unintentionally sent me into a sudden, screeching meltdown. I watched myself as if from a distance, clawing at the door of the washing machine, sobbing as the sheets tumbled through the suds, swilling any last lingering traces of Freddie's skin and scent down the drain.

My mother was beside herself, trying to lift me from the floor, calling out for my sister to come and help. We ended up huddled together on the stripped kitchen floor-boards, watching the sheets, all of us in tears because it is just so bloody unfair that Freddie isn't here any more.

I haven't been to bed since. In fact, I don't think I've properly been to sleep since. I just nap sometimes: my head on the table beside my uneaten breakfast; on the sofa huddled underneath Freddie's winter coat; standing up leaning against the fridge, even.

'Come on, Lyds,' my sister says now, shaking my shoulder softly. 'I'll come up with you.'

I glance at the clock, disorientated because it was broad daylight when I closed my eyes, but now it's shadowy enough for someone, Elle I presume, to have flicked the lamps on. It's typical of her to be so thoughtful; I've always thought of her as a better version of me. We're physically similar in height and bone structure, but she's dark to my light; her hair, her eyes. She's kinder than I am too, too kind for her own good a lot of the time. She's been here most of the afternoon; I think my mum must have drawn up a rota to make sure I'm never on my own for more than an hour or two. It's probably pinned to the side of her fridge, right next to the shopping list she adds to all week and the food diary she fills in for her slimming class. She likes a list, my mum.

'Up where?' I say, sitting up straighter, clocking the glass of water and bottle of pills in Elle's hand.

'Bed,' she says, an edge of steel to her voice.

'I'm fine here,' I mutter, even though our sofa isn't actually all that comfortable to sleep on. 'It's not even bedtime. We can watch . . .' I bat my hand towards the TV in the corner, trying to remember any of the soaps. I sigh, annoyed that my tired brain can't muster it. 'You know, that one with the pub and the bald men and the shouting.'

She smiles and rolls her eyes. 'You mean *EastEnders*.'

'That's the one,' I say, distracted as I scan the room for the remote to turn the TV on.

'It'll have finished by now. Besides, you haven't watched *EastEnders* for the last five years or more,' she says, having none of it.

I screw my face up. 'I have. There's . . . there's that woman with the dangly earrings, and . . . and Barbara Windsor,' I say, lifting my chin.

Elle shakes her head. 'Both dead,' she says.

Poor them, I think, and their poor families.

Elle holds her hand out. 'It's time to go to bed, Lydia,' she says, gentle and firm, more nurse than sister.

Hot tears prick the back of my retinas. 'I don't think I can.'

'You can,' she says, resolute, her hand still outstretched. 'What else are you going to do? Sleep on the sofa for the rest of your life?'

'Would that be so bad?'

Elle perches next to me and picks up my hand, the pills in her lap. 'It would, really, Lyds,' she says. 'If it was

Freddie left here alone rather than you, you'd want him to get some proper sleep, wouldn't you?'

I nod, miserable. Of course I would.

'In fact, you'd haunt him rotten until he went to bed,' she says, rubbing her thumb over my knuckles, and I half choke on the permanent ball of tears that I've been trying to breathe around since the day Freddie died.

I watch her shake a small neon-pink tablet into her palm. Is that all it's going to take to put me straight? A few weeks of solid sleep and I'll be ship-shape-shiny and good to go again?

Elle holds my gaze, unwavering, and tears slide down my cheeks as I realize how shattered I am; I'm as emotionally and physically low as I can go. Or at least I hope I am, because I don't think I'll survive if there's further to fall than this. Taking the pill with trembling fingers, I put it in my mouth and wash it down. At my bedroom door, I turn to Elle.

'I need to do this on my own,' I whisper.

She brushes my lank hair out of my eyes. 'You sure?' Her dark eyes study my face. 'I can stay with you until you're asleep, if you like?'

I sniff, looking at the floor, crying as usual. 'I know you could,' I say, catching hold of her hand and holding on tight. 'But I think I better . . .' I can't quite find the words I need; I don't know if it's because the tablet is having an effect or simply because there aren't any adequate words.

Elle nods. 'I'll be just downstairs if you want me, okay? I'm not going anywhere.'

My fingers close around the handle. I've kept the door shut since the day Mum changed the bed linen, not even wanting to catch an accidental glimpse of the pristine bed on my way to the bathroom. I've built it up into this thing in my head, this alien place, as off limits as a crime scene criss-crossed with yellow tape.

'It's just a bed,' I whisper, pushing the door slowly open. There's no yellow tape blocking my entry and there are no monsters under the bed. But there's no Freddie Hunter either and that's every kind of heartbreaking.

'Just a bed,' Elle says, her hand soothing on my back. 'A place to rest.'

But she's lying. We both know it's so much more than that. This room, mine and Freddie's bedroom, was one of the main reasons we bought this house. Airy, bathed in daylight thanks to the low-slung sash windows and honey floorboards, striped by bright slices of moonlight on clear summer nights.

Someone, Elle presumably, has been in already to turn on the lamp on my side of the bed, a pool of mellow light to welcome me, even though the sun hasn't quite set yet. She's turned the bed down too; it's all more hotel than bedroom. The overwhelming scent in here when I close the door is line-fresh bed linen. No traces of my perfume mingled with Freddie's aftershave, no office-crumpled shirts slung carelessly over the armchair or shoes kicked off before they could make it as far as the bottom of the wardrobe. It's neat as a new pin; I feel like a visitor in my own life.

'It's just a bed,' I whisper again, sitting on the edge of the mattress. I close my eyes as I lay down, curling on to my side beneath the quilt.

We spent more than we should have on bedding befitting of our Savoy bed; white cotton sheets with a higher thread count than most hotels I've ever stayed in. As my body slides against the sheets, I realize they're already warm. Elle's put a hot-water bottle in here for me, my lovely sister, taking away the chill of clean sheets. My bed, our bed, envelops me like an old friend I feel guilty for neglecting.

I lie on my side of the mattress, my body wracked, painful with sorrow, my arms outstretched to find him as always. Then I push the hot-water bottle to his side, warming the sheets before I move across and lie there myself, clutching the heat of the bottle to my chest with both arms. I bury my wet face in his pillow and wail like a wounded animal, a noise as alien as it is uncontrollable.

And then, little by little, it subsides. My heart rate begins to steady and my limbs turn lead-heavy. I'm warm, cocooned, and for the first time in fifty-six days, I'm not lost without Freddie. I'm not lost, because as I slide under the coat-tails of sleep, I can almost feel the solid weight of him depress the mattress, his body spooned around mine, his breath steady against my neck. Save me from these dark, uncharted waters, Freddie Hunter. I pull him close and breathe him in as I fall into a deep, peaceful sleep.

Friday 11 May, asleep

You know those blissful dawn moments, summer mornings when the sun rises before you do, and you half rouse and then fall back asleep, glad of a few more hours? I turn and find Freddie still here with me and the relief is so profound that it's all I can do to lie perfectly still and try to match my breathing pattern to his. It's four in the morning, too early to get up, so I close my eyes again; I don't think I've ever known such absolute comfort. The bed warmed by our nested bodies, the golden half-light before dawn, the muted music of birdsong. Please don't let me leave this dream.

Friday 11 May, awake

I know before I open my eyes for a second time that he's gone. The bed is colder, the six a.m. sunlight harsher, the birdsong like nails down a blackboard. Freddie was here, I know he was. I burrow my head into the pillow and screw my eyes tight shut, searching the darkness behind my eyelids for sleep again. If I can only sleep, I might find him.

Panic starts to bubble low in my gut; the harder I try to relax the more my brain fires up, preparing itself for the day ahead, full of dark thoughts and desperate emotions I don't know what to do with. And then my heart judders, jump leads on a dodgy battery, because I remember: I have sleeping pills now. Pink pills designed to knock me out. I reach for the bottle Elle has placed on my bedside table and clutch it in both hands, relieved, then unscrew the lid and swallow one down.

Friday 11 May, asleep

'Morning, Lyds.' Freddie rolls over and kisses my forehead, his arm heavy over my shoulders as our alarm informs us it's seven a.m. 'I don't want to play today. Shall we stay in bed? I'll call in for you if you call in for me.'

He says something along the same lines most mornings and for a couple of minutes we always pretend to entertain the idea.

'Will you make us breakfast in bed?' I mumble, sliding my arm around the warmth of his body, burying my face in the soft down of his chest hair. There is a solidity about his body that I love; he's a commanding physical presence thanks to his height and broad shoulders. People at work sometimes underestimate his business brain because of his stereotypical rugby-player build and he's more than happy to play that to his advantage. He's competitive to the core.

'As long as you want breakfast at midday, yeah.' I hear the laugh behind his breastbone as he strokes the back of my head.

'Sounds about right,' I say, closing my eyes, breathing him in deep.

We stay like that for a few lazy, exquisite minutes, clasped, half sleeping, knowing we need to get up soon. But we linger, because these are the moments that matter, the ones that make it Freddie and me against the world. These moments are the bedrock our love is built on, an invisible cloak around our shoulders when we are out in the world going about our business. Freddie won't return the interested look from the striking girl on platform 4 waiting for the 7.47, and I never allow Leon, the barista in the café I sometimes buy lunch from, to cross the line from messing around to flirting even though he's movie-star gorgeous and writes outrageous things on my coffee cup.

I'm crying. For a few seconds I don't know why, and then I remember, and I suck down great lungsful of air, like someone breaking the surface after falling into deep water.

Freddie startles, jerking up on one elbow to stare at me, concern on his face as he grips my shoulder. 'Lyds, what's the matter?' His voice is urgent, ready to help, to soothe whatever pain I'm in.

I can't breathe, my breath burns in my chest.

'You died.' I sob out the shocking words, my eyes scanning his beloved face for telltale signs of the accident. There's nothing, no hint of the catastrophic head injury that claimed his life. His eyes are an unusual blue, dark enough to be mistaken for brown unless you're close enough to really look. He sometimes wears a pair of black-framed glasses for important work pitches, clear glass, an illusion of weakness where there isn't any. I stare into those eyes now and run my hand over the harvest-blond stubble on his jawline.

A soft laugh rumbles from him and relief passes through his eyes.

'You daft cow,' he says, hugging me in. 'You were dreaming, that's all.'

Oh, how dearly I wish that were true. I shake my head, so he takes my hand and lays it over his heart.

'I'm fine,' he insists. 'Feel, my heart's beating and everything.'

It is. I press hard enough to feel it jumping beneath my palm, and yet I know that it isn't, really. It can't be. He covers my hand with his own now, not laughing any more because he can see how distressed I am. He doesn't understand, of course; how could he? He's not real but, God, this doesn't feel like any other dream I've ever had, either. I'm awake in my sleep. I can feel the heat of his body. I can smell the trace of his aftershave on his skin. I can taste my tears when he leans down and kisses me, tender. I can't stop crying; I try to take shallow breaths as I hold him, as though he's made of smoke and will blow away if I breathe too hard.

'A nightmare, that's all,' he whispers, stroking my back, letting me cry it out because there's nothing else he can do.

If only he knew that this is the opposite of a nightmare; nightmares come when you're impatiently waiting for your boyfriend to arrive on your birthday, your family already assembled at the table in the restaurant on the High Street.

'I miss you. I miss you so very much,' I gulp. I can't keep a limb still and he folds his arms around me, really tight this time, and he's telling me that he loves me, and that he's fine, that we're both fine.

'We're going to be late for work,' he says gently after a few minutes.

I lie still, my eyes closed, trying to memorize the feel of his arms around me for when I wake.

'Let's stay here,' I whisper. 'Let's stay here for ever, Freddie.'

His hand slides into my hair and he draws my head back so he can look me in the eyes. 'I wish I could,' he says, the trace of a smile on his lips. 'But you know I can't. I'm chairing that meeting this morning with the PodGods,' he says, reminding me of something I know nothing of.

'The PodGods?'

He raises his eyebrows. 'The coffee-pod people? Remember, I told you? They all turned up to the pitch wearing Day-Glo green PodGod T-shirts and baseball caps?'

'How could I forget them,' I say, even though I've no clue.

He untangles himself from me, kissing my cheek.

'Stay here this morning,' he says, his eyes concerned. 'You never take a day off. Do it today, yeah? I'll bring you a cup of tea.'

I don't argue with him. I haven't been to work in fifty-six days.

My life has been entwined around Freddie Hunter's since the first time he kissed me, breathing himself into my DNA one late-summertime afternoon. It had been coming between us for a while, building like steam in an engine – his seat always beside mine in the school canteen so he could steal my ice cream, flirty comments batted back and forth across the classroom like tennis balls. He began to walk home the same way as Jonah and me even though it was out of his way, usually making up some flimsy excuse about collecting something for his mum or visiting his nan. When Jonah came down with chicken-pox and had to stay home for a week or two, I didn't stand a chance. I get nostalgic butterflies thinking about it even now: Freddie gave me a yellow plastic flower ring, the kind you get from a Christmas cracker, and then he kissed me sitting on my neighbours' front wall.

'Won't your nan be worried about you?' I asked him, after the five most exciting minutes of my life.

'Hardly. She lives in Bournemouth,' he said, and then we both laughed because it was at least a hundred miles away.

And that was that, I was Freddie Hunter's girl, then and always. The next morning he slid a chocolate bar into my bag along with a note telling me he was walking me home. From someone else it could have come off as possessive; my tender teenage heart saw only thrilling directness.

I watch him move with purpose now, heading into the bathroom to switch the shower on, pulling a clean white shirt off the hanger.

'I don't want to jinx it, but I think this one's in the bag,' he's saying, answering a work call briefly, his mobile tucked under his chin as he grabs underwear from the drawer. I watch his everyday moves, my answering smile shaky when he rolls his eyes at me because he wants whoever is on the phone to wind it up.

He disappears into the bathroom and I sit up and push the quilt back when I hear the water sluicing around his body.

'What's happening to me?' I whisper, lowering my feet to the floor, sitting on the edge of the bed like a hospital patient after open-heart surgery. Because that is what this feels like. As if someone opened my chest and massaged my heart back into working order.

'I don't believe in fairy tales or magic beans,' I mutter, biting down on my trembling bottom lip hard enough to taste blood, metallic and harsh.

Freddie emerges from the bathroom on a cloud of steam, shoving his shirt into his trousers as he buttons them.

'I better go,' he says, reaching for his phone. 'If I stick the kettle on, can you make the tea? I'll make the train if I dash.'

We chose this house for exactly this scenario, mornings when we were running late and grateful to have a train station around the corner. His city-centre job demands long hours, so the less time added for travel the better. My own commute to the local town hall is shorter: ten minutes and I'm in the car park at work. It wasn't just location that made us fall for the house though. We viewed it early one spring weekend morning, the sun at just the perfect height to show off the honeyed stone and deep bay window. It's mid terrace, and decorating it proved to be a bit of a nightmare because there isn't a straight wall or door in the place. It all adds to the charm, I argued, every time Freddie banged his head on the low exposed kitchen beam. I like to think the decor has echoes of Kate Winslet's cottage in *The Holiday*, all stripped boards and cosy clutter. It's a look I've cultivated carefully at car boots and flea markets, occasionally reined in by Freddie's preference for more modern things. It's a battle he was always set to lose: my magpie eye loves pretty things and my Pinterest game is strong.

A couple of days ago, after I'd forced myself to get dressed and nip round to the off-licence for wine supplies, it occurred to me that I didn't want to go home. It's the first time I've felt that way about the house since the morning we collected the keys, and another piece of my heart snapped off at the realization that home wasn't home any more. I could never have conceived of the idea of selling the house, but in that moment I felt cut adrift and I walked in the other direction, two circuits of the children's play park before I could face going home. And then, curiously, once I was back inside, I didn't want to leave again. I am a mass of contradictions – it's no wonder my family are worried to death about me.

It was our house, and now it is mine, though there is little pleasure to be gained from becoming mortgage-free at twenty-eight when I'm Freddie-free too. We both felt as if our financial advisor stitched us up like a pair of kippers on life insurance at the time; the concept of something happening to either of us before the house was paid for seemed ludicrous. How wonderfully lucky we were to feel so secure. I pull myself out of my thoughts, realizing I'm close to tears again. Freddie is looking at me questioningly. 'Okay now?' he asks, cupping my jaw, rubbing his thumb over my cheekbone.

I nod, turning my face to press my lips into his palm as he kisses the top of my head. 'That's my girl,' he whispers. 'I love you.'

As undignified as it would be, I want to cling to him, beg him not to leave me again, but I don't. If this is to be my final memory of us, I want it to seal itself around my heart for all of the best reasons. So I stand up and hold the lapels of his suit jacket and look up into his beautiful, familiar blue eyes.

'You're the love of my life, Freddie Hunter,' I say, forcing the words out clear and true.

He lowers his head and kisses me. 'I love you more than Keira Knightly.' He laughs softly as he plays our game.

'That much, huh?' I say, rounding my eyes because we

usually start low and work our way up – to Keira in his case and Ryan Reynolds in mine.

'That much,' he says, blowing me a kiss as he backs out of the bedroom.

Panic rises from my gut, hot and bilious, and I curl my toes into the floorboards to stop myself from running after him. I listen to his footfall on the stairs, the sound of the front door closing, and I run to the bedroom window to watch him half stride, half jog towards the corner. Too late, I open the windows, struggling with the old catches, yelling his name even though I know he won't hear me. Why did I let him leave? What if I never find him again? I clutch the windowsill, my eyes pinned to his back. I almost expect him to fade away, but he doesn't. He just rounds the corner, lost to the world, to some corporate coffee client, to the girl on platform 4, to all the places I cannot be.

Friday 11 May, awake

My face is wet and my mouth is caked with what tastes like blood when I wake. I grab my phone and on closer inspection I've bitten the inside of my bottom lip quite badly; I can see the indentations my teeth have left and my lip has swollen as if I've had bad Botox. It's not my best look – Freddie would have no doubt found my uncanny resemblance to a pufferfish amusing.

Freddie. I close my eyes, winded by the hyperrealism of my dream, or whatever it was. I can only liken it to when you go into an electrical store and see the latest, flashiest TV, the kind that costs a small fortune. The colours are brighter, the edges sharper, the sounds clearer. It was Technicolor brilliant, like watching a movie at an Imax theatre. No, more like being in a movie at an Imax theatre. It was too real to not be. Freddie was alive, and showering, and running late for work, and making Keira Knightly jokes once again.

I wrack my brain, trying to dredge up a memory of any mention of a corporate coffee client before he died. I'm sure there wasn't one; it's as if Freddie has been living the last fifty-seven days behind a veil, going about his day-to-day business without a care in the world.

I'm once more overcome with the need to try to fall back asleep, to go back and find him, back to the life where Freddie's heart is still beating, but in that world he's already out slaying the advertising world with a flash of his cufflinks and a smile. For someone who didn't even want to go to bed last night, I now find myself absolutely unwilling to get up and face the new day. It takes me a good fifteen minutes to convince myself that leaving the bedroom is even a remotely good idea. In the end, I strike a bargain with myself; If I get up and do Friday, if I shower, eat, and maybe even leave the house for a while, then I can take another pill. I'll have an early dinner, come back to bed, and maybe, just maybe, I'll get to spend the evening with my love.

Saturday 12 May, awake

'I've been dreaming about Freddie,' I say, wrapping my hands around my coffee mug for comfort rather than warmth. Elle looks at me across the kitchen table, nodding slowly.

'I do that every now and then too,' she says, stirring sugar into her drink. 'I'd be more surprised if you didn't dream about him, to be honest.'

'You would?' I look at her sharply, willing her to meet my eye and pay full attention because this is important. 'It hasn't happened to me before.'

Disappointment twists in my gut. What's been happening to me felt too intimate to be a run-of-the-mill kind of thing.

Elle glances up at the kitchen clock.

'Ready to go?'

We're going to Mum's for breakfast; it's something we've started to do most Saturday mornings before I visit Freddie's grave, Mum's way of adding structure to my weekend, I think. Elle doesn't pass comment on my unbrushed hair and yesterday's T-shirt. It's one of Freddie's. My hair was for him too; he loved it long so I've barely had more than a trim for years now. I mean, I can't sit on it or anything yet, but it's slowly become one of my defining features. Lydia, Freddie's girlfriend, the one with the long blonde hair.

Had this been last week, I probably would have shrugged on my denim jacket and dragged my hair back into an elastic, tangles and all, and considered myself good to go. But it isn't last week. If my recent encounters with Freddie have taught me anything it's that I am alive, and people who are alive should, at the very least, be clean. Even Freddie, who technically isn't alive, took a shower.

'Give me ten?' I shoot Elle the barest of smiles. 'I think it's time I put on some make-up.' I haven't so much as touched my make-up bag since the funeral.

She looks at me strangely; I can tell that I've surprised her.

'Well, I didn't want to say, but you have been looking a little bit shit lately,' she says, making light.

Her joke makes my stomach lurch, because we've always been as close as, I don't know, two close things. Two peas in a pod? I don't think that's quite it, because we aren't very alike to look at. As close as sisters doesn't cut it either, because there are sisters like Julia at work and her elder sister, Susan, who she denies could even be from the same gene pool because she's such a cow, and then there are sisters like Alice and Ellen, twins I went to school with who wore matching clothes and finished each other's sentences, but would throw each other under a bus to get picked to captain the netball team. Me and Elle, we're . . . we're Monica and Rachel. We're Carrie and Miranda. We have always been each other's loudest cheerleader and first-choice shoulder to cry on, and it's only now that I catch a glimpse of how much I've withdrawn from her. I know she doesn't for a minute resent it or blame me, but it must have been hard on her; she's lost me as well as Freddie, in a way. I make a mental note that one day, when I'm better, I'll tell her how sometimes on the dark days she's been the only light I could see.

'I won't be long,' I say, pushing my chair back, a scrape of wood against wood.

'I'll make myself another drink while I wait,' she says.

I leave Elle in the kitchen, comforted by the sound of

her running the tap and clattering around in the cup-boards. She's always been a frequent and very welcome visitor here. Not nearly as frequent as Jonah Jones, mind – he spent almost as much time here with Freddie as I did, very often slumped on our sofa watching a movie no one had ever heard of or eating pizza out of boxes because neither of them were exactly Jamie Oliver in the kitchen. I never said as much to Freddie, but I sometimes felt as if Jonah resented having to give his best friend up to me. I guess three is always an odd number.

'No David today?'

Mum looks past us as she opens the front door; I some-times think she's fonder of David than she is of us. She was the same way with Freddie; she enjoys fussing over the men in that mothers-and-sons way.

'Just us this morning, sorry,' Elle says, not sorry.

Mum sighs theatrically. 'You'll just have to do. Although I was going to ask him to change the fuse in the plug on my hairdryer – it's packed up again.'

Elle catches my eye behind Mum's back and I know exactly what she's thinking. David is terrible at anything DIY-related. It's firmly Elle's department if they have a shelf to go up or a room to be decorated or indeed a fuse to be changed, but our mother insists on clinging to the outdated suggestion that David is the man of the family and will do all the manly things. She could change her own fuse perfectly well: she raised us single-handedly and we didn't die, she knows her earth wire from her live. She seems to think it imbues David with an added sense of self-worth if she looks to him for odd jobs, and he in turn looks to us with panicked, help-me eyes. He can't even climb a step ladder without breaking out in a sweat; I had to distract Mum in the kitchen a few weeks ago while he held the ladder for Elle to clear out the guttering. It's a game we all play; Freddie was the natural doer of the family, and in his absence David has been unwillingly promoted to family fixer.

'I'm making cheese and onion omelettes,' Mum says as we follow her down the hallway. 'Testing out a new pan.' She twirls a bright pink frying pan at us.

'The shopping channel again?' Elle asks, dropping her bag by the kitchen table.

Mum shrugs. 'It just happened to be on. You know I don't usually buy off the telly, but Kathrin Magyar was so impressed by it, and the handle had just fallen off my old frying pan, so it seemed like it was fate.'

I supress a smile and Elle looks away. We both know that Mum's kitchen cupboards are stuffed with unnecessary purchases the super-glam TV presenter Kathrin Magyar has convinced her will revolutionize her life.

'Want me to chop the onions?' I say.

Mum shakes her head. 'Already done. They're in the mini-chopper.'

I nod, noticing it on the kitchen surface. I don't ask if that was from the shopping channel too, because of course it was, along with the motorized cheese grater she's used for the Cheddar.

I make coffee instead, thankfully unaided by superfluous gadgetry.

'Did you try the pills?' Mum asks, cracking eggs into a bowl.

I nod, winded by the reminder of Freddie.

She rifles through her jug of kitchen implements until she finds the whisk. 'And?'

'And they work.' I shrug. 'I slept through.'

'In bed?'

I sigh, and Elle shoots me a small smile. 'Yes, in bed.'

Relief smooths the lines from Mum's forehead as she whisks the eggs. 'That's good. So no more sleeping on the sofa, okay? It's no good for you.'

'No, promise.'

Elle lays the table, three place settings. Our family swelled to five, and now it's reduced to four, but in its purest form it has always been three: Mum, Elle and me. We don't really know our dad. He walked out five days before my first birthday, and Mum has never really forgiven him. Elle was two and still in nappies, I was a handful, and he decided that life with three females wasn't his gig and moved to Cornwall to take up surfing. He's that kind of man. Every few years he sends news of where he is, and he even turned up on the doorstep unannounced once or twice when we were still at school. He's not a bad person, just a flighty one. It's nice to know he's there, but I've never really needed him in my life.

'I'm thinking of buying a new kitchen table,' Mum says as she places our plates down and takes her seat.

Elle and I both stare at her. 'You can't,' I say.

'No way,' Elle says.

Mum raises her eyes to the ceiling; she'd obviously anticipated resistance to the idea. 'Girls, this one's on its last legs.'

We've sat around this battered, scrubbed wooden table

our entire lives, always in the exact same spots. It's seen our school-morning breakfasts, our favourite weekend bacon and beetroot sandwiches and our family rows. Our mother is by and large a creature of habit; her home hasn't changed much over the years and Elle and I have come to rely on it staying more or less the same. Come to think of it, you could say the same for Mum – she's had the same ash-blonde bob for as long as I can recall. Elle and I inherit our heart-shaped faces from her and we all share the same deep dimples, as if someone screwed their fingers into our cheeks when we laugh. She is our safety net and this house is our sanctuary.

'We did our homework on this table.' Elle lays a protective hand on it.

'Every Christmas dinner I've ever had has been around this table,' I say.

'But it's drawn all over,' Mum tries.

'Yes,' Elle says. 'With our names from when I was five years old.'

She gouged each of our names deep into the surface with a blue ballpoint not long after she learned her letters. The story goes that she was terribly proud and couldn't wait to show Mum what she'd done; they're still there now, childish capitals beneath our place mats. Gwen. Elle. Lydia. A scrawny little bird after each of them.

'Would you like to take it to your house?' Mum says, looking at Elle, who has a screamingly tidy home where everything matches or complements, and absolutely nothing is battered or gouged.

'It belongs here,' Elle says, firm.

Mum looks at me. 'Lydia?'

'You know I don't have the room,' I say. 'But please let it stay. It's part of the family.'

She sighs, wavering. I can see she knows it's true. I don't think she really wants to lose it either. 'Maybe.'

'Omelettes are lovely,' Elle offers.

A thought occurs to me. 'Did Kathrin Magyar sell you a new dining table?'

Mum reaches for her coffee and pats the tabletop like an old friend. 'I'll cancel the order.'

Kathrin Magyar might be good, but she never stood a chance against the Bird family collective.

He just wanted a decent book to read ...

Not too much to ask, is it? It was in 1935 when Allen Lane, Managing Director of Bodley Head Publishers, stood on a platform at Exeter railway station looking for something good to read on his journey back to London. His choice was limited to popular magazines and poor-quality paperbacks – the same choice faced every day by the vast majority of readers, few of whom could afford hardbacks. Lane's disappointment and subsequent anger at the range of books generally available led him to found a company – and change the world.

'We believed in the existence in this country of a vast reading public for intelligent books at a low price, and staked everything on it'
Sir Allen Lane, 1902–1970, founder of Penguin Books

The quality paperback had arrived – and not just in bookshops. Lane was adamant that his Penguins should appear in chain stores and tobacconists, and should cost no more than a packet of cigarettes.

Reading habits (and cigarette prices) have changed since 1935, but Penguin still believes in publishing the best books for everybody to enjoy. We still believe that good design costs no more than bad design, and we still believe that quality books published passionately and responsibly make the world a better place.

So wherever you see the little bird – whether it's on a piece of prize-winning literary fiction or a celebrity autobiography, political tour de force or historical masterpiece, a serial-killer thriller, reference book, world classic or a piece of pure escapism – you can bet that it represents the very best that the genre has to offer.

Whatever you like to read – trust Penguin.